Tradit

Thr

Robert L. Cauley

Q.E.S.

Quantum Eccentric Studios

First published by Quantum Eccentric Studios 2025

Author: Robert L. Cauley
Editor: Carlo DeCarlo
First edition
ISBN 979-8-9919904-3-4-51499

To my beloved wife, Elizabeth,
you have always been my muse

Contents

Opening: Tri-Synergy

I couldn't fall back asleep, so I held my wives tighter, my mind filled with them. I found myself captivated by the peace of their quiescent state. The dreaminess of being the romantic partner of two extraordinary women swirled into a spectrum of vivid life. I pondered the long road our loving fable had traveled. It was beyond an average romance.

However, this was not achieved without effort. There were many trials, yet here we stand. Our souls now synchronized into the perfect combination of love, jest, solidarity, and sanctuary. Our bond was something unbreakable, an eternal love unlike any other.

Victoria was the abyssal entity, wild with the incendiary heat of passionate desire. A defiant ravishment of the soul. Her independent moxie flourished in a decisive flurry. Her tongue was razor-sharp, often eviscerating any opponent with her words. Yet her maternal caress soothed the soul.

Sarah was the celestial spirit, whimsical with the empyrean of tranquil tenderness. An acquiescent, loving soul. Her warmth was apricity, marked by empathy for all things in life. Her heart was overflowing with devotion. Often, it melted all those around her. Yet her playful effervescence and spunk brought out joy in those around her.

The eclectic nature of their personas harmonized lovingly with the harsh realities of life. My love for them grew daily, along with my need for them. I couldn't ask for better wives than Victoria and Sarah. They had fully taken my heart. Every piece of me belonged to them. Both my benevolence and darker side were now theirs completely.

I ruminated about the mystique of their origins and the serendipity of our tryst. At first, I excused it, but the thoughts lingered. Soon, the sleuth in my core was about to stumble upon answers.

I reflected on the events that led to this unifying revelation.

Chapter 1: A Day in the Life

The October sun broke through the window. I felt its warm glow against my face as it started to wake me. The timbre of light snoring was always so cute to hear. We'd reveled in our engagement bliss since that day in July. I couldn't believe it had been three months since I'd proposed—since they had accepted.

Protectively folded tightly around them, my arms felt like I was holding the whole world. They were my world. Opening with a sense of crowning accomplishment, my eyes glanced at each. They were so radiant, even in their sleep. Unwavering in her deep snoozing, Sarah's delicate tenderness was on display. The fire of Vicky broke all the rules, even in a peaceful slumber. Waking up next to them would never get old.

I gently leveraged myself from their warm bodies, trying not to disturb their rest. Once off the bed, I turned to admire them. Just a few months ago, I was a loner with no prospects. No true understanding of love. But now, I stared at the women to whom my affections had been bestowed so deeply. Their embraces had become my sanctuary—love's warmth within their caresses. They had become everything to me.

I turned toward the door. Hazily, I made my way into the living room. It was Saturday, my turn to cook. I was going to prepare breakfast for them, which had become routine for us.

During the week, they took turns cooking; on the weekends, it was my turn. My food had improved, but not as well as theirs. Sarah made gourmet-style dishes, which were always delicious. Vicky cooked simple meals, but her food tasted better than mine.

Wasting no time, I made breakfast: eggs, bacon, and toast. The table was set carefully as I poured each a glass of orange juice. I always wanted them to feel loved, so I ensured that all the dishes I made suited their preferences.

I stood back for a moment, admiring the meal. Vicky liked her eggs poached hard, while Sarah preferred her eggs sunny-side up. Strawberry jam on Sarah's toast and butter on Vicky's. Perfect. This would be an excellent wake-up for them. It was time to get my lovelies. I moved toward the bedroom.

Opening the door slowly, I peered in on them as they slept. Watching their chests rise and fall was mesmerizing. It was time to wake my incredible women. Maneuvering to the foot of the bed, I sat on the edge.

The soft flesh of their soles peeked out of the blanket, giving me an idea. Rushing with care, my hands wrapped around their ankles and tugged them upward. I put their feet together and licked their toes. My tongue played along their big toes for a moment. Then I plunged between their digits, softly kissing the web of each of their feet—Sarah first, then Vicky.

"Ooh! That feels nice." Sarah squealed as grogginess seeped from her lips.

"Mm-hmm, what a way to wake up," Vicky said, her face peering down at me.

"Good morning, my sweets."

"Morning, sweetheart," Vicky responded as she sat up. Her disheveled hair fell over the left side of her face, hiding it from my view.

"Good morning, Master. Wake us like this every day, please," Sarah purred, cocking herself up on her elbows. Her soft breasts fell to the sides as she lifted herself.

"Today, we won't need clothes for breakfast," I announced. My eyes darted between them as I took in the surprise forming on their faces.

"Hmph, dirty boy. Let me have some coffee first," Vicky said with a playful eye roll. She slid off the mattress without much effort.

"Yay, no clothes! I love naked breakfast time." Sarah giggled excitedly before lazily rolling out of bed.

My hand motioned them to the door. "Breakfast, then I have a surprise." My voice assumed that Noncommissioned Officer tone.

Vicky side-eyed me as she grumbled, "Coffee first. It's too early for funny business." She moved toward the kitchen.

"It's never too early to play with Master," Sarah sheepishly murmured. Her body moved lazily past me.

As we walked, my eyes couldn't help but dreamily gaze at them. The way their bodies moved, the curves flowed sensually. The complex nature of each body's uniqueness pulled all my fancies into a dazzling display. These women were my dreams in motion, clearing away all my fears. Tandem in my heart, both claim it without much effort. It was no wonder that I had proposed to both.

"Breakfast looks delicious, Master." Sarah rejoiced as she sat at the table, giddy. She took a whiff of the breakfast, closing her eyes to enjoy the scent.

"Hmm, breakfast and a surprise," Vicky said before her lips tugged into a dark and sensual grin.

"Let's eat, then I'll share the surprise," I said as I took my seat.

The ladies sat in silence as they started munching on the food. I waited to eat until they took their first bite, our usual routine. Then, I started chatting about the week.

"David is making a pretty good hand. I enjoy working with him," I explained before I took a bite of my toast.

"He seems like a nice guy, Master," Sarah said. "How is the coffee shop?"

"It seems good. We should get the first owner's draw sometime this month," I explained.

"Remind me why we have to wait?" Vicky asked as she rubbed her hands.

"Per the partner agreement, payouts to the owners, Howard and us, are quarterly. But it clears after that quarter has ended," I explained, pausing to watch Vicky. My mind filled with concern. "What's wrong with your hands?"

"I'm worn out. My hands feel like they're petrifying. I didn't think I would gather so many massage clients so freaken fast," Vicky lamented, then stared at her hands as she tried to grip her fork.

"Too many happy endings, huh?" Sarah winked at Vicky.

"Eww. The only one who will ever get a happy ending from me is Mas— Kyle," Vicky said. She stopped herself from calling me Master. She wasn't mad at me anymore. However, she still felt I hadn't earned the title back, which was fine.

"So, I take it the masseuse needs a massage tonight?" I asked, looking at Vicky.

"With your tongue," Vicky answered, then sipped her orange juice. Her hands seemed to be feeling better.

I shook my head before I spoke. "Anyway, last month was the end of the quarter, so the money should hit the bank in the next week or so."

"When do we get our house?" Sarah broke back into the conversation.

"Yeah, when?" Vicky asked before she playfully flicked her fork at me, and some eggs hit my chest.

"No, no, Vicky. You've gotta do it like this." Sarah tutted, demonstrating the proper technique with a playful smirk. Then, she used her fork like a catapult and landed a bigger scoop of eggs on me.

"Haha, you two always cause trouble." I chuckled, shaking my head. "If you both behave, I might take you shopping. That was the surprise," I said calmly as I cleaned up the eggs.

"For?" Vicky asked, her brow arched.

"Shopping! I'll be good. Swear. I'll behave, Master," Sarah stammered with excitement. She bounced in her chair a few times, her hands rhythmically tapping the table.

"Well, two girls said they wanted to decorate for Halloween, but... since they are being naughty..." I smirked with an evil grin.

"Fine, I'll behave." Vicky huffed, then looked at me with a feigned sad pout.

"Okay. Once we finish and clean up breakfast, we will go," I said. Sometimes, it was hard to say no to them, especially when they acted so cute.

"You didn't answer my question," Sarah said as she looked at me sternly. Quickly, her face returned to her cheerful smile.

"When things are right, but we have other things to worry about for now," I answered her coldly, trying to mask my intentions.

Over the past month, I'd worked with Howard and Elle to set up a few surprises for them—ones they'd love. But I didn't want them to know just yet.

"Didn't want us to know what?" Vicky asked slyly.

"Nothing, just thinking out loud again," I replied quickly. *That was close, Sergeant. Keep those thoughts to yourself; you'll tell them when the time is right.*

Vicky snarled as she crossed her arms; she seemed upset with me. "Secrets got you in hot water last time."

"It's not like that. I'm just working with Howard on business stuff. And Elle asked me to be her backup for visitation exchanges," I calmly explained. Both statements were true.

"Then say it next time." Vicky huffed before uncrossing her arms and returning to eating.

It was hard to plan nice things for them, given the lingering effects of my mistake a few months ago. But this wasn't like that. I was planning things to help them.

"Did you ever fix that chair, Master?" Sarah asked, pointing to the living room. I assumed she was trying to break the tension I had accidentally caused.

I had forgotten about that chair. We'd just avoided sitting in it for the past few months, which had become a habit. I was sure that we would eventually need extra seating again.

"No, I was thinking about replacing it," I said as I cleared the table.

"That's a great idea," Vicky said as she brushed against me, putting her dishes in the sink. "While out, we can pick up a new one."

The warmth of her skin felt like electricity as her flesh touched mine. I was sure she did that on purpose to tease me.

The three of us worked to clear the table and clean the kitchen, occasionally bumping into each other. When their smooth skin touched mine, my desire ached to take them, but I needed to remain stoic. I wanted today to revolve around decorating for Halloween and finding a costume for all three of us.

As the girls were finishing the dishes, I swept the floor. Staring at them intensely, my eyes roamed over their bodies. The mechanics of their movements made them seem so enchanting; it was a gateway into my daze. Sarah's body moved with feline grace; her hourglass shape had the proper movements of elegance. Vicky's body was slightly more rigid; her sculpted muscles caressed the strength of her persona.

Fascinated by their uniqueness, I was always caught between lust and love. I could not think of life without either. Sarah's softness reassured me, while Vicky's harshness challenged me to improve myself. This sentiment was not just reflected in their bodies but in their words, actions, and, yes, in their love for me.

I always felt euphoric around them, always happy. I could never put into words how they made me feel. The only words I could think of were that my heart was whole. And to reciprocate, I wanted to do things to support their dreams.

Howard helped me find two places of business—one for my HVAC company and one for Vicky's spa idea. We'd close on them later this month. Howard had begun compiling a list of beauticians and masseuses who might be interested in working in that part of the city. He also assisted me in writing a business plan and proposal for the spa.

Elle had found a nearby college offering night, weekend, and online courses. Sarah could choose to return to school without compromising her job. I began researching various scholarships and grants that she could apply for. I stumbled upon the Reginald Payne Developing Teachers grant. A substantial amount was offered, so I entered Sarah's information. They needed an essay. I was going to discuss it with Sarah sometime next week. However, I wanted to confirm the validity of the grant due to the high monthly stipend.

I enjoyed doing things for them, seeing them happy. They had taken over my mind, and every thought was about them. All the years of loneliness from before had become distant memories. Just a few months and a lifetime of despair had been forgotten. I felt as though this had always been my life—or at least it should have. How could life have been anything else before?

As I pushed the dirt and egg pieces into the dustpan, I started thinking about the wedding again. I still hadn't figured out the legal route to it. Leonard, Howard's dad, explained that we had no lawful avenue to marry simultaneously. He suggested a long-shot approach, but with no guarantee. Sue the state for the privilege to marry both under my First Amendment right, claiming religious freedom. It felt awkward and dishonest to me since religion and I had a rocky relationship in the past. However, I knew that I was destined to marry them.

"All cleaned up, Master!" Sarah exclaimed. She leaned down, her face inches from mine. Her pearly white teeth sparkled in the dim light; her eyes twinkled with excitement.

"Now, can we get ready?" Vicky asked as she looked up at me; her smile gleamed just as bright. Her eyes dared me to say something offbeat.

"Go get dressed," I ordered in that dominant voice, lazily waving them on.

They both made their way into the bedroom to choose their outfits. I followed them, gathering a pair of jeans. They had insisted that I expand my fashion sense, so they added jeans, slacks, and a few more button-down shirts to my wardrobe.

I pulled on the blue jeans. I'd started to get accustomed to going commando these days; my ladies felt it was better. But on workdays, I cheated and wore boxers. Chafing was a concern. My days in the Army taught me not to chance something like that. I pulled over a black T-shirt. I now wore more solid-colored shirts. But I still always had my combat boots; they comforted me to my sense of self.

"I'm ready." I sighed as I watched them.

Sarah wore blue jeans and a flannel shirt. Vicky had a long-sleeved belly top and Tripp pants. I shook my head slightly. Their styles were unique yet always enticing.

"We're ready for Halloweenie, Master," Sarah announced. She swayed with her bubbly attitude.

"Ready," Vicky responded as she briefly glanced at Sarah. She gave a playfully annoyed sigh before heading out.

As we approached the front door, I let them go ahead. It was the gentlemanly thing to do. Besides, my eyes watched their rears as we exited the apartment. It was always a great view.

"Master, you gonna stare at our booties all day?" Sarah asked coyishly.

"How can he not, Miss Halloweenie. Tah." Vicky mocked as she shook her head.

"Coming," I said as I rushed up to take my place between them. Instinctively, our hands locked into each other's, fingers lovingly interlacing.

"Miss Halloweenie? What happened to Miss Pushover? Huh, Brattypants?" Sarah questioned Vicky as we walked down the hallway.

"Hey, you're the one who made a wiener joke about Halloween," Vicky answered as her face leaned past my chest to catch Sarah's attention.

"Jealous of my wienie, now," Sarah quipped with a hint of mischief. Then she blew a raspberry at Vicky.

"Be nice, girls." Mrs. Helderman interrupted as we made our way to the stairwell. She seemed to be waiting for something as she stood at the landing. Her body was straight, almost like she was standing at attention. Her gaze scanned our faces, as if tracing our features for signs of something. Then her eyes snapped back down the stairway.

"Good morning. How are you today?" I asked.

"Good morning, lovebirds. I'm just waiting on the delivery guy," Mrs. Helderman replied, seeming worried about the delivery.

I held the girls back for a moment. "If you want, we can stay to help carry it in for you."

Her face turned back to us, giving a slight sideways smile as she waved us on. "No, my boy, it's fine. Just paperwork. Nothing these old bones can't handle," she responded, her voice smooth, yet with a hint of tension pulled through.

"You sure?" Vicky asked, turning to view Mrs. Helderman.

"Yeah. We can stay if you need, Miss Wanda," Sarah said.

"Nah, I'm fine. You kids have fun." Mrs. Helderman insisted with no room for argument, then waved us on. "Besides, it can be all day. Deliveries aren't as reliable as they were in my day. Punctuality is lost in this newer generation." Her words seemed rehearsed. Finally, she nodded at us, glancing at how I was holding Vicky and Sarah. "Well, on some things."

"Okay. Have a great day, Wanda. I look forward to dinner next week," I said as I descended the stairs. I shook my head; there was no arguing with this seventy-two-year-old broad.

We made our way to my beater. Even though Vicky and Sarah had better vehicles, they always wanted to ride in mine. I assumed they liked me taking the wheel, controlling our destination. After we were all in, I started the car and pulled out.

The road was busy for the morning, but I seemed to navigate it easily. Sarah sat up front, so the radio blared with the country station. Vicky was in the back; I glanced at her through the rearview mirror. She was lost in thought about something.

My hand turned the radio down. "Have you thought any more about that spa?" I asked.

"Was just thinking about it." Vicky sighed.

"Sis, you need to go for it." Sarah turned in her seat. "Besides, we'll support you. I'm sure Master could even get Howard to help."

"But what if I can't keep up?" Vicky sighed. "My hands are having problems with what clients I do have."

My eyes briefly looked at her through the mirror. "Hire more people; you won't have to do all the work yourself," I explained.

"Maybe," Vicky muttered, then deflected. "And what about college, Miss Pushover?"

"I've been thinking about night classes lately."

I said, "I hear they also have weekend and online classes."

"Weekends are a no-no, Master. I can't leave you two alone that long."

Vicky leaned forward in her seat. "And why is that?"

"Hmm... it'd be no fair." Sarah stroked her chin. "While I studied, Vicky would get to spend all weekend with Master."

"Haha, you're worried about missing out?" Vicky teased.

"Maybe." Sarah giggled before blowing a kiss to me. "But I know Master loves me the most," she said in her childlike voice.

"Loves you the most, huh? Miss Pushover is full of herself today. Maybe we should hold a book burning to knock her down a peg or two. Yeah, her whole collection."

Sarah gasped. "You wouldn't!"

"Ya never know."

"Play nice, girls," I commanded in my NCO voice. Since July, their banter had become more spiteful toward each other. I wondered if that was my fault. "There are no favorites. I don't want to hear any more about burning books or paintings. Understood?"

"Yes, Master," Sarah said.

"I was just messing with her. I wasn't going to burn her precious books," Vicky explained, annoyed.

I pulled into a parking spot. The place seemed semi-busy this morning, at least busier than usual for this early. I stepped out of the vehicle; they joined me, locking into my arms. We always seemed to walk this way.

"I know they have all kinds of decorations. Should have stuff to suit each of you," I explained. I had scouted stores yesterday to find one that would have things for both of their tastes.

"Do they have costumes, too?" Sarah asked.

Vicky clicked her tongue. "What do you think, Miss Halloweenie?" she retorted.

"Yeah, they have costumes," I responded. "What do you want to dress up as?"

"An elf maid, from my new favorite book."

Vicky scoffed. "Ha, an elf. Big goofy ears, yep, so you."

Sarah moaned sensually. "Big ears for Master to tug on when I'm on my knees." She leaned across me. "What about you?"

"Only a child of the night would understand my insatiable thirst for blood," Vicky said.

"Vampire?" I asked. They seemed to be getting along better.

"Um... yeah, kinda got a thing for vampires," Vicky admitted shyly. "Well, a vampire kink."

I wanted to encourage Vicky to open up. "That sounds like it could be a fun kink."

"I saw they have these expensive vampire fangs, but..." Vicky appeared torn, half excited and half humiliated.

"We can probably get them," I encouraged her. I wanted them to express themselves and be who they were, to embrace their unique ideas and passions.

"Yeah, but I'm a bit embarrassed," Vicky said coyishly. I had never seen her act coy like this. Was there something that she was afraid we—I—would judge her for?

I turned to her. "We can talk about it later if you want."

"Okay. It's just a dirty idea." Vicky sighed. "One I might ask for some time."

I didn't press Vicky anymore. It was odd, though. She was never shy, always open, and always seductive about topics like this. But I left it alone; she would tell me in time. Our feet moved in step as we drew near the store.

"Kinks. Reminds me. Last night, I just finished reading a juicy, steamy book," Sarah interjected dreamily.

"Let me guess, billionaire aloof playboy?" Vicky huffed with annoyance. "And for some reason, he is unfazed by all except that mediocre and bland female lead."

"Not to mention his insanely good looks," I mocked. "Or when someone barely mentions a skill, he has already mastered it."

"No fair. You two are always making fun of my stories," Sarah said, feigning upset before shifting back to her childlike voice. "But yeah, all of that's true. But, he was into some really kinky stuff."

Vicky rolled her eyes. "They are always into kink."

"Well, yeah. But this one is different, gotta explain this kink. It's crazy but hot," Sarah spouted.

"Hmm... something tells me you want to try it," I said, arching my eyebrow in intrigue. They were both confessing secret kinks; I was more than willing to listen. The more I learned about them, the closer I felt to them. The more I loved them.

"Ha! That's if Miss Pushover can handle it. Whatever it is." Vicky said in a sexy rasp. She tossed around her free hand before glancing at Sarah.

Sarah hastily let go of my arm and quickly walked behind me to Vicky. I heard a loud pop as Vicky was briefly jolted forward. Then Sarah was like the wind as her feet started into a solid sprint.

"I can be rough, too, Brattypants!" Sarah quipped with a slight chuckle as her pace quickened.

"It's on." Vicky released my arm and bolted after Sarah.

Sarah briefly turned to blow a raspberry at Vicky. "Thought you liked spankings?" She rushed to the store, keeping her distance from Vicky.

I shook my head as I continued my leisurely pace. Watching their playful antics as we walked through the parking lot was so much fun. I like that we were always in our own world, playfully bantering with each other. When we were together, the rest of the world didn't matter—it was just us three.

They were my fiancées, the women I always wanted to see playing with our wild banter.

As I reached them, I found Vicky tickling Sarah; they were laughing. I reached out to tickle Vicky.

"Hehe, I knew you'd join the fun." Vicky wiggled away from me.

Sarah started straightening her clothes and composing herself. "Yeah, Brattypants thinks she has won. But wait 'til we get home." She panted, catching her breath.

I motioned toward the automatic doors. "Now, can we go shopping?" I asked with a slight chuckle.

Vicky stared at me with a composed look. "Ahem, yes."

Sarah finished fixing her attire. "Ready, Master."

"People these days." A lady pushing a cart past us scoffed. "Not an ounce of decency with this generation."

I ignored the lady and locked my arms with my beauties again. We entered the sliding doors. Sarah grabbed a cart and slid it over to me. I pushed the buggy as they walked in step beside me, arms still locked into mine.

"Where to first?"

"Halloween stuff, duh, Master," Sarah mocked.

"Yeah, let's go." Vicky yanked my arm toward the aisle.

I aimed the cart at the Halloween stuff. As we walked through the store, many eyes were on us. The sounds of scoffs filled the air, and the disapproving glares cut through me. It was always random women who found my relationship distasteful. I ignored it all and continued toward our destination.

As we entered the section, strobe lights flashed on a lower shelf, and creepy sounds emanated from several of the props.

Sarah let go of me and ran down the aisle, examining items on the shelves. Vicky stayed close to me; she seemed to be looking for something really spooky. It wasn't long before Sarah came rushing back to the cart, holding something.

"Ooh, look at this cute little guy!" Sarah's eyes sparkled with childlike wonder as she held up a grinning ghost figurine. "Isn't he just adorable?"

Vicky scoffed. "Cute and Halloween? We need something more... sinister." She rifled through the shelves, her lips curling into a wicked grin as she unearthed a bloody severed head prop.

"Cute goes with anything," Sarah explained before asking, "Right, Master?"

"Cute goes good with Halloween. Cute can even be scary."

Sarah stuck her tongue out. "See, Halloween can be cute—cute and spooky."

"Ugh! You two." Vicky made a throat-cutting motion. "Halloween is severed heads, blood, and pus oozing out."

Sarah feigned a barfing sound. "Gross."

"Eviscerated torsos with guts hanging out. People walking around with eyeballs dangling around their cheeks," I added.

Sarah recoiled. "Yuck! Halloween is not an autopsy on display. And whose side are you on?"

"I agree with you both."

"Both? Turncoat." Vicky stuck her hands on her hips, a sly look of playful disdain spread on her face. "Think you can work both sides all the time?"

I chuckled awkwardly, "Duh. I'm always on both sides. Because I love you both equally."

Sarah giggled, a mischievous glint in her eye. "Oh, really, Master? Think you can get away with such a lame answer?"

Vicky smirked as her arms crossed. "Yeah, soldier boy. That's not very commanding of you."

Sarah put the ghost figure in the cart, then turned to Vicky, "I think we need to teach Master a proper lesson in communication."

Vicky tossed the severed head prop in the cart, her eyes gleaming at me with a dark, sensual gaze. "I've a few ideas."

"Teach *me* a lesson? You girls think you're badasses now, huh?"

They ignored me and started to conspire with each other.

Sarah picked up another cute item and inspected it. "Ooh, sis, remember me telling you about that book last week?"

Vicky mirrored Sarah and picked up a gory item from the opposite shelf. "You mean the one where the villainess kidnapped the hero? Mm-hmm, I see where you're going."

"Master just gave us the perfect opportunity for it. I say we tie him down to the bed," Sarah explained.

This piqued my interest; I could go for something like that.

Vicky caressed Sarah's cheek. "Then we make him watch us play together."

This "lesson" was getting interesting. The aura around them felt calculating and sensual, like a scary kind of sexiness. I was getting excited in the store.

"We finish with each other, making him not be able to stand how hot it is to watch us..." Sarah trailed off.

"And when he is all worked up..." Vicky continued.

Sarah exchanged a knowing glance with Vicky. Playful smirks tugged at the corners of their lips. The anticipation of their answer was driving my libido into flames of desire. I was readying myself for an answer that would make me crave lessons from now on.

They narrowed their gaze upon me, mischief dancing in their eyes. Vicky leaned toward Sarah as a silent communication filled the void between them. "Lay down beside him to sleep, leaving him tied up to cool off," they said in unison, conveying sensual superiority.

They got my engine revving, then took their feet off the gas. Would they really leave me in that kind of state? My body craving theirs yet left without. Why did they want to be so evil? Was it that bad that I tried to balance our lives between their tastes?

"Why so cruel?" I asked. "I didn't do anything to warrant that."

"Maybe you did," Vicky said as she playfully slapped my cheek.

"Or maybe we want to watch you suffer, Master." Sarah giggled, then she winked at me. "Besides, something like that will make you want us more when we untie you."

"I'll remember that, you brats," I said with a wicked grin forming on my face. "Anyway, don't I get a say in our decorations?"

"Of course you do, Master," Sarah said, then stuck her tongue out at me. Her lips slowly pulled into a coy smile. "After all, you have to love us both equally."

Vicky elbowed me in the ribs. "Yeah, better love us equally." She warned, winking at me. "Or you might find yourself tied up with none of the good stuff."

I raised my hands in mock surrender. "Wouldn't dream of it." I leaned in and pressed a tender kiss to each of their foreheads, savoring their delighted giggles.

We busied ourselves trying to find an eclectic balance between their personalities. Balancing their tastes with each item we placed in the buggy was fun, but tedious. Crude and gory for Vicky, cutesy and lighthearted for Sarah.

I made sure to get the specific items they had mentioned. For Sarah, I found some elf ears that she could glue on. And for Vicky, I got some nice vampire fangs. As she stated, they were expensive, but I added them to the cart anyway.

As we attempted to achieve an equilibrium of decorations, I had fun laughing and carrying on with them. Soon, I looked down at the cart, which was filled to the top. We moseyed our way to the checkout; I felt a surge of pride. They seemed to be gushing over the items I helped them pick to decorate. We had a fun day out. Now it was time to go home and set up our apartment.

"Are we going to buy a chair, Master?" Sarah asked.

I had forgotten about the chair. On our way back, we could stop at Big Al Furniture. I was sure they would have a better choice.

"The furniture store down the street might have a nicer selection," I suggested, glancing between them.

Vicky slid some items from the cart to the checkout counter. "That's a great idea. And it's on the way home."

After we finished the checkout and walked back to the store, I couldn't help but feel content—I had made them both happy.

We joked about their little threat on the drive to the furniture store. About the sexy consequences their coup would have. And the sensual wrath that I would unleash upon those sexy bodies.

Chapter 2: Opening the Door

I was satisfied with the new recliner they'd picked, which was scheduled for delivery next week. After dealing with the paperwork, we made our way home. As we pulled into the apartment complex, I was reminded of how unique yet similar my fiancées were. My heart was thumping with a rhythm of wholeness in their presence.

Quickly, we exited my beater and gathered arms full of bags. Sarah, of course, skipped ahead, excited to start decorating.

The soothing breeze infused the October air with a seasonal chill. The excitement to decorate bloomed around us. Yet, I felt an eeriness at how quiet the world had seemed these past few months. Was life really coming to a tranquil measure? Perhaps a storm was brewing on the horizon? Or was it just my paranoia from the war that was trying to sabotage my happiness?

Vicky elbowed me, breaking the sullen thoughts. "Looks like Sarah's all fired up," she muttered.

I chortled. "Obviously." Turning to Vicky, I asked. "What about you?"

"Decorating will be fun." She smiled, but the excitement faded from her face. "I'm worried that being in the apartment, we won't get trick-or-treaters, like Sarah thinks."

"It'll be fun either way."

We caught up to Sarah on the stairs, and her childlike wonder was bursting.

As Sarah made it to the second floor, she looked back at me. "Master, can we hang Mr. Ghost by the front door?"

"No way!" Vicky snapped.

"Brattypants thinks she gets to tell everyone what to do," Sarah huffed, stomping her foot.

"Yeah, because I can handle more than Ms. Pushover."

"More? Ha, like what? Cry about your hands?" Sarah mocked.

Vicky looked down at her hands, her face crinkled with hurt and anger. Their vicious attacks against each other were getting out of hand. This was beyond their typical playful bickering.

"Enough, you two!" I roared before lowering my voice. "Let's bring everything inside. Then, we'll decide where things go."

Neither spoke again.

Lately, it had felt like I was babysitting two angsty teens. Were these the women that I had asked to marry me? Was the three-way relationship taking its toll on their sisterhood?

Mrs. Helderman said love must be shared equally in this relationship, with all three of us loving and caring for each other. Otherwise, this marriage would fall apart, like Elle and Stephen's. I couldn't bear to see either of my loves hurt. If we were to have a happy life together, I needed to solve this.

Once we got inside, I pointed toward the kitchen. "Let's get this stuff sorted before we start putting it up." I offloaded my arms onto the coffee table. Setting their bags down on the kitchen counters, they whispered back and forth to each other.

I glanced at the chair. I knew we needed to carry it to the dumpster. "Would you mind helping me get this downstairs?" I asked as I was rummaging through the bags on the table.

"Guess so." Vicky sighed as she stared at the La-Z-Boy. Then she walked over to the chair and leaned down, easily picking up the bottom of it. I quickly moved to catch it as we pulled it upward.

"Need me to help, Master?"

I grunted. "Thanks, Sarah. Can you get the door?"

"Sure. Be careful, you two," Sarah said as she walked to the door.

As Sarah held the door open, Vicky and I tilted the chair to maneuver through it. We scurried down the hallway. This chair was heavier than I remembered, and my back was starting to ache.

"I'll go down the stairs backward," I said as we neared the stairwell.

"Are you sure?" Vicky asked.

"I got this."

I stepped down one stair at a time, and as we descended, the chair in my arms felt like I was carrying a whale.

We made it down the stairs to the outside, rounded the corner of the building, then tossed the chair next to the dumpster. Surprisingly, Vicky didn't seem to have broken a sweat moving it. But I was slightly winded and the pressure on my lower back was increasing with a sharp ache. I slumped over, huffing to catch my breath. A sharp pain shot through my lower back, and my hands instinctively reached to the area. When had I become so broken?

"You okay?" Vicky asked, as her hand slid onto my shoulder.

I gazed into her eyes; those blue pools always captivated me with their mesmerizing allure.

I wheezed. “Yeah. Just let me catch my breath.”

Gracefully, she glided behind me. Her hands, so strong yet tender, worked magic on my aching muscles. It wasn’t just the pain easing; she was unwinding the tension in my soul. Only the touch of Vicky and Sarah could do that. That silent understanding between the three of us went beyond words.

Vicky leaned into my ear, her voice carrying that motherly gentleness. “You know, those pain meds the VA gave you aren’t just for decoration in the medicine cabinet?”

“Yeah, yeah.” I waved my hand dismissively. “When we get back up to the apartment, I’ll take them,” I said in defeat. It’s one thing to feel the pain, but an entirely different matter to admit that at a young age, my body was so broken.

Recently, Vicky and Sarah had ensured I visit the VA regularly. These visits are not only for my psych meds but for all the issues that have been troubling me.

Vicky lifted her hands and gave me a quick pat. “There, that should help you get back up the stairs.”

“Thank you, baby.” I turned to her. My lips pressed against her forehead for a moment. Lacing my fingers with hers, I took her hand, stepping off together.

Vicky whimpered. “Is that all?”

She looked at me, a sad pout on her face, but her eyes held the flame of desire. It was a potent invitation, forcing my body to respond instantly. But it was more than raw lust; it was a deep yearning for the loving intimacy they offered. Those shared moments of passion intertwined our three souls as one, closing the distance between the trio of hearts as we tightened into the embraces of one another.

The parking lot was no place for that. And Sarah deserved to be part of that embrace, that unity. The desire burned into me as a silent promise for later.

I released her hand and slid my arm around her waist, gently squeezing her. “Later, my sweet,” I whispered. “We need to decorate, eat, then meet Howard and Elle at the dance club.”

As we walked toward the security door, the cool autumn breeze blew with a slight howl. It felt comforting against the skin. I had walked in this comfort for months now. This love, this relationship, had come to define me as a person. This morning, I succeeded in acquiring decorations that suited both my fiancées. I felt accomplished in the task.

As we climbed the stairs, Vicky matched each step as we moved up, and I felt so in sync with them. At first, these women were an annoyance, then sexual fascinations, but now...

Vicky's raspy voice broke me from my thoughts. "Kyle, I know you're hiding something. If it's bad, please tell me."

I cleared my throat. "I've been working on surprises for you and Sarah. It's nothing bad, it's... well, a surprise." I paused to stroke a stray lock of hair behind her ear. "Besides, I'm my own boss now, so I don't see me firing myself any time soon."

"Okay, so when do we get these supposed surprises?"

I smirked. "Patience, my dear." A flash of the future spa and a college admissions letter ran through my mind, but was soon pushed aside. I didn't want to slip, saying too much.

Making sure my thoughts weren't broadcast, I opened the apartment door, waving Vicky inside. As soon as we crossed the threshold, we saw it. Sarah had organized the decorations: cutesy stuff on one side, gory on the other, and neutral ones in the middle.

Vicky stifled a laugh. "What happened here? It looks like Halloween exploded all over the apartment."

"Yep." Sarah replied before pointing at the cache of severed body parts props, "And your nasty stuff is over there."

They wasted no time decorating. Both seemed to enjoy transforming our love nest into a celebration of All Hallows' Eve.

And of course, I was the one on the stepladder, mounting cobwebs in the corners and hanging a ghoulish skull from the ceiling. As my hands worked on decorations, my mind worked through the marriage.

I thought about the wedding. I had found one preacher, Father Piercy, who was willing to hold the ceremony for us. He usually performed non-sanctioned marriages for gay couples. When I approached him to explain my relationship, he was intrigued. He seemed excited about the three-way marriage.

It made me feel accepted that others understood this kind of relationship. Father Piercy seemed happy to hear about my deep feelings for Vicky and Sarah. He gave me some encouraging words about love.

As I was hanging another spiderweb, I glanced over at Sarah. She flitted about, posting her funny Frankenstein banners everywhere. Her spirits seemed to be up.

I stepped down from the ladder to find a new position. My eyes drifted to Vicky, who was strategically scattering her more grotesque decorations. I went back to my work—and thoughts.

Watching them, they were so different, yet so perfectly in sync. I always felt a quiet joy when sneaking glances at them. It was comforting how they blended into a vibrant life.

Sarah was a whirlwind of glitter and laughter, sporadically placing her decorations. Vicky was methodically placing her grotesque props with an exacting artistic eye. This messy, beautifully controlled chaos was our home, reflecting the vibrant, sometimes wild, love we shared. Father Piercy was right to be excited about our three-way relationship.

I've spoken with Mrs. Helderman about him; she seemed to know Father Piercy. However, she cautioned me again not to get so caught up in marriage with Vicky and Sarah just yet. I wasn't sure why she was apprehensive about the union. Helda and she had "married" Jimmy within two months of returning from Vietnam. Their ceremony was held at a hippie commune by the compound's spiritual leader. How was my relationship any less than theirs? The love between the three of us was so raw and powerful.

War had taught me to survive, to be hard, to be a monster. But my two beautiful, fierce women were teaching me to truly live. Their hearts taught me to feel again. To love with an intensity I had never thought possible. Every bat Vicky hung, every goofy Frankenstein Sarah taped up, was not only a testament to the life they'd breathed back into me, but a physical representation of it. I wanted this to last the rest of my life. How could I *not* want to marry them?

"Master, can you staple this to the bedroom door?" Sarah snapped me out of my head. Her green puppy eyes tugged at me.

My hands reached for the plastic drape, which featured an image of a dungeon door. "Sure, honey."

After the handoff, Sarah disappeared behind me. She soon walked past me into the bedroom, her arms filled with plastic jack-o'-lanterns, all with different goofy smiling faces.

I moved the stepladder to the doorway of the bedroom. I stepped up, holding the door drape with one hand as I stapled across the top. After pinning the final staple, there was a knock at the front door.

Vicky had just entered the bathroom. I knew I was the only one who could answer the door, so I hurried off the ladder and rushed to it. As I flung it open, there stood a scruffy man. He was slightly muscular, with a bicycle helmet under his arm.

"Mr. Forester?" the man asked.

"That's me."

The man cleared his throat. "Correspondence for you, sir." His right hand lifted a letter, revealing a wolf tattoo. It was on the back of his hand, between his thumb and index finger. I glanced at the manila envelope.

I heard a growl come from down the hall. I poked my head out further, scanning the direction of the growl. Mrs. Helderman had her door cracked; her head turned toward my apartment. Her eyes burned through the courier with anger. I figured she was angered because she never got her delivery today. Then she looked at me with shocked, wide eyes before retreating behind a closed door.

I turned my focus back to the courier. "Thank you."

"Ahem..." The man turned his palm up. "Tip, sir?"

His eyes stared into mine as I reached for my wallet. I pulled out a five and handed it to him.

"Good day, sir," he said. "And remember, Garou Couriers lead the pack. Ah-woo!"

"Have a good afternoon," I said, shaking my head. He walked off toward the stairs. I closed the door and did an about-face.

"Whoa!" I yelped. To my surprise, Vicky and Sarah were standing right behind me.

Vicky chuckled. "Did we scare ya?"

"Who's the letter from, Master?"

"Yeah, you scared me. And I have no idea."

I looked at the parchment. No stamp, return address, or even my address—just my name, nothing more. I flipped it over. It was sealed with red wax—how odd. The sigil on the wax was a skull.

Sarah watched me look over the letter, her eyes studying the stationery. I took out my pocketknife, opened the letter, retracted the blade, and put it away.

Inside the envelope was a neatly folded paper. I unraveled the letter, and three tickets fell to the ground. Sarah quickly bent down to pick them up.

I started to read the letter, foreboding washing over me.

Fellow crusader,

Death has known thee before. Yet he rests barely from thine door. Though I am a stranger, heed me, thou art in danger. Puzzle not who I be, beware the shackles that bind are bound to three. Cherish those in the lines of L-O-V, for the moons navigate the sea. Do not disregard in reproach, for darkness is ever on approach.

'Til we meet,
Anima Mortis

P.S. Enjoy the gala.

L.O.V. the memo... A half-formed memory struggled to surface, a vague unease prickling the back of my mind. In the moment of recall, Vicky snatched the cryptic letter from my hand, dissipating the memory.

Her brow furrowed as she began to re-read to herself. "The hell is this?" Her voice trembled slightly.

"No clue." A joke or prank? But something didn't feel right.

Sarah, however, beamed as she held up ornate black tickets. "Exclusive museum fundraiser! Before the public opening!"

I examined the tickets that Sarah was waving around. They were on black cardstock, with golden, ornate lettering. Odd symbols framed the edges of the tickets.

"Oh, yeah?" Vicky huffed as she let her hand holding the letter fall to her side. "And what museum would that be?"

Sarah waved the tickets again. "Magus Artifacts and Relics Museum," she exclaimed.

"Never heard of it. Have you, Kyle?"

"I heard of it, never been," I explained, reaching out, holding Sarah's hand still to get a better look at the ticket. "It sounds interesting. But..." I trailed off.

"Wondering why we were invited, Master?"

"Yeah." I released Sarah's hand.

"Anima Mortis? Sounds like a heavy metal band or a crappy horror film," Vicky mocked, ridiculing the letter's author. "But a dusty museum filled with creepy stuff does sound interesting."

"It's Latin. I think it means the 'soul of death' or something like that." Sarah explained coolly. Her eyes were fixed on the letter in Vicky's hand. "Let me see that, please."

Vicky gave Sarah the letter. Their hands gently caressed each other for a brief moment. At least they weren't being catty anymore. I felt relieved about that.

Sarah read the letter immediately, snickering at the contents. "Mr. Death or whoever has a poetic sense to his pranks."

"Yeah, that death stuff made me feel uneasy." Vicky sighed as she looked over at me. Her face seemed to be forming into a concerned scowl.

I found it odd that neither mentioned the letter's L.O.V. portion. I finally remembered that L.O.V. was the project mentioned in the memo I saw in the girls' stuff when I moved them in, yet neither acknowledged that part of the bizarre letter.

I gave a light hum before opening my mouth. "So, I guess that means we aren't going to the museum thing?" I questioned.

"Hell yeah, we're going," Vicky said. "We're more badass than some emo poet. Besides, I kind of want to see what kind of friends this oddball has."

Sarah glanced between the tickets and the letter. "You think this could be some cheesy Halloween party to get people to donate?" Her voice suggested that she didn't trust the author or the invite.

"Well, whatever it is, we can mess with it later." I pointed toward the decorations lying on the table. "But for now, we gotta get done decorating, eat, and get ready. We meet Elle and Howard at the dance club after dark."

"Dancing! I can't wait." Sarah bounced as she returned to her playful self.

Vicky shook her head. "You're right. We can play cloak and dagger games later."

I went to the kitchen to start dinner, while Vicky and Sarah returned to decorating the apartment. The entire time, I stayed quiet, my mind racing over what that letter meant. And L.O.V., I had to get more information on that project. It seemed to be a ghost that would haunt us until I got a solid answer—a ghost that others could see but was invisible to me.

I didn't have time for that now; I needed to cook my wives dinner. I opened the fridge, scanning its contents. Leftover chicken breasts—yes, I could make something with that. I reached in, grabbing the container. I retrieved the chopping board and knife and began slicing the chicken into small chunks.

Cheesy ranch chicken sounded good. And easy. I gathered the ingredients: a can of mixed vegetables, a bottle of ranch dressing, a couple of shredded cheeses we had on hand, and noodles. It was a simple meal, but I knew they would both like it.

"Looks like Master is experimenting again." Sarah chuckled as she pointed toward me.

Vicky shook her head. "Hope it doesn't turn out like the last disaster he tried."

"Hey, I'll have you know those biscuits made excellent shooting targets," I shot back.

The apartment started to return to its lighthearted goofiness. That ominous atmosphere from the letter was not entirely dispelled, but had receded enough for us to return to reality: our reality, our little world of three.

However, as I cooked, my mind kept returning to that letter. It mentioned death not once but twice—once in the poem and once in the signature. I looked at Sarah and Vicky. Who would want to bring death to my beloveds? I didn't have an answer. But I knew I had to protect them—keep them safe from whatever that letter implied. Or was it just my paranoia creeping up?

As I stirred the mixture, my gaze drifted to them. I watched my gorgeous treasures in amazement. Vicky was on the stepladder hanging bats, and Sarah was handing her other little items here and there. They may never know how they saved me. They brought me back from the war, not physically, but back to myself as a person.

War taught me to be a monster, but they taught me to love. And love I do, I love them both. That's why I need to vow to myself to make sure this life is peaceful for the three of us.

I pushed the darkness from my mind once more and started setting the table, but my eyes couldn't stay off of them. My body hummed with a different kind of hunger. Vicky's washboard stomach looked kissable in that shirt. And the way Sarah's body gracefully stretched as she handed things up to Vicky stirred me.

Every move, every curve was a silent promise to our nights together. The time of day when we mesh beautifully into one being, as our desires for each other took hold. The tender whispers of affection, the silent moans of pleasure, the muffled cries of release. All circling us, making the three of us at one with each other.

I was getting myself worked up, so I calmed down. Besides, it was time to feed them. *Mmm, feed them—no, down boy!*

"Time to eat," I announced as I moved the food over.

"Coming." They responded in unison. It wasn't creepy anymore that they did that. Instead, I found it cute and sexy that they were on the same page, saying things in perfect harmony.

They finished hanging the last item, quickly folded the ladder, cleaned up, and sat at the table. I sat back watching them take their scoops, then took mine. Being responsible for them, I kept my military decorum of rank eats last.

"You think someone is watching us?" Vicky asked as I was taking a bite. This intense question quickly set the mood on edge.

"No, I don't think so. Not with my paranoia from the war not alerting, anyway."

"Who would be watching us, sis?" Sarah held her fork up with a piece of chicken stabbed to the end. "Miss Wanda?"

Vicky let out a sigh before shrugging.

We chatted and ate. Our conversation moved from the disturbing letter to more fun topics. We had made plans for the night. And none of us wanted our fun to be spoiled by some haunted house bull crap.

"You know, this isn't half bad." Vicky snickered as she looked at her fork full of the dish.

"Master, it's terrific," Sarah confirmed as she put another bite into her mouth.

"Thank you." I rejoiced. My fork twirled noodles before I took a bite. "I knew you both would enjoy it."

After finishing, we cleaned the kitchen together. I washed the dishes as they cleared the table.

As I was busy with my hands in the suds, Vicky and Sarah slid the last dishes into the sink. A sudden, familiar, and comforting embrace overtook me. My beauties had wrapped their arms around my sides: Sarah on my left, Vicky on my right.

The combined heat of their bodies, the soft press of their breasts against my back, sent a shiver of pure contentment through me. At that moment, I felt their love wash over me in waves. A teasing giggle escaped their lips. But this wasn't just teasing, it was an affirmation, a silent acknowledgment of our bond. The caress was an act of showing appreciation for my spirit.

In that moment, surrounded by their warmth, the mundane act of washing dishes felt like the most sacred of rituals, a statement to the beautiful, messy, and perfect life we were building together. A life of playful happiness I knew we deserved.

After cleaning up, we found ourselves in the bedroom, readying for the club.

Sarah wore a jean skirt and a flowery western-style shirt. She tied the shirt to accentuate her cleavage. Vicky chose a long black skirt that hugged her curves and a top that looked more like two black ribbons that wrapped her in an X, barely covering her breasts.

They always dressed so pleasingly, but tonight, they were masterpieces. Sarah's playful tie, Vicky's daring ribbons—each choice a deliberate invitation, a declaration of their confidence and their desire to captivate my eyes. My gaze lingered, indulging in the sights they created, like a child drawn to candy, but with a man's deep, appreciative hunger for the women who were truly his.

As I selected my club clothes, I wondered if it was a good idea to accept the invitation to the museum. My hand slowly buttoned my shirt as I tried to shake off thoughts of that letter. It's just spook-house advertisement for the museum. It's what it has to be. Besides, I'd soon get to dance with my beauties and hang with my best friend and sister. That was the perfect antidote for the unsettling letter.

Tonight wasn't just a night out; it was a celebration of the fierce, unconditional love that defined us. I had no time for all the nonsense about the boogeyman note. It couldn't touch the joy we found in each other. The happiness our life together brought

Mr. Mortis, we'll probably go to your gala. Prove it's just some Halloween-infused thing to garner donations. But still... L.O.V., what exactly is that? And how is it connected to me... us three?

It said, "the shackles that bind are bound to three." It must mean us as a throuple, right? Or was I reading too much into it?

Whatever it was, it didn't matter—time to enjoy a fun night, free of worry. However, I just needed to ensure my guard stayed up, just in case. Keeping Vicky and Sarah safe was my priority.

"Are we ready, ladies?"

Sarah slanted her head to one side as she put on her earring. "Coming, Master,"

Vicky slid her feet into her heels and jumped from the bed. "Ready and willing."

As we exited the apartment, I gave them both a quick slap on the butt. They both jolted forward, letting loose frolicsome giggles.

"Ooh, Master is feeling frisky." Sarah bubbled.

Vicky turned her head to gaze at me with a lustful stare. "Frisky, huh. Slow down, cowboy, you haven't even liquored us up yet."

I smirked. "Just want to give you two a one-handed applause for such nice asses."

"Get going, mister, or we'll be late," Vicky said.

We navigated to Vicky's car; she wanted to drive this time. I jumped into the back seat as they got in up front. For some reason, I felt a pang of dejection.

I settled into my seat, and a desperation spread in me at not having their warmth next to me. Their distance seemed a million miles away as this desire built a fire in me. The intoxicating scent of their perfumes was driving me crazy. My hunger for them was spurring the need for their touch, yet I was exiled to the back, alone.

I watched the sky darken as the vehicle passed street signs. Pedestrians walked to a beat that seemed passionless. Was the danger the letter posed an aphrodisiac, heightening my cravings? Or was I more than ready to claim them, having restrained myself all day? My soul ached to be complete, to feel their embraces. Taste the sweetness of their kiss.

Stop working yourself up, Sergeant. Just sit back and relax. We're on our way to the dance club for a fun night out.

Still, the silent promise of passion lingered in the car. There was no quick fix for my need to have them. It was a journey with a destination and a treasure waiting to be discovered. I knew, without a doubt, that later they would be fully and completely mine. All I had to do was be patient. To wait, which I would, because that treasure was worth every agonizing moment.

Chapter 3: Nightclub Blues

Day melded into night, and darkness edged into the retreating day. As the sun gave way, the moon made its way into the sky. I felt the revelry of the shadows wash over the city, the neon glow fill the air.

The nightclub was pulsating with a sense of defiance, almost primitive, against the modern, civilized urban atmosphere. A large neon sign hung over the door, shining brightly. *"Full Moon Lounge"* was highlighted against the red brick, hinting at a mystical allure for night owls—an invitation to indulge in hedonistic dance.

We parked not far from the club. Next to the place was a guy standing in the parking lot. He looked like a thuggish teenager in baggy pants and a jersey. He seemed more like he was swimming in the fabric than wearing it. The red bandana on his head made him look nefarious. I immediately felt my guard go up.

We exited the vehicle, and I locked it—a task I usually didn't do. I kept my gaze focused on the suspicious young man. Soon, I felt two warm bodies next to me, and without hesitating, we moved forward. As usual, Sarah walked to my right and Vicky to my left. I held both of them by the waist, guiding them away from that young man. I wanted to protect them from him.

My loves walked close beside me. Sarah slouched as she gripped my arm, radiating an almost fearful vibe. But Vicky stood tall, confidently holding my waist. This would be a fun night, finally hitting the dance floor with my beauties.

"That guy looks creepy," Sarah whispered.

"Just stay close," I commanded. "I'll protect you both."

We walked toward the club, not acknowledging the guy.

"Hey, my dude! What ya doin' with two hot snatches?" The thug walked up to us. He had a faint, musky smell, like a wet dog or something.

We ignored him and kept walking. But this kid didn't seem to take the hint; he rushed beside Vicky.

"Shawty, ya know ya need a good dicking down. Girl, why ya with this loser? Could have a real man's cock in ya."

This kid was becoming annoying. Wasn't it his bedtime? Could his mother be around here somewhere? Or a father with a leather belt to dole out some discipline?

The boy started walking backward in front of Vicky, continuing to do so. "Come on, ya bitches know ya need this young dick." His hand made a rude gesture at his crotch.

He didn't know he'd just said the wrong thing, calling my wives bitches. How dare this punk!

"Watch your mouth, boy," I growled. I felt my muscles tense as I halted our movements. My arms dropped from my fiancées to my sides, my body square with the kid. I was going to protect my loves from this thug.

But before I could say or do anything else, I felt a soft hand on my shoulder, giving a light tug back.

"Aww, aren't you just the cutest wittle thing?" Sarah said with a patronizing sneer. With a flick of her hand, she tossed her hair backward. "Where's your mommy, huh?"

"Hmm, bet his blood would be delicious," Vicky purred, baring her teeth in a menacing grin. She chomped her teeth at the thug as she growled. "Rawr!"

The boy flinched back, looking shocked. His stance shifted into a sloppy defensive posture. I was sure this kid had never fought a day in his life. I eased from my stance. Sensing my aggression wane, Vicky released my shoulder.

"Careful, dude. My fiancées are dangerous," I stated sharply. An air of command filled the space around me as I wrapped my arms around the girls' waists, drawing them nearer. My eyes narrowed into a piercing glare. "Maybe you should back off. Unless you're eager to find out exactly how dangerous they can be."

He said nothing as he trudged past us, deflated and embarrassed. I watched his every move until he faded away from my view. It was only then that my muscles began to relax.

When he was out of earshot, Sarah asked. "Rawr? Really, Vicky?" She tapped her sister playfully. "What's gotten into you?"

"It just came out," Vicky tittered. Her hand ran up my back.

Sarah squeezed my butt roughly, "Oh, and look at you, almost laying hands on that punk. Tsk-tsk. Master, I'm disappointed in you," she teased, wagging her finger at me.

"I'm not the one who wanted to drink his blood." My eyes darted to Vicky.

"She's just getting into her vampire mood," Sarah explained, shrugging. "Tis the season."

"The season of you crazy shawties," I joked.

My sessions with Holly seemed to have a positive impact. If that punk had tried this a few months ago, I might've banged him up pretty good. But now, I was able to hold myself back. Sarah and Vicky handled him well. They didn't seem to want me dirtying my hands and sully our night out. Vicky and Sarah had often told me I no longer needed to be a soldier; I could simply be their lover. This idea of being a lover made me feel better about myself and my titles.

I started thinking about the names we called each other in the Army. Killer sounds silly now, but that was what we called each other. Killer and Battle were names that once held a special place for me, like brotherly names of endearment. But I no longer wanted to identify as a killer—simply a man—a man in love with his fiancées.

"Maybe that was Mr. Mortis?" Sarah chuckled.

Vicky rested her head on my shoulder. "If that idiot is our doom letter guy, then I'm the fucking queen of the world." She laughed.

"Haven't you guys watched horror films? It's always the person you least suspect. So maybe Mr. Shawty and Mr. Death are the same person," I teased in a spooky voice.

As the last sentence left my lips, we approached the club entrance. The doorway was framed by neon blue lights, making it seem like a dream to enter. A red velvet rope was all that stood between us and the inside, guarded by a giant who reminded me of someone from a Conan movie. His biceps, outlined through his button-up shirt, were as big as my thighs. I was sure he could easily toss around most riffraff like a ragdoll.

He stood tall beside the doorway, clipboard in one hand, eyeing me with an odd stare. It was the look someone would give when they had already neutralized a threat, a brush-off of potential danger.

"Good evening, sir," I greeted him with a slight nod. His eyes stayed fixed on me. I smiled, letting him know I wasn't intimidated by his size.

The bouncer held out his arm to halt us. His wrist extended past his shirt cuff; it was hairier than most. "Members only." He said in a soft, squeaky voice.

For some reason, a thought flashed in my mind of a small mouse attempting not to get caught in the kitchen with a hunk of cheese. I snickered to myself at the odd contradiction of his stature with that shrill voice.

Sarah held her hand out as she presented our IDs to him. His large fist snatched the cards with the smoothness of a flowing river. I wasn't sure if I could win in a tussle with him. Not only was he massive, but he was agile, too. That combo might land me a lovely vacation in the ICU.

"We're members," I stated firmly, confident that Howard had already gotten our memberships to this club.

"Never seen you guys before," he mumbled. Immediately searching the clipboard.

Vicky looked over at me with affection, then back at the bouncer. "We don't get out much."

"Surprisingly, you three are on the list," he said as he handed our driver's licenses back. "Right this way." He opened the velvet rope, inviting us in.

"Oh, and there is some weirdo harassing members over there," I explained, pointing in the direction we had encountered the thug.

"Mm-hmm." He acknowledged with a nod as we passed by him.

As we entered, the pungent aroma of alcohol wafted into our nostrils. Numerous paintings of wolves in various scenes hung along the black walls. The hallway was illuminated by light strips along the floor and in the ceiling corners, resembling an airport runway. Near the take-off point were two black swinging doors with crescent moon windows. We moved forward; the music grew louder as we approached the end of the hallway. Shoving through the door, we made it inside.

The lighting was dim, with neon strips strategically placed to enhance the wolf motif and spotlight the thematic elements throughout the space. Two large wolf statues stood majestically at each end of the bar, emphasizing the overall ambiance.

The club was semi-packed. Most patrons moved along with the DJ's music on the dance floor. Around the bar, singles seemed to be waiting to find a partner for a dance, either on the dance floor or in the sheets. Booths lined the outer walls.

"Sarah. Vicky. Please bring my hermit brother over here." Elle's voice sounded from the closest booth as she waved us over.

I glanced toward the booth; Elle was seated next to Howard. It was always an interesting sight to see them together. Her slender, twig-like figure beside his ridiculously stacked muscles was a stark contrast. The only comparisons that would come close are Mutt and Jeff or Popeye and Olive Oyl.

Our feet carried us over; we slid into the bench opposite Elle and Howard.

"I win the bet, ya owe me a dance," Howard smirked, looking mischievously at Elle.

"Okay, Steroids, you win," Elle grumbled. "But we drink first."

My brows furrowed, "What bet?"

Howard rubbed his hands together, like he had just stolen a precious jewel or something. "Ya sista bet that ya wouldn't come."

Elle elbowed Howard. "Well, he usually stays in that apartment," she said dismissively. Her gaze flicked to me with a hint of envy in her eyes before her smile lingered a bit longer on Vicky.

"Anyway... how are you, Elle?" Vicky leaned forward over the table.

I bristled, a pang of betrayal hit me as Vicky seemed to ignore the fact that my sister had practically insulted me.

"Good. How are my favorite ladies?"

"Awesome, Miss Elle!" Sarah bounced in her seat.

"Doing alright," Vicky responded. Her eyes glanced at her hands. "My instruments have been troubling me."

Elle eyed Vicky's hands. "What's wrong with your mitts?"

"Too many massages, I guess."

My sister and fiancées started conversing. I paid attention to Howard. His presence seemed lighter than usual, happier even. I smiled, knowing that maybe he and Elle were getting closer.

"How are things, bro?" I asked him as I nodded toward Elle.

Howard gave me a quick, stiff smile before speaking. "All good." His voice was loud and elated before he whispered. "That thing next to the thing, we can close on it next week."

I understood immediately what he meant. The building for Vicky's spa was almost ready. Then I could present her with the keys and see the look on her face as her dream came true.

"Cool, we'll get into the details later."

"Hey, ya get the insights about Sentinel's new project I sent over?" Howard asked. He flashed a quick smile. "Sounds like a good add to our investment accounts."

"Yeah, but I don't know what consciousness transference means. So, are they downloading people's minds into computers?"

"Ya know, I didn't fully understand all the science mumbo-jumbo myself. But I think so." Howard looked up, his gaze distant. "From what I gather, there are a lot of people who'd pay to have the service."

"Okay. Guess I'll add some to the project's investment," I said. A sigh of resignation soon escaped my lips.

Howard knew more about investments than I did. He had helped me set up the account in the first place. Not surprisingly, it had grown significantly under his tutelage. This was his domain anyway.

"Cool." Howard nodded. "Oh, Rylon-Tek, that arms company I was telling ya about, they got the contract to make some kinda plasma guns or something for the military."

"Plasma guns?" I was stunned. "Like in the movies?"

"Yeah, uses electro-whatever converted from, get this, a special sap from a tree outta Germany. It shoots a bolt of energy. Ya might want to read over the investment proposal."

"Send it to me. I'll look it over," I said. A thought struck me. "In June, you mentioned some R&D project involving cloned organs to help people be removed from the donor list. Is that still a thing?"

"Yeah, ITI, ya soon-to-be ex-brother-in-law's company, was ramping up for it back 'bout six months ago." Howard shrugged. "Why ya ask?"

"Just curious what happened," I replied.

"Another company beat 'em to it. Prodigy Life or something. Anyway, my ITI stocks never shot up."

"You two never stop working," Vicky interjected. Her finger poked me in the ribs. "Don't make us put you in a corner."

Howard shook his head. "Damn, brah." His hands rising in mock surrender. "Jus' got here and ya already in trouble."

"No more work talk for you either." Elle jabbed a finger in Howard's face. "Unless He-Man doesn't want the dance I promised."

"Good evening, what would you like?" the barmaid interrupted as she came over. Her smile seemed forced, but it made her approachable. "We're running a special on daiquiris."

"Ooh. Daiquiri sounds super yummy!" Sarah squealed.

She looked at me for approval. I gave a slight nod.

Sarah looked back at the waitress. "I'll have a tropical daiquiri, please, ma'am."

Vicky raised her hand from the table, pointing toward Sarah. "Yeah, let me get one too, please."

The waitress looked at me. "Just a Mountain Dew for me, thank you." I sighed.

I was the designated driver for the night. However, though I may not be drinking, I will enjoy the benefits of Sarah and Vicky being intoxicated later. They were even more sexually wild and adventurous when they got tipsy—more than a fair trade-off, if you ask me.

Elle snapped her fingers in front of my face, a teasing smirk playing on her lips. "Did you go off to perv land or something?"

The look on her face was a playful scowl tinged with a hint of jealousy, which then softened.

"No, just, uh, thinking," I stammered before coming up with a proper response. "Hey, did either of you get a weird invitation to some kind of museum spooktacular or whatever?"

"Spook what?" Howard asked, eyeing me with bewilderment. "Nah, ain't got nothing like that."

Elle looked stunned, as if she had stepped in dog crap. "Museum?"

"We got tickets to a museum event," Sarah explained.

Vicky halfheartedly chimed in. "Meh, it came with a weird promotional letter."

A fleeting feeling of unease washed over me. Why were Vicky and Sarah dismissing the strangeness of that letter?

"Can't say that I've gotten anything like that." Elle shrugged dismissively, though her fingers tapped impatiently on the table. There was a flicker of envy in her eyes as she looked between the three of us. "Booze is flowing like mud around here," she added, trying to sound casual but failing to hide her anxiousness.

Not a few seconds after Elle voiced her concern, the barmaid brought our first round. We sat for a while drinking, and round after round came in. We discussed this and that, but I didn't mention the weird letter again. However, the topic of my engagement came up as the second round of drinks arrived.

"Brah, you talk with my dad?" Howard asked before downing his whiskey shot. "'Bout the wedding?"

"He said that we could try suing for our First Amendment right," I explained. The hope in my voice faded as I took a small sip. "But it's a long shot."

Elle gently patted my hand. "Well, it's still worth a try, little Bro." Her warm voice sounded hollow. A cold flicker lingered in her eyes before she masked it with a smile.

Her insincerity seemed weird. Or maybe I was reading too much into it?

"Love is always worth a try! Right, Miss Elle?" Sarah beamed.

"Besides, if Kyle doesn't marry us soon, we might be old maids put out to pasture in a few years." Vicky laughed, trying to bring the mood back to a playful beat.

Elle rolled her eyes. "My brother's heart and perviness belong to you two." The way she emphasized "two" seemed like a gibe at our throuple, but maybe it was just my imagination.

The music suddenly changed. The rhythm entranced me. My feet were bouncing with the drums. Sarah looked at me with a knowing gaze.

"Let's dance, Master." Sarah tugged on my arm.

Vicky gave me a gentle push before saying, "Dancing, yes, come dance with us."

"See you two in a minute." I looked between Howard and Elle. He had a big, goofy grin as he playfully shooed me with his hand. She waved at me, a slight flicker of something sharp crossing her face before she rolled her eyes. Then I scooted out of the booth. The music started taking hold of me as we moved toward the floor.

"We'll hold down the fort for ya," Howard said, adding while glaring at Elle. "Ya still owe me, ya know."

"After they get back, dickwad," Elle retorted. "You told me that you would explain that ITI project."

Howard started to speak, but I couldn't make anything out because Sarah and Vicky were dragging me away. We soon found ourselves on the dance floor.

Our bodies started to move in sync with the rhythm of the music. Although the dance floor was packed, it felt like we were the only three there. My movements mirrored those of Sarah and Vicky perfectly.

I held them close. They knew that even though the dance floor was crowded with bodies, they were the only people present to me. Our feet moved to the music, our hips swaying in sync. Heating up with sexy movements, we expressed the need that the three of us had—a need to touch each other, to feel the soul of the other two. I would turn to one, then the other, ensuring equal time with them.

Vicky and Sarah started dancing provocatively together; I stepped back to enjoy the sight. Their heads turned to me as they were grinding onto each other, their hands roaming over each other's bodies. Our three pairs of eyes studied one another, hungry for the soul of the other. I was struck in amazement at them.

"Want a taste, Master?" Sarah asked in that cute baby voice, her hips gyrating against Vicky. Their movements were divine.

I moved forward, embracing them both as I began to maneuver with them. Faucets of their radiance showered over me into a carnal cleanse with our dancing. I felt their hands exploring my chest as our bodies intertwined into a sensual sway. My heart was thumping in my chest, and my breathing was erratic. They were incredibly intelligent and humorous. Beautiful and sensual. But most astonishingly, they were mine. And I was irrevocably theirs.

The raw fragrance of their skin infiltrated my senses; the wonder of these awe-inspiring women surrounded me.

I reached down, fringing Vicky's hair, pulling her soft cheek to mine. Hammering my lips against hers, the crimson pucker of firm gloss sealed a curl of my tongue into her wanting smile. I began to taste the harsh and wild nature I had come to know she was. Our tongues fought against each other as we struggled to take control of the other. Clashing as we always did in our eternal war. We fought mouth to mouth, tongue to tongue for dominance. I was soon the victor, claiming Vicky once more. I felt like a king in her wake, conquering her.

I broke from Vicky and turned to Sarah. My hand reached up, caressing Sarah's smooth face. Sold to the dirty innocence of her elegant movements, I was compelled to taste her lips. Her face glowed with warmth as her eyes caught sight of my happiness. The happiness that she enthralled me as my lips sipped in her softness. Belted into an expression of affection, her mouth accepted mine. Whipped with the delectable sugar of her salivated hearth, I gathered her candy in with gluttony. Her breaths into my lungs were life's joy poured into my spirit.

Breaking my kiss with Sarah, the music swept the three of us into a perfect harmony of movements. I could hear gasps from the crowd. But I wasn't concerned with what others thought of us; my only cognitive thought was them, us, our three souls engaged in merriment, celebrating our love.

In their presence, I always felt as though I wore a crown, jeweled with their never-ending love. I was complete with my beauties. They were like a drug to me, making me high—high on life... high on love.

My mind wandered, hearing them moan in pleasure. Their cool sweat pressed against me. The unforgettable feeling when their moist velvet walls surrounded me. My manhood felt like it could jump out at any moment to take them. To own them.

But just as I was in the throes of this feeling, I felt Sarah suddenly be tugged away with great force. The movement was so fast that I was momentarily stunned. I looked over to see the thug we had encountered in the parking lot, his hand tightly gripping Sarah's wrist. She instinctively pulled back her arm to no avail.

"Let go of me, asshole!" Sarah yelled as her free hand slapped him. The loud pop didn't seem to faze this thug. For a fleeting moment, his eyes appeared to glow like a cat or dog.

"Think ya so fucken tough, bitch. I'ma fuck ya!" he shouted, pulling Sarah away. Sarah kicked him between his legs. He leaned forward, doubling over, but quickly straightened up. However, his face was still twisted with pain.

I snapped out of my shock and moved to intercept Sarah from him. Before I could step in, a massive arm flew right past my face. The knuckles smashed into the thug's jaw with a loud crack. The thug let go of Sarah as he was knocked backward. He fell onto his back, startling a couple dancing nearby. Blood seeped from his mouth as he whimpered in pain.

"Don't ya fucken touch my sister-in-law, ya dirty mothahfucka!" Howard bellowed, readying to strike again.

It was at that moment that the bouncer came over. He glanced at the four of us, then he glared at the thug.

"Get your ass up, Deshawn," the bouncer said in that high-pitched voice, "before I finish knocking your damn teeth out."

The thug got up; embarrassment cascaded over him. He looked like a child being scolded. Two more bouncers came over, escorting the thug to the entrance. My eyes glared at him with disdain as I pulled Sarah into my arms.

"Are you okay?" I asked, my voice slightly wavering.

"Yes, Master. I'm fine," Sarah replied before her face looked down at me. "And happy that you didn't get into a fight."

Turning to Howard. "Thank you, bro," I uttered with relief.

"No one touches my brah or my sistas," Howard stated with pride. His arm reached out to briefly pat my shoulder.

Elle stepped close to Vicky. "Damn, Howard. That was one helluva punch," she said with a hint of admiration in her voice.

"I guess we're in trouble now?" Vicky implied as she scratched her head.

"No, ma'am. I'm going to talk with the owner," the bouncer explained as he looked toward a large mirror on the other side of the dance floor. "Please enjoy some refreshments on the house." He pointed toward our booth.

The five of us got the hint and soon exited the dance floor. We returned to our booth. The barmaid brought a round to the table as we cozied back into our seats.

"This round is on the house." She smiled as her hand started passing each drink over.

"Gotta give it to you, Bro. When that creep grabbed Sarah, I thought you might wreck his shit," Elle said before taking a sip of her daiquiri. "But you didn't. I'm proud of you."

Vicky clinked her glass with Elle's. "I second that. Holly has made great progress with him."

"Master has been far less angry than he once was," Sarah disclosed, her hand briefly caressing my shoulder.

"Whatta 'bout me?" Howard interjected. "I'm the hero here."

I smiled at Howard. "Thank you, again, bro. I really appreciated that you stepped in."

"You did well, too," Elle said, turning her face to Howard. "My hero," she sarcastically swooned.

Even though she was picking on him, I could see in her eyes that she admired his actions. Perhaps I should consider a career as a Cupid, playing matchmaker for lost souls.

Howard beamed. "Hero enough to lick ya holes?"

“How about you lick a toilet bowl instead?” Elle responded with an icy chill.

On second thought, maybe I should stay in HVAC. Being a matchmaker for someone like Howard might end with my balls being chopped off, and I’m sort of attached to them. Sorry, all you lost souls. I’m just not up to the job.

“Excuse me.” A man’s voice sounded outside the booth. “I’m—”

“Jamal?” Howard asked. “Fuck. Ain’t seen ya ass in forever.”

Jamal acknowledged Howard. “Yeah, been a while, Howey.” “The last time I saw you was in seventh grade.”

“Was that the time in the bathroom when ya buddies held me down so ya could give me a swirly?” Howard asked as humiliation washed over his face. His eyes darted to Elle; he gulped hard.

“Sorry about that. I was a scumbag teenager.” Jamal shuddered; he seemed to be ashamed of that time as well. “I truly am sorry I did that to you when we were kids.”

“It’s all good,” Howard murmured. His cheeks flushed red as he noticed Elle looking at him. “Water under the lake.”

Well, I can see Howard still hasn’t learned his idioms. Or is he purposefully messing them up to keep up his facade persona?

I looked over Jamal, trying to determine what kind of man, boy, had tormented my brother. He was of average height and athletic, but nowhere near as muscular as Howard. Howard had mentioned that during high school, he started working out and weightlifting to become as big as he could. Was Jamal the reason? And possibly the reason for Howard’s carefully crafted hard-edge persona.

Sarah cleared her throat, snapping me back from my thoughts.

Sarah’s eyes stared Jamal down with laser accuracy. “Are you the owner?”

“Yes, ma’am, I am.”

“I should call the police!” Sarah snapped. I’d never seen her so angry. She was usually the calm one, the peacemaker.

“I apologize for Deshawn, ma’am. He’s just a pup. No need for police, ma’am,” Jamal said with sympathy. “We’ll handle it; he doesn’t understand the Lycan ways, yet.”

Lycan? Lycanthropy? I glanced over to the wolf décor. Oh, this must be one of those themed clubs. It’s probably catering to werewolf cosplayers or lifestylists. Once in the Army, I stumbled off post into one of those vampire-themed places. Friendly people, but they took the fantasy too far for my tastes.

I looked over Jamal one last time, paying closer attention. Then I saw it on the left side of his neck—a wolf tattoo, the same one the courier had on his hand earlier. The black ink was barely noticeable against his dark complexion, but it was there. The courier had howled earlier, something about a pack. Don't wolves run in a pack?

"Thank you for the apology," Vicky said, reaching her arm behind me to caress Sarah's shoulder. "My sister doesn't like strangers touching her."

"Again, I apologize," Jamal said with remorse. He briefly hung his head low. "And to make up for it, your tab for the night is on the house. Drink all you want."

"Thank you, sir," Sarah whispered, her body relaxing back in her seat. She seemed to let go of all the frustration.

"Enjoy your night. If there's nothing else, I will take my leave," Jamal said as he started to turn away.

"A word with you, sir," I said. That tattoo had me intrigued. Was it a gang tattoo or something? "Privately," I added.

"Sure, we can go to my office," he said as he turned toward the other end of the club.

Vicky sighed as she pulled her arm back. "Don't do anything stupid," she cautioned.

I didn't respond. How could I? I didn't know how I would react to the answers he could offer.

Sarah briefly stepped out of the booth, letting me exit as well. I began to follow Jamal. His movements were fluid, like the doorman's. Being so close, I caught a whiff of something. It wasn't cologne but something damp and earthy, like overturned dirt after heavy rain combined with a sharp tang of ozone. It felt completely out of place in the crowded club.

I glanced around; the eyes of most patrons followed him. Was he their leader? Alpha wolf? I chuckled inwardly at the idea. These cosplayers are often overly dramatic about the theme.

We moved to a door next to the large mirror that overlooked the dance floor. He went inside. As I entered, I noticed the office was neat and clean. There were a few shelves scattered here and there, lined with books. A dark-stained wooden desk sat in the middle of the room. I noticed half a dozen wolf figures of various sizes on the desk. Behind it was an office chair, and a circle of four chairs faced it. A large window overlooking the dance floor was in the same spot as the dance floor mirror. He had a two-way mirror to watch over his club—a genius move.

He sat in the office chair, motioning me to sit in front of his desk. His posture seemed tense. His expression was apprehensive but strangely hopeful. "How can I help you?"

"That tattoo," I stated coolly as I sat down. "I'd seen it earlier on a courier."

Jamal visibly relaxed. "Garou Couriers, another business of mine," he said as a smile formed on his face. "Looking for a job?"

"I don't need a job." I leaned back in my chair. "I need information."

"On?"

"A strange letter was sent to me through your courier service. No name, no return address," I explained.

"Our client information is confidential, and if the client did not place their name on the parcel, it is their right." He shrugged, looking at me with an annoyed gaze.

"It was signed Anima Mortis." My NCO voice rang harshly. "It was a creepy note. Freaked out my fiancées."

"Anima Mortis? Spirit of death. Doesn't ring any bells." Jamal shook his head. "Now, if you don't mind, I'm a busy man. Please see yourself out."

"Tickets inviting us to a museum fundraiser were in it," I calmly stated. His eyes widened at the mention of a museum. "Magus Artifacts and Relics Museum, to be exact."

Jamal choked when I named the museum. His body tensed with terror, as if a monster lurked there.

"Did he send you?" Jamal asked in a shaky voice.

"Huh? No. I have no idea who *he* is," I replied. "That's why I asked to speak with you when I noticed the tattoo. Figured you might have something on him."

"A dangerous man. Far more dangerous than me," Jamal admitted as he looked away. His eyes scanned the window. "That's all I can say."

"So, you know him? I assume really well?"

"Yes, but I dare not speak about him. If that is all, please leave my office." Jamal grunted and pointed to the door. "Enjoy your evening. And never mention him again. To anyone."

I didn't press for any more information. I got my answer. The letter was not an advertisement. It wasn't a joke. Something was happening. And it was happening to my family, my beauties. I didn't want them to be dragged into something vile like this. Something that felt like a war. A silent declaration, or a whispered warning.

I was a soldier once, but now I yearned for peace and a simple life with my loved ones. However, this letter might disrupt my sanctuary. Jamal seemed genuinely afraid of my mystery man. Poetic as the letter was, it didn't convey anything pleasant.

I left the office, plastering a fake smile on my face. I didn't want to ruin what was left of this night. My mind reeled over eventually meeting Mr. Mortis and hearing what he had to say about Project L.O.V. A familiar voice rang out, breaking me from my thoughts.

"Kyle." I looked over at the dance floor where the voice came from to see Myra. Her blond hair had grown out a little since I last saw her; she no longer had a pixie cut. It looked like an angled bob.

"Myra, how are you?" I asked, turning toward the dance floor.

"Good, I guess," she said with an awkward smile. "You?"

"Doing great," I said, then excitedly explained. "Started my own company. Even got engaged."

"I knew about the business. David left not long after you were..." She trailed off. "Anyway, he said he was going to work for you. And congratulations on your engagement."

"Thank you. So, how's it at McKellen's these days?"

Myra shrugged, "I was laid off a few weeks ago."

"Sorry to hear that."

Myra walked closer to me as she said, "It's cool. I've wanted out of that place for a while." Her voice seemed filled with hope. "So, who's the lucky lady?"

I breathed deeply. "Well, that's a funny story..."

"Oh?" Myra eyed me with an intrigued glare.

"My fiancées are Vicky Schein and Sarah Jones."

Myra's face instantly changed. She stared at me, beguiled. "Come again?" She fidgeted for a moment. "Did I hear you right? Two?"

"Yes, I'm engaged to two women."

"Um, okay." She averted her eyes to the dance floor for a moment. She seemed unsure how to react to the news of my dual engagement. Then a husky sound rattled from her throat to find a way to change the subject. "Are you setting up for Halloween?"

"Yeah. We decorated the apartment earlier."

"It's only the sixth, and I already have my house set up. I hope you get lots of trick-or-treaters. I love Halloween. Seeing the kids have fun is my favorite part," she said, beaming with a large grin.

"That's my favorite part, too. What brought you to the club?"

"A girlfriend... Well, not a girlfriend. I'm not into that." She stammered, pausing to collect herself. "My friend said I needed to get out and meet a cute guy." She suddenly seemed even shyer.

"Well, it's always good to get out, let loose sometimes," I said. I pointed toward the dance floor. "I take it you like to dance."

"Y-yes, I love dancing," Myra revealed enthusiastically.

"Me too. That's why my fiancées dragged me here," I explained, waving my hand around. "The wolf décor adds to the mood."

Myra let out a soft, brief snort. "Yeah, it fits with Halloween."

"What are your plans for work? Do you have a job lined up?"

"No job lined up." Her voice seemed somber.

I smiled wryly. "Would you step back in as a dispatcher? Or are you looking to do something else?"

Myra sighed and stared at me oddly. "I could dispatch again if the pay was right."

"Well, when I get my office set up, I might have a position for you." I glanced over my shoulder at the booth. Vicky and Sarah seemed caught up in conversation; then Vicky gestured emphatically. Sarah nodded at Vicky as they seemed to be staring in my direction. I turned back to Myra. I felt my lips unconsciously curl into a slight smile uncontrollably.

A pained look washed over her face. "What would your fiancées say? Would they... be okay that you'd be working with me?" Her voice seemed filled with apprehension. Her eyes reflected what might be unrequited affection. But I wasn't entirely sure.

"I don't think..." I started to speak, but was interrupted by Vicky's booming voice.

"Found him!"

I briefly turned back to see Vicky and Sarah taking significant steps toward us. I looked at Myra, who seemed embarrassed. Her head hung down.

I felt the warmth of an arm wrapped smoothly around my waist as Vicky leaned into me.

"We were waiting for you, Master," Sarah said softly with a slight slur as she mirrored Vicky on my other side.

"Master?" Myra whispered in confusion to herself. Her brows furrowed, then arched.

"Girls, this is Myra; we worked together at McKellen's. Myra, this is Sarah and Vicky, my fiancées."

"Gorgeous," Myra whispered to herself again, then spoke energetically. "Nice to meet you."

"Hi." Sarah smiled as she tilted her head. I felt her fiery locks brush against me. The strong scent of alcohol was on her breath. "Myra, is it?"

"Yes, Myra," she announced as her face twisted momentarily, then smiled brightly again. "Are you Vicky?"

"I'm Sarah. The cute one." Sarah beamed with her childlike attitude. I could tell she was starting to feel the effects of the alcohol.

Vicky perked up her chest. "Vicky would be me."

"You still have my number, right?" Myra asked, looking at me with a strange stare.

"Yeah, I still have it," I answered apprehensively. I gave a brief smile. I didn't know how to react to this situation.

"You should come hang out with us sometime," Sarah suggested, her words slurring a bit.

"Uh, I don't want to impose."

"Don't be silly. Kyle told us that you were always kind to him," Vicky interjected. "We've wanted to meet you for a long time."

"Okay, I have to ask." Myra seemed to be nervous about something. "Why both?"

Sarah and Vicky gave a light snicker, but soon contained themselves.

"Because love..." Sarah shrugged, shaking her head; she seemed confused by the question.

"Does it bother you?" Vicky asked.

"Well. No. Just..." Myra stammered; she couldn't find the words she wanted to say. "I don't understand."

"Most people don't," I said as I pointed to a small crowd that had gathered on the dance floor to observe my interactions. Myra looked over at the crowd, her face flushed.

"I know, it's a lot for some people to take in," Sarah slurred as she glanced at the crowd, a coy smile emerged on her face. "But we're making it work."

"I'll think about hanging out," Myra told Sarah, her face showing embarrassment, before she looked at me. "Thank you for the job offer. Text me when it's open." Then she started back toward the center of the dance floor. She had an odd but happy look on her face. She briefly turned back to us. "Bye, Kyle," she said. "Nice meeting you, Sarah and Vicky."

"Bye, Myra, nice seeing you again."

"Have a great night, Myra," Sarah happily said, waving. "I hope to hang out sometime."

Vicky mirrored Sarah. "Nice meeting you, too. Enjoy dancing." She waved lazily at Myra.

Myra turned back and continued until she faded into the crowd on the dance floor.

Vicky whispered into my ear, "I'm gonna ride you raw later."

Sarah seemed to have heard Vicky and echoed her whisper. "Raw, real raw."

My face flushed; I could feel the surge of embarrassment. The heat of their bodies was doing little to help me contain myself.

"She seemed cool. A bit awkward but cool," Sarah commented.

"Yeah, it seems like she would make a good friend," Vicky affirmed, then her voice got serious. "But we still have a problem."

The tension felt thick in the air.

"Ugh, whatever," Sarah huffed, crossing her arms petulantly.

"What?"

"Where the hell were you? We needed you, and you ran off with that owner guy." Vicky's eyes narrowed, pointing a finger toward the booth. "Then we got ditched by Elle and Howard."

"But they look cute together," Sarah exclaimed as she swayed in her intoxicated state. Her hand pointed toward the dance floor.

I glanced over to see Howard and Elle slowly dancing in the crowd. It seemed my efforts as a Cupid were not in vain. I smiled, looking back at Vicky and Sarah. They both seemed really tipsy, drunk even. Maybe I should get them somewhere safe; tonight had been a barrage of crazies.

"Maybe we should head home. It's been a long day."

"But, Master, I want to have more fun with you!" Sarah pleaded childishly. "We got interrupted by that guy."

"And I think you're drunk," I scolded.

"Kyle is right, we might want to get home," Vicky said.

Howard and Elle glanced our way. I waved goodbye to them, then pointed at Sarah, who was almost falling over. They nodded in acknowledgement and waved us on. I soon tried to help Sarah stand properly with Vicky's help.

Vicky walked on one side of Sarah; I walked on the other. We helped to steady her movements. She couldn't hold her liquor too well. Vicky and I stayed in step with Sarah; occasionally, Sarah would lean heavily on one of us.

We made our way out of the club and hastily got in the car. I started it with ease. Vicky's car was a much better drive than my rusted old beater. On the drive home, the car was silent, eerily so. Forcing me to think about that letter, its contents, and most of all the enigmatic and dangerous author. I will figure out what this means. If I want to live a good life with my wives, I must solve it.

Chapter 4: Secret Needs

As we drove home, the lights from the road flickered rapidly, casting shadows in and out of the vehicle. My eyes focused on the jagged yellow center line, trying not to worry. But I was worried, concerned about my beauties. I knew I had to protect this life from whatever was lingering over us and that I might need to put my training to use. But from what I didn't know; I just had a strange feeling.

I lifted my eyes from the road and glanced at Sarah in the passenger seat. She seemed to be sobering up. My eyes darted to the rearview mirror to be met by Vicky's. She watched the front intently, almost as if she wanted to say something.

"What is it?"

Vicky averted her eyes. "While you were with that owner guy, Sarah and I conversed."

"About?"

"Master, I want to feel the way Vicky does," Sarah blurted. Her words didn't slur; she was more lucid than when we left.

"Um, okay."

"And I want to be treated the way you treat Sarah." Vicky hesitated before gaining courage. "To feel your softness."

"Use me, Master. Rough and hard," Sarah explained with clarity. "For one night, I want to know that side of you. Please, Master."

"And just once, I want to feel how tender you can be," Vicky admitted.

I focused on the road for a moment, stunned. How do I respond? I thought I was giving them the type of love they needed. Was I wrong? Or maybe this was what their current rivalry was about? My love for them was unique yet equal. Could they've needed to see the other side, to feel it?

"Say something." Vicky quavered, slightly embarrassed. She seemed more vulnerable than I'd ever seen her before.

"Is this what all the squabbling between you two has been about?" I asked.

"Part of it," Sarah admitted. She became increasingly sober as the conversation continued.

I was the cause of their strife, breaking their sisterhood apart. I felt the sting of that in my heart. I didn't want there to be any issues like this. I'd always tried to balance things evenly. I hadn't thought they would like to feel different portions of my love.

Had I been so caught up in balancing the relationship that I neglected them? Had I failed to realize that they each needed the complete version of me? Or at the very least, have them feel those portions individually. Maybe so.

"Just for tonight?" I questioned, a loving hesitation lacing into my words.

"Yes," they responded in a sexy unison.

The revelation hit me not as a challenge but as an invitation. It wasn't that my love was wrong. Instead, it was that they each needed—craved—the vastness it carried. I needed to embrace and encompass every corner of their desires. To meet them emotionally where they needed, precisely when they craved my affection. Granting them the different portions of praise I had for them.

Their willingness to share this vulnerable longing was, in itself, a deepening of our love. A wave of fierce joy washed over me, eager to explore these new depths of our passion and love. I'd made up my mind. Tonight, my softness would be Vicky's, and my savagery would be for Sarah.

"As you wish, my beauties."

We soon pulled into the apartment complex. After killing the vehicle, I strode toward the apartment with knots of anticipation tightening in my heart. Their request was unexpected. Their desires, their thoughts, were so raw and honest. I felt a sense of happiness stir, knowing they could share these desires I hadn't fully comprehended. Neither seemed as intoxicated as they were at the club; a focused intensity had replaced the giddiness. Was this what they truly desired? Would they enjoy it?

We hastily entered the apartment building. As we ascended the stairs, the air between us felt charged, as if oxygen itself was an aphrodisiac. My mind raced, replaying their words, the vulnerability that filled their eyes. I, too, had fantasized about doing something like this.

Our feet halted at the door as I unlocked it. Sarah was close to me, her hand brushed against mine, igniting a spark where our skin met. The heat of her body on mine radiated against me, promising the delights to come. I reached out, tracing my finger along her delicate jawline. A reminder to her that she was still cherished even if I beastly took her. Then my hand fell with restraint, trying not to make a scene in the hallway.

As the apartment door sprang open, our eyes locked. A deep, unspoken understanding passed between us. I grasped Sarah by the waist and pulled her near. My lips collided with hers with a nova of lust—a prelude to the fiery storm that beckoned to be unleashed.

As I fiercely kissed Sarah, my feet led her inside. The soft milk of her skin against my cheek seared me with coals of ripping flames. My body transformed into a furnace, burning hotter and hotter for her delicious taste. I wanted her... I needed her. There was nothing that could satisfy my thirst except her passion. I broke from our kiss, my eyes staring into her green gems.

I heard the door close as I walked Sarah to the dining table. I glanced to Vicky, who had sealed our privacy with a sensual smirk on her face. I returned to Sarah; my desire tore through me. I needed her more than ever.

"Tonight, my sweet, I will show you how I adore you," I whispered. My lips less than an inch from hers. My warm breath on her sent a shiver down her body. "You get to know the beast in me as I devour your sexy body."

I couldn't hold back any longer; the arson of her flame crazed me. My body was on fire, sweat dripping from my brow. I slammed her on the table; she gasped as her back fell flat on the hardwood. Her eyes looked up with fear and hunger. Then she looked over toward the cabinets. I followed her gaze to Vicky, standing nearby, watching us as her hand rubbed smoothly under her skirt. I quickly turned my attention back to Sarah.

I leaned forward over her, staring at her as if she were my prey. She was so close to me that her fire heated my body. I wanted nothing but to rip her clothes off, to take her into pleasure. Our lips laced into a dancing play for a hasty force of desire.

Her nails scratched along my chest as she pulled my shirt collar down fiercely. I knew at that moment that we were heading into deep lust. I palmed her breast, tearing open her blouse, exposing those perky, luscious bulbs. The dark areolas pulsed with blood, her nipples stood erect, and I could smell her getting wet.

The warmth of her skin on mine didn't just drive me wild; it ignited a beastly need in my core—a desperate, undeniable hunger to consume her. A calling from my primal instincts to possess her in a way that made her feel completely unburdened. This was more than lust; it was a furious devotion—my devotion to her. A soft moan escaped her lips under the lure of my sexual gaze.

"Please, Master," Sarah whimpered, her voice dripping with wanton lust. "Claim my body, like a king claims the spoils of war. Unchain the dirty whore I want to be."

Her words were a torrent of raw desire that resonated deep within me. They didn't diminish her; they amplified her fierce, untamed spirit, the very essence of Sarah that I adored. In that moment, the innocent beauty I cherished transformed, not into something strange, but into something magnificent: a bold creature, a beast like me. Brave enough to lay bare her hidden, darker fantasies. The ones stored away in the romance novels she read.

And seeing that, feeling her trust, made my own blood sing with a feral love, native to the passion of this primitive monster in me.

I hastily undid my pants, letting them fall to the floor at my feet. Hiking her skirt up, I ripped her panties with ease. Without another thought, I slammed in hard and roughly.

"Aah!" she squealed under me. "Tonight, I'm a slut. Own me."

Her words pushed me further and further. She was mine; I took her as I owned her.

This wasn't degradation; it was a sacred surrender. A fierce trust that I would meet her deepest, hidden need. A need to make her feel utterly cherished. Consumed by my love, in all its primal glory. She was drawn to my wild, untamed expression of affection; she craved it. I aimed to meet this need, this desire.

Every thrust was a declaration of possession, yes, but also a loving act of devotion to her wildest longing. Each slam of my body into hers was a loving vow to her, answering the deep, beautiful cry of her soul.

"Take my cock, slut."

My lips traveled to her throat; I dragged my lower lip over the tender flesh of her neck, the place I desired to bite down. I closed my lips, placing a small kiss, before my teeth clamped onto her pulse, causing a painful pleasure. As my teeth sank in, I roughly caressed her.

The vulnerable fabric of her neck made me groan with wantonness. Whimpers of pain spilled into moans of ecstasy as her body was delivered from the agony of bitterness into the compelled action of my hunger to be inside her. Her hands grappled my head as she began to nibble at my ear.

She was in wonder of my raw power; my instinct to possess her took me into her depths. I loved her with wanton jolts of lust.

"Ravage me, Master!" she demanded before her voice quieted to almost a whisper. "Take me from behind, I want to feel every inch of your control." Her body arched with heated passion.

I grabbed her arm, tugging her up; she got to her feet, turning around. I roughly shoved her forward, bending her over, her hands planted with a loud bang on the table.

"Take it like the bitch you are, my little cum slut."

The roundness of her rear stuck out, a sight I always enjoyed. Her body bowed into me, arching her round cheeks into my hips. I speared myself into her hot pinkness without warning, rougher than before. I felt the heat of her flames around me. Reaching up, my hand grappled her mane, tugging on it with rage. My rod pummeled her, taking her as if I were a barbarian.

"Fuck... Me... Harder!" Sarah huffed loudly between breaths.

With the thirst for her sensual aura to pour bounties of pleasure over me, I assaulted her with all my manhood's fury. I pulled her hair tighter as my thrusts became vicious. Her body tensed, and I knew she was close. I punched my erection into her walls more brutally with a quickened haste. I felt my own release building.

"Pound my cunt, Master!" she screamed. "Make me... Make me break," she whimpered. Her essence of love flowed upon me. It wasn't just a release; it was the flood of her pent-up desire, an uncontainable tide washing over me—a devotion to her self-care.

"Ah! Fuck!" I growled. Bolts of my savage spunk shot deep into her womb.

Her screams of pleasure, my own release, it was a symphony of shared abandon. A savage scripture to the boundless depths of our connection. Her essence, flowing freely, mingled with mine, was a worldly way our souls intertwined in this raw, beautiful chaos.

I slumped forward onto her for a moment. "I love you," I whispered.

She heaved and panted, catching her breath from the intensity before turning back to look at me. Her eyes twinkled with a newfound revelation of acceptance and admiration.

"I love you too, Master."

I pulled out of Sarah; a mixture of our love flowed from between her thighs. Vicky moved into place, lapping up every drop.

I was spent, yet I knew that Vicky needed me next. I pulled out a chair from the table, sitting as I caught my breath. I watched as Vicky licked all the fluids from the floor. Then she turned her attention to Sarah, her tongue whipped in and out. It was always a delightful sight to watch them pleasure each other. Vicky moved her head up and down between Sarah's cheeks until she was sure that Sarah was clean.

Vicky stood, twirling Sarah around. Sarah's head tilted down as Vicky stood on her toes, their faces meeting. Locking a kiss into each other, their mouths caressing into a spiral of lingering lust for the other. Still locked in their kiss, Sarah slowly peeled off Vicky's shirt. I watched this fantastic scene as my member started to recover. Both broke their kiss as they looked over to me.

"Please, make love to me," Vicky purred, her voice dripping with a sensual need.

I stood up without a word. My hand took Vicky's as I gently pulled her to the bedroom. Sarah followed behind us.

As we entered, I kissed Vicky with a tenderness I'd never shown her. This tenderness was not weakness; it was strength that unveiled a deliberate and kind love.

My hands tenderly roamed her body, each touch a silent promise. I felt the hardened muscles under my fingers, caressing them with gentle reverence, in awe of her strength. And yet she whimpered onto my tongue as our kiss deepened, melting into me.

My hand ran up her back, feeling the smooth contours. My heart swelled with fierce, protective admiration. My fingers smoothly grazed up the nape of her neck; she felt like a treasure under my touch. A fragile, exquisite bounty only for me to cherish and claim. Not just with my body, but with every fiber of my being.

The tip of my tongue claimed her mouth, our kiss. The passion her lips bestowed was solemn and gentle.

Every soft touch, every lingering kiss, was an unspoken whisper of how deeply I cherished her. How precious she was to me.

Watching her eyes soften as I guided her body to the gentle side of my soul was heartwarming. Her body melting under my tranquil embrace spoke volumes without a word.

Breaking our kiss, I guided Vicky to the bed. Sarah was seated at the head, enjoying the show as she slowly strummed her soaked bud.

“Let me love you in the softest way I can,” I whispered.

She gazed deeply into my soul, those blue pools swirling with admiration. I smiled. “Touching your heart with mine.”

I gently laid Vicky on her back, following her down. My tongue danced along her breast, softly flicking her nipple. I pried my hand between her legs. The heat of her flower sent shock waves through me; I had to touch her softness. Two fingers pressed into her, the moisture of her warmth was slick on my tips.

"I want to feel your love.” Her plea, a hymn of vulnerable desire, stirred deep into my soul.

The timbre of her voice blended with the moist feel of her on my fingertips, driving me to thirst for her more. My rod strained against the heat of her stomach. I dug my hips with a grind into her, letting her know I wanted her. Her muscles tensed around my fingers; I worked them in and out, painstakingly slow. My thumb rubbed her bud with gentle circles. I looked deep into her sapphire eyes.

“You need my love?”

“Yes.” Vicky sobbed. “I need it inside me.”

Her voice was sweet like an erotic hymn. This wasn’t just about physical penetration; it was the merging of two hearts—a complete surrender to the gentle, overwhelming warmth of our love. I pulled my hand from her ocean, positioning myself between her legs.

I slid my member into her silky wetness, the feeling was like coming home, a soft embrace that settled deeply into my soul. My slow, methodical thrusts were a promise whispered without words, a steady rhythm of devotion poured directly into her. With every push, every gentle withdrawal, I focused on ensuring she didn’t just feel me, but felt every ounce of my adoration filling her. A tenderness so palpable that it felt like it truly besieged Vicky. Wrapping her in the safe, cherished love she craved.

I briefly looked past Vicky to see Sarah romantically relishing the spectacle. Her hand was rubbing vigorously.

I turned my gaze back to Vicky, staring deep into her soul. Our eyes never broke as each drive of my love fell deeper into her. Her hands explored my back, pulling me closer to her. Her legs wrapped around me, enveloping me as she was greedy for my love.

"Can you feel my heart, my love, inside you as we join?" I murmured. My pace slightly quickened.

"I feel it. Feel me." Vicky purred. "Feel my love surround you."

I felt her moist walls tighten around me. My tempo hastened again as I could feel my climax rising. I felt the warmth of her love around me, her body growing tense. I knew she was there. She felt my love for her.

"I love you!" she purred.

Her words were a raw, beautiful cry that pierced through me. A confirmation that she felt the depths of my love as I felt hers. The satin tunnel of her cove flowed with ocean tides of her liquid love; my efforts made her feel admired. The halo of adoration floated around her as she fell into the gentleness of my caress.

"I love you, too," I whispered.

I flooded her with every ounce of my love. My essence mixed with her liquid devotion that had showered me. This fusion was the ultimate act of shared tenderness, written on the other like a new verse for our sacred communion of souls.

I rolled off of Vicky; Sarah moved from the bed to complete their promise of every drop. Tired from the long day, I lay on my side watching Sarah clean the mess with her tongue.

My mind uncontrollably drifted back to that letter and the dangerous author. I had to keep my women, my brides, safe. They were my everything, my world. Their voices were the only soothing to my dreads. I stayed in a daze throughout the day, wishing to feel their lips against mine. Locked in kisses to feed them my affection, tasting theirs in return. I loved them. How could I let anything happen to them? How could I live with myself if it did?

I pushed those thoughts down, peeled off the rest of my clothes, and threw them on the floor. I scooted over to the middle. Vicky and Sarah slid into their respective spots next to me. We pulled the cover over us in an embrace. My arms cradled them both.

"How was that?"

"Fun, Master," Sarah whispered in a swoon.

Vicky nuzzled into my chest. "Wonderful."

I kissed their foreheads. "So why the switch?"

"Your gentleness makes me feel safe and adored," Sarah said. "But sometimes I want to feel your unbridled passion too."

"That makes sense." I turned to Vicky. "What about you?"

"I crave your dominant and primal lust most of the time," Vicky explained. She let out a low sigh. "However, sometimes I need your gentle lovemaking to feel truly cherished."

"I'm sorry I didn't pick up on this before."

"It's not your fault, Master." Sarah comforted me with a gentle pat. "You are always good at giving us exactly what we need."

Vicky ran her hand through my hair. "It's just, sometimes we want something different." Her voice was laced with admiration.

My hands caressed their bodies. "Today was a full day."

"You can say that again," Vicky said.

Sarah lightly bit my collarbone. "You didn't tell us why you wanted to talk with that guy at the club."

"He had the same tattoo as the courier with the letter."

"So, you what?" Vicky teased. "Thought he would have answers about our doom letter?"

"He actually did."

"What?" Sarah perked up.

"He didn't want to talk about our Mr. Mortis. He was terrified." I sighed. "So, it's not a prank or advertisement. It's a real threat."

Vicky continued to run her hand through my hair. "What can that letter mean?"

"I don't know. Whatever it is, I want to protect you both."

Sarah kissed my cheek. "Aw, Master..."

"The three of us need to protect each other," Vicky said. She ruffled my hair. "You're just as precious to us as we are to you."

"Can't we call the police?" Sarah interjected.

"Tell them what? We got a creepy poem with free tickets to an exclusive event?"

Vicky chimed in. "He's right, sis." She snuggled closer. "There isn't anything in the letter that can be considered a direct threat."

"If we want answers, we might have to go to the gala," I said.

"Sounds scary, I don't think we should..." Sarah trailed off. She trembled with a hint of fear.

"It's settled," Vicky roared. "We show up at the museum and get to the bottom of this, busting doors down if we have to." The fire in her ignored Sarah's apprehension.

I chuckled a bit at Vicky's enthusiasm, but then realized Sarah might be right. We may need to think it through. At the very least, figure out if it's worth messing with. Worth putting them in danger.

"Hold your horses, Magnum PI, just chill," I chastised Vicky, kissing both their cheeks to prevent an argument. "You're a 'yes,' I'm a 'maybe,' and Sarah is a 'no.' We've got all week to decide."

"I just... I'm worried about what could happen," Sarah said.

"I know," I whispered before my voice went to that NCO resonance. "But for now, we need to get some sleep. Good night, my beauties. I love you both."

"I love you, too, Kyle. Good night, sweet dreams."

"Good night, Master. I love you always."

I lay in bed holding my lovelies. I watched as they both fell into their dreamlands, their chests rising and falling as they peacefully slumbered. I hoped to keep them safe, shielding them from harm. My arms snuggled tighter around them.

Tonight was special; they showed me that they need all the forms of love I could give. That each one of them cherished all aspects of my personality. I hoped to be forever showered in their passion and show them my fiery admiration. To give them my heart, soul, and body. I wanted to remain with them. Remain loving them for all time. I wanted to feel their soft kisses on my lips forever. I wanted to spend every moment with them both.

Although I've braved the carnage of war, they're the most powerful things I've ever encountered. I love them each with all that I am. Neither night nor day shall our love fade; I desire, greedily, to keep our time together eternal.

There are no other women like these two. I want to see them succeed in their dreams. That's why I've worked so hard to surprise them with Vicky's spa and Sarah's college, ensuring that they only know happiness in this life.

I swore to myself I would keep them from the horrors I've seen. That is why I need to be their shield and, if necessary, their sword. I can't live without them. They are the two pieces of my heart, completing it. The two tender chains that bind me to what I now know as love.

Chapter 5: Unanimous Decision

The weekend came and went. Sunday was a balm to the distance and disarray in my relationship. I spent that day making up for my neglect of Sarah's and Vicky's sexual needs—the desire to be treated with the care I had given the other, experiencing my love completely.

That day unfolded into a tapestry of whispered secrets, lingering touches, and the joy of simply being together. We rediscovered the smooth rhythm of our affections, our shared intimacy. Every glance, every brush of skin, was a silent conversation—a reaffirmation of the deep connection we shared. It was as if words were unnecessary to convey our affections.

After experiencing my harshness, Sarah lost herself in the curl of a smile as she nuzzled into a book. Her contentment was a song in my soul, an orchestra playing the depths of her trust in me.

Having felt my tenderness, Vicky danced around as she created two paintings that day. Her movements were fluid as her spirit radiated a newfound lightness.

Both my beauties seemed more alive, vivid in the colors of our love. Each reflected different hues of the endless pastel river of affection that flowed between us.

After that, they wanted things to return to normal: my harshness toward Vicky and my tenderness toward Sarah. For them, it was a release, an escape from how they usually experienced my passions. But for me, it was a learning experience, teaching me to pay closer attention to their needs so that I may anticipate and appreciate them better.

The thought of failing Vicky and Sarah, of not nurturing the fierce love they'd freely given me, had been a lingering shadow. It was a love that constantly pulled me from the brink—saved me from a life of isolation and despair. A love I was sworn to protect.

I failed them once by lying to them. Thought I'd lost them forever. But I got a second chance and wouldn't fail them again.

We'd almost forgotten the strangeness of that letter and that terrifying author. Or at least they had. In the quiet moments, my mind circled it. The danger it imposed became an obsession. My only distraction from its danger was work and my relationship.

Our relationship had grown tremendously in just one weekend.

Late Saturday night, Vicky sat on the couch beside me, watching a movie. Her hand gently caressed me, a fleeting touch different from her usually firm embraces. It sparked a memory of the tenderness she had longed for.

On Sunday, at dinner, I explained how I handled an issue with an HVAC supplier the week before. Sarah interjected with a playful, "Master, are you sure you managed that right?" Her teasing challenge held an air of that commanding dynamic we'd explored.

And just this morning, before I left for work, I absentmindedly ruffled Vicky's hair. Sarah caught my eye across the room, and we exchanged knowing smiles. There was now a more profound understanding between the three of us.

As the weekend's reprieve came to an end, Monday inevitably arrived. The week started with the usual rush. Work was like any other day: work, work, work. Mondays were always busy. Seventeen-thirty hours, it was time to drop off David and head home.

"I thought we'd slow down by now," David said as he entered the work van.

"Me too." I exhaled, turning the ignition on. "But I'm glad it hasn't."

"Do you think that lady will buy a new system from us?"

"I don't know." I shrugged. "She wasn't too happy when we told her that old heat pump was shot."

"True." David retrieved his cigarettes.

A smile tugged at my lips as I pulled the van onto the busy street. We'd had a productive Monday, making some impressive profits. I felt happy that I could go home to share this success with Vicky and Sarah. To watch their faces light up with pride. Their smiles beaming bright, knowing that every achievement was a step closer to our shared dreams.

"For this being only the start of the week, we've already doubled what we made last week." I beamed with satisfaction.

"It's hard to believe," David acknowledged, pulling a cigarette out of the pack. "But we make a helluva team."

"That we do." I nodded, glancing over at him. He lit the cigarette and took a drag.

I smirked at his statement. The excitement was hard to contain. Our talk throughout the drive wasn't all business. After exhausting the topics of the day's events and tomorrow's workload, the conversation naturally drifted to our personal lives.

David complained about his girlfriend, Ava, again. She was pestering him to marry, but he opposed the idea for some reason. I offered some sound advice about whether to pull the trigger or let her go. Then he turned his sights to me.

"I'm always going on about Ava, but you've never said anything about your girl," David said coolly.

I'd never talked about my romantic life with David before. I didn't know how he would take it. I didn't want any strife to affect our working relationship. Should I tell him? What would he say? Would he think it was wrong that I was engaged to two women?

Only three months into the creation of Forester Heat and Air, the name had already made an impression with many high-profile clients. I couldn't take all the credit; David was a damn good technician. It didn't hurt that Howard handed us some of my earlier clients, allowing the company name to grow. However, the company would suffer a massive setback if I messed things up with David.

"It's complicated," I admitted.

"Complicated?" David asked, "What? Are you fucking the mayor's wife or something?"

We stopped at a red light and saw a billboard for a new AI companion app—a sexy woman in 1950s attire holding cookies. It targeted lonely men. I shook my head at those saps fooled by something so fake—a subscription to love. The real thing is messy, intense, and far more rewarding, like it is with my beauties.

I could feel David's anxious look bearing down on me. His question finally sank in. "No, no, nothing like that."

"I promise I won't judge." His eyes darted to the billboard. "Swear."

I sighed deeply. "I'm engaged to two women."

His face turned to utter confusion. His shocked expression was one I'd seen a million times now. I'd always get the same look when I took them in public: the odd stares, the gasps, the mean comments. However, those things only pulled the three of us closer together. Inspiring and infusing an "us versus the world" mentality into the relationship. I smiled, thinking about the solidarity and raw power of my shared union with Sarah and Vicky and of the renewed affection that this last weekend gave us.

David and I sat in silence for the rest of the red light. I felt that my admission may have awkwardly changed the van's mood. I glanced over at him. It seemed he was processing the words I'd just spoken, like they were some profound, philosophical logic or something. He finally spoke up when we reached the next red light.

"Man, how do you keep up with two?" He asked. "Ava is a fucking handful."

I couldn't help but sigh. Keep up? I was barely treading water; this past weekend proved that. I'd neglected that they both needed to have all the pieces of me. A mistake that had caused them to snap at each other.

"It's not easy."

David took a drag from his cigarette. "Shit, I'd think not. But do they know about each other?"

"Huh? Oh, yeah, I get your confusion now. Honestly, they kind of made the first move as a pair. We live together now."

"Oh, um... ohhh-kaaaay..."

I didn't respond, I let silence reclaim the van.

"Wait, how can you be engaged to two women?"

"Easy. I simply proposed. Now the marriage part, legally, I can't be," I lamented. "However, I'm going to sue the state, hoping I can legally marry them."

"I wish you luck, man." David's voice was laced with hesitation.

"Thanks."

David tossed his cigarette butt out the window. "Do you love them?"

"Yes, very much so."

David turned to look out the window. "Do they love you back?"

"I would say so."

David turned back to me. "Then you're a lucky man."

"To be honest, I sometimes feel that I'm failing them."

I turned down his road. Just a few more blocks, and I could escape this awkward conversation.

"Just keep being you." David patted my shoulder. "You're a good man."

"So are you. And you're a damn good tech."

I stopped the van in front of his house.

"Thanks, boss." David hopped out. "See you in the morning."

"See you after my appointment," I replied. "And marry that girl, for God's sake."

He chuckled as he closed the door.

I felt relieved when he left. However, I was surprised he didn't berate me or look down on me for my relationship. I pulled out of the driveway to go home. At least maybe I hadn't screwed up my rapport with David. But only time could tell.

As I moved the van onto the busy street, my mind was still ringing over the day's success—a welcome distraction from the shadow of that letter. Even with the newfound success in both my business and my relationship, I couldn't shake the concern that the letter might cause, the harm the author could inflict.

A flicker of movement in a shadowed alley caught my eye. I saw only a vague outline, but the hair on my neck prickled. My grip tightened on the wheel as the soldier in me was readying for war.

Just as my heart was icing up, rationality hit me. It was probably nothing, just a trick of the light, but the image lingered, a grim reminder of the letter's author and the promise of impending danger. I had to be ready for anything. *Chill Sergeant. Just chill.*

Those thoughts carried on for a while before I pushed them back. I soon reminded myself I had an appointment with Holly first thing; the therapy was actually helping, and I was feeling better about most things. This small matter of that cryptic letter, I couldn't let it derail my progress. I promised myself I would be better for them, for my fiancées, my wives.

As the streets whizzed by, I listened to music to distract my mind. I didn't want that awkward admission or the letter to pull down my good mood. I sang along as I passed street after street.

My thoughts drifted to Sarah's quiet contentment and Vicky's radiant ferocity. The knot in my stomach loosened. Our love wasn't a distraction; it was a tether. A point of contact on our shared climb to a better life. Grounding me to the world, a loving tether to them.

Home was my destination. Home to them. A sense of belonging filled me, knowing that they greeted my nightly returns. That my world had expanded to the sphere of my beauties. I couldn't wait to see them, those smiles brightly greeting me. Their soft scents intoxicated me with happiness. And the feeling of those warm embraces filled me with acceptance and harmony.

As I parked the van, I was ready to head upstairs to my real life, my loves, to the scents of what Sarah had cooked. I bet it would be delicious, like always.

I shoved the van door open, my feet moving with a purpose. I made it upstairs in record time. As my hand turned the knob and the door opened, I was graced with a wonderful aroma, a familiar comfort. The delicious scent filled the apartment with love.

But as I closed the door, my gaze lingered on the mail slot, evoking a brief, unwelcome memory of the envelope and its unsettling contents. I shook it off, forcing myself to focus on the warmth within.

"Good evening," I said, crossing over into the threshold.

"Dinner is almost done, Master," Sarah announced.

My eyes followed her bouncing around the kitchen. "Is Vicky home yet?"

"Not yet, she had a late client." Sarah removed a pan from the stove.

I figured it might be time to chat about college, now that we finally had a moment alone. I gathered my courage.

I walked over to the kitchen. "There's something that I've been meaning to talk with you about."

"Oh, what is it, Master?"

"I um..." I stammered. Not sure if my meddling would be seen as just that: meddling.

Sarah walked over, fiddling with the plate. Her movements were graceful and delicate, a sight that bolstered my courage.

I stood inches from her. "I signed you up for college classes."

Sarah put the plate on the dining table. "Really, Master?"

Her eyes studied me for a moment, not with suspicion, but with an overwhelming vulnerability. Her lips pulled into a large grin before the sheer weight of the reveal made it fall.

"But we don't have the tuition money, let alone for books or..." Her voice was barely a whisper, laced with a familiar self-doubt I longed to erase.

I interrupted her by gently placing my index finger over her lips. "I found a grant that will be more than enough." My stance held the power of my NCO presence, yet with that gentleness they knew so well.

"Thank you, Master," Sarah whispered as tears started to fall.

"You're welcome, my sweet."

My arms closed around her in a deep hug. She embraced me tightly; I felt the warmth of her happy tears on my shoulder. As we were entangled, I explained everything about the school and the grant. She wiped tears from her eyes, but her smile seemed permanently pinned to her face. Seeing her so happy filled my heart with joy. This was a tangible expression of my love and devotion to her happiness, a foundation for the future we were building.

"Campus is almost halfway between your job and home."

"Awesome!" Sarah roared with excitement. "But no weekend classes."

I smiled, remembering her jealous reason for no weekend courses. "No weekend classes."

I felt her embrace grow tighter at my words. We held each other for a while before retreating. Then I helped her as she set the table.

Sarah pulled a bowl of vegetables from the counter to the table. "Master, when do I start?"

"January, for the spring semester."

"I have a couple of months to prepare," Sarah said to herself before turning around. She looked down at me with a gaze of admiration when we had finished. I stared into those green sparkles with as much love in my heart.

As we savored the quiet joy, a sound broke our entanglement. The front door sprang open. Vicky had made it home; her face looked weary and worn out.

"Welcome home, my lovely."

"Hello, sis. Long day?" Sarah tilted her head in empathy.

"Hello," Vicky said, giving a lazy wave. "These damn hands keep acting up, almost cost me a client."

I rushed over to Vicky, taking her hands and rubbing them to soothe her pain. Her blue oceans washed over me as our eyes locked. The love in her eyes filled my heart.

"Maybe it's time to see a doctor about it."

"Maybe," Vicky said. "Or maybe it's time to take me out back, put one in my head."

"Don't talk like that," Sarah chastised. "We can figure it out."

"Let's just eat for now," I said, releasing her hands.

We sat at the table. The girls piled their plates full after I picked bits for my plate: pork chop, mashed potatoes, green peas, and some weird bread. I waited for them to take the first bite before I took a bite of the pork chop. The juiciness was mouthwatering.

"Ooh, sis. I didn't get a chance to tell you yet," Sarah said, leaning forward in her seat. Her fork hovered over her plate. "Master found a school grant for me, so I can start in January." The happiness in Sarah's words was exploding through the apartment.

"That's pretty cool," Vicky said. "I hope you get in."

"Actually, Elle found the college and helped pick the classes; I just signed her up." I didn't want to take all the credit.

"It's still a nice gesture, Master. So, thank you," Sarah said. "And I will be sure to thank Miss Elle, too."

"I'm excited for you, sis. I hope you get to teach kids like you dreamed of."

"Thank you, sis."

Dreams and wishes filled the dinner table as we discussed Sarah's college plans. But even as I smiled, a cold shiver traced down my spine. The image of the distorted handwriting from the letter flashed through my mind, a fleeting, unwelcome shadow on an otherwise perfect evening.

I noticed Vicky occasionally peered at her hands with slight pity in her eyes throughout the chat. This spiked my concern about that situation. Could she be showing signs of early arthritis?

When the fun had died and we started clearing the table, I spoke up. "What are we going to do about your hands?"

"Fuck if I know," Vicky growled. Her eyes blazed with fury.

"No need to get nasty." Sarah's voice was harsh before pulling back to bubbly. "Master is just concerned about you."

"I can deal with it for now." Vicky sighed. Her gaze fell into an apologetic look, as if she was asking for my forgiveness. I smiled and nodded at her, letting her know that I took no offence.

"As for that gala on Friday night," Vicky said, attempting to change the subject, "what are we planning?"

"Not sure."

"I have a bad feeling about this gala," Sarah said, her voice shaky. "Can we just not go, Master? I feel like something bad is going to happen. Staying home in our jammies would be way safer."

"I'm going," Vicky crowed, her hands planted on her hips. "This doom guy needs to be unmasked; I'm not waiting around for him to make the next move."

The room was silent for a moment. However, with Vicky's ferocity, Sarah seemed to gain courage.

"Me too. I'll go. I can do this." Sarah's voice trembled.

I could tell this was going to be a tough conversation. So, I decided to try to ease the tension. What would be an appropriate joke for this situation?

"So, am I Fred or Shaggy?" I chuckled.

Sarah and Vicky stared at me for a moment, as if I had scratched a chalkboard with my nails. Then, out of nowhere, they both burst into giggles.

"Shaggy, of course." Vicky quipped. "I'm Daphne," she said, pointing at herself, then to Sarah. "Which makes you Velma."

"Velma? Why Velma?" Sarah pouted.

Vicky placed the last dish in the sink. "You're like a genius and stuff."

Sarah strutted around with even greater confidence as she began to wipe down the table and counters. I moved to the sink, my hands instinctively getting to work cleaning the dishes. Vicky quickly grabbed the broom and dustpan, sweeping the floor.

"That's right, I'm the smartest one in the room," Sarah boasted. She stood sharp and commanding—a flicker of the weekend strength dancing in her eyes.

Vicky shook her head. "Watch out. Shaggy might get the wrong impression."

"Does Shaggy get a Scooby Snack tonight?" I asked.

"Maybe." Sarah giggled, then her voice rose with that newfound power. "Depends, you gonna be a good boy?"

Vicky bumped into me, poking the broom into my back. "Yeah, only good boys get snacks." She continued to move along, sweeping.

I shook my head. Damn teases. They always tease me like this, knowing I'm always ready to take them. I sighed, resigned to the coldness of their playful mockery.

Feeling their warmth was more than sex. It was our souls connecting through our bodies, as if I were one with them—a tangible foundation of our love. Ethereally, a scripture of unspoken affection manifested in touch.

I shook my desires as I drifted off into more concerning thoughts. I needed to convince Vicky to go to a doctor. But cutting through her stubborn, independent attitude was like stabbing a steel plate with a foam sword. And Sarah was still hesitant about the gala thing.

I continued with my work. Halfway through the dishes, as my hand pulled from the suds, I felt two warm bulbs press into my back. An arm reached around my waist, slipping a hand into the front of my pants, gripping my manhood with tender pressure.

Sarah whispered into my ear, "Jinkies, looks like we have a mystery on our hands."

A feeling of being adored washed over me, filling my heart with a playful, yet sensual ache. The role of being Shaggy in this game appealed to me. Love rippled through me as I enjoyed her slow motions on my throbbing rod.

I played along. "Zoinks, I think the creep is coming back."

"I think he'd rather eat pussy than solve a mystery," Vicky coolly stated in her raspy vixen voice.

I spoke with my best impression of Casey Kasem. "Mystery or pussy? What a dilemma."

Sarah and Vicky shared a light snicker before I was pushed around. My hands were still dripping with dishwater as I turned. Eye to eye with Sarah, her face moved closer to mine, her lips gently brushing against me. I welcomed her tender kiss, our tongues dancing in the whimsy of this game. The sweetness of the kiss lingered as a bead of saliva trailed out from my mouth.

Sarah fell to her knees before me. "My cock! I can't do a thing without my cock," she said as her hand undid my fly, freeing me from the restraints of the fabric. "Found it."

Her lips circled the girth before sealing around me. The moistness of her mouth closed around the stiffness; I huffed out with an erotic growl.

Vicky leaned into me, the heat of her breath on my cheek, whispering. "You'd do anything for your snacks."

I took her hand in mine, briefly glancing at it. A silent promise lingered in the air between us that I would tackle her ailment. Her hand aggressively recoiled from mine. Then she stared at me with an angered glare, before softening to a sensual gaze.

The defiance of pulling away from my concern for her stirred the loving dominance inside. Instinctively, my hand reached out, grabbing a fistful of Vicky's hair, pulling her face close to mine.

"Watch the hair," she scolded. My tongue whipped across her chin. She lightly bit it before wildly fencing her tongue against mine.

The raging sexual fire was building in the three of us. Sarah bobbed the length of my shaft as her throat took me completely. My knees were buckling from the sensations Sarah was creating. My mouth assaulted Vicky, locked in our eternal war for control. As I won the battle against Vicky, Sarah pulled away from my member.

I gazed into those green eyes, searching for the desire within them. Vicky helped her up; they guided me to the bedroom. As we entered, their hands slipped away from me as they began to disrobe. I followed their lead, hastily peeling off my clothes in a flash.

"Jeepers creepers," I said in my Shaggy impression. "I need a sexy sandwich to calm my nerves."

Vicky's hard body closed in on Sarah, their arms embracing each other. Both staring at me with a hungry, sensual stare.

"If given a choice," Vicky gloated, turning to Sarah, "he'd choose this."

Their mouths claimed one another with a need to quench the thirst for love. Their hands roamed around each other's bodies, caressing the heated flesh of the other with passion and love. I relished the sight, taking in the beauty of both my wanton wives.

Unable to stand it any longer, I approached them. My arms protectively folded around them, encapsulating both. I snuggled my cheek between them, their tongues fiercely lashing out at mine, our three-way kiss stoking the need in all of us. After the melee, they slipped from my grasp.

Vicky lay flat on the mattress, her head at the foot of the bed. Sarah mounted Vicky's face, her body arched, pushing her rear to me. Gripping Sarah's cheeks with hunger, Vicky's tongue reached out, lovingly caressing the folds of the flower hovering above. Sarah's head slumped down over Vicky's crotch; I assumed she was returning the pleasure.

I watched with sexual intrigue as they started to lap at each other's warmth, their tongues granting delight to the other. The silvery slickness was moistening the beauty before me. The sight was inviting, and there was no need to negotiate the terms. We all knew the high stakes.

I moved behind Sarah, my tip near her entrance; I felt the moist heat of her pinkness. Filled with a yearning to take what I knew was mine, I couldn't hold back any longer. Gently sliding into her warmth with ease, I felt Vicky's rapid breaths on my sac, driving me into the rapture of this union.

My pelvis gyrated slow, steady rhythms into Sarah, my hands gripping her hips. Sarah, with a muffled moan onto Vicky's dark cove, made both their bodies twitch as my pace stayed steady and robust.

Pulling a hand free, I tenderly ran it along her back, starting at the shoulder. She shivered as my fingertips traced the silk of her skin. My pace quickened at the reaction her body was giving.

Vicky's face pulled from Sarah's moist bud, huffing in ecstasy. "Eat... me... fucking... God... eat..." she gasped. Her hands clapped over Sarah's butt cheeks and tightly grasped. Her nails dug into the soft flesh, leaving a trail of passion.

My hips moved into overdrive, hastening my piston movement. I knew Vicky was close, so I wanted Sarah to finish with her.

"Ah... I'm caah... cumming!" Vicky screamed beneath us.

I felt Sarah's soft spritz form around me. My pace picked up once more. I needed to get her there. Her moans were muffled by having her face deep inside Vicky's thighs. Then her body's faucet poured Sarah's bountiful juices on me.

At that moment, I shoved deep into her, releasing the first load of this pent-up frustration. I pulled from Sarah, the warm fluids of our union mixing. Our love dripped down to Vicky, who quickly indulged, lapping every drop.

I moved to the head of the bed, kneeling before Vicky's spread legs. The crimson curtain of Sarah's mane draped over my destination. It was Vicky's turn; I had enough libido for her, too.

Sarah lifted her head from Vicky, eyeing me with a mischievous grin. Without warning, I rammed into Vicky roughly. Her body immediately tensed under Sarah. With a giggle, Sarah went back to her work on Vicky. Occasionally, her tongue would lather my shaft as I moved in and out of Vicky's fiery walls.

Thrusting hard, I pounded Vicky with the brutality that she enjoyed. My eyes caught Sarah's hair dangling over Vicky's dark cave. I could hear the sloppy sounds coming from behind Sarah as she was worked into another orgasm by Vicky's tongue.

Sarah's head moved away from Vicky as she panted. "Damn... Damn good... I'm there... I'm cumming again!"

As Sarah reveled in the throes of her orgasm, my hand instinctively reached out, grabbing a fistful of her hair. I pulled her face up to watch the agonizing expressions as she rained down her love onto Vicky's face for a second time.

I vigorously assaulted Vicky with all the passion my hips could muster. Violent in my attack, I could feel the rising heat of her body; she was getting to the point of no return.

Then I felt the hurricane inside of her burst out, flooding me with her furious wonder. Sarah glanced down at the mess I was making of Vicky; she smiled. I released her hair as Sarah slumped back down, greedily lapping up Vicky's ooze.

Finally, the lethal blow of my attack shot through Vicky as I exploded all my love inside of her. Her body accepted it with grace. Pulling free of the melee, I lay to my side watching Sarah clean the mess of this battle.

Once all was cleared and every drop collected, we moved into our positions on the bed. With me in the middle, Vicky to my left, and Sarah to my right.

Vicky's breathing slowly evened out against my side, a soft, contented sigh escaping her lips. Sarah laid her head on my chest, cuddling affectionately into me.

Vicky huffed, trying to catch her breath. "That was fun."

Sarah's head snuggled onto my chest. "Gee, willy, gosh, was it."

This was more than fun; this was the sacred heart of us. A shared union of lighthearted banter mixing into the melding of our committed love. The blending of our very essences into one cosmic happiness, shared with laughter and snarky jokes.

"It was... different," I replied, the words played on my tongue.

"Different?" Vicky asked as she leaned up for a moment, playfully slugging my shoulder. "That was better than different."

Sarah smirked. "Ruh-roh."

I shook my head, thinking these women were insatiable. "Okay, it was fun."

"See, Master, sex doesn't have to be all serious every time," Sarah teased as her hand playfully slapped my chest.

Vicky sighed before whispering, "Yeah, now let's get some sleep."

We nestled closer, the warmth of our bodies intertwined into a unified spirit. Contrasting the cold unease that stirred on the edges of my heart. Even though the sexual adventure we'd just shared was still fresh, I couldn't help but think this gala thing was a trap. I may be placing my beauties in danger by taking them there. The vibrant afterglow of our passion was slowly dimming, replaced by that lingering shadow of Mr. Mortis and his intent.

"This museum visit could be dangerous," I said.

My words fell heavily over the night, spreading worry for the once-heated pleasure. The room was still for a moment before it filled with determination.

"So what?" Vicky roared. "This beatnik can't scare us."

Sarah punched her hand, thundering resolutely. "Yeah, as long as we're together, we can't be beat."

Vicky's hand softly played in my chest hairs. "See, even Sarah is getting into it, now."

"I was getting scared earlier, because I don't want anything to happen to my two favorite people," Sarah admitted, her voice hoarse, as if fighting back tears. "But now, I'm ready to kick ass."

"I guess it'll be okay. If we stay together on this, everything will be alright." I kissed the top of both their heads. "Now let's get some rest. Good night, my beauties. I love you, both."

Sarah snuggled tighter. "Good night, Master. I love you."

"I love you, too, my mystery machine. Sweet dreams." Vicky gently kissed my cheek.

I smiled to myself. I had to give it to them; they may be scared, but they were willing to face the enemy at the gates. They were a powerful force, for sure: my warrior women, my Valkyries. I still needed to figure out a way to keep them safe during all this, since they insisted on going.

Chapter 6: Earnest Dissuasion

Wednesday's work faded fast. I felt the week was flying by; there didn't seem to be a system that David and I couldn't face together. Calls were piling up, so I might need to hire Myra sooner than I had expected.

I'd been thinking about it for most of the week. I can't keep answering the phone while out on calls.

I sent Myra a text, explaining that if she wanted the job, she should meet us at the restaurant the following Monday for the meeting with Howard. I included a generous salary amount to entice her. She didn't reply.

David slung his tool bag into the van, drawing my attention away from my phone. "Did you get the gauges?" he asked.

I hung the gauges on the shelf. "I got 'em."

"Quitting time yet, boss?"

I closed the back door. "Yep. Hop in. I'll take you home."

I slipped into the driver's seat; he jumped in quickly. As we pulled away from the client's house, he recovered his cigarettes and then tapped the bottom of the pack repeatedly.

"Ava's gonna be pissed that I'm late for dinner." He pulled a cigarette from the pack. "You're ol' ladies gonna be pissed?"

"Nah, they understand." I braked at a stop sign.

"So, uh... kids. How are you planning for some rugrats?"

I glanced over at him; he seemed intrigued as he lit his cigarette. Is he really that interested in my love life?

"We've had a few chats."

"And?"

"Waiting until marriage." My desire for children was shackled by fear and duty inside me. "I want to do it the right way."

"Sounds fair." David took a drag of his cigarette.

"How about you? Kids with Ava?"

He gave a self-deprecating laugh. "Man, I swear you two are talking."

"I take it kids are off the table?"

David sighed. "For now. I'm only twenty-two."

An awkward silence filled the van for a while. The thought of fatherhood was weighing on both of us—the roads passed by as the quietness filled the air. I could hear the roar of the engine as we cruised along. David broke the silence.

"That business partner, we'll meet him next week, right?"

I smiled at the idea of them meeting. "Howard is treating us to lunch around noon on Monday."

"He a good guy?"

"Yeah, a bit rough around the edges, but a cool guy. Don't take his words to heart; he means well."

"No problem, boss."

As we pulled into his driveway, Ava was standing on the porch, her arms crossed. Her face had an angry scowl. He wasn't kidding; she seemed livid. I put the van in park and stepped out.

"Sorry for keeping David out so late."

"That's quite all right, Mr. Forester," Ava said with a syrupy voice before turning mean. "That's not why I'm pissed."

Ava glared at David with an evil stare.

David started pleading. "Baby, on my mama, I don't know that girl."

Another woman? Ouch. Realizing the real reason Ava was not happy with David, I decided it was time for me to exit the situation.

"Ah, okay." I smiled, waving at them both. I started walking back to the van, leaving David in his mess. "I'll pick you up in the morning."

"He'll be ready, Mr. Forester." Ava snapped before David could say anything.

"Alive, I hope," I said. "And please call me Kyle."

"Alive but not well, Kyle," Ava shouted back.

"Bye, boss," David slumped into his words.

I bid him farewell as I got into the van.

Backing out of his driveway, I saw him get to his knees, groveling. I understood what that felt like, just a few months ago, that was me, groveling for Sarah and Vicky to take me back. I felt his pain, but there was nothing I could do to help. I pulled into the right lane; it was time to pop smoke.

On the way home, I thought about that museum gala again and that letter. I'd read it many times these past few days, trying to figure out what it meant. I even looked for that memo from ITI that mentioned project L.O.V., which I'd seen months ago. However, it was gone. I couldn't find it anywhere. Did Sarah or Vicky hide it?

They'd said it was Naomi's. Could they have returned it to her? Wasn't it something about A.I.? I couldn't remember clearly.

All I knew was that it was related to my relationship. That was obvious from that line in the letter, "bound to three."

Lost in these unsettling thoughts, I barely registered pulling into the apartment complex. I sat in the van for a minute, trying to shake that eerie feeling. Before long, I plastered on a smile and decided to go inside.

Today, Mrs. Helderman should be at our place for dinner. We kept the tradition of eating together on Wednesdays. She loved seeing the growth of my three-way relationship. Recently, she started calling us her little lovebirds. Out of everyone in my circle, she was the most excited about my relationship, always praising our domestic dynamic. But she was very critical of the marriage idea, cautioning me more times than I cared to count.

I made my way up to the second floor, passing by a young couple ogling over a baby cooing. I gave the couple a brief smile. The man gave me a quick nod before tickling the child's nose.

I thought about the conversation I had with David. It must be a wonderful feeling to be a father. I wondered if that day would ever come for me. Sarah and Vicky were still taking birth control. Some days, I felt like they should stop taking it. That maybe, even without the legal document allowing us to marry, we should still have kids.

Both Vicky and Sarah would make great mothers. Sarah would be the fun mom, always playing with the kids, and Vicky would be the mother who would protect our babies no matter what.

That dream house came to mind again. We always fantasized about our dream home—the place where we would raise our children and live out our lives together. I could imagine the three of us running around the backyard, playing games with the kids.

I wondered what Mrs. Helderman would say about the pregnancies. Or Elle, for that matter. Maybe they'd be happy for us. And Jenny would finally have cousins to play with.

But other days, I was afraid I might not be a good father. I mean, look at Vicky and Sarah. I neglected a basic relationship need. Would I neglect my children's needs? I'd never want my children to feel neglected. I'd want them to feel seen, heard, understood, and loved. I'd want to keep my kids safe, yet at this moment, I couldn't figure out how to keep their future mothers safe.

If harm came to either of my beauties, it would crush me. And I couldn't bear to be without either one. Pushing these anxieties from my mind, I found myself approaching the apartment door. I could hear chattering voices on the other side. I opened it and went in.

Sarah beamed from the kitchen as soon as I entered. "Master! Welcome home!"

I looked around. Mrs. Helderman was drinking from a mug in the new La-Z-Boy, which was obviously delivered sometime today. Vicky was sitting on the couch with a mug in her hand.

"Hello, my boy." Mrs. Helderman's voice rang out, calming from a laugh.

"Hi, honey. I was just telling Wanda about that punk in the club." Vicky tittered before sipping her mug.

"Hello, my beauties. Good evening, Wanda."

"I still say you should've drunk his blood," Mrs. Helderman said. I let the two of them talk; they seemed engrossed in gossiping.

I walked into the kitchen. A familiar warmth filled my heart as I moved past Sarah to the coffee mugs. My hand lightly grazed her butt, a silent greeting, before I gave a quick, affectionate squeeze.

A playful "ooh" escaped Sarah's lips; her soft sound always thrilled me.

"You okay, dear?" Mrs. Helderman glanced into the kitchen from the living room.

"Fine, Miss Wanda. Just thought I dropped something, guess I didn't." Sarah's eyes burned a hole in me, but her lips playfully pouted.

I mouthed with a facetious smirk. "I'll behave."

Sarah rolled her eyes, lightly slapped my crotch before turning back to the stove. I poured myself some coffee and headed toward the living room.

On my way out of the kitchen, Sarah slapped my butt really hard, making sure to get her payback from earlier. I turned my head, smiling wickedly at her. She blew me a raspberry. I softly shook my head as my feet carried me to the couch.

"You let Howard be the hero?" Mrs. Helderman asked as I plopped on the couch.

"I was stunned at first," I explained. "By the time I could react, Howard had already knocked the guy on his rear."

Vicky rested her hand on my thigh, roughly squeezing before relaxing her grip.

"That wasn't what upset us." Vicky huffed before explaining. "He left us in the booth to talk with some people."

"It wasn't like that," I said, sipping my coffee. "I talked with the owner of the club."

"Hmm," Mrs. Helderman seemed puzzled. "Why talk alone with him?"

"I thought he had information on something."

"My boy, you don't abandon your girls after something like that." Mrs. Helderman reprimanded me, then she eyed me with an unsettling gaze. "What kind of information?"

Vicky leaned her head on my shoulder, acting cute as if she didn't just cause me to be scolded.

Sarah answered as she removed the pan from the stove. "The spooky kind."

I got up from the couch and went to the letterbox on the kitchen counter. I quickly retrieved the letter from the drawer and placed it in front of her on the coffee table. I sat back in my spot, sitting closer to Vicky. My hand played in her hair as I sipped my coffee. Vicky side-eyed me with a lustful gaze, forgetting we had company for a moment, but quickly straightened up.

Mrs. Helderman reached out and picked up the letter. She mumbled the words as she read them, and her face seemed concerned. I couldn't tell if it was shock or amusement. After she finished reading, she placed the letter back on the table. She stared at it for a long while before glancing up.

"Spooky? Jimmy wasn't so easily scared, my boy," she announced with a slight cackle as she shook her head. Her body sank back into the chair, and her face relaxed into a smile.

"It sure seems like a threat to me," I mumbled.

Mrs. Helderman frowned. "That poem isn't a threat. It's more of a warning." She hurriedly placed her hand over her mouth as if she had said too much.

My eyes narrowed on her, trying to understand the sudden behavior. "A warning? For what?"

"Nothing, dear," Mrs. Helderman assured, taking a sip. "Just an observation."

“Sis, can you set the table, please?” Sarah called from the kitchen.

Vicky let out a groan before hopping up to help. “Coming.”

Mrs. Helderman leaned forward in her chair, waving me over. I moved closer to her, leaning forward too.

“Are you still on about that marriage idea?” She whispered so Vicky and Sarah couldn’t hear her. Here we go again.

“Yes, Wanda. I still want to marry them,” I whispered, my voice deliberately louder than hers.

She sighed deeply. “Give it a few years. Don’t rush into things.”

“Look at how we are. Things are wonderful.”

“The future isn’t certain; you need to wait,” she whispered a bit louder. Her concerned voice seemed filled with regret.

“Kyle, you wouldn’t be hitting on Wanda, would you?” Vicky chuckled loudly. I looked over to see her staring at us as she put plates around the table.

“No, we were discussing the wedding,” I admitted.

“Chow time,” Sarah announced.

We sat around the table. I led the blessing, as Wanda always required before every meal. I’d finally memorized the Lord’s Prayer and could recite every word in my sleep.

“Amen,” I said. “Dig in, looks good.”

Sarah had cooked steak strips wrapped in bacon. It smelled delicious. After everyone got their plate full and started eating, I got mine and followed suit. The table was quiet as everyone ate.

Sarah excitedly broke the silence first. “Friday, we’re going to a night museum exhibit.”

“How nice.” Mrs. Helderman matched Sarah’s excitement. “Why at night? I thought most museums close around five.”

“It’s an exclusive gala,” Sarah offered before she forked some steak into her mouth.

“Gala? From that letter?” Mrs. Helderman’s spoon froze mid-air.

“Yeah, we thought it would be fun,” Vicky shared. “Besides, how will we learn who sent the letter?”

“That’s a bad idea.” Mrs. Helderman sighed, her face turned ashen, before hissing. “I forbid you from going.”

“Miss Wanda, what’s wrong?”

"We're adults, you can't forbid us from anything," I stated matter-of-factly, the words harsher than I intended.

Mrs. Helderman stared at us oddly, as if she had just realized she had overstepped her authority. She gave a light, forced chuckle. "Haha, you kids are so silly."

"You had me there." Vicky laughed, then imitated Wanda's warning. "I forbid you."

"We elderly have to find some way to pick at you youngens." Mrs. Helderman smiled, but it seemed forced.

The girls and Mrs. Helderman bantered back and forth about the differences between young and old. But as the laughter died down, so did the mood.

"Be careful, my little lovebirds."

"We usually are, thanks to Mr. Paranoid over here." Vicky chortled as she kicked my foot.

Since the topic was on my paranoia, I figured I would ask about the Project L.O.V. while Mrs. Helderman was here. She might be able to help me find answers on the subject.

"I still find it strange that Mr. Mortis mentioned Project L.O.V. in his poem." My casual observation was like the opposite of a stone in a still pond. Instead of disrupting the stillness, it reinforced it. The room went dead silent. I felt the warmth of dinner drain away, replaced by an unsettling coldness.

Mrs. Helderman's eyes, usually so kind, now held a guilty flicker; her hand flew to her mouth as if to trap unspoken words. Sarah and Vicky had both tightly held their forks, knuckles white against the steel. They looked utterly aghast, their silence mirroring Mrs. Helderman's.

The apartment, only moments ago filled with chatter, now had a disquieting calm that saturated the ambience, a stillness so profound it sent a chill down my spine.

"I didn't see project, whatever, on the letter," Mrs. Helderman eventually muttered. Her voice, thin and strained, felt forced. "It looked like someone tried to spell 'love' but forgot the 'E'." She offered a brittle, apprehensive smile that didn't quite reach her eyes.

I didn't understand what had happened, but I knew this topic was too sensitive to discuss at the moment.

"Yeah, what an idiot to misspell a simple word like love," I said.

"Spelling, hmm. A couple of weeks ago, Kyle left us a note; he put two k's in my name." Vicky chortled as she playfully poked me in the ribs.

Though the atmosphere eased, tension still lingered beneath the surface as everyone resumed talking and enjoying themselves. After the meal, I told the ladies to chat in the living room, and I would clean up.

I shuffled through the cabinets. Finding the right Tupperware to put food in sometimes feels like playing Tetris. Does it fit here? No. How about here? Nope. It's got to fit here. I found the right-sized Tupperware for each item and put it all in the fridge.

While washing the dishes, I couldn't help but think that maybe I'd misremembered that memo. Maybe Mrs. Helderman was right. It wasn't L.O.V.; the author meant "love" but couldn't spell it. Or maybe "love" didn't fit the rhyme scheme? But if you spelled it out, wouldn't the "E" rhyme with sea? I put the dishes in the dry rack.

"Master, Miss Wanda is about to leave."

Mrs. Helderman stood from the chair. "Getting older means bedtime comes earlier," she said sheepishly.

I walked toward the door, escorting her out.

"Good night. If you need anything, we are just one door over." I bid her farewell.

"Thanks for coming," Sarah said as she waved from the couch.

"A pleasure as always, Wanda," Vicky added.

"Good night, my little lovebirds."

After closing the door, I moved to the couch between Vicky and Sarah.

"Want to watch a movie?" I asked.

"I was about to start painting," Vicky announced as she gracefully slid off the couch, her movements fluid and captivating. My hand brushed against her rear, lingering for just a moment. She turned her head back to meet my gaze, her eyes sparkling with a playful allure, drawing me closer to her world of creativity.

"Enjoy. I can't wait to see what you create next," I said.

"Master, can we play a video game instead?" Sarah asked in her childlike voice, redirecting my attention from Vicky.

"Sure."

As I turned the Xbox on and gathered the controllers, I watched Vicky in the kitchen setting up her easel. Her headphones fit snugly around her ears.

I reclined comfortably on the couch, gently passing a controller to Sarah. With a playful smile, she shifted to face me, resting her feet softly in my lap. Our competitiveness mingled in the warm air.

"I'm gonna beat your ass, Master," Sarah insisted.

I chuckled at her enthusiasm. "I'll make you cry to mama."

As the night unfolded, Vicky lost herself in her brushstrokes, creating a stunning waterfall scene that shimmered with life.

Meanwhile, Sarah and I engaged in playful banter as we challenged each other in *Halo* matches. Time slipped away until she finally triumphed in every game with a gleeful sparkle in her eye, leaving me both impressed and charmed by her competitive spirit.

However, I was distracted during the matches. My concern and suspicion about that letter and L.O.V. kept my mind wandering, as I tried to anticipate what to expect at the gala. I also pondered the source of the awkwardness at the mere mention of Project L.O.V. during dinner. All three of them resembled children caught stealing a pack of gum or something similar. One thing was for sure: I had no idea what I was up against.

Yet as Sarah cheered, throwing her arms around me in a triumphant hug, I felt the warmth of love. And Vicky's presence surrounded us as the scent of her paint mingled with the comfort of home.

This was my strength, my power. Them... our love. Their laughter, their happiness. The playfulness of our relationship. The creativity and the joy they spread across the bleak, barren wasteland of life. These were my anchors in the storm of this complex and changing world.

I wrapped my arms around Sarah. "You're incredible, you know that."

She giggled, her lips less than an inch from mine. "Only because I have the bestest Master in the world." The warm purr of her voice spiked the senses on my chin.

A moment later, Vicky emerged from the kitchen, a smudged streak of blue paint on her right cheek. She caught my eye as a beautifully soft, knowing smile of happiness blossomed across her face. She didn't need words; her gaze conveyed a deep understanding, a shared quiet appreciation of the affection and harmony that echoed in the apartment.

Vicky walked over, gently nudging Sarah, then settled on my other side. Her head rested on my chest, that dark veil a scattered fluff on me. Her hand found mine, lacing our digits together.

Sarah mirrored her, with that fiery mane draped over my shoulder. Her face nuzzled lovingly into my neck. And her fingers traced my free hand before interlocking.

I squeezed their hands with a tender caress. The silence of the room spoke louder than words to our shared unity. An unspoken promise to each other, that no matter what, we would protect this peace, this love. Come what may, the mysteries, the bad guys, whatever. This was worth fighting for.

With them, I felt invincible. With them, I felt at home. The world outside could be a chaotic and destructive place. But within these walls, within their warm embraces. I had everything I needed.

Chapter 7: Triad of Magical Exhibits

Friday was a blur of a workday. David and I had a few calls, but we knocked off early. The jobs were simple, and we completed them quickly, working together. By fourteen hundred hours, I was at home, seated comfortably on the couch, thumbing through to find something to watch.

I lounged back on the sofa, finally coming across *Stardust* with Michelle Pfeiffer. I loved how the movie seamlessly blended fantasy, action, and romance. It seemed to fit the enchanting sense of my extraordinary relationship. That she was a living star from the heavens reminded me of my stars, Vicky and Sarah. That divine way they blessed my life. The main character, Tristan, fights everything to be with Yvaine, the star, even facing off with the witches who wanted to harness her power. In the end, Yvaine and Tristan save each other. Of course, they marry and spend eternity loving each other. A happily-ever-after.

My heart swelled at the scene where they saved each other. It reminded me of Vicky's words that the three of us protect each other. Knowing they wanted to protect me as much as I tried to keep them safe was a strange feeling. From one angle, it felt emasculating. As an adult, I'd been the one saving, the soldier, the one sacrificing to ensure no harm came to those I loved. But from another angle, it felt good, like I was valued enough to be worthy.

Was that how love really worked? How marriage was designed to work—really work? A partnership of mutual respect, love, support, and protection. Then a happily-ever-after. A true testament to the power of love overcoming the most daunting of obstacles. Could we face this darkness, and many others, to achieve that ending? Or was I simply like a little boy dreaming?

I turned off the TV. Then my mind strained to the dread of facing whatever awaited us at this gala. Would Mr. Mortis be there? Would he show his face, make his presence known? And if he did, what would be the outcome?

I felt like we were sheep being led to slaughter. Yet if we wanted an answer to anything—if I wanted answers to L.O.V.—we needed to go. And if that happily-ever-after was for us, we would have to fend off all the darkness—every bit of it. I thought back to a few months ago, when Stephen had almost pushed the killer in me to the surface. Could Mr. Mortis draw that monster out as well?

As I thought deeply about it, I heard the lock on the apartment door click. The door whooshed open with an excited voice.

"Master"—Sarah's voice rang loudly from the door—"how was your day?"

I smiled. "Fine, my sweet." My eyes followed her as she walked toward the bedroom. "How was yours?"

"Hmm, okay, I guess. Had an author in my office all day crying about his advance," Sarah announced perfunctorily, then boomed, "but I'm ready for the gala tonight!"

I was amused by her enthusiasm. We were obviously walking into a trap, yet she was excited.

"Are you wearing your blue dress?" I hurried after her. When I caught up, I leaned in, kissing her cheek quickly. We moved into the bedroom easily; her steps hastened to the closet door.

"Yes, and Vicky is wearing her black cocktail dress." She began rummaging around in the closet. "You wearing your suit, Master?"

"Of course, it's a gala!" I sat on the bed to admire her animated enthusiasm.

Sarah handed me the hanger with my sports jacket. "Oh, Vicky called me; she should be home in a few minutes."

I stood up from the edge of the bed. "Are you still up for this?" The words fell from my lips with concern as I approached her.

Sarah slid her blue evening gown up her curvy body while I absentmindedly fastened my button-down shirt.

Sarah looked at me when she pulled the shoulder straps into place. "Why wouldn't I be?"

"You seemed afraid a few days ago."

"I can do this," Sarah said confidently to herself before turning around. I knew what she needed, so my hand instinctively reached out and zipped her dress closed.

She turned back with a giggle. "Besides, you still owe us a wedding and a house."

"That's if we don't become corpses by the night's end."

Sarah tittered at my comment; we heard the front door open.

"Sis, we're in here," Sarah called.

I was lacing my belt through my pants when Vicky entered the bedroom. "Hello, my lovely." I greeted Vicky as I buckled my belt.

"Hey, sexy man," Vicky said before looking at Sarah. "Hey, sis."

"I got your cocktail dress ready." Sarah picked up the dress from the bed and held it to Vicky.

Vicky took the clothing and held it in front of her before her voice broke through the air. "So, we're really going to Scooby Doo this thing, huh?" Her eyes scanned us, the curl playing on the corner of her lips said she was ready to dive into mischief.

Her words and that look reminded me of the sexual adventure the three of us shared the other day. "Yep," I said with apprehension, then snapped into the commanding NCO resonance. "But our love will protect us."

Sarah and Vicky both leaned in, kissing my cheeks. "We will protect each other," they whispered in unison.

At that moment, I felt as though Mr. Mortis was the one who should be afraid—afraid of our united front. I quickly threw on my jacket, readying for the gala and what tonight might bring.

Vicky rushed out of her work clothes and wiggled into her cocktail dress. I watched my strong beauties as they strapped on their heels like soldiers lacing boots. It's time, Sergeant. It's time to show the world that the three of us are stronger than some emo poetry and scary people lurking in the shadows.

Without another word, we headed out. We heard a familiar voice as soon as we were outside the apartment. It startled all three of us. My body reflexively tensed, ready for combat.

"My lovebirds, are you off to a date?" Mrs. Helderman asked as she stood in front of her door. I relaxed when I saw it was her.

"Miss Wanda!" Sarah gasped; she jumped slightly at the sound.

"Yes, ma'am," Vicky stated calmly. "A Halloween party."

"How nice," Mrs. Helderman said with a chill. This was odd; I had never heard her sound so disconnected, so cold. Her eyes studied us for a moment. The look she gave was almost scolding, as if warning us. But I wasn't sure.

I finished locking the door before turning to Mrs. Helderman.

"We're heading to that museum gala," I explained, my keys twirling on my index finger. I wasn't going to lie to her. Mrs. Helderman's face seemed ashen as my words landed in her ears.

"Behave." That was all she said before turning back into her apartment. The door shut hard—not violently, just rougher than her usual nature.

I locked arms with the girls and started toward the stairs.

"What was that?" Vicky spoke low so only Sarah and I could hear her.

"No idea. But it was weird," I admitted.

"Miss Wanda may have been serious on Wednesday," Sarah suggested.

"Maybe," Vicky said, "but for now, we must figure out who our brooding letter guy is."

After Vicky's nugget of wisdom, we seemed lost in thought as we made our way to the parking lot.

"Here, Kyle," Vicky said as she tossed her keys to me. I caught them with ease. "Drive us there in my car."

Quickly, we moved to the Dodge. Vicky took the passenger seat while Sarah sat in the back. I moseyed into the driver's side, starting the vehicle, then launched us on this adventure.

Sarah was beaming with excitement and nervousness, but a determined strength burned in her eyes. Vicky maintained a stern composure with clenched fists, as if she were ready to rip off Mr. Mortis's balls. They both seemed prepared to charge into combat.

"I forgot to tell you both," Sarah announced, leaning forward from the back seat. Her face was hovering over the center console. "The school accepted me, and I got the grant." Her happiness exploded through the car as she did a small victory dance.

Vicky rejoiced. "Awesome! I'm happy you're finally going to be a teacher." Then, she slowly gazed at her hands sullenly. "At least one of us can accomplish something."

Vicky's hands were worsening and taking a toll on her spirits. It had been getting worse with each passing day. I glanced over and saw a strange, distant look in her eyes.

"Once we get you a spa, you can relax a little."

Vicky didn't say anything else; she looked out the window momentarily before her hand reached out to turn on the radio. She quickly turned the dial to the rock station. The intro to Dire Straits' most famous song came through the speakers.

"You know, the riff at the beginning," Vicky started to say, her words a punch more upbeat. "It is considered to be a very unique and hard-to-replicate riff."

I figured Vicky wanted to change subjects, maybe before the topic erupted over her hands—the nagging of sending her to a doctor to get an answer. But I let her have the distraction. We had other things to do tonight.

"That's cool," Sarah said from the back seat. "How did he get it to sound like that?"

Vicky air-guitared. "I think he suppressed his pinky on the chords while playing."

"I never played the guitar, but that sounds tough," I said.

Vicky shook her head. "Not as tough as us. We got a creep to take down tonight."

"Yes, we do," Sarah agreed, her voice charged with aggression.

The rest of the trip to the museum was filled with questions we might ask if we found Mr. Mortis, as well as possible reasons why he sent the letter. Even though the conversation felt lighthearted, an undercurrent of unease seemed to flow around us.

Getting close, we could see the massive and weirdly shaped building. My eyes gazed up at the sky, taking in the layers. I glanced back down and pumped the brakes.

A crowd adorned in high fashion crossed the street in front of us, which was the reason for my sudden braking. The parking lot was mostly full. I noticed we were one block away as I pulled into the lot. I figured the destination of those highly dressed individuals was the same as ours.

Circling for a while, I saw the sun fading against the city horizon as the day fell into darkness, like we were about to do. Once parked, we hurried out. Sarah and Vicky eased over to me, taking their places on cue. Instinctively, my arms reached around their waists, pulling them near to safeguard them.

"Master, I'm a bit..." Sarah trailed off, her head cantered slightly toward me. Her steps started to stiffen.

"It's okay, my sweet," I explained, my voice a softness against the cool breeze. "We have each other's backs."

"We can handle some moody beatnik," Vicky reassured her. She hooked her arm around my shoulder. "Besides, our hunky soldier boy is with us."

"Ahem, I prefer badass soldier man," I joked, trying to pull down the fear welling up.

Sarah's movements relaxed as she started to prance forward. Her hand reached down, giving my right butt cheek a quick squeeze. "Or just a nice ass."

“Just remember, even though we are here to find out about that letter, we can have fun too,” I said with swagger, confidence, and love. “Think of it as a date... with an added agenda.”

“A date. Yes, everything feels like a date with you, Master.” Sarah bubbled, regaining that fire of strength.

“That’s the spirit.” Vicky’s hand gently caressed Sarah’s shoulder. “Now let’s go kick some ass.”

“Ass kickers on the way,” Sarah said. Her feet moved with a determined stride.

Our movements halted when we reached the front of the building, as though our feet were compelled to pause in front of the overwhelming and almost sinister structure before us.

The towering building evoked a sense of both dread and amazement in the pit of my stomach. The structure was monolithic, seemingly defying the natural order of the city. It was like a modern pyramid, its tiered layers ascending skyward, each smaller than the last. It was as if the building itself was a staircase to some unknown realm, a mystic portal to the divine or... the damned.

Cascading down the pristine white marble were rivers of blue light casting a wraith-like aura on the stone, which heightened my unease. In the fading dusk, the museum appeared more like a magical temple, an invitation to venture deeper into the shadows that clung to its very foundations.

Those foundations were guarded by ominous sentinels: two massive stone dragon heads. Their gaping maws poured forth streams of water as if the building were exhaling its dark secrets. Carved with intricate detail, these mythical beasts felt more like gatekeepers than ornamentation. Daring the unwary to cross the threshold and face whatever lies within the walls. Walls that raged with undead fury, casting doubt in the most courageous of heroes.

The fountain in front of the entrance only compounded this sense of dread. The two knight statues centered in the reservoir stood frozen in violent fighting poses, their swords crossing in eternal combat. The still skirmish seemed to beckon us into a realm of conflict and strife. The lights that illuminated their frozen melee flickered with an eerie glow, as if the very spirits of the fallen stirred restlessly, eager to join the fray.

Staring at the knights, I felt a surge of courage rise inside me. That was what I needed to be tonight—a knight, a warrior. The soldier in me focused on my mission: to gather information and ensure my lovelies stayed safe.

"Whoa, that's a big building," Sarah exclaimed, shocked at the museum's size.

"Duh," Vicky dismissively huffed. "It's jam-packed with all kinds of history stuff. So, of course, it will be big."

"It's a pyramid," I stated coolly.

"Ziggurat." Sarah corrected. "It's a step pyramid, known as a ziggurat."

"Why would anyone want a cigarette building?" Vicky chuckled.

"It's a zig—" Sarah started to say, but then laughed. "Never mind." They giggled together momentarily, as if trying to dispel the feelings this place evoked.

As we marched forward and made it to the dragons, it felt like a fatal funnel as we continued through to the doors. Being surrounded by car-sized heads gave the hairs on my neck the chills. Hold it together, Sergeant. Stand fast.

This was no mere museum; this was a temple to worship the past, one that seemed to have eluded humanity for eons. Venturing to the doors was like moving further into the heart of darkness. None of this seemed real.

I felt it in my bones. Something about this place was way off. I was sure it was a trap, like that day in Uday's palace. Nothing was for sure in Iraq, and it was the same with this place. The only certainty I had was that tonight, things would change forever.

Two large, shaded glass doors marked the entrance; I couldn't make out the interior. However, the usher at the door looked sharp in his suit. The scruffy beard on his face contrasted harshly against the elegant nature of his attire.

"Invitations?" the doorman asked, raising his head. Cheers and pleasant chatter seemed to be coming from inside the museum. Moussorgsky's apropos classical piece "Pictures at an Exhibition" reverberated against the glass doors.

Sarah quickly retrieved them from her purse and showed them to the man. He briefly glanced at them before opening the door.

He bowed as he waved us in. "Right this way."

Stepping inside the Magus Artifacts and Relics Museum, the oppressive sense of dread that had gripped us outside quickly dissipated. I stood stunned just past the doorway.

The grand hall was filled with the palpable energy and vibrancy of a party. The atrium, which once seemed as if it would devour us, was alive with activity, buzzing with infectious enthusiasm.

Gone were the towering shadows and cryptic, sinister atmosphere. In its place were warm golden lights shining everywhere. The chandeliers hung from soaring ceilings, casting down a radiance that danced across the pristine marble floors.

All around us, well-dressed patrons mingled and socialized with Champagne in hand. Pleasant conversations filled the air, a stark contrast to the eerie stillness and silence of the outdoor promenade. This seemed less like a temple of doom and more like a celebratory gathering of elites.

An intriguing display caught my eye at the center of the grand hall. The perfectly preserved fossils of several dinosaurs. A testament to the endless fascination of the mysteries the past holds. I felt the little boy in me push to the surface; being faced with such colossal creatures—even just their bones—was awe-inspiring.

Behind the magnificent exhibit stood a circular desk manned by three highly attentive ladies. They greeted and offered a pamphlet to everyone who walked by. Their warm smiles and gracious nature put me at ease.

I glanced around. Ornate doorways lined the walls, each leading to a different era of exhibits. The bottom nine floors had many different doorways to explore the myriad wonders of the past.

Finally, at the back of the grand hall, a towering elevator flanked by two beautifully carved staircases. The sight was an invitation to ascend and delve deeper into the past.

"This is not what I'd expected." Sarah sighed, half-released and half-disappointed.

"Me neither," I echoed, shocked as my eyes took in everything.

"Come on." Vicky nudged us. "Let's explore."

Gone were the ominous whispers and sense of imminent danger. Instead, the ambiance felt charged with an excitement of discovery. The museum seemed to promise that the extraordinary was waiting for us. As Vicky, Sarah, and I moved through the bustling crowd, I couldn't help but feel my own trepidation melt away. I no longer needed to safeguard my beloveds; I could simply enjoy uncovering this place's treasures with them.

A waiter holding a tray approached us. "Champagne?"

“Thank you.” I reached for a Champagne flute. Sarah and Vicky followed suit, grabbing a glass from the young man’s tray.

“Ooh, can we get a pamphlet?” Sarah asked in her baby voice, seeming more relaxed. “I wanna know where to go first.”

“I still don’t trust this,” Vicky sighed. Her eyes darted around as if waiting for something crazy to happen.

I smiled and nodded to Sarah, then looked Vicky in the eye and commanded, “Stay on guard.”

Gently pushing through the crowd, we reached the circular desk. Black marble topped a wooden base, harshly contrasting the purity of the white marble floor and walls. A redhead behind the counter motioned us over.

“Good evening. Tonight, there are some exclusive exhibits only available for gala attendees,” the redhead said in a soothing voice. Her hand slid a pamphlet across the desk. “They are highlighted in the October section.”

“Thank you, ma’am.” Sarah excitedly grabbed a brochure. She started thumbing through it.

I sipped Champagne, still trying to process everything. I was expecting something... different. I guess I could enjoy the night out, spending a wonderful evening with my fiancées. We locked arms again as Sarah started guiding us toward an exhibit.

“Pirates are this way.” Her bubbly voice rang out against the roar of the crowd.

“Pirates?” Vicky asked.

“Arr, me booty.” I jested as I looked between them. They rolled their eyes.

“Do an impression that bad again, and you ain’t getting no booty,” Vicky said.

Sarah batted her eyelashes. “I don’t know. I could go for Master being a pirate.”

“Miss Pushover would be in heat even if Kyle wore a garbage dumpster.”

Sarah shook her head. “Nuh-uh. I would spray him down with Febreze first, Brattypants.”

“Okay, just settle down,” I commanded. “Since things are going better than we thought, let’s enjoy this as a date.”

Sarah blew a raspberry at Vicky before composing herself. Vicky rolled her eyes. They were back to their playful bickering. At least things were going back to normal—sort of.

Approaching the pirate archway, I felt a childlike wonder soaring inside me. I couldn't believe they had a pirate exhibit. Stepping inside, I felt the joy of exploring history with my fiancées.

I was immediately immersed in the world of piracy. The sound of ocean waves came from the speakers strategically placed around. The salty smell of the sea wafted as we walked by each showcase. I was transported to the high seas, which felt like a dream.

Drawn to the gleaming swords and daggers lined up in the "Arsenal" case, my eyes widened. I could almost feel their weight in my hand—the daringness and adventure they might have brought.

One sword caught my eye; the spine appeared covered in dark red scales. The plaque read *"Demonbane Cutlass wielded by Captain William Holymight 1706 CE."* I smirked to myself that the rum was named after a real pirate. I walked on.

Nearby were weathered compasses sprawled atop old maps. The faint scent of aged parchment and tarnished brass filled the air. The speakers sounded with cannon fire and sword clashing, bringing the feeling of being there even closer.

Vicky and Sarah moved with reverence, their fingers trailing the glass cases, almost as if they were tracing the stories of each artifact with their fingertips. Their eyes were bright with fascination.

I watched them, enthralled by how they seemed to breathe life into these trinkets, their spirits kindled by the promise of adventure.

It was as if we were pulled to another time, when the world was wild and untamed, a ripe frontier for the taking. The weight of the present was no more; we were giddy with a sense of high-seas exploits. At that moment with my beloveds beside me, we could take on the world, be our own kind of buccaneers, daring and dashing.

"Master, you really like pirates, huh?"

"As a boy, I was fascinated by them," I admitted.

"Hmm. Would you pillage our petticoats?" Vicky smirked coquettishly before sipping from her flute.

"Maybe," I felt my face flush. "As a teenager, I fantasized about being a pirate. Plundering, swashbuckling, and ravaging beauties."

"Master," Sarah said with a teasing grin, playfully smacking my shoulder a few times, "we have an audience."

Vicky leaned into my ear, whispering seductively, "Well, I've always wanted to be ravaged by a sexy pirate."

As Sarah and Vicky teased me about my youthful fantasies, their amusement felt endearing. Yet I couldn't help but entertain the idea of taking them like a pirate, imagining the three of us standing on the bow of a ship. All the while, my roguish desires to ravage their bodies and plunder their panties aroused me.

I scanned the area; our banter had caught the attention of a small crowd standing nearby. It didn't matter; I needed to taste them. To live one moment in my teenage fantasy. The whole world could watch me kiss my wives for all I cared.

I don't know what came over me. I leaned over to Vicky; my lips smashed into hers as my tongue waged war against her mouth. The flame of our passion was enough to burrow deep within our souls as her tongue parried my assault. We fought in our kiss for a moment before I turned to Sarah, her head leaning to meet mine.

Our lips were drunk in each other's caresses, and the tender lovingness of our kiss formed a divine union. Sarah seemed to be affectionately roaming through my mouth, longing to be reassured of my love for her.

As I broke my kiss with Sarah, my eyes lingered on my gorgeous ladies. My gaze shifted as I looked around. The crowd had grown, and many patrons were gawking at us; they seemed shocked. I could see the disgust in their faces. They were whispering among themselves. I wasn't sure of the words, but I could guess the gist. However, I didn't care. Instead, I found my courage to speak again.

"I think that's enough of my fantasies for now." I became slightly embarrassed that my passion got the better of me. "Let's move on."

"Wh-what?" Vicky stammered. "You can't just kiss us, expecting us to move along without…" Her voice trailed off.

"People are watching." My hand waved toward the crowd.

"Okay." Vicky obediently submitted. "But this isn't finished." Her eyes flashed with that dark vixen glare before softening.

"Where to next?" Sarah asked as she opened the map for Vicky and me. She was trying to shift the focus away from the crowd.

I glanced at the crowd that had just witnessed our kiss; they avoided my gaze. I nodded at the crowd, and a tall, chubby man in a tuxedo tipped his glass to me. His deep smile was approving.

Even though the intensity was starting to wane, we were still summoned here under weird and serious circumstances. I needed to stay sharp. Ease up, Sarge. Maintain a composed yet vigilant mind.

"Prohibition and gangsters?" Vicky asked before she gushed. "We gotta go there next."

"Okay," I agreed. "But that's on the second floor. Is there anything else we want to see on the first before we head up?"

"Nah, we can go to Vicky's speakeasy room." Sarah shrugged. "The one I want is on the fourth floor."

We soon stepped out of the archway. I noticed the patrons on the first floor had thinned out. I figured everyone was off roaming through different exhibits, just like we were. With the floor cleared, we reached the elevator without any issues. The ding to the second floor happened in a flash.

Stepping off the lift, Sarah pointed toward the left side of the hall. "Map says it's over there." She paused with apprehension.

"Good, I can't wait." Happy anticipation rose in Vicky's voice. Immediately, she hurried away in the direction Sarah had mentioned. Sarah and I followed Vicky's lead.

For some reason, I felt as though someone was watching us. I glanced around but saw only patrons enjoying Champagne; no one held a lingering gaze for us. The museum had proven itself as a place of wonder and discovery, yet I couldn't shake that dark feeling from before. The darkness might be hidden, but I could feel it. My senses sharpened to my vigilance.

Rounding the corner, we were met with the opulent splendor of the mobster exhibit. The air was thick with the scent of fine liquor and the thrill of illicit activities. Vicky's eyes gleamed with the sights, her earlier apprehension seemingly forgotten. The usually cool exterior she had was now a giddy childlike prance.

Sarah and I assumed our places beside Vicky. Sarah took her hand, swinging their arms like carefree schoolgirls. I stayed a step behind them, enjoying that maybe this place would aid in mending their sisterhood.

Whiskey steels and brewing pots fit neatly along the wall. Swing music softly played from the speakers.

I watched my beauties, torn between the desire to indulge in the museum's adventure with my fiancées and the need to stay attentive to our surroundings. This was not just a museum visit; we were summoned here for a reason. One that could determine the course of our relationship.

I scanned the area for signs of danger, but there were none. I felt myself relax, being taken over by the lure of this place. Maybe it was all in my head? Perhaps this place wasn't so bad.

Vicky, enraptured, ran her hand along the glass as she marveled at the firearms and flasks. The containers once held the most illegal spirits of the time. Sarah was just as enthralled.

I couldn't deny the thrill that coursed through me, watching their excitement at the visit to the past. On the outside, we were museum-goers, quietly adventuring into bygone eras. On the inside, we were soldiers, here on a specific mission.

Vicky broke our silence, pulling me from my thoughts. "I always wanted to be a mob boss." She beamed as she turned to me. "Bootlegging, booze running, speakeasies, all of it."

"Mob boss?" Sarah said with hesitation.

"I wanted to be a 'made man,' or in my case, a 'made woman.'"

"I can see you bossing everyone around," I replied, "a cigar between your lips and a Tommy gun propped on your shoulder."

"The thrill of being wild, of being in control, of being dangerous..." Vicky trailed off.

"Boss lady Brattypants, what she says goes." Sarah raised their joined hands. "Or you'll be sleeping with the fishes, see."

Vicky and I both chuckled at Sarah's goofy joke. It seemed Vicky had always yearned to be hedonistic in a way—a savage playing by rules she created, a desire to live life on her own terms.

I shook my head. "My savage woman, what will I do with you?"

Vicky's eyes fixated on me. "Fuck me into oblivion." Dark sensuality soaked through her words.

My senses were ensnared by her sensual nature, yet I couldn't let myself be taken off guard. I quickly suppressed the desire boiling over within me. My hand pointed to the vintage cars. "That's what I like about this era," my voice cooling the seduction to a freeze.

"Giving me the cold shoulder?" Vicky slyly inquired. "Or playing hard to get?"

Sarah stared at me with a sensual coldness. "I think Master is toying with you. Maybe we should actually go through with that punishment we had in mind."

Their sultry gazes fell upon me. I tamped down the flames of desire that threatened to consume me. As much as I wanted to succumb to their seduction, I couldn't. I needed to remind them of the danger.

I put my hands up in mock surrender. "The letter thing is not completely extinguished. I need to keep my wits, at least until we are home." My voice assumed that NCO smoothness, trying not to let them know I was struggling to maintain my composure.

"Fine, mister. But once at home, you're ours," Vicky said as sexiness rolled from her lips.

Crap. Was this going to be a fun "ours"? Or that punishment thing they'd teased last week? Well, doesn't matter at the moment. I had to protect them.

"Can we go to the medieval exhibit now?" Sarah pleaded in her childish voice. "I wanna see the knights."

"Of course, my sweet," I said. "Or do you want to stay here a bit longer, Vicky?"

"We can head out," Vicky's voice was laced with hesitation. "I could stay here daydreaming all day; that wouldn't be fair to Sarah."

We headed to the lift and took it to the fourth floor. A sense of calm washed over me. The girls were uniting in their sisterhood. Not only that, but we were sharing this experience and our childhood dreams. This made me overflow with my love for them.

Shuffling to the next area that was on our list of must-sees, the unease of being watched crept in again. I instinctively glanced around but found nothing that seemed out of place.

"My knights are this way," Sarah exclaimed as she tugged me along, Vicky following close behind us.

"Slow down, Miss Pushover." Vicky huffed, trying to keep up.

When we reached the entrance of the exhibit, a chill ran down my spine. Two suits of armor stood guard at the door, swords at the ready, evoking an eerie undercurrent of that ominous exterior. But when we stepped inside, that lingering foreboding was quickly overshadowed by the wonder of this display—a far more massive collection of artifacts than the previous two. Soft lute and harp sounds strummed from the speakers.

Ancient tools, weapons, armor, and clothing from the era were displayed beautifully. Each item seemed to hold its own story, each item a testament to the brilliant artisans of the time.

Sarah bounced with glee, her eyes sparkling with delight. She gravitated toward a beautifully adorned female mannequin, wearing a purple gown trimmed with gold. Her fingers traced the ornate designs embroidered on the fabric in the air. She seemed in a trance, staring at the dress.

Vicky, on the other hand, drifted to the collection of swords, pikes, and axes. Her gaze swept over the blades with fascination.

I watched them with admiration as my heart swelled with pride. These were my fiancées, my partners in this adventure we call life. As I stood there surrounded by these relics of the past, I knew that together we could face whatever challenges were ahead of us. Our love is the shield, the light that fends off the darkness in this world.

Sarah turned to us, her voice was spilling over with happiness as she spoke. "As a little girl, I dreamed of being a princess."

"I can see that." I nodded.

"And now that I'm about to marry a handsome prince, I feel that dream has come true."

Warmth burst through me. I was the prince in her heart. The man she saw walking beside her in life.

Vicky chuckled. "And the three of us live happily ever after."

"Hey, I didn't make fun of your mob boss ambitions." Sarah's righteous indignation was palpable in her words.

"I wasn't making fun of you, sis." Vicky sighed as if Sarah's accusation hurt her. "I was stating what the three of us truly desire. A happy life together."

"I'm sorry, sis." Sarah wrapped her arms tightly around Vicky. "I love you."

Vicky embraced her as well. "I love you, too."

I feigned a pout. "Hey, I'm feeling left out over here."

"Good," Vicky said, giving me a wink. "Besides, Mr. Badass Soldier Man, wasn't it you who wanted to keep his wits?"

"Yeah, yeah." My hand lazily waved her off.

They broke their embrace; I just stood there watching them. The way their dresses contoured their unique body shapes was a tempting invitation.

"Hey, I gotta go to the girls' room," Sarah said, her legs together at the knees, swaying.

"I'll go with you." Vicky patted Sarah's head. "I gotta piss too."

“Okay, I’ll stay here,” I turned to the weapons racks. I heard their footsteps fade away as I admired the swords. Being amid armor and swords, I felt that instinct to be a knight again. Honor and valor cascaded into my sense of self. Protection. Shield.

Tonight hasn’t been dangerous; it felt more like a date with my lovelies. Nothing seemed crazy, no psychopaths wanting to murder us. Just the three of us enjoying the exhibits and sharing our childhood fantasies.

Maybe we had gotten ourselves worked up about that letter. Perhaps I was overly cautious when it came to their safety.

As I stared intently at the weapons, a curved sword caught my eye. Strange symbols were engraved along the blade. The metal had a peculiar, bluish-silver hue. The plaque read *“Turkish Rune Scimitar of Alev Bengi, 1217 CE.”*

A sudden, inexplicable rush of warmth bloomed over me, siphoning the air in the exhibit. Each breath felt thin and dry, as if my face were near a fire. My eyes locked on the blade. It seemed to drink in all the ambient light. For a moment, I thought the blue-silver metal had a faint, pulsing red core. A hunger, sharp and possessive, snapped in my chest. It wasn’t just a metal; it felt like a dormant, potent force calling out, summoning the soldier in me, demanding I reach out, claim the sword, and wield it.

My vision blurred, and a blinding red, flame-like haze—not a trance but a targeted annihilation of all rational thought—filled my mind. My hand, now heavy and strangely possessed, devoid of my own will, lifted. It felt as if it were a puppet, being yanked by an invisible thread. Each finger instinctively clawed the cool glass, hunting for a seam, a latch, a way to seize the treasure. I was a passenger in my own body, watching myself commit a crime. The command was simple: *take the sword.*

Suddenly, a voice pierced the air, violently ripping me out of the compulsion and back into the world. “Mr. Forester.” A mature man’s voice rang out from behind me.

I did an about-face. The haze slowly drifted from me. I didn’t know what that was, but it was strange. I regained my focus to assess the person who pulled me from my trance.

A thin man stood in a tailored suit. His face looked pale, like a corpse devoid of life, with features that were sunken, almost skeletal. Those dark eyes seemed to hold a hint of a smile. His small frame and short stature weren't too intimidating, but he carried himself with an air of creepiness.

"Have we met?" I asked, trying to place his face. A copper scent wafted from him. It reminded me of how pools of blood smelled, a sinister aroma I could never forget, even if I wanted to.

"Not formally. I hope the gala is to your liking," the man said as he walked beside me. His stance was wide, his arms folded across his chest. He seemed detached from this place, yet commanded the space with authority. He glanced knowingly at the sword I was looking at, then turned to me.

"It's wonderful. But again, how do we know each other?" I couldn't figure out who he was, and it annoyed me.

He looked back at the sword before he spoke. "The shackles that bind are bound to three." I felt a chill creep down my spine.

That ominous feeling from earlier returned. I gulped. "From the letter." My voice was low, not yet a whisper.

I turned my head to look at him. A flash of light reflected on my face. I saw a pen in his breast pocket. It was an odd-looking pen with a silver skull carved on the top.

He turned to me with a brief smile, tilting his head. "The what?" he asked cryptically and gave a sly wink.

"Um... yeah. What was your name again, sir?" I asked, my eyes studying him. He seemed like a dangerous man—a man who could make that nightclub owner cower in fear. I could feel the soldier in me on high alert.

"Apologies, I never introduced myself. Ira Kuolem," he said, then did a slight quick bow. "Chief curator of this enchanted museum."

"Nice to meet you." Should I offer this man a handshake? Something told me I might pull back a stub instead of my hand.

"Well, enjoy the exhibition, Mr. Forester." He added, with an unusually detached voice wrapped in creepiness. Then he turned away from me. His head turned back before his final words to me. "I'll come find you later for a private chat. You and I have a business matter to discuss."

"Ooh-kay." I sighed once he was gone. But his creepy presence lingered.

"Ah, senator, how nice to see you." I heard Ira's faint voice as he faded into the crowd.

Business? Was this Ira guy our Mr. Mortis or one of his lackies? I quickly turned to find Vicky and Sarah emerging from the restroom as I approached. They seemed unharmed. Should I tell them about Ira? Or should I wait it out? Figure out what this "business" he had with me was? See if he was our Mr. Mortis?

"Master, why do you look so pale?" Sarah asked, concern filling her voice.

"Nothing, was looking for you two."

"Scared we'd gotten kidnapped?" Vicky joked and lightly elbowed me on the shoulder. "Thinking the pirates and mobsters had their filthy way with us?"

"Maybe it's Master who wants to have his filthy way with us."

"Maybe," I chuckled, trying to mask my worry.

For the next hour or so, we moved from exhibit to exhibit. I didn't tell them about my encounter with Ira right away simply because I didn't want it to interfere with the fun they were having. I also enjoyed seeing their smiles and laughter. However, my guard stayed up, poised for a fight.

When we arrived at the exclusive, gala-only Black Forest exhibit, Sarah turned to me.

"What's wrong, Master?" Sarah asked as her smile froze. "You've been stiff ever since we stopped in at the knights."

Vicky eyed me. "Yeah, like you swallowed a bug or something."

"When you two were in the bathroom, I think..."—I faltered for a moment—"I think I met our Mr. Mortis."

"Why the hell didn't you tell us?" Vicky's harshness drew the attention of other patrons.

"He said he would find me later, talk business or something."

"Huh?" Sarah looked confused. "What kind of business?"

"I don't know. But I've been waiting for him to show up again."

At the moment the words left my lips, a man in a suit marched over to me. His eyes seemed feral, like a wild dog.

"Mr. Forester, Ira wants to have that chat now." The man said in a deep voice. He waved toward the elevator. I felt the chill of war fill my body. The soldier in me was ready to fight, to kill if needed.

I commanded Vicky and Sarah with icy dominance. "Get to the car. Lock the doors. If I'm not out in thirty minutes, call the police."

Sarah looked the man up and down, sizing him up.

Vicky scowled at me, her eyes burning through me. "No," she protested. "We're in this together, we protect each other."

"Who do you think you are to take our Master away?" Sarah exploded at the man. "I'll scratch your eyes out if you hurt him."

"I assure you, ladies, this is simply a business matter." The man tried to assuage their fears, his hand moving up to signal a halt.

Vicky eyed the man; her fierce face was intimidating even to me. Sarah gave me a pleading look, as if to say, "Don't go."

"I'll be fine." I smiled at them, my teeth gritting hard. Vicky seemed to become aware of my killing demeanor. I watched as a corner of her lips tugged slightly before falling.

"Thirty minutes, not a second more." Vicky's fierce eyes remained on the man.

"Master..." Sarah started to say, but Vicky grabbed her hand and led her away.

"Lead on," I told the man. He seemed to pause for a moment, staring at me. Then we started walking to the elevator.

I wasn't sure if I was returning to my beauties or not, but this meeting needed to happen. I needed answers about Project L.O.V. Definitive answers. Ira was going to provide them, one way or another. Moreover, sending them away ensured their safety.

As I entered the elevator, I sensed a change in the air around me, charged like a battlefield waiting for the first shot. The first to draw blood. The bodyguard pressed the button for the tenth floor with a lazy motion. This was it.

Chapter 8: Dossier of Intrigue

Stepping off the elevator felt like I was facing Death all over again. The whispers of my conscience screamed that this was the wrong thing to do. Yet, I had to see this through. The sharply dressed man led me through the hallway. I glanced at the bodyguard, whose demeanor was professional, not intimidating, in his movements.

Our echoing footfalls on the cold marble were the only sound. This place was devoid of even a mechanical hum, silent in comparison to the bustling event just below. The air felt cool and moist, like an ancient mausoleum.

The marble walls contrasted with red wooden doors, lined on either side of the professional corridor. Plaques naming the museum's personnel and their positions were centered at eye level on each crimson door.

At the end of the hallway was a large gray door, a carving of a reaper sitting high above the souls harvested by his scythe eerily imprinted on it. As we approached it, a hint of cigar smoke and that copper scent wafted by from the other side. The sense of battle was bursting inside me; I just wished my Valkyries stayed safe.

As we reached the door, the bodyguard pulled it open with ease, his hand gesturing for me to go inside. I nodded before entering.

The room felt like the hollowness of a crypt, cold and petrifying. Shadows danced along the walls, clinging to the corners like ghosts of the past. Many shelves lined the oppressive space, overflowing with ancient tomes, their leather bindings weathered and cracked, whispering tales of forgotten languages and dark, forbidden knowledge. An old, large astrolabe sat on a tripod at the back of the room. Life-size statues of an angel and a devil faced off across the dark wooden desk. The massive desk at the room's center felt less like a workstation and more like a judge's bench, as if Ira's word was not only final but absolute.

This obscure room mirrored the emptiness of going at this alone without my beauties. I was sure Vicky would have some sharp-tongued thing to say about this place. Sarah would be bouncing around, running her finger over the books in a playful discovery of the content. But I couldn't get distracted.

Ira was pacing behind his desk, phone to his ear. "What do you mean it's gone?" Ira's frustration was palpable, sending a shiver down my spine. "Locate it. Immediately!"

He ended the call with furious finality, looking out the large window behind his desk. The city's night sky was blazing in, suggesting that perhaps I wasn't supposed to hear his conversation. Slowly lowering the cell phone, his grip seemed painful, as if the weight of it was unbearable.

"Reggie, you're too slick sometimes!" he snapped to himself, the words more exhausted than angry. Staring out the window, he released a frustrated sigh. The reflection of his gaze through the glass looked troubled, as if lost in a storm of thoughts. He caught my reflection behind him in the glass, his eyes penetrating me, but he didn't acknowledge my presence for several counts.

When I finally cleared my throat, he pretended that I'd broken him from some deep contemplation. He turned sharply, forcing a smile. That darkness in his eyes pierced straight through my soul.

"What was this business you mentioned?"

"Mr. Forester, it's wonderful to have you here." His voice was warm and inviting, with no trace of the frustration or anger that had just been there less than a second ago. He gestured to the chair in front of his desk. "Please, take a seat."

I moved toward the desk, sitting with caution. He soon took the chair behind the desk. His smile seemed like a wry attempt to appear less... weird.

"I initially intended to arrange a trip that would showcase something of interest," Ira explained, oddly detached from the current discussion.

"What happened?"

"The assets were moved—again." He answered solemnly.

"What was it?"

"As a former military professional, Mr. Forester, I trust you're aware that situations often reveal more complexity than initially apparent."

I looked him over once more, certain he seemed creepy and nerdy, yet somehow harmless in an odd way, as if he meant no ill against me. I couldn't explain it, but I felt it, the iciness of the soldier starting to fade. I lounged back in the chair, my hands calmly planted on my lap, listening with intrigue.

"Consider this location; many would presume it's merely a museum." He spoke with assuredness. "However, it serves as a repository of ancient wisdom, housing exhibits that represent some of the most extensive collections globally."

Was he stalling? Sidetracking? ADHD? I couldn't wait any longer to cut to the chase. "Why the weird letter?" Agitation rose in me, remembering how it shook my beauties.

A subtle smile played at the corner of his mouth, though a hint of weariness never left his face. "I possess a flair for theatrics, though opportunities to write poetry have become scarce lately."

"L.O.V. was in the letter, why?"

"A wise observation." Ira regarded me with a sympathetic expression. He raised his hand briefly, pointing his index finger in my direction. "The more pertinent question is, how is that project relevant to you?"

"Okay, you got me," I admitted, shrugging. "What does it have to do with my life?"

"Do you believe in magic?" Ira asked, quickly following up his question with another. "The principles of science?"

"Magic? No. But science, we live in the era of technology," I responded. "Of course, I believe in science."

"What if you were informed that your current life is not a coincidence of the universe but constructed?"

"Like a lie? My entire life?" I was trying to understand where this conversation was heading. "What is this? The Matrix?"

Ira chuckled softly, crossing his arms over his chest. "Do you perceive the current circumstances of your existence as an outcome of fate?" He paused, his gaze becoming intense. "You reference a belief in science, Mr. Forester. Have you ever contemplated the synergy of life?" He stared at me, gauging my reaction, then shook his head in a barely imperceptible way. "No, that's not the appropriate term. The sophistication of authentic synchronicity?"

"What the hell does that mean?"

Ira exhaled slowly. "Consider, Mr. Forester, the beautiful solace inherent in a reflection."

"A reflection." I sighed. "That's what this entire thing is about?"

He continued. "A mirror image that resonates with your every thought and aspiration. It manifests a harmony that penetrates the soul, presenting itself as a form of destiny."

"Okay..." Was this guy nuts? Was I for listening to this crap?

"Then the reflection begins to crystallize, vivid and assertive in its insistence on reality." He reclined in his chair, a subtle pause pulling his voice deeper. "Refusing its existence as a mere illusion, insisting everyone accept the fabrication is now made flesh."

"You lost me. What are you talking about?"

Ira was quiet for a moment, a look of deep disappointment blurring his features, as if he'd hoped for a glimmer of understanding that hadn't come. Unfolding his arms, his hands began to animate his words as he started to speak again.

"Let me speak plainly, Kyle. Your destiny, your life, is not a marvelous feat of the gods. It is a meticulous design. A design with sinister intent."

My life feels anything but precise. It's been messy and uncertain from the start. Is he really implying that I'm being controlled? That my choices aren't my own? That I'm just following some kind of preconditioned programming. And if *my* life was a lie, what would that mean for Sarah and Vicky? What would that make our relationship?

"What would anyone want with designing my life? What would they gain, manipulating things, like you imply?"

Ira leaned forward in his chair, adopting a seriousness. "The value of your life can be quantified in data."

My brow furrowed, eyeing him with a distrustful glare. "I have nothing. No data for anyone," I murmured. "I'm just a regular guy."

"I'm confident that isn't the case, Mr. Forester."

"Then what data?" I asked, my back straightening on the chair.

"Empirical data," he answered, certainty rooted in his words. Ira stood from his chair and moved to gaze out the window again. "Pure, raw data that can't be manufactured." His words echoed off the glass in front of him. Dropping to an almost whisper, he seemed to carry a conspiracy theorist's demeanor. "And there seem to be those who seek to harvest it. Far less... gentle than I."

"Sure," I huffed, the corners of my lips tugging upward. Yet that last part he said clawed at my heart. What would harvesting data mean for my beauties?

"The phone call you overheard was to arrange that trip I mentioned."

"A trip, huh. That's where you planned to lure me into a warehouse to harvest my organs?" Sarcasm dripped from my every word. Vicky was starting to rub off on me; that was for sure. Ira gave a light chuckle as he turned around.

"You're here seeking answers regarding Project L.O.V., Mr. Forester. Given your skeptical nature, you will not be convinced unless you witness it personally." He sighed in resignation as he moved toward the desk.

"Okay, what am I supposed to witness?"

"Genesis. Regrettably, I'm unable to demonstrate what you need today. However, you'll not leave without obtaining something of value." Ira, barely concealing frustration, softened. "Consider it due diligence or a gesture of good faith; the label is yours to choose."

Ira opened a desk drawer and retrieved a manila folder. With a graceful push, he closed the drawer, then flicked the folder onto the desk. It spun in the air before landing softly on the hardwood.

"We're not enemies, Mr. Forester," he murmured dejectedly. He walked back to the window, his shoulders heavy with sorrow. "In the future, I hope we can be friends."

I pulled the folder close and opened it to find a single paper—a research update on Project L.O.V. I snapped it closed, gripping the spine tightly. Finally I had a clue. Not everything, but it was a start.

"What does all this mean? For me?" I was hoping for an unfiltered answer.

Instead, I got nothing.

Ira stood at the window, gazing out at the city skyline, longing for something. He was finished with the conversation.

"Thank you, Ira," I said softly as my feet carried me to the door. I glanced back at him as I turned the knob. "Maybe we can be friends." My words blazed across the room, warming it slightly. "Goodbye for now."

Ira sighed nearly inaudibly. "Maybe so." Then his voiced boomed. "Have a good evening, Mr. Forester."

He never turned, but simply stared into the night. He seemed restrained, lonely even. The silhouette he cast from the window looked like an isolated king, head heavy from the responsibilities of the crown. A feeling I knew all too well, at least I once did.

Vicky and Sarah. I had to get to them. I sent a text.

[Master] Friday 21:17

You 2 safe?

[Vicky] Friday 21:17

Yes, we're safe

[Sarah] Friday 21:17

R u?

[Master] Friday 21:18

I'm good, no cops needed

Be out in a minute

[Vicky] Friday 21:18

hurry ur ass up

I felt relieved they were safe. Nothing had happened to them. A sigh escaped my lips as the weight of the universe lifted from my heart. And though that phantom chill of Ira's office still clung to my clothing, the thought of Sarah and Vicky started to warm me.

I walked to the elevator at the end of the hall, assuming the bodyguard had returned to the festivities. The hallway, devoid of life, warmed under the pressure of knowing I was moving toward them. My home, my loves.

I pressed the elevator button and looked back at the unsettling door. The reaper seemed less frightening now, revealing a sense of hollowness and loneliness in its task of guiding souls to the next world. That must be how Ira felt—lonely in a harsh world. Friends? Yes, Ira, I think we could be.

Was he a friend or just someone trying to take advantage of me? Time would tell. His methods were not completely upfront.

The cold metal doors opened, inviting me to step in. I moved with haste to leave this tomb.

Inside the elevator, I pressed the button for the first floor. I opened the folder, glancing at the document and reading the research update dated the previous December.

Project: Lineage Oversight Vindication (L.O.V.)

December 20, 2011

Genetically identical subjects from batch 048 began with twelve test models. However, only five models completed the incubation process and were transferred to the birthing apparatus. The models are hereby referred to as Subjects 01 through 05.

All subjects were integrated into Organoid Intelligence (O.I.) via the modulation of the encephalon during the fertilization period. O.I. integration permitted access to the central A.I. node, granting a higher development of mental faculties than previously achieved. This has allowed all five subjects to mature mentally alongside their physical development. An improvement that requires sustainment in further iterations. However, the aging process remains a significant issue.

The deterioration of Subjects 01–05 has not ceased in the current iteration. All five subjects currently possess signs of accelerated aging. The root cause of such aging has not been filtered through the genome harvesting of the genetic source. Nor has the process of incubation inhibited such deterioration of cells.

The telomeres of both Subject 02 and Subject 04 are beginning to show signs of fracture. Thus, after two years, the bodies of both subjects have aged rapidly to a typical human body in their mid-twenties.

Subjects 01, 03, and 05, while aging at a rapid rate, do not yet exhibit signs of telomere fracture, having reached typical human pubescence in the same two-year time span.

No solutions are currently available to correct the aging issues or fractured telomeres. Subjects will continue to deteriorate unless intervention can be formulated.

Dr. Lilianna Ambrosio

That's weird. What in hell does all that mean? Telo-what? Uh... Yeah, I barely remember my high school science classes, let alone whatever this is. At least I know what L.O.V. stands for: Lineage Oversight Vindication, whatever the hell that is.

The elevator dinged, and the doors opened to the first floor. The clamor of voices, the scent of perfumes and stale Champagne, hit me like a tidal wave, a jarring contrast to the grievous necropolis upstairs. The crowd felt too loud, too vibrant, from the intense quiet

I just retreated from. I shook loose from my mind and that document, closing the file once more.

I made my way through the crowd. The first floor was once again flooded with patrons. Bumping my way to the door, I found the entrance. I left the ziggurat with a relieved feeling, as if a week of worry was now flushed from our lives. But it's been replaced by a piece of paper, a document I can't begin to understand.

On my way out, crossing the courtyard, I gave a brief salute to the knights locked in their eternal poses. Their fight, forever cast into this world unresolved, mirrored the seemingly endless loop I found myself in.

Ira said this project would tell me my life was a lie. Was I one of those genetic things? Is that what he was hinting at? What did all this mean? I should have asked more questions. But would he have given me answers? Doubtful. He said I needed to see it for myself.

I briskly walked in the night air alone, filtering my thoughts before I reached the car and had to explain this to my beauties. What a conversation: hey lovelies, I'm a genetic mutation thing.

Fitting this would happen now, around October. A spooky mystery, to heighten the allure of Halloween. I smirked, as the irony and timing seemed too convenient. I looked at my feet, the boots that comforted me in my sense of self felt like impostors trampling the sidewalk.

Was I Kyle? Or had he been replaced by this thing, this body? Or was I just being taken in by some grifter, trying to swindle me out of something?

My mind fell back to Iraq, where the bazaars in the cities were filled with street vendors acting politely: all smiles and nice words. Yet beneath the surface, they wanted your money, your information to sell to the insurgents.

Row after row of cars lined the parking lot, yet through the array, I found the Dodge. Vicky was sitting on the hood, eyes staring at the ziggurat, phone in hand. Sarah was leaning against the driver's door, her hips cocked to the right, her torso pressed against the cold surface. The moment I saw them, a wave of relief surged through me, starting my heart once more. Sarah spotted me.

"Master!" Sarah rejoiced, shifting her body away from the car. The calling was a beacon I'd craved since I left with that bodyguard.

"See, I'm fine." My arms raised as I did a quick spin. Stepping closer, I could smell the intoxicating aroma of their perfumes, which soothed my spirit. I inhaled deeply, taking it all in.

The rustle of their dresses swaying in the wind began to clear away the phantom chill, as the sense of their radiant presence took hold. Their voices broke the sterile, muted feel of Ira's office.

"Good," Vicky replied, her voice sharp yet relieved. "Now, mind telling us what the hell happened?" Vicky demanded. I knew I needed to bring the conversation in softly.

I pointed at Vicky. "If you weren't sitting cross-legged, someone might get a nice beaver shot," I quipped. Her eyes fluttered for a moment, then her gaze fell on me, stern yet warm.

Vicky jumped down from the hood. In a blur of blue, Sarah ran to me, crashing into my side, her arms tightly wrapping around me. Vicky slowly walked to me, her black dress contoured her curves as she swayed her hips with determination. She gave me a playful slap before hugging my other side. I was engulfed in their embraces as my arms folded around them. I closed my eyes, enveloped in this feeling.

Sarah's fiery locks and Vicky's raven hair whipped in the night air, caressing my face. Though their bodies were distinctly different, contrasting even, they fit neatly against me. We were a complete puzzle, one that fit perfectly into our shared union, our love.

The rhythm of our three hearts beating was in sync; the cool night breeze was heated to the power of our embrace. This was the warmth missing from that cold, lifeless office. Not just their bodies but the fire of their souls against mine. The warmth that I needed to protect. Breaking from our shared hug, the drama started.

"A dress won't stop me from kicking your ass." Vicky huffed.

"Yeah, Master, we were supposed to protect each other."

"We did," I tried to reassure them. "I met with the big bad, and you two covered me with police support."

"Bullshit. You abandoned us to play hero," Vicky grumbled, a hurt-filled look crossing her face.

I sighed. "I didn't abandon you; I protected you. And you protected me. And we won." I opened the driver's side door, stepping halfway in. "Let's go, I'll explain on the way home."

I tossed the file on the dashboard. They got in without saying another word. Pulling out of the parking lot, Vicky was breathing heavily in the seat beside me. Sarah was leaning over the center console from the back seat; her face filled with intrigue. I felt as if both were stewing with a mix of emotions.

The car was silent for a few blocks before Vicky busted the conversation open again. "What did our killer poem guy say?"

"I think I'm a pet science project." My words fell heavy like a mountain boulder tumbling down, crushing the conversation.

"A science project? Like what? A baking soda volcano or something?" Sarah asked innocently.

"The fuck... The hell does that mean?" Vicky stammered with confusion. Her whole body shifted in her seat toward me.

I glanced over, and both she and Sarah seemed to be eyeing me with a complex expression.

"The file," I stated calmly, pointing to the folder on the dashboard. "There's a document in it about Project L.O.V." The car fell into deep silence again, so silent that I began to hear the ringing of my tinnitus that I usually ignored.

Vicky opened the file in a flash. The streetlights we passed provided her with enough light to scan it and get the gist. Once done, she passed the folder to Sarah, who leaned back in her seat.

Maybe they could figure this out. I started recounting the entire encounter I had with Ira to them, trying not to leave out a single detail. Sarah gasped while Vicky sighed during my entire rant.

"So, let me get this straight," Vicky said, reiterating the conversation. "Our death poem guy is this Ira character. He gave you a file with literally a single printed page. That is supposed to prove you are what? A mutated beast man or something? Flimsy."

"Not a mutant," Sarah corrected. "Genetically identical, meaning clones."

Clones? I sometimes felt her uncanny wealth of knowledge was scary and clashed with her bubbly and innocent persona, but I think she was right. Wait, ITI had a cloning project. But it wasn't this big; it was just organs to help people on the donor list. Or was that a smoke screen for this project? I needed answers, not just a vaguely connected report.

"What does the rest of that mean?"

"No clue," Vicky said.

“O.I. is... Well, an experimental form of computing that uses human brain cells,” Sarah said. “It’s supposed to be theoretical, at least that’s what I read.”

“So, a computer chip made from someone’s brain. Sounds kinda cool,” Vicky said.

“That sounds a little morbid. I wonder where they get the brains.”

“Not a chip, more like the hardware for processing and storage,” Sarah said, leaning forward in her seat. “And it is grotesque. But you might be able to imitate a person, or even make an entirely new personality that way.”

“That’s actually neat,” Vicky acknowledged. “But what about the tele-whatever things?”

“Telomeres. They are... well, like caps to the genetic code. It replicates endlessly until you die.” Sarah paused as she stared at me. “Over time, the cap gets distorted, causing aging. This is natural.”

“What does a fractured telomere mean?” Vicky asked.

“Simply, the code can’t be held anymore.” Sarah took a shaky breath, placing her hand on my shoulder. “It means the body is failing.”

I choked on her words. “So, uh, basically, the person dies.”

“Basically,” Sarah admitted.

Vicky turned to look out the window. A sniffle came from the passenger’s seat. The car was awash in silence, consuming the realities of everything. Turning down our street, I resigned myself to the thought that this conversation would consume our night. Parking in Vicky’s spot, we exited the vehicle in silence. Sarah handed me the folder with a trembling hand.

Trudging through the parking lot, they kept glancing at me. No one spoke as we climbed the stairs. Even as the apartment door opened, there was not a whisper. The quiet was deafening.

Once inside, Sarah and Vicky disappeared into the bedroom. I moved to the living room. Tossing the folder on the coffee table, I sat in the middle of the sofa, my hand reached for the remote. The glow of the TV shone upon me as I sat in the thickness of this unspoken implication.

I slid my sports jacket off, draping it over the couch behind me. I played with the remote, searching for a movie or show that would remind me of myself, that I was human, that I was me.

A thought formed in my head: the report said the clones were dying, rapidly aging to an early death. Does that mean I was dying? As a soldier, I had accepted my death as a fact of life.

But... I was no longer a soldier; I was a lover, a husband. The thought of leaving my wonderful women sent an ache piercing deep in my chest. I wanted to stay in this world. To feel their touches, taste their kisses. See those smiles beaming as I made their dreams a reality.

Vicky and Sarah reemerged, both in sexy nightgowns. Each took a place on either side of me. Sarah nuzzled her face into my neck, planting kisses. Vicky took my hand in hers, interlacing our fingers.

"What does that piece of paper mean to us? Nothing. It doesn't change a damn thing," Vicky said, her voice a sexy growl tinged with raw vulnerability. "We are yours and you are ours."

"There's nothing we can't face together," Sarah said in my ear. Her finger lightly traced along the line of my jaw, a seductive reassurance. "Said so yourself, Master."

Before they could say anything more, I kissed them, reclaiming my humanity. Sarah first, her lips fluttering over mine like butterfly wings. Soft and gentle, our tongues tasted the tranquil warmth of the other. Her aggression started to appear as she fought me with fire. The depths of our souls battled, not for conquest but for beautiful surrender. Sarah broke from me, her hand gently turning my head toward Vicky.

Without warning, Vicky assaulted my lips with vigor, reengaging our eternal struggle for dominion. But then her mouth muted the melee to grant me a kinder expression of her affections. The fibrillation of her sweetness poured over me like a gentle caress to the heart. She was like liquid fire, yet a calm burn in my soul. Breaking away, Vicky gave me a playful slap on the cheek. My hand played in her dark veil.

"See, Kyle, you are real," Vicky assured me, her blue eyes gazing deep into my soul. "So is this... us."

Vicky turned my head toward Sarah. Sarah's green gems sparkled with tears. I caressed her cheek, wiping the tears that fell.

"We are one, all three of us. Never forget that, Master." Sarah sobbed, tears of devotion welling up. Her hand softly traced along my chest.

Their calibrated words reaffirmed my existence, filling me with contentment. I was going to live. Live for them. Live to build a life together. Live for us, the trio of affection.

"I love you, my beauties."

"We love you, too," they said in unison.

Design? The thought was like a bitter taste of surrealism. How could something like this be anything but real? This was raw, unapologetic, real love—a unity that was written about in dime-store novels but rarely seen in practice.

The night proceeded with heated passion, our shared love language of becoming one. The sensual prowess of our shared youthful fantasies played out deep into the early hours of the morning. Every whisper, every kiss, every touch left no room for further deliberation.

After the fires of our passion died out, I lay in bed, cradling my loves. The neatness of how the three of us were pieces only made whole by being together reeled through me. Their light snores a rhythm that filled me with joy; however, I was unable to fall asleep.

I inhaled the intoxicating scents of their hair, aromas that filled me with joy. Sarah, the summer rain, and Vicky, night-blooming jasmine. The tickle of their breath on my skin, the heat of their bodies caressing me. Their chests rising and falling, the flutter of their hearts against mine. This was not a fabrication. This was a living, breathing testament to the reality of us, our union. This was home. This was everything. My whole world wrapped tightly in my arms.

Our love, our shared life, comforted my soul, but my mind couldn't be tamed. Even with my beauties pressed close, somehow, I still felt like a still-wooden Pinocchio claiming he was a real boy.

That document—and Ira's words—lingered.

Chapter 9: Chaos at Lunch

The weekend only deepened our shared love and understanding, as we grew closer to each other with each new day, cherishing each other more. Each passing moment was vibrant with life. Their power truly awed me. I saw more of their Valkyrie presence and the strength of their spirits, which complemented my warrior nature. Our promise to protect each other was more than words; it became a vow to our relationship, to our love.

The laughter from their lips rang with joy in our apartment. The way our hands caressed each other, as the warm hugs closed our bodies to each other. The way their hands found mine as we sat on the couch together. The unspoken language our hearts sang loudly, further intertwining our souls. Each shared moment became another sturdy, unbreakable piece of foundation for our life together—a life built on trust and love.

Sweet moments unfolded, nurturing our ever-growing relationship with the nectar of love. I'd sit on the sofa to watch Sarah lounging in the new La-Z-Boy, the book in her hands completely spellbinding to her senses. A smile pranced across her lips as she engrossed herself in a romantic fantasy. And Vicky, dancing around the kitchen, paintbrush in hand, was filled with vibrant energy. I found myself swaying along with her, even though I couldn't hear the music, simply caught up in her joy.

Their presence filled the air with fortified love. Our days were filled with devotion; cozy movie nights overflowed with popcorn and shared secrets. The shared delight on Saturday as we explored the new store that recently opened. It had things that catered to our individual tastes. On Sunday, we had a picnic at the waterfall, with stolen kisses under the heavens as the Sun shone its beauty down upon our love.

A warmth surrounded me as I basked in their joyous radiance. These moments solidified our beautiful, united heart, reinforcing our life together.

The topics of L.O.V. and clones were forgotten, unintentionally or intentionally avoided. I wasn't sure which. Neither Vicky nor Sarah mentioned it after Friday night. For me, however, the disturbing topics circled my mind. Death. Being taken from them.

After they fell asleep, my nights were consumed with research. I tiptoed to the living room, hit the computer, and surfed the web.

I searched for Dr. Lilianna Ambrosio first, since her name was on the report. Surprisingly, there was a lot of information about her. She held a dual doctorate in Biomedical Engineering and Molecular and Cellular Biology from Harvard. If that wasn't impressive enough, she also wrote a research paper about cloning techniques.

I skimmed it; it was filled with medical and scientific jargon I barely understood. However, the premise clearly expressed an argument for the morality and benefits of using such a technology. She cleverly advocated for the legality of cloning.

I couldn't find which company was her current employer, so I turned my attention to the topic of cloning. But there was very little practical information, beyond the chilling fact that human cloning had been banned since the Nuremberg trials.

I did find, for some odd reason, that the World Health Organization had a "watch list" for genetically altered or synthetic humans. This seemed to be a bizarrely specific rule.

The questions it raised were a cold dread in my gut. Would I have to register under this? Was I already on it? How would this affect my life, my relationship with Sarah and Vicky? And the most terrifying question, the one that twisted my gut the most: would they allow us to have children? Would the beautiful family we dreamed of even be possible if I was... this?

Then the thoughts of the aging thing swirled around. Would I die early? If so, how would it affect Vicky and Sarah? Would they be okay? Could they have the life we wanted without me? Find happiness when I was gone? All the questions of this reeled in my head, causing me to stumble around in a haze. I wanted to find answers, to protect our love. But I was at a loss.

Monday was a straight jump into the deep end of work. David and I completed four jobs before lunch. All the while, I was in a daze, barely there. David carried the weight of the day's workload without complaint.

When lunch came, I drove us to the restaurant Howard had agreed to meet at. David and I barely spoke all day; he seemed to understand that something was bothering me.

While parking, David finally spoke up. "You okay, boss? You haven't been yourself all day."

"Yeah, no worries." I forced a smile while the thoughts of clones seared deep into my brain.

"If you say so," he muttered.

How could I confide in him? What would I say? *Hey man, I think I'm a clone.* Yeah, real smooth. Get the straitjacket ready.

We exited the van and walked toward the restaurant. Inside, the hostess ushered us to a table next to the kitchen, where the smell of hamburgers and pancakes filled the air.

"What would you two handsome men like to drink?" the waitress asked as she approached.

"Coke for me, sweetie-pie," David hurriedly answered, his cheesy smile spread across the table as if he were trying to flirt with her. The waitress gave him a soft chuckle before turning to me.

"Mountain Dew, please," I responded in a dull voice. "No ice."

"Be right back." She flicked her hair back with her hand.

"Man, she's cute," David said with an excited gleam in his voice.

"One word: Ava," I reminded him.

"Did anyone ever tell you that you're a cockblocker?"

"Wouldn't have to be if you kept it in your pants." My eyes narrowed on him for a moment before glancing at the door.

"Shit, boss, I was just flirting." David sighed. "Not like I'd ever cheat on Ava. Just like the thrill of flirting every now and then."

I shook my head. "Is that why Ava is always pissed at you?"

"Yeah. She doesn't understand I'm a flirt." His voice filled with a sense of regret. "Don't mean anything by it; it's just who I am."

"You never cheated?"

"Hell no. I'd be dickless by now," he said, his hands pointing under the table. "Ava would probably cut the damn thing off and sell it to science or something."

The waitress interrupted as she placed our drinks on the table, trying to hide a chuckle after hearing the last bit of conversation.

"You ready to order?" she asked.

"Not yet, we're waiting on another guy," I explained, my hand pulling my drink close.

"Okay, handsome," she said, smiling sincerely at me. "Be back in a bit."

When the waitress left, I leaned toward David. "Maybe you should make an honest woman out of Ava."

David ignored my suggestion; instead, he put the focus on me. "How about you? Ever cheat on your girls?" David probed, fishing for what was concerning me.

"Nope, never would," I said, my voice half stern.

"Not even flirting?"

"To me, flirting is still cheating. My devotion to Sarah and Vicky runs deeper than I can put into words. And flashing a smile at some random girl gives me no satisfaction." I took a sip. "Look, I don't know how to explain this, but those two women are my world. They are the compass that points me in the right direction."

His brows furrowed and his lips tightened as he puzzled over my loyalty. "How is flirting cheating?"

"Emotional cheating," I answered quickly.

"Man, boss, you really are deep into these two women."

I was about to answer him when Howard's voice boomed across the restaurant.

"Bro, how are ya?" I turned to see Howard's hulking stature standing at the entrance, briefcase in hand.

I stood up, embracing Howard in a brief hug before answering. "Good, how are you?"

"Fucking traffic almost made me late."

I looked at Howard's attire, disheveled, almost as if he dressed himself in a hurry.

"Traffic, huh?" I quipped before sitting back down. "This is David, our journeyman. David, this is Howard, the other owner."

"Nice to meet ya," Howard said, offering a handshake to David.

David's eyes widened, briefly intimidated by Howard's size. He immediately shook Howard's hand. "Heard a lot about you," he said with a slightly higher pitch.

Howard sat opposite me, placing the briefcase at his feet. He studied David for a moment before talking again.

"I see the business is going good. We sign on the building this week. Ya still up for it?"

"Yep, good to go. We get the permits for the place next door?"

"Yeah, but ya gotta let me be there when ya give her the keys to it," Howard said, a cheery look twinkled in his eyes.

David looked confused. "What other building? And who is she?"

"My sista-in-law, Vicky," Howard proudly declared, his voice erupting with happiness. "And it's the spa she wants."

"Spa?" David whispered to himself before his face dinged with realization. "Wait, you mean Kyle's girl, Vicky?"

"Uh... don't know any other Vicky."

"So, you know Kyle is engaged to two women, right?"

Howard stared at me with an odd look, as if he couldn't fathom why David was so interested in my love life.

"Yeah, Vicky and Sarah. So what?"

"Man, I need this in my life," David spoke to himself.

I cleared my throat. "Anyway, back to business. I found a truck for me; the same dealership we got the van."

"Good, good. Ya should buy it soon, before it's gone." Howard's demeanor shifted back to his assertive business acumen.

"Why do we need two vehicles?" David asked, seeming lost in the business talk.

"You're getting the van and an apprentice," I announced excitedly. "And a raise."

"Apprentice, of my own?"

"Yep, ya gonna be service manager," Howard explained, his voice starting to lower. "That's the job title, right?"

"Uh-huh. David, you'll be taking over as the company's service manager."

"Really, boss?" His eyes widened as his breath broadened. "Never been a big boss before."

"You'll do fine. I have faith in you." I assured him, my hand gesturing with my words. "Next week, you and I will start to interview applicants for your apprentice. I want your input on the applicants. Basically, pick the person you want."

"Pick who I work with? Hell yeah." David's voice filled with appreciation. "Thank you for the promotion, boss. I mean bosses."

Howard shook his head, then chuckled. "I'm just the money behind the scenes, he's ya boss."

"Speaking of money, I got my half of the owner's payout from the coffee shops. It was less than I thought it would be." My words fell short of how I meant it.

"Coming out of summer, it's to be expected. Checks get bigger in winter, rest ya big head bro." Howard's body movements were informal and unworried. "Didn't ya read the projection model?"

"You mean that paper with the charts and graphs... maybe," I answered apprehensively. "I mean, I skimmed it."

"Shit, bro, ya gotta read all that shit."

The waitress stood at the table's edge. "Handsome, you guys ready to order?"

I glanced at the door. I guess she wasn't going to make it. Then I looked back at the waitress. "Yes, ma'am, I'll have the steak, rare, with mashed potatoes, please."

"Same, done up the same too, thank ya," Howard echoed.

"Me too, but make mine medium, please," David said in a playful voice.

The waitress's gaze fell on Howard. "Drink, darling?"

"Sweet tea, thank ya," he replied, giving her a brief smile.

"Alright, get that right in for you," she said before leaving.

"You two own a coffee place together, too?" David asked, his face turning even more confused than earlier.

Howard puffed out his chest. "Bought it a few months ago."

"Wait, Nolan? Howard Nolan?" David seemed to have an epiphany. "*The* Howard Nolan, as in the stock billionaire?"

"Ya know it." Howard beamed, the smile on his face curled so high I thought it might reach his forehead. He loved being recognized, not by the masses, just on an individual level. Then his smile folded into a straight line. "Not yet a billionaire though, 'bout hundred million or so short. Still just a millionaire."

David was silent for a moment, his mouth agape. His eyes danced between Howard and me, as he tried to piece together the connection.

"A bill... I mean, a multimillionaire is your business partner. How the hell did you meet him?" David's face was stiff from shock.

Howard chuckled with amusement. "Beat my ass and throws a pretty good hook."

Immediately, the image of that first night we met rushed to my mind, and how he smashed my Harley Quinn bust. "Yeah, I did kick your ass that night." I laughed.

"W-what?" David asked, his shock more pronounced as he shook his head.

I looked at the entrance, still waiting to see if the last person would show. She hadn't replied to my text from last week, so I was starting to worry. Just as I looked toward the door, I saw that Myra had finally arrived. She was dressed in professional attire—a different sight compared to the dance club the other night.

“Kyle, David. Hello.” Myra’s voice travelled across the diner. Her eyes seemed never to lift from me as she walked toward us.

“Hello, Myra. Have a seat. You just missed the waitress.”

“Myra, what are you doing here?” David asked, his face turning a deep shade of red. “When Kyle and I left McKellen’s, you were still working there.”

“Kyle hired me to dispatch for you two. All HVAC companies need a good dispatcher,” she said with pride in her voice. Her smile, while polite, never reached her eyes.

“Howard, this is Myra. Myra, Howard. He’s the business partner I told you about.”

“Nice to meet ya.” Howard gently shook her tiny hand.

“Howard, nice to meet you. You look familiar,” Myra said, sitting opposite David. Her gaze lingered longer on me than was necessary. Or maybe I was just imagining it. I’d been staying up almost all night for the past three nights researching cloning junk.

“Yeah, he’s Howard Nolan, the almost billionaire,” David announced, his brow furrowing as if he couldn’t believe the words coming out of his own mouth.

Myra seemed to connect the dots. “You were at the Full Moon Lounge the night I bumped into Kyle there. I remember seeing you on the dance floor with a woman.”

“Yeah, Elle, Kyle’s sista. We’re sorta dating,” Howard said, his eyes immediately darting to me. His body stiffened and tensed. He seemed embarrassed, ashamed even.

I just smiled and shook my head. It wasn’t as if I didn’t expect it to happen at some point. I was the one trying to play Cupid with them, lining up a brother-in-law I could actually get along with.

Thinking about Cupid and his arrows, I couldn’t help but think about how Vicky and Sarah owned every fiber of my being. I felt gratitude for the genuine connection we shared—a bond built on something far more substantial than a fleeting flirtation or simple convenience.

“Um… you’re dating his sister?” David asked, his voice sounding even more confused with a hint of awe in it.

“It’s cool.” I nodded to Howard. A look of relief washed over him. A thought popped into my head. He was always informed about cutting-edge tech. “You heard anything about a project known as L.O.V.?” My heart hammered in my chest. Perhaps he could help me find a solution to this puzzle. Discover a way to stay with Vicky and Sarah. But this was quickly interrupted.

The waitress came over, placing the plates in front of us. Her hands moved with a graceful purpose. Her eyes stayed on me during the entire process, as if she were waiting for me to say something.

"Thank you," I said as she served me. Her smile brightened, but she seemed disappointed about something.

I focused on my plate. The steak smelled delicious, the mashed potatoes were smothered in brown gravy, the green beans were peppered, and the two rolls on the side were perfectly golden.

"Thanks," Howard said as she put down his plate. His hand quickly picked up his fork and knife, busily focusing on the steak.

"Thank you, sweetie-pie," David flirted again. His cheesy smile was almost too much. This time, the waitress rolled her eyes at him, annoyed by his advances, before turning to Myra with a smile.

"Ma'am, can I get you anything?" she enthusiastically asked.

"Since the boys got steaks, let me get one too. Medium well, please. And a Dr. Pepper," Myra said, her voice gleeful before tittering coquettishly. "My new boss is flipping the bill, might as well go all out."

The waitress chuckled, "You got a good boss. I'll get that right out." She left smiling even wider.

Howard dove back into the conversation. "Nah, nothing like L.O- whatever." Howard dismissed the topic, taking a sip. "Do anything fun with ya girls, lately?"

"What about clones, I mean more than transplant organs?"

"Ain't that illegal?" Howard asked. "Ya know, something 'bout morals and all. But I guess someone could."

That seemed to be a dead end. I hoped Howard would have some information, even if it were just a little. Just a hint that could send me down another branch of this clone thing. Yet I am met with a disappointing "no."

"Sarah and Vicky seem nice," Myra interjected, her smile again not quite reaching her eyes.

"Was I the only one who recently found out about his two women?" David asked, shaking his head.

Damn, my personal life just can't stay out of the limelight, can it? I was here to discuss business, but instead I was ambushed by everyone. I remained silent for a moment.

"Hey, almost forgot, Dad told me he filed ya lawsuit against the state," Howard said as his knife sawed his steak with precision.

"Yeah, I knew he filed," I replied, my voice faltering a bit. "Not sure when the court date is."

"Lawsuit?" Myra stared at me with confusion.

"To marry them both." I cut into the meat with ease.

"You're seriously going to marry them both?" Her voice was tight with a mix of disbelief and something sharp. Jealousy? Anger?

"I can't live without either one," I calmly replied, my voice absolute. "I love them both."

Myra softened, her body slouched in her chair. "You better not be taking advantage of them. Not Sarah. Not Vicky." Her voice was low, almost a warning, cutting through the din of the restaurant.

"Shit, more like they run his ass over," Howard interjected with a mouthful of food. "We got drunk at his place, both 'em girls and Elle chewed out our asses the next mornin.'"

"Ma'am, your steak." The waitress placed a plate in front of Myra and a glass to the side of the plate.

"Thank you." Myra nodded, her voice gentle. With hesitation, Myra picked up her steak with shaky hands and bit a chunk out of it like a nervous creature. Her eyes fixed on me as she chewed, almost as if eating the steak in this manner was soothing her anxiety.

"Damn, girl, ya eat like a crazy person," Howard exclaimed, his eyes large with surprise and fear.

"You okay, Myra?" David asked, putting his fork down to watch the spectacle.

"Fine," Myra huffed after swallowing a big bite. She wiped her mouth with a napkin, her gaze distant for a moment, as if trying to gather herself. Then her eyes snapped back to me with a raw vulnerability. "So, if you're not taking advantage of them, what is happening? The other night, meeting them, it... it shocked me. At first, I thought you were joking or trying to avoid me." She took another large, almost aggressive bite, the habit still present but laced with a desperate need for understanding instead of judgment.

"Well, first, why don't you eat normally?" I sighed, trying to cut through the sudden tension. "Second, I wasn't avoiding you."

"Kyle, I liked you when we both worked at McKellen's." Her voice was weak, her eyes welling with tears, though she blinked them back. "But you never got any of the hints I dropped."

“I’m sorry, Myra.” I was genuinely sympathetic. “I wouldn’t have gotten their hints either, had it not been for them forcing their way into my apartment. Things with them are... well, complicated.”

“Uh...” Myra stared at me, her intense glare softening, replaced by confusion. “Okay, tell me what happened; this changes things.”

For the next few minutes, I recounted my relationship with Vicky and Sarah. From the beginning until now. Everything, from most of our first dates to moving in, the issues being fired from McKellen’s had on my relationship, the proposal, and our shared life. Myra sighed, laughed, shook her head, and even cried when I explained the time I thought I’d almost lost them. David just nodded the entire time; his face locked in a look of envy. I left out the letter, Ira, and the L.O.V. project.

Myra sat processing everything, her steak forgotten for a moment. Her gaze drifted, then fell back to me, with a new sense of consideration and possibly understanding. “Okay, okay. I believe you. Sorry, I acted that way. I was a bit out of line.”

“So, you started dating two women after they wrongfully tried to deliver your neighbor’s pizza to your apartment?” David asked in disbelief, his brows furrowed with deep contemplation.

“Yeah, basically.”

“Um, Kyle.” Myra’s posture straightened, asserting her previous stance. “I don’t really approve of your relationship. I don’t understand it, frankly. But don’t worry, it won’t affect our working relationship. You’ve always been a good guy, so I can give you the benefit of not clumping you in with creeps and losers.”

I smiled, admiring her convictions; at least she was firm on them. “Fair enough.”

“By the way,” she added, a genuine yet mischievous smile playing on her lips. “I’ll be taking up Sarah and Vicky’s offer to hang out. I wanna see this for myself.” She reached over the table, giving my arm a playful but firm punch.

“Good, they will love it,” I said with a smile, relieved that I hadn’t messed up my company, just as I was getting things on track. And now maybe the girls would have someone other than Elle and Naomi to hang out with.

I looked over at David again, and he simply shook his head, mumbling under his breath. I caught a word or two here and there, but one phrase stuck out: “Lucky son of a bitch.”

"Damn, bro, ya can get people all fucked from ya life, huh?" Howard smirked, shaking his head. "Now that my bro's love life is out there, ya two wanna get back to business?"

At that moment, when the table was reaching some semblance of normalcy, a person in a drab, tattered gray hoodie stumbled over to the table. Head hung low, the oversized hood shrouding her face, concealing it almost completely. Her body trembled and wobbled with each deliberate and anguished step. Her movements were stiff yet desperate, as if every motion was painful.

"Kyle, Kyle." A vaguely familiar yet feeble female voice wheezed from under the hood, barely above a whisper.

"Ma'am, do I know you?" I leaned forward in my chair toward her, trying to get a glimpse of her face. She recoiled, a shiver racked her frail frame, as if even mild curiosity was an invasion.

"L-O-V, L-O-V," she croaked. Though her words were incoherent, I heard them as if they were crisply funneled into my ear. A wet rasping cough followed her mumbling, her voice raw and desperate. "Find serum. Save us, save us all. You must."

Her hand, a skeletal claw mottled with large red blisters, reached out trembling violently as she touched mine. Thick greenish-yellow pus oozed from the lesions, slick and sickening. Without a thought, I instinctively pulled my hand away.

"Eww!" David's face distorted in horror and disgust.

"Ma'am, what's wrong? Are you sick?" I questioned; my heart tightened with pity. I wanted to help her, but I didn't know how. Her condition seemed beyond my simple medical skills.

"Serum, get serum. Save us. Please. Only one who can... you." The hooded woman sobbed before breaking into a coughing fit.

Then she puked a torrent of thick, dark red fluid on me, the warm liquid soaked through my shirt. Before I could fully process everything, her unstable legs buckled completely. I lunged forward from my chair, trying to catch her. I was too slow. Her face crashed with a loud, sickening bang on the tile. Blood bloomed into a splatter on the floor beneath her head.

With her last bit of agonizing strength, she dipped a shaky finger in the blood, scribbling something on the ground. I barely registered her action. Scooping her into my arms, I cradled her. The fragile body I was embracing felt cold.

"Call 911." Instantly, all three of my companions pulled out their phones and began dialing. But only Howard walked toward the entrance, phone to his ear.

I peeled the hood off the woman, exposing a face hideously disfigured by a constellation of angry, swollen blisters that rendered her unrecognizable. Her eyes, open and staring, were bloodshot and vacant, a silent plea frozen in the depths. Several of the patrons gathered around with their phones to record everything, but I paid no attention.

Think, Kyle, what was it that they taught you in your combat lifesavers class? There was blood from her mouth, a sign of internal bleeding. I started patting her down for any external wounds; her body had an uncountable number of festering bumps underneath her clothes. I found no other injuries. I checked for a pulse and heartbeat—nothing. I immediately started chest compressions.

"Get away from her, Kyle," Myra cautioned. I looked up. Her face was a mix of concern and revulsion. "She may be contagious."

I looked down at the person under me; her eyes were fixed in a lifeless stare. She wasn't moving, damn it.

Breathing and airway, yeah. I checked for breathing, but there was nothing. Nothing I was doing seemed to be working. But I continued chest compressions; I had to try.

It didn't take long before Howard returned, accompanied by the medics and police. I was pushed aside by the medical technician, who took over. I stood up, glancing at what she had written: *"MNV."* What was that? MNV? Save us? I sat down in my chair. The voices and noise around me faded into a muffled hum.

She asked for my help to save *us*. Who is this *us*? Clones? What is MNV? I looked down at my shirt, which was covered in her blood; the pungent smell finally registered. Being saturated in so much blood, flashes of combat rapidly flipped in my mind, as if channel-surfing at hyper speed. I felt my muscles tense, my eyes sharpen. My body was reacting as if I were in a combat situation.

I closed my eyes, trying to gather myself. *Please don't fall into the trap.* I couldn't have a flashback, not at that time. Vicky and Sarah weren't there to rescue me. *Breathe, that's what Holly taught me. Just breathe. Deep breaths. Remember the calming techniques your therapist designed for you. Recite their names, Sarah, Vicky, Sarah, Vicky, Sarah, Vicky.*

Reciting their names was a quiet prayer, an incantation to hold me to this world. The only reality that I could truly hold onto in times of need. Breathe in, breathe out. I soon regained my wits. The noise of the commotion finally reached my ears. I glanced down, staring into those hollow, lightless eyes, a sense of remorse striking me like a slap in the face.

"Sir, I have to take your statement about what happened." The male voice came from above me. I looked up and was met with a black uniform and a badge. It was the officer who had arrived on the scene first.

"Sure, officer. Anything to help," I muttered softly, guilt torn into my words.

The gurney wheeled away, a white sheet draped over the body as if it were a bright shroud. A final send-off for that poor soul, her pain no longer ripping through the core of her being.

My hands trembled from the incident, shaken but no longer on the verge of a flashback. The pain of not being able to save that lady surged through me, a brutal reminder of the world's harsh reality.

The medical staff had deemed her noncontagious. I was relieved to receive a clean bill of health. The excitement of the scene faded, and the bystanders grew bored, stopping their recordings.

After taking my statement, the officer seized my shirt as evidence. I wasn't sure why, but I complied. The chilly air in the restaurant sent shivers over my skin, creating goosebumps. I wasn't sure if it was the cold air or that haunting face burning into my mind that caused them.

Howard saw my trembling body, quickly identifying the goosebumps. Giving me a pat on the shoulder, his eyes watched me with concern.

Howard comfortingly said, "I got an extra shirt ya can borrow," his voice strained and hoarse. "I'll go get it."

Disappearing to the parking lot for a moment, Howard returned with a button-down shirt. It was clean and crisp, pressed perfectly with neat creases—a stark contrast to the messy, wrinkled shirt he, himself, was wearing.

I quickly washed what I could in the restroom sink and slipped on the massively oversized shirt. Staring in the mirror, I shook my head. I looked like a child drowning in his father's clothes. It was sometimes hard to believe how large Howard's muscles were.

The feeling of being a failure rose inside me. I failed her, whoever she was. She died in my arms, and I was powerless to do anything. The burden of that pierced my entire being.

I trudged to the door, putting on the air of a hardened soldier—the armor I needed to carry on, even if just to make it home.

Stepping back out into the world, I gathered my courage to lead again. I sent Myra and David home with a guarantee of a full day's pay. The relief on their faces washed away all the insanity of the incident that had plagued our luncheon.

I tossed the keys for the work van to David, explaining that it was now his. I asked Myra to come by the office in the morning after we finalized the real estate paperwork.

And Howard, my chosen brother, stayed with me. A piercing gaze stared at me with a weary look in his eyes. He led me to his vehicle, away from the chaos. "I'll take ya home, bro."

I didn't respond as we got into his car. The day felt too unreal for me, like a fever dream or lucid nightmare. I sighed, sinking back in the passenger's seat, resigning my heart from this place.

Chapter 10: Cleansing the Soul

As Howard and I left the restaurant, neither of us spoke for a long while on the drive. The silence in Howard's sports car contrasted with the horror of the scene we'd just witnessed. The roar and thrill of the car's engine were lost under the currents of gory fright. Echoing in my mind were the phantom rasps that rattled the lady's final breaths. Her pleas for help—my help—sliced deep into my core, bisecting my heart with her need for my aid to solve the puzzle that is L.O.V.

Streets whizzed by as I stared out the window; the beauty of the city was blurred, replaced with a guilt that I had failed to save her. Her disfigured face mounted in my mind. Her eyes stared at me with that lifeless unreality, pain tearing through her fragile body. These were the same things I saw at war. Broken bodies, painful cries, and spirits eviscerated.

Howard's normally obnoxious nature had subsided, and he was unusually quiet. His hands were tight on the steering wheel, focused solely on the road. He noticed my stare and glanced over at me.

"Ya okay, bro?" His eyes were sorrowful with threatening tears.

I swallowed; the inside of my mouth felt like a desert. "I think so," I replied, my head hanging low. "It's just a lot."

"Yeah, it was," he echoed, his voice a little upbeat. "But we got the business stuff going good."

"Yep." My one-word answer came out sullen and hollow. For some reason, I couldn't feel any excitement about business at the moment.

"Ya did all ya could, bro," he said, his voice cracking.

"Thanks, bro. I know," I mumbled, my words seeming to disconnect from the fog of reality.

The car fell back into the pit of silence. Only the roar of the engine fought against the hungry quietness consuming the desperation that seemed to sink into our hearts. It wasn't until we pulled into my apartment complex that I started to feel like I was regaining some bit of humanity.

I sat in the car, looking up at the second floor of the building. I still had no answers to any of my questions, only more questions. MNV? Yeah. And the weight of that woman's death crushed me underneath the guilt of not... not being enough to keep her alive. Good job, Sergeant. Someone else died on your watch. What kind of warrior is unable to save lives?

"Bro, ya want me to come up for a while?" Howard's question broke me from my thoughts. "Stay wit ya 'til the girls get home?"

I didn't answer him immediately, my mind weighing his offer. Then I spoke with a clear voice. "Nah, bro. I'm good. Go home. Mom needs you more than I do. Is she able to get around?"

"Barely. She finally started using her walker," Howard said, his eyes showing concern. "Ya sure ya don't want me to stick around?"

"I'll be alright, bro," I affirmed, gracing him with a brief smile.

His eyes studied me for a moment before saying, "No crazy death thoughts, bro."

"No crazy suicide thoughts. I'm good. No worries."

Howard hesitated briefly, still studying me. "Pick ya up in the morning?" He asked.

"Yeah. We got a truck to buy and a couple of buildings to start setting up."

"Did ya tell Vicky to not have clients around ten?"

I opened the car door and turned to Howard. "Yep, she'll meet us at the new HVAC office."

"Cool, I hope she likes the surprise." Howard's mood lightened.

"I think she'll love it." I slid out of the car, then leaned my head in. "Goodbye, bro."

"Bro, ya... ya did good." Howard's words felt soothing against the chill of sorrow. "Sorry ya couldn't save her."

"Thanks, bro, you did good too." My compliment was genuine. To me, Howard was the real hero of the day.

Howard smiled, his eyes welling with tears again. "Tomorrow, bro," were his final words before I closed the door.

My feet carried me toward the apartment. I trudged through, still dazed by the day's events. On the stairs, my steps felt heavy, wabbling toward my sanctuary. As the apartment door opened, I felt the slight ease of the bricks bearing my shoulders down.

Shower first. Wash away this failure. Then what? I didn't know. Once in the bathroom, I tossed my clothes in the basket. I started the shower, running my hand under the water until I got the right temperature. When it felt comfortable, I walked under it, head back, letting the torrent cascade over my chest. I lathered the soap between my fingers and scrubbed along my flesh. But the suds weren't helping.

My head dangled beneath the cleansing drizzle—an attempt to drive her from my mind, to wash it away thoroughly. The horrifying spectacle of her demise remained burned in my eyes. And her haunting request to be saved clung to my unclean soul.

I stepped out of the shower, toweling off, not having gained anything. No epiphany of what MNV was. No revelation of L.O.V. and what the project meant to my life. No grand plan to save anyone. And the guilt of not rescuing the life of that nameless woman ripped at my conscience like hellish claws.

My legs felt weak as I walked to the bedroom. Trepidation flooded me like a tidal wave of regret. Gathering a pair of pants and sliding them on, I dressed in haste as my thoughts took me over. Was there something more I could have done? Could I have acted quicker? Who was she? Did she have someone who loved her like I do? Or was she alone, facing the weight of this by herself?

As I returned to the living room, I set my remorseful, heavy heart firmly on the plush couch. I settled into its comforting softness, staring listlessly at the blank TV screen, a reflection of my inner conflict. My thoughts were a messy battlefield. Vivid details of every tactical error I'd made were displayed. Each thought crashed into the next like relentless waves against the once peaceful shore.

The apartment's silence pressed in, a smothering isolation. This contrasted against the vibrant banter and laughter that usually filled the halls. When my beauties were home, joy filled every room.

I craved their touch, their gentle caresses to soothe the roar of despair inside me. But more than that, I craved *them*. Their boundless energy, showering color into my dull life. The way their mere presence breathed wholeness into my soul, transforming the world from a menacing monster into visionary beauty.

Their sincerity crafted a realm of wonder, removing the constant reminder of the horrors that lurk in the shadows—replacing my need to be the soldier with an aching desire to be a lover, *their* lover. A void grew within me as a sharp ache pierced deep. This hollowness echoed with my despair. Waiting to be filled by Vicky's fierce spirit and Sarah's gentle warmth.

My body physically ached for their caresses to soothe the storm within. And a yearning to taste their kisses, for the breath of those divine women to breathe life back into my lungs, resurrecting my heart from this coldness.

I longed for my beauties, yet the emptiness of the apartment left me locked in solitude. And silence swallowed my thoughts.

Questions whirled around my mind like a destructive tornado, twisting and turning with relentless ferocity. Thoughts of "woulda-coulda-shoulda" raced through my consciousness, pounding like a harsh drumbeat, running an endless marathon of anxiety, one thought to another, raging in a chaotic scramble.

Suddenly, a sharp click of the lock alerted my senses. The metallic sound rang loudly in the quiet space. The door abruptly flung open, slicing through the thick fog of my thoughts. Jovial laughter, bright and familiar, swept through the air. The noise of happiness began to melt the ice that had formed in my heart.

My head snapped up, a spark of warmth overriding the guilt that had been my companion for hours. My eyes watered with salvation—the simple sight of Vicky's bold stride and Sarah's skipping cast the haunting shadows aside.

"Maybe we should show Master when he gets home tonight," Sarah continued, unaware that I'd arrived home way before them. "Or put them on now and watch his reaction when he comes in."

Vicky chuckled, lifting up the bag in her hand. "You think his blood pressure will rise?"

"Along with other things." Sarah pointed at Vicky's crotch. "He is our dirty man, after all."

Vicky walked toward the kitchen, setting the bag on the table. "I like riling Kyle up, watching him struggle to stay composed."

Sarah giggled, putting her purse down. "It's so cute, the way he tries not to rip our clothes off."

"It's the little things, you know." Vicky sighed in a swoon as she rummaged through the bag. "How he is always so thoughtful to make meals just the way we like. Holding doors. Even his pervy yet affectionate stares."

"Or the way his arms tenderly hold us, like we're treasures he has to guard." Sarah giggled, bouncing in glee. "Feels so safe curled up next to him. And the fire you pour in solidifies the warmth."

"Me? You're the warmth of our trio. Always caring for him and me," Vicky said, placing something on the kitchen table. "I just make sure he stays in line. Whip him into shape."

"Things before are such a distant memory now—loneliness has totally flown the coop!" Sarah's voice bubbled with joy. "This wild, crazy, wonderfully messy life the three of us share, always bursting with energy and love!"

"I know what you mean. He's my rock, and you're my safe harbor." Vicky walked over to the light switch, her hand pausing for a moment. "I think it's time to have *the* talk with him finally. The one about our pills."

"Really, sis, you want children right now?" Sarah asked, her voice softer now, hinting at a vulnerability underneath her usual playfulness.

"Yes," Vicky replied. "More than anything." She turned to Sarah with unwavering resolve. "And I want them with *him*."

Sarah bounced with joy. "Me, too, sis."

"The thought of tiny versions of us running around makes me want to scream with happiness," Vicky explained, her words dripping with affection. "We deserve this, sis."

"But we have to make a pinky promise that no matter how many little ones we have," Sarah said with mischief edging her words, "we find time for our dirty man and each other."

"Deal." Vicky flicked the switch on. As the soft glow of the lights flickered to life, illuminating every corner of the living room, they both gasped in unison. Their beautiful eyes widened in surprise as they finally acknowledged my unexpected presence.

The atmosphere was charged with an electric stillness; the room was screaming with silence. Frozen in their poses like mannequins, the initial shock wore off as the sudden revelation finally sprang them to life again.

"Master?" Sarah squealed, her voice pitched higher than usual.

Vicky walked over to the couch, playfully slapping the back of my head. "Damn, Kyle, you scared the shit out of us."

"Sorry, wasn't trying to," I said in a stale voice, almost hoarse.

Sarah leaned over the back of the couch, examining my face. "Master, why do you look so pale?" Her voice was full of concern.

"An interesting development at work," I responded, trying not to alert them. I didn't want to break their joyful moment, although I may have already done so with the jump scare.

Vicky sat down beside me. "Where's the van?"

"With David." My answer was stern and absolute.

Vicky stood and sighed with relief. “Oh, okay. Well, we have something to show you.”

“Yeah, Master, we’ll go to the bedroom and be right out,” Sarah explained, then took the bag from the table.

Vicky started toward the bedroom, Sarah in tow. I sat on the couch, trying to find a way to tell them what happened today. They soon reappeared in the dim light of the living room.

Vicky was wearing a slip of a nightgown, barely covering her just below her belly. Walking toward me, her stride made the fabric slide up, allowing me to see the dark fur between her thighs. Sarah wore a blue teddy, which hugged her curves in all the right places. With each step, her body flowed underneath the silk like a river of passion. They sat on the couch, one on each side of me.

“Whatta ya think?” Sarah asked in a voice that conveyed that innocent sexiness.

Vicky took my hand and ran it along the fabric just under her breast. “Yeah, we met up after work and bought them just for you.”

I reluctantly pulled my hand back. Gulping hard, I began the difficult conversation. “Today was a rough day.”

“Why?” Sarah asked. “Is something wrong with the business?”

Vicky stayed silent, as her brows furrowed. Her eyes showed signs of hurt, and a look of dejection filled her face.

“The business is fine, doing great really,” I answered, shifting forward in my seat. Sighing, I placed my elbows on my knees, hands coming together. “I promoted David; he’s our new service manager. That’s why he has the van.”

“What are you going to drive?” Vicky asked, her voice carried a spiteful and hurt quality.

“Howard and I are going to buy a work truck in the morning,” I replied in a flat voice. “Before we head to the new building.”

Vicky sighed, my solitary mood confusing her. “I gotta meet you there at ten, right?”

Sarah shot me a knowing glance.

“Yep,” I said, then leaned back on the sofa. The coolness of the couch filled me with some ease. “I also hired Myra today.”

Sarah gave a single clap. “Awesome, now maybe she’ll hang out with us.” As she spoke, her voice was filled with excitement.

“Okay, but why do you look like a ghost tickled your butthole?” Vicky caressed my shoulder.

"An incident happened at the restaurant in the middle of our meeting." I sighed nervously as I adjusted in the seat. "A lady came over to us; she had sores all over."

Sarah cuddled with me, her face nuzzling my neck. "Is she okay?"

"No, she's dead. I tried to save her, but nothing I did helped."

Vicky sighed, her face pulsed with life again. "Are you okay?"

"Not really. She begged me to save 'us,' and mumbled stuff about L.O.V." A shiver ran through me.

"L.O.V.?" Sarah rubbed her neck, releasing hints of her perfume. "That document that Ira gave you was for that."

Vicky's grip on my shoulder tightened. "Did she say anything else?"

"Something about a serum, that I am the only one who can save this '*us'* she was talking about." I rambled on, my mind trying to retrieve every notable detail. "Um, and she wrote in her own blood the letters MNV on the floor."

"M-N-V," Sarah muttered slowly to herself.

"You're upset that you couldn't save her, aren't you?" Vicky asked. She was perfectly in tune with my current thoughts.

"Yes. I performed CPR on her, but she didn't make it."

Sarah shot up. "That's not your fault, Master."

Vicky met my eyes. "You look depressed."

"Maybe," I shrugged. "I keep seeing her face. Her eyes pleading for me to save her. But I couldn't. I... I wasn't enough."

The room fell quiet for a while. However, it became alive with activity. Animated by the powerful current of our trinity, tethered by the threads of its connection.

Sarah's lips brushed my cheek, a soft, feather-like kiss that sent a sensation of warmth through me. "She said save *us*, not just her." Her fingers, usually so playful, now moved with tender certainty as they stroked my bicep. "And you do every day. Now, let us be enough for you. We can wash away the pain with love."

From the other side, Vicky's strong, familiar hand moved through my hair, gently massaging my scalp.

Their actions were silent comfort, an unspoken promise soothing the pain uttered in a ciphered language that could only be translated with our unity. Yet I still felt the bloodied stain of not only that woman's death, but the questions she raised.

The calming affection from their caresses felt like the warmth of the sun. The luminescence of their love shone brightly in the darkness, scattering the shadows to the corners. Their light cut through the haze of my guilt.

Vicky moved, settling gently on my lap. The warmth of her body on mine contrasted with the cold dread that had crept in. Those blue oceans met my eyes; they stared with loving determination. I felt the nexus of life start to pull me back into them, my beauties.

Vicky hovered over me, her face inches from mine. "Listen to me, you didn't fail. The pain in your heart is not yours alone. Let us share it," she said, her voice a low, fierce vow. Her hands, gentle yet urgent, found my pants. Her intent was crystal clear, as she had hastily undone the fly, ripping the fabric down to my knees. This was more than desire; she was reclaiming me, reclaiming the power of her soldier.

Leaning forward, her forehead rested on mine. Her eyes burned with a need to see my strength once more. "Give me, give us your guilt. Don't be depressed, our brave soldier," she whispered endearingly. A devious grin spread across her face, then she growled with seduction, a loving, savage demand, "Fuck me instead."

Her words dripped with ferocious spirit, like a shield against the darkness. My thoughts wrapped in the tempting notion, the demand of her body. The intoxicating smell of her skin fueled my desire.

I felt Sarah's hand on the back of my head, her fingers twirling my hair. "Be with us tonight." Sarah's low voice was warm against my ear; she playfully bit down on it. "Let us heal your soul."

The sudden, all-encompassing moist heat of Vicky engulfed my manhood. A low, breathy moan surged from her throat as she impaled herself upon me. Her slick, comforting embrace soothed to the core of my being.

As Vicky's hips rocked a slow, deliberate rhythm, I felt it—not just the physical sensation, but the first true shift in the suffocating weight on my chest. Each movement was an unspoken, sincere testament of her fierce love—a tangible, carnal devotion to pull me from the abyss.

They weren't just my lovers; they were my home, my solace, the very breath filling my lungs. They were my salvation, my loves, my wives. In this moment, they were my everything.

This raw, vulnerable act became a sacred exchange of pain for unconditional love. I let the passion take over me, take me into the depths of them, away from the incident.

Sarah's breath on my skin felt safe. "That's it, Master, let her show you what you mean to us."

Vicky took my head in her hands, pulling my face to meet hers. Those blue oceans stared deep into my soul. "Yes, my warrior, let me show you." Her whisper, oozing with a caring sensuality, began to lift the bricks from my shoulders.

I claimed her mouth, our tongues battling. As our kiss deepened, so did her ecstasy. Fiercely, her motions hastened, she began riding as if to take the sorrow by force. My hands reached out, gripping her hips, pulling her harder with each stride. The passion of her heart started to make me feel the panacea of affection.

The rapid assault shoved her body into overdrive, her head rolled back, and her breaths were rapid. She was close to the edge. Before long, she showered me with her alleviating love.

"Feel... fuck... feel my healing powers," Vicky gasped as the flood of her affections reached me.

Her hips continued to gyrate, guiding me to the first salvation of the day. The torrent of her healing essence pushed the first bricks aside as I became lost in her. Then the bolts of my love shot deep within her.

"Ah, damn, baby," I growled, then leaned forward, kissing her forehead. "Thank you."

Vicky's body relaxed, she patted my head, then she leaned down. "Good boy, now let Sarah help." She slid off me, her body slumping into the sofa.

"Now, Master... let me give you peace," Sarah said, her words were like a song that filled the wounds in my soul.

My eyes snapped to Sarah, those green gems peering deep into my soul. Her face nuzzled into mine as her body moved into place, straddling my hips. She enveloped me, fully accepting the fragile man beneath the soldier's hardened armor.

Her warmth felt like a balm to my soul. The fiery wetness of her swallowing me whole stitched the invisible wounds with her tranquil demeanor. Without a thought, I grappled with her hair, bringing her face near.

“That’s it, Master, use me...” She whimpered; her body trembled with a triaged ecstasy. “Use my body to feel whole again.” Her words were like a vow of healing, mingled with the rhythm of our breaths.

Instinct took her over as her lips gently fell upon mine. Our kiss was a salve easing the pain within. Our tongues played in the mending power of our shared need. Tasting the wild passion alongside the sweet peace, blossoming the final resilience needed to pull me from the darkness.

I obliged her pleas, indulging my senses in her regenerative spring. I felt the soothing sensation of her wet walls fall upon me. The depths of her stealing into the core of me. Slowly, her pelvis rocked into mine, taking in the entirety of my being. My hands tenderly traveled down her back, feeling the silk of her nightie smoothly on my fingertips.

Grasping her cheeks hard, I pulled her body closer. The pestling motion of her on my rod threw me into the chasm of her healing light. I returned her affections as my hips met hers. The shifting tides of dark to light reigned upon me. Her body tensed, then she flowed with the fountain of a revitalizing waterfall.

“Oh... God... Master...” Sarah whimpered, her fiery mane draping over me like a curtain of red.

My thighs tensed as I felt the pain leave my body for the second time. The fire of my attenuated fluids erratically erupted inside of her. Sarah slouched on me, her breath shallow.

I felt the safety and security of life return to me. I was not completely healed, but this was a good start on the path. As Sarah rolled off me, both she and Vicky began to lap up the mess, ensuring that not a drop was missed.

After the wounds of my heart were sutured through their love and devotion, we lay on the living room floor. Sweat was soaking through the laminate beneath us. Our breaths were rapid with the falling passion as we snuggled into each other’s embraces. Our hearts beat in sync, tangled in the joys of our love.

“Thank you, my beauties.” I kissed each atop their heads.

They stayed silent, both cuddling deep into my sides. With them, I could face any danger, any insane thing. So long as I could always come to this, to our love. Sarah’s voice cracked the silence.

“Did you want to talk about it?” Sarah whispered against me.

"I think the sores on her were from the telo-things breaking down."

"Are you okay?" Vicky asked, her hand playing in my chest hair. "I mean really okay."

"Sort of." I choked back my words. "What if that happens to me?"

Sarah kissed my cheek, "Is that why you've been staying up lately?" she asked, each word filled with understanding.

"Uh... yeah. How did you know I've been staying up?"

"You act like we don't sleep in the same bed," Vicky quipped with sarcasm flowing from her lips.

"Yeah." Sarah sighed. "We were waiting for you to come to us about what was bothering you."

"What if I'm one of those clone things?" I asked, my words ripping through the air. "Society already ostracizes our relationship because we're a throuple."

"What does it matter what society thinks?" Vicky barked. She leaned up. "We love each other."

"The World Health Organization has rules about genetically altered humans."

"Fuck 'em," Vicky declared, her voice blazing with a protective fire that burned through external judgment. She wasn't just dismissing society; her statement seemed to defend our shared future, our love.

Sarah chuckled, a soft, knowing sound, before leaning on me. "Yeah," she murmured, her voice warm against my ear. "What Vicky said. Because our family is *ours*, no one else's. They can shovel it."

Vicky snorted. "Sis, it's 'shove it,' not shovel it."

"It's not that simple," I lamented, my voice cracking. The reality of those rules began to sink in. "They can force us not to have children."

"Again, fuck 'em," Vicky added, her words defiant and absolute against all judgments.

Sarah snickered before speaking. "Besides, they can't keep us from having kids," she explained, rubbing her belly in mock pregnancy. "We've already decided you need to be a daddy."

"Damn, right!" Vicky burst with willful rebellion. "Ain't no egghead in some office a million miles away gonna stop that."

"Are you two serious?"

“Fuck yeah,” Vicky exclaimed, her hand giving my chest a playful slap. “Our little monsters will terrorize those prudes at the World... whatever organization.”

“Are you ready for that, Master?”

I thought about it for a moment. Maybe this was something natural for us. Maybe having kids would ground us even more. But I felt the hesitation rise in my chest. No. We needed to wait until we were married before we started having children. I couldn’t have a child growing up without all their parents.

“Can we wait until after the wedding?” I asked, the hesitation in my voice felt devoid of complete sincerity.

Neither of them spoke for a moment. The silence filled the void around us, as if I had killed their joy with a single hesitation. Then the vacuum I created was filled once more.

“Since kids are still a sensitive subject”—Vicky sighed in defeat—“what about the sores? Are you afraid the sores will form?” Her words seemed rhetorical. “Afraid you will die?”

“Yes. That, and I failed to save that lady; her body was wracked with so much pain.”

Vicky rubbed her hand along my side. “And you want to save these others she mentioned, huh?”

“Yes, my sense of duty wants to help them.” Then selfishness set in. “And myself as well. I don’t want to leave you two, die before we have a life together.”

“Then we’ll solve this.” Sarah beamed, her excitement shattering the sullen mood in the air. “We can save all the clones, no problem.”

Vicky playfully bit my collarbone. “Your Valkyries are here to help.”

“I don’t know where to start.”

Sarah leaned up on her elbow, her eyes locking into mine. “What do you think MNV is?”

“Don’t know,” I admitted. The letters were a confusing mess of nothingness to me.

“That’s where we start,” Vicky said.

We lay back in our quiet reprieve. The idea of facing this challenge together made me feel a sense of unity and love. I was blessed to have such women that I could call my own.

Held captive by their warmth, this was sanctuary. I hoped they always remained the life-giving kisses upon my lips. Stay the essence of love and fire in my heart. Forever held every moment that I'm with them both as a treasure. A bounty that no gold or jewels could ever compare to. A flame of love never to fade into the cold night of this mystery. Instead, burning bright in the glow of each loving day together. Eternal in our bliss, our life.

Just as I was lost in the feeling of us, a knock came rapping on the door. Sarah and Vicky retreated from me, straightening their nightgowns. I rushed to put on my pants, then stood with determination, moving toward the door.

As I opened it, the courier from Garou was staring me in the face. His dark tan clothes seemed faded, as if he had ridden for a millennium to bring this letter. Before I could say anything, his voice boomed.

"Mr. Forester, another letter," he said, a smile not quite reaching his eyes pulled at the corners of his lips.

I peered down at his hand; another manila envelope sat between his fingers. Nothing other than my name on the front, in that same messy handwriting. Ira, back at it again.

I reached out to receive the letter, but stopped myself. Tip: I needed to tip the courier. I patted my pockets, but remembered I left my wallet in the bedroom. As I was about to turn around, an arm slid next to me, holding out a twenty-dollar bill.

"Thank you, sir," Vicky said as she exchanged the bill for the letter.

He smiled brightly, taking the bill. He gave a light whistle as he quickly bowed his head. Making his exit, he turned to leave. "Garou Couriers lead the pack. Ah-wooh!" His words faded down the hallway.

I closed the door, staring at Vicky. Her hand ripped open the letter. With gusto, she read it aloud.

Fellow crusader,

All is but a mesh, tearing deep into flesh. The phantom of her name is yet to drive you insane. The sight of her death leaves you sore, you can't seem to find what's in store. For now, let it be. And

remember the shackles that bind are bound to three.
Worry not of M-N-V, for in time you shall see.
Answers will unfold, so don't let the night go cold.

Your Friend,
Anima Mortis

P.S. I have your shirt. See me next Tuesday.

Ira had sent a new letter, and evidently he knew about my lunch visitor, even the weight of her death on my heart.

"With creepy friends like Ira, who needs enemies?" Sarah shuddered at the words read aloud.

"Creepoid." Vicky shivered, her voice a torrent of emotions. "Your beatnik buddy is really fucking spooky."

"Yeah, he does have a flair for theatrics."

Soon, Ira's intrusion with his new cryptic letter was discarded and replaced with affection. A swirl of soothing passion marked the rest of the night. The lingering warmth of Sarah and Vicky's bodies was a comforting weight on me. Their soft breaths were a lullaby that calmed the beast within me. The peace of our trinity was a slice of life I always enjoyed. The unity was something that I knew caused envy.

We laid in bed with discussions about Ira's new poem. Vicky was right: he was a creepy beatnik. Yet somehow, he was the only one who was actively helping us solve this L.O.V. thing. I'm sure he had an agenda of his own, but that didn't matter so long as he got answers for us. And maybe, when all of this was over, we might actually become friends, real friends.

But when I next visited Ira, he'd better have answers: no more riddles, no more games. I would beat this thing. But for now, I would, each day, enjoy what time I had with my beauties.

Chapter 11: A Spa Treatment

The day started with a bang. Howard picked me up from the apartment at seven-thirty, so we could buy the work truck. He talked with the dealership yesterday after leaving my apartment. With cash in hand from the business account, we quickly processed the purchase agreement and transfer.

By eight-fifteen, we were at the abstract office where the deeds were researched and transferred. We signed the deeds for both properties in no time. And by nine on the dot, I was ready to unlock the office for Myra and David. Howard had to leave briefly to attend to his parents, asking me to wait for him to return before showing Vicky the spa we had purchased.

The exterior of the building was clad in red brick, and large windows encircled the front half of the structure. The sturdy glass security door conveyed an inviting and professional appearance.

As we approached, Myra said, "Hey, about yesterday, I thought you were fearless."

"Yeah, boss, a true badass," David interjected with excitement before falling into yesterday's despair. "Too bad about the girl."

"Thank you." I graciously accepted their admiration with a nod. "But let's not worry about yesterday; we have things to do today."

Though yesterday's fiasco was far from over, at least for me, I didn't want it to bring my team down. Turning on my soldier's compartmentalization, I pushed the thoughts of death away.

Glancing toward the road, I felt a sense of achievement. The sign structure was still standing, but it was blank—at least for now, but not for much longer.

Then I thought about how today marked a significant leap forward in my life with Vicky and Sarah—financial security. Every step forward, every successful deal, felt like another brick laid in the foundation of the dream house we fantasized about. Brick by loving brick, the three of us moved toward that beautiful life we were building together with our love. I slipped the key into the lock, and I stepped inside, followed by David and Myra.

David quickly snooped around. "Wow, this place looks good."

The beige walls were freshly painted. The large, solid windows wrapped around the office area, allowing sunlight to bathe the interior in a warm glow. The main area featured a dark gray carpet that contrasted with the walls. Two enclosed offices sat at the back of the spacious open floor, flanking the bay door. A restroom was located on either side of the side walls: one marked for males and the other for females.

"Yep, it's also centrally located." I smiled as the achievement of finally walking into my own shop hit me with a surge of excitement.

Myra walked over to an area near the front door. "When is the office furniture getting delivered?" she asked, her voice tingling with anticipation. Her hand was waving in the air, almost as if she were imagining a desk in the empty space.

"Should be any time, now. Your desk is ergonomic."

She beamed. "Oh, Kyle, you're such a thoughtful boss. You thought of everything to support us in our work."

"I try."

David roamed around to the back area. He opened the entrance leading to the bay, his eyes widening in surprise. For a moment, he stood stunned at the sheer size of the fabrication bay.

Myra's eyes trailed up my frame for a moment before she turned away. The tips of her ears flushed red. "A sturdy desk should help with *stamina*." She paused for a moment, turning around. "You're way better than McKellen, more thoughtful."

David turned to me, his body halfway in the bay door. "Holy fuck, so much room."

"And before you ask, no smoking in the office," I announced, pointedly, directly at the bay door.

David looked at me with a mischievous smile spreading across his face. Then he walked into the bay area, the door closing behind him. I was sure he was going to light one up. But it was the first day in our new office, so I let it slide.

Myra immediately drew my attention, her hand pointing toward the back wall. "Which one is yours?" she asked as she started walking toward the rooms beside the bay door.

"I hadn't really thought about it." I shrugged, following behind her.

"This one catches the light better," Myra stated as she moved to the one on the left. Her cheeks briefly flushed red. "Will give you a better view."

I smiled in agreement. "That's a great choice."

My eyes were soaking in the area, trying to picture in my head how to arrange the furniture. I felt the heat of her body next to mine as she leaned into me.

"Plus," she murmured, placing a hand on my shoulder, "it has a perfect line of sight to my desk. For... easy communication."

I felt a strange unease wash over me but ignored it. At that moment, a beeping sound came from outside. I spotted the delivery truck. The driver had begun moving into a position to offload the office furniture. I walked to the bay door and knocked on it.

"David, gotta cut the smoke short. We've got furniture to build."

"Coming, boss," he said back through the door. I could hear him shuffling around, probably trying to wave off the smoke from his cigarette. I just chuckled to myself.

The delivery workers busily offloaded a variety of professional furniture pieces into the shop's open space. Among the items, a few were already assembled and ready for use. This gave us an idea of what the interior could look like after everything was set up.

However, Myra's work desk remained flat and disassembled securely in its box. Without wasting a moment, David and I rolled up our sleeves and set to work, eager to piece together Myra's desk. Myra sat off to the side, supervising. I was sure she was imagining how it would transform the space once completed.

While we were busy, Vicky showed up in black pants and a dark gray T-shirt. Her eyes narrowed at me. Then she walked over toward Myra, propping herself on the wall behind her.

Vicky greeted the room. "Good morning, everyone."

I looked up from my work. "Good morning, darling."

"Good morning," David said, then he straightened up, looking directly at Vicky. "Sarah or Vicky?"

Myra chuckled, shaking her head at David. "Good morning, Vicky." Her warm words held an undertone of harshness that seemed to go unnoticed by everyone but me.

"Good morning, beautiful," Vicky responded, giving a brief nod in my direction. "I see you put the boys to work fast."

"Hard work being a woman." Myra's words carried a challenge. "Real women have to keep men in check, don't you agree?"

"Maybe some women," Vicky crowed, her voice sharp like a sword striking a combatant. "But it's easy to be a good woman with a man like Kyle. He seems to bring out authenticity in everyone."

Myra didn't respond; she leaned against the wall next to Vicky. Both stood still with arms crossed. A silent battle was taking place between them. Myra watched Vicky with a cold stare, as if she were sizing her up. Vicky simply smiled with a wide grin.

I ignored their exchanges; instead, David and I were almost done setting up the desk. The delivery guys came over to us with paperwork. Myra took the initiative to look over the receipt and sign the document.

"There, all done, boss," David said as we flipped the desk over to its proper position. "Looks expensive."

"Wait until you see some of the new tools." Then a smirk grew on my face as my eyes wandered over to Vicky. She and Myra were whispering back and forth. "What are you two yapping about?"

"Girl talk," Vicky announced perfunctorily, her eyes fixed on me with a dangerous seduction glinting in them.

Myra cleared her throat, as if she were caught doing something she shouldn't be. "Just talking about this spook-house that my friend invited me to."

"Cool, maybe I should take Ava. Scare her into needing cuddles later." David snickered with a chill. "Then maybe more."

"Eww, such a sleaze, Dave," Myra muttered as she walked past us. She grabbed an office chair and slid it over to the desk, then sat down immediately.

"So, why do I have to be here?" Vicky kicked away from the wall, launching her body forward. Her hips swayed seductively as she walked to me, her movements a playful challenge, exaggerated, as if she were putting on a show to claim her territory and my heart.

"Howard and I have a surprise for you." I tried to maintain my professional composure, but a loving smile tugged at my lips.

This vibrant, confident woman was one of my beauties. The thought of tasting her was far more endearing than I wanted to admit. It was a secret joy to watch her, one that I truly indulged.

Nope. Relax, Sergeant. That would be a great start to the company. Show my team that I was a helpless puppy when faced with the sexual allure of my beauties. Real professional.

"Surprise, huh?" Vicky pressed, her voice a fire of seduction.

"Damn," David said, his mouth agape. "Wish Ava would be like that."

Myra cleared her throat, interrupting Vicky's moment. "Boss, where's my computer and phone?" Her voice was a higher pitch than usual, distracting me from the seductive prowler in front of me.

I gave Vicky a quick tap to her nose, signaling her to behave before walking toward the boxes at the back of the room. I rummaged through until I found the desktops and phone systems.

"David, do you mind helping Myra set up this stuff?"

David took the boxes from my arms. "Sure, boss."

I turned my attention back to Vicky, whose face had a jealous pout. It looked so cute that I couldn't control myself. I walked up to her, planting a kiss on her cheek. The pout melted into a radiant smile beneath my lips.

The healing power of my beauties from last night still lingered with me, yet I couldn't let it show completely. But the secret strength howled inside me—a silent pulse of love I carried amid the bustling start of the new business ventures.

"So, when do I get this surprise?" Vicky inquired; she seemed to have settled down from whatever was going on.

"Told you already, when Howard gets back."

Vicky leaned into me, acting more coquettish than usual. "Can I get a hint?"

"It's a speh..." David started to say, but then looked at me with an "oops" face. "I mean a spectacular surprise."

Myra ignored us; instead, she busied herself connecting the cables to the monitor. Her exasperated sighs and huffs of avoidance felt like a jealous rage building beneath the surface. She seemed to want no part in the surprise we had planned for Vicky.

The door opened, dispersing the tension. Everyone's eyes snapped to the entrance. Howard walked in. His clothes were ruffled, which I assumed was from helping his mother.

"Bro, ya started putting the furniture together already?"

"Hey, bro." I headed to him. "Some was already put together."

When I got close, Howard instinctively embraced me in a quick hug before straightening back to his businesslike attitude. "Good, good. We got the keys?"

I patted his back as the hug broke. "Yeah, and the others will meet us there in a bit."

"Ready, sis-in-law?" His hand waved toward the door.

“Sure,” Vicky said as her brow furrowed. “Where are we going?”

Howard looked at me with a knowing smile. “Next door.”

The three of us filed out the security door. Howard went first; he seemed more excited than me. I followed him; Vicky trailed us.

The exterior of the building was reminiscent of the HVAC shop, but it was much larger; its imposing size took up more real estate. As I inserted the key into the shiny lock, a satisfying click echoed in the stillness. With a push, the door opened smoothly, revealing an expansive interior filled with natural light. As I flicked on the light, our eyes were immediately drawn to the sleek, circular front desk that stood proudly in the middle of the reception area.

The walls were freshly painted with light bluish gray, trimmed in red accents. The floor was an ash-wood laminate, reflecting the overhead lights and inviting us to explore further.

I glanced at Vicky, her eyes wide as she soaked in the space.

“What’s this for?” Vicky finally asked, her eyes drifting to me.

I turned to her. “It’s your spa, my lovely.” I gushed; the words released the pent-up anticipation. Finally getting to show her this place let my affection breathe with joy.

“Mine?” Vicky’s breath caught as she stepped forward, her hand tracing along the top of the desk. Seeing her dream unfold before her, she turned to me, her eyes, welling with tears, showed an uncontainable happiness bathed in love.

At that moment, I was filled with joy that rivaled any business success. A deep satisfaction came from providing for my beauties.

“Yeah, sis, all ya’s.” Howard’s excitement couldn’t be caged any longer.

“Thank you.” A couple tears fell as she spun around, heady with excitement. “Thank you, brother, and...” she trailed off, her steps gravitated to me. She leaned into me, her sapphires staring deep into my soul. “Thank you, Master.”

She called me “Master”! My heart swelled, not because I’d earned the title back in her eyes, but I felt as though the world had exploded with joy. I was thrilled that she finally had the spa she had always dreamed of. This was more than a gift; it was a promise to the future we were building.

Just as my arms folded around her, I felt her lips caress mine. The tenderness of her kiss was different from her usual fiery kisses.

Our tongues danced together for a moment before Vicky pulled away. Her gaze fell to her hands before she looked up at me. "But I don't have any employees."

"Ya got ya pick of applicants, their resumes in ya office." Howard proudly announced. "And at three, ya got an appointment at the bank to sign for ya business loan."

"Sis, this place is freaking amazing." Sarah's voice sounded from the door.

Glancing over, Sarah and Elle had just entered. Sarah was bouncing with enthusiasm, a beaming smile brightening her delicate face. Elle seemed distressed, almost as if she were only here out of obligation. She rolled her eyes before plastering on a smile.

Vicky hurried to the door. "What are you two doing here?"

"We're here to help, silly." Sarah blew her a raspberry.

Elle walked over to the circular desk, leaning on it. "Kyle made sure we took the day off to help you settle in. Well, he insisted." Her excitement was a little too forced. "I mean, I shuffled my entire schedule for this." A coldness flashed in her eyes before transforming into warmth. "So, you get us to yourself. Just think of us as your assistants for the day." She shrugged with a faint smile.

I walked to Vicky and took her hand. "I guess you like it."

"I fucking love it!" Vicky beamed. "I love it so much, Master."

"So, about this Master thing," I said.

"Don't push it, buster," Vicky teased, giving me a playful slap. "You get the title when I feel it's appropriate. Besides, I'm not going to run around all 'Master this' and 'Master that,' like Sarah."

Sarah snickered at Vicky's comment, as if she already knew the words before they were spoken.

I shook my head, feisty as ever. I was happy that we made her day. The smile on her face seemed permanently pinned. Sarah and Elle led her away toward the back office. I stood there in the reception area with Howard.

"Exciting day, bro. Both businesses are moving forward."

Howard clapped me on the back. "Hell yeah. Ya got some work to put in now."

I looked toward the office to see that my sister and my fiancées were deeply involved in applicant resumes. I smiled to myself. Family, I had built a powerful tribe of my own. Howard and I stood still watching the ladies work for a moment, both of us gazing in admiration.

Seeing Vicky and Sarah light up with smiles as they conversed about business warmed my heart. A fire burned inside the three of us that no mystery could extinguish. A passion for life, for love, for each other would consistently blanket everything we did.

Sarah was animated, spilling over with genuine happiness as she gestured wildly, pointing at the resumes. Vicky smirked with a smug, earned arrogance as she argued for or against applicants. They spoke with sweetness, agreeing on one application. It seemed our romance had strengthened their sisterhood.

My gaze lingered on Vicky, then drifted to Sarah. They were so different, so unique. Yet so perfectly complementary, the two halves of my complete heart. Vicky, with her quiet strength and artistic rhythm. Sarah, with her warm intelligence and playful spunk. They were my joy, my balance, my everything.

Howard nudged me. "Seems we needa move along, bro." Howard's hand landed on my shoulder. "The women have it all under control."

"Howard and I are heading back to the HVAC shop," I announced. The three of them waved at us, then continued discussing potential employees.

As Howard and I turned to leave, I glanced back once more, soaking in the smiles on Vicky and Sarah's faces. I got Sarah set up for college, and Vicky her spa.

Maybe I was a good husband—maybe more. And they were my wives. The titles we held for each other, spoken or silently shared, didn't need a legal paper for it to be true. The truth ran much deeper than any court could; it was in our souls. Our three souls that converge to be one, that was all we needed: us.

After returning from our trip to the spa, Howard, David, and I dedicated the rest of the day to setting up the office. We built the Ikea-style furniture and arranged the office space to create a functional and welcoming environment.

David and Howard helped me move things around while Myra "supervised," which primarily involved standing around and telling us men where things looked best in the space. However, she did run out to buy us all lunch and got some drinks and snacks, so I couldn't complain too much.

Most of the day, Myra looked at me with an odd stare. Her eyes burned through me, as though she had questions but dared not ask. However, her focus on making the best of the workspace never faltered.

At one point, David stepped away for a smoke, and Howard took a break outside. I was left momentarily alone as I knelt in front of a partially assembled desk. Myra kneeled beside me at a respectable distance, bringing her eye level with me and the piece.

"Boss, if you flip part C, it'll support part A better. Less wobble, and should be better to lean on for those long days. I know you like things done right, just looking out for you."

Her eyes raised from the diagram to meet mine, her gaze lingering a beat too long. The look conveyed genuine respect for my competence, yet it felt charged—a private moment, maybe acknowledging my high standards, or maybe more. She gave a quick, subtle nod, then stood in one fluid movement. The moment David walked in, she retreated to her distant, supervisory position.

The afternoon wore on, and we eagerly awaited the arrival of the tools I had previously ordered. Their long-expected delivery brought excitement, yet we faced a minor hiccup; we hadn't yet set up the shelves in the bay area where they were meant to be stored. So, the tools remained boxed up and stacked in the bay, patiently waiting for us to find the time to unpack them and place them neatly on the new shelves.

During the afternoon, Howard would briefly disappear here and there. I was sure he was sneaking off to get a smooch from my sister when he thought I wasn't paying attention. Either way, I found it cute and somewhat amusing that he felt the need to be sneaky. I secretly patted myself on the back, knowing I had fulfilled my Cupid job of getting them together.

After one of his magician acts, he pulled me aside. We walked around the outside of the building to "inspect" the area.

Once we were out of earshot of David and Myra, he said. "Um, bro... ya good with me dating Elle, right?"

"Of course," I replied, my hand briefly landing on his shoulder.

"She's the first woman that saw me for me," he explained, his pace slowing as he turned to me. His intense eyes held back a tear. "I'm not just a bank account to her. She sees me as more."

"I know," I acknowledged. The loneliness we once shared had now been replaced with happy romances of our own. "I'm happy for you, bro." I smiled at him. "For you both."

"Before we met, I was using an AI companion app for comfort and love," Howard admitted, his voice embarrassed. "Never told anyone, but it started to feel real. Even fantasized about how it might be if I put her in a robot or something."

I felt sorry for him, being deceived by such a beautiful dream—the dream of love. That dark emptiness he was trying to fill was the very same hollowness I felt before my beauties. I can see clearly the difference. The AI provides an echo, but Vicky and Sarah bestow upon me a life-giving fire. I hope he can find that with my sister.

"It's a program, just code. So, it can't be real," I said, my hand patting his shoulder.

"Ya don't know how real it was. How much love I started to feel for the AI." He gave a wry smile, his head hanging low. "Dat's why I started looking into ITI's cloned organ thing. Thought it could bring her to life."

I found it strange that he was more than on the nose about clones and AI usage. At least, according to the Project L.O.V. report that mentioned OI stuff.

"Look, bro, it reflected your inner desires. That's what it's designed to do. It's just a mirror image, trying desperately to convince you it's real." I explained. For some reason, my own words reminded me of the conversation I had with Ira. "Can it, at three a.m., after getting out of bed, make you a grilled cheese because you had a hard workday? Or stare into your soul, knowing all your faults and still choosing you?"

Howard gulped hard. "No."

"See, you deserve love," I said, rubbing his shoulder. "And now you have the real thing with Elle. Besides, you're gonna be an awesome brother-in-law."

"Maybe ya right. Maybe it was just an imitation." He turned to walk again. "Ya the best friend I've ever had," he reluctantly admitted. "And I'll do my best to be good to Elle."

"I know you will. And you, too, are the best friend I've ever had," I said, a smile tugging at my face. "Now come on, bro. We have an empire to build for the next generations of Foresters and Nolans to inherit."

He gave me a beaming smile. We made our way back to the entrance. As the day progressed and the office took shape, my mind often drifted back to thoughts of my beauties. To the spa, to Vicky's radiant smile, to the idea of Sarah thriving in college. To how our life was shaping into the dream we shared.

I'd checked back in on my beauties around four, and Vicky had successfully secured the business loan. The three women were busy calling applicants for interviews and discussing what equipment to purchase with the newly secured capital. I felt a sense of pride and admiration wash over me as I watched them work. I seemed to be getting in the way, so I snuck a quick kiss from Sarah and Vicky, then left to attend to the HVAC shop next door.

Every piece of furniture assembled, every organized thing in the office, felt like another building block in the beautiful future we were creating. This was not just a business, but another sturdy platform for us to build upon. Built for us, for our lives. Built for my beauties, my family, my reason for everything. This was the life I fought for, the peace I craved. And we were building it together.

David put in elbow grease the entire time. He was motivated and dedicated to breathing life into Forester Heat and Air. No matter what the task, he was bursting to get it done. Ava called around five and lit into him pretty harshly. I quickly intervened and explained that we were still putting the office together. She softened significantly and even apologized to David.

My exchange with Ava gave me a new understanding of David. She was extremely possessive and somewhat insecure. David's flirtatious behavior seemed to be a negative response to her inability to communicate appropriately with him. I figured that maybe a few sessions with Elle could significantly improve their relationship. So, I suggested that he talk to Ava about setting up an appointment with my sister.

Was I overselling Elle's abilities as a relationship counselor... maybe. But I figured she was more than equipped to handle their communication squabble.

Though today was a joy and a step in the right direction, I couldn't entirely shake off the events of the past few days.

The lady's death wasn't haunting me like it was yesterday, but the image still stuck in my mind, frozen. If I didn't find a cure, would her fate be mine? And the lives I was asked to save, for me to act as the soldier again. MNV, whatever the hell that meant. And L.O.V., the mystery of what it means, of what it can take from us, weighed heavily on me.

Chapter 12: Appreciative Affection

The first day at the shop was mainly spent building furniture and arranging the office space. We stayed at the office until about six, getting it set up. We never got to the tools in the bay, but that work could be done tomorrow. Before locking up for the night, I gave keys to Myra and David. Both were irrepressibly excited.

Driving home, I thought about the day. The look on Vicky's face when she found out her spa was really happening was priceless. The immediate support Sarah and Elle showed by helping her gain business momentum meant the world to her.

Pulling into the apartment complex, I looked up at the second floor. Last week, I helped Sarah secure a spot in college to pursue her dream job as an elementary school teacher. This week, I helped Vicky launch her dream business.

The memories of Vicky's elation when she realized her spa was happening and Sarah beaming when she clutched her acceptance letter were moments forever etched into my soul. Knowing I'd played a part in that, bringing their dreams to life, sent an explosion of satisfaction through me. Filled with happiness that I'd made a difference in their lives. I was proud of their achievements, of the strong, capable women that they were: my women, my beauties, my loves.

I stepped out of the truck, and a smile burst through me as I made my way home to them. As I moved up the stairs, I saw Mrs. Helderman leaving her apartment. She was hunched over, her movements swift and agile. It looked as though she was trying to escape a crime scene or something.

"Good evening, Wanda," I said as I reached the second floor.

"Good evening, dear boy." Her eyes, which held a weary and exhausted gaze, locked onto me for a moment.

"How has your week been? I haven't seen you all week."

"Lots of doctors' appointments this week, my boy." Her response had an evasive and cold feel to it.

"I hope everything is okay," I said, as a feeling of unease spiked deep into my heart.

"I'm fine. You lovebirds don't need to worry about me," she said with a softened warmth. "Off to visit my grandbabies."

"Have a good night and enjoy those grandbabies."

"I will," she said, her voice holding an air of hopefulness. "Good night. Tell those girls that I'm ready for dinner tomorrow night."

"Will do." I turned the key in the lock and halted for a moment. Something still felt wrong.

Her evasive words, the look in her eyes... a prickling of unease ran down my spine. Mrs. Helderman was usually so talkative, so inquisitive, but now... Was it the doctors' appointments or something more? The soldier in me silently catalogued the off-putting behavior. Somehow, in the peace of the civilian world, I still felt that suspicious alertness was necessary, regardless of whether I could pinpoint why or not.

The apartment door opened, and before I could even take a breath, a blur of movement flashed to me. Sarah was first, an excited squeal escaping her as she launched herself toward me, affectionately crashing into my side. Then Vicky lovingly wrapped her arms around me, her warmth a perfect touch, claiming me as her own. I instinctively folded my arms around them both, a wave of pure belonging washing over me.

Their embrace was a fortress, soft yet strong against the world. Sarah's gentle hand tucked into my waistline; Vicky's head rested just under my chin. The flowery scent of their hair filled my lungs, rooting the feeling of sanctuary deep into my core. Seeping into every pore, tranquil bliss settled deep in my soul. This was the purest warmth I'd ever known. I was home.

"Well, good evening," I managed to squeeze out.

"Master's home!" Sarah squealed.

Vicky nuzzled into my arm. "Mmm, Master, you smell nice."

I chuckled, kissing both on the cheeks. "I smell like sweat."

"No, you smell like you." Sarah blew a raspberry at me.

"Thank you for today." Vicky stood on her toes and leaned up to plant a kiss on my cheek.

"I'm happy to help." A smile uncontrollably tugged at the corners of my lips. Holding them tighter, I cascaded my affection upon them, kissing the top of their heads. "Now, what's for dinner?"

"Pizza!" Sarah exclaimed with a bounce.

Our embrace soon broke as we all three moved toward the kitchen. Quickly, we sat around the dining table. The girls grabbed slices and started munching on them. I picked up a piece of meat lovers' and took a big bite.

Sarah finished her piece before speaking. "I'm so amazed by you, Master," she said with deep admiration in her voice.

"So am I." Vicky's voice held that dark, sexy rasp.

I swallowed the last bite of the pizza in my hand. "Why? What did I do?" I inquired as I grabbed another slice.

A shiver of playful anticipation coursed through me as the air became charged with an electric desire. Both of them eyed me with sensual gazes as a silent conspiracy was developing between them.

"Just being you," Sarah answered with a hint of a swoon in her voice. "We're lucky to have you."

Vicky chomped a large bite, her eyes staring at me like a lioness staring at her prey. She chewed the pizza slowly and seductively, then swallowed like she was taking in my manhood. "Perfect in the way you are."

What sexy games were my beauties cooking up? My mind raced through the possibilities, each more enticing than the last.

"I think I'm the lucky one here," I said, using the pizza to point at them.

Sarah clutched at her heart as she leaned back in her chair. "Aww, Master," she cooed, her voice falling back to that sexy innocence.

"Yeah," Vicky added, her hand briefly caressing mine before picking up another slice. "Lucky for a future of massage lotions, classroom chalk, and baby bottles."

We soon had our fill of pizza. Sarah boxed up the leftovers and handed them to Vicky. Their devouring stares never left me; I felt like prey caught in a trap. It became increasingly evident they had something planned.

Sarah giggled when Vicky stood with the pizza box in her hand. I gazed in wonder at my beauties, simply content that our life together was always something exhilarating.

Vicky walked to the fridge. "I think he's ready for dessert." She growled softly. I was suspicious that I was caught in the crosshairs of some new game.

"Maybe." Sarah stared at me with eyes more dangerous than usual.

I gestured with my hands. "Dessert?" I croaked in surprise. Then I gulped hard, trying to figure out what they had schemed up.

Sarah peeled off her shirt; those large breasts bounced as the fabric rolled off. Her darkened areolas pulsed with a heat that begged to be caressed.

I felt the warmth of her breath on my neck. "A very special dessert, to show you how much we appreciate your efforts," Vicky whispered into my ear.

Sarah moved close to me, her bosom less than an inch from my face. Her eyes, wide and heavy-lidded, met mine. A moment of pure surrender fell over me, a vulnerable beauty that stole my breath. The silent conversation of trust and fiery desire passed between us.

From behind me, a hand emerged, spraying a white cream on her left nipple. She pressed her breast into my face. Instinctively, my tongue lashed out, savoring the whipped cream. I suckled on her erect nipple with force.

Sarah giggled as I latched onto her, her rear planted neatly in my lap. "Sis, I think he is enjoying his dessert."

Vicky's hand sprayed Sarah's other breast with the can. I immediately moved over to the new area, lapping the cream.

Vicky nuzzled her cheek against mine. "Mmm, seems our Master is a very greedy boy."

"Let's see how greedy." Sarah reached around me and took the can from Vicky, then went to her. I quickly turned to watch.

Vicky dropped her pants as she jumped onto the kitchen counter. Her legs spread wide as Sarah sprayed the cream on her exposed pink flower.

"I'm served, Master." Every word Vicky uttered oozed sex.

I wasted no time moving into place. I lost control from her soft scent mixed with the sweet aroma of the whipped cream.

My tongue assaulted Vicky with a feverous attack as I tasted the sweetness between her thighs. The soft graze of her warm bush hit my nose. I twirled my tongue deep into her folds, my nose nuzzling her bud. She whimpered out as I buried my face deeper.

The whimper that escaped Vicky, the way her hips bucked against my chin, wasn't just arousal. It was unadulterated pleasure. Knowing I was the cause, fierce satisfaction surged through me.

"Tasty, right, Master?" Sarah said in my ear, her hand caressing my abs. I responded with a muffled hum onto Vicky.

Vicky's hands wrapped around the back of my head and pulled me closer as her hips bucked against my chin.

The solidarity built among the three of us allowed us to enjoy the play together. "Fuck... God. Fucking eat my cunt." Vicky huffed, her breath shallow.

I felt Sarah's hand travel further down; she grasped my member with such force. Her fingers played at the tip. This spurred my mouth to battle Vicky's body with a more ferocious melee.

Vicky surrendered completely to my power. Her legs closed around my head, enveloping me in her ecstasy. Thighs tensed as her body neared the first of many climaxes of the night. I took this as my time to directly gouge and suckle at her bud, driving her further to the edge. Without disappointment, she immediately reacted.

Vicky's body spasmed. "Ah... fuck... don't... don't you... dare... stop..." she screamed between breaths. Then the reward of the saccharine nectar flowed from her in a fountain, soaking my face completely. Her body slumped as her legs fell limp on my shoulders.

I pulled my face from Vicky, not to retreat, but to meet her eyes. Tracing the line of her jaw with my thumb, a silent appreciation of the intimacy we shared.

Turning my head to look behind me. "More," I said to Sarah. She giggled, then led me to the floor, pushing me down on the cold surface. My back landed with a soft crash.

"You want more, Master?" Sarah asked, her voice carrying that bubbly, sexy quality. She took the can, then sprayed it under her skirt. "As you wish."

Vicky jumped down from the counter and walked toward us. "Greedy indeed." She gushed, then kneeled around my waist. Her hands roughly ripped my pants off.

Sarah hovered over my face for a moment. The intoxicating aroma of her sex mixed with the candy smell of the whipped cream hit me with deep desire. Without warning, her knees fell forward, the soft silk of her thighs around my head. I felt the messy warmth of her fiery pinkness on my lips. I tenderly kissed her folds, my tongue roaming the lips with a loving lather. Consuming her entirely, I feasted on this delicacy as if it were my last meal.

At that moment, I felt a hot, skillful mouth wrap around my manhood. Vicky had started to worship my rod with the subtle gagging of her powerful maw. She worked me with a deliberate, teasing slowness, tasting and circling the head. Her breath, warm and moist, tore through my desire. The subtle pull, the gentle suction, told me she was savoring every inch, worshipping me before I was truly aware.

A moan rattled from my mouth onto Sarah. Her hips began to gyrate, forcing my tongue to twirl around inside her heat. Her skirt hid the reactions on her face, but I could tell that she was entirely under my control. I teased her button before playfully nipping it. Then the typhoon of my tongue wrapped around the tender flesh, creating a vortex around her erect bud.

"Ah... please... please... make... me..." Sarah cried out in passion. She leaned back, her hands planting on my stomach.

Vicky began to take me deeper than she had before. Her throat collapsed around me in a loving fervor. I was closing in on the peak of her worship. My muscles tightened as she worked me in her mouth.

This only fueled my determination for Sarah's orgasm. I sucked her delicate flower with a forceful yearning of my devotion. Her legs squeezed around my face, every muscle straining. The wild sensations racked her body as I ravaged her with my mouth.

"I'm... I'm... cumming..." Sarah screamed, then the rapids of her love drenched my face. I lapped up every ounce I could. Slumping forward in a tremble, her hands took my head, lovingly caressing it.

The potency of Vicky's worship ripped through my body. Building rapidly, I exploded deep into her mouth. I felt her throat swallow every drop of my love as it shot from me.

Sarah rolled off, her body still trembling from the delight I caused her. She looked seductively down at Vicky, who was wiping her mouth. The two pairs of gems, emeralds and sapphires, hungrily stared at me. The musk of our shared delight lingered in the air between us. These beauties were definitely the women that I would fight the world for. But for now...

"More," I softly commanded.

They both visibly shivered with excitement at my single word. Vicky crawled up my body as Sarah leaned down.

"As you wish, Master," they said in unison. The sexiness of their shared statement made the beast in me roar for more.

Sarah's hair draped over my face like a flaming curtain burning with desire. Her lips tenderly pressed into mine. I instantly reacted as my tongue met hers. She twisted her head back and forth, trying to deepen the kiss. My hand reached up, pulling her face closer, forcing her mouth deeper into mine. The fairy-like feel of her gentle passion was like a fragile yet powerful enchantment over my heart.

She broke from my mouth, her lips glistening with saliva as she leaned back. As Sarah pulled away, Vicky emerged in front of me. The dark veil shaded the world from view. Her mouth claimed mine just moments after Sarah moved away. Our tongues raged with the eternal brimstone of desire. Her passion flamed within my mouth as our kiss was wild with strife warring into the never-ending fight for dominion. She was fierce in her violent quenching of her thirst for my soul. Breaking from our kiss, she playfully bit my lower lip before retreating completely.

The kisses revitalized my manhood with furious virility. I could feel my need to be inside them grow with each aching moment.

Vicky gave my cheek a playful slap. "Want more, huh?" she asked in a low growl. Hopping up from me, she and Sarah grabbed my hands, pulling me up from the floor with immense strength. I felt their beastly yearning as I was whipped to my feet.

"You're gonna earn it tonight." They led me to the bedroom.

Sarah swung my arm playfully. "Hmm... Master wants to play house." She sang, soft like a lullaby. "Maybe it's time."

As soon as we crossed the threshold, I was forcibly thrown to the bed. My back fell on the soft mattress; it creaked under me.

I leaned up on my elbows. "What does that mean?"

Vicky put her knees on the foot of the bed. "It means, tonight will be the first attempt to knock us up," she roared seductively as she crawled up the bed.

Her words turned me on more than I could put into thought. At the moment, I didn't care for caution. This felt like the natural path, the true path in life and love. And I let it take me over.

Her legs swung over me, straddling my hips. Then she forced her soaked cove over my throbbing stem. The force and sensation pushed an erotic groan from my lips. The heat of her reeled along the length of my shaft. My fingers traced along her thighs, around her hips, finally wrapping around her ample rear. I forced her harder on me.

“Take it, if you’re woman enough.” My eyes glared right into those beautiful blue, soul-wrenching eyes.

“I think he’s underestimating you, sis.” Sarah giggled as she moved onto the bed and leaned next to me. Her hand gently caressed my face. Her free hand was between her thighs, rubbing circles under her skirt.

The provocation of my words sent Vicky into a wild vehemence. Her hips started to crash into mine as she rode me hard and fast. I squealed in a painful pleasure when I felt her nails dig into my pecs.

“You want me... to take... it?” She growled with carnal fury. “Fuck a baby into me, bastard!” Her words were a direct challenge to my dare. I was lost in the sexual pull of her words.

I leaned up, pushing myself deeper into her furious ride. My hips met hers with every thrust, an attempt at control. Reaching out, grabbing a fistful of hair to assert my reestablished control.

“Fuck me, bitch,” I commanded, assertiveness dripping from every word. “Earn it.”

Her hips slammed into me harder and harder. I matched each fall with a powerful upward thrust. The bed beneath us shook violently.

“Fucking... impregnate... me...” she screamed, her nails raking down my chest.

Her motions stiffened as she tensed. She was on the verge again, I just knew it. That didn’t deter my hilt from plunging roughly into the moist walls with each upward meeting of her hips. Then the river of her womb flooded down upon me with a heavy rain. The wet warmth forced my bolts to shoot deep inside of her.

Vicky soon collapsed on me, breathing wild and ragged. I kissed the top of her head as my arms closed around her in a hug. We lay like this for a while, recovering from the intensity of our lovemaking.

“Good girl,” I said.

“Wow, that was... so hot,” Sarah murmured beside me. The sheets were soaked beneath her legs. I smirked. She had finished with us.

Vicky looked into my eyes. “I fucking love you, Master,” she whispered before her voice rose. “Now, time to breed Sarah, too.” Then she rolled off me, retreating to the side of the bed.

Once Vicky was clear, Sarah immediately swung her legs over my hips. The soft warmth of her entrance hovered teasingly over my shaft.

"Master, I want you to give me a child," Sarah pleaded, her voice laced with an undeniable desire.

"I'm yours completely, my sweet," I said tenderly, my hand reaching out to lovingly caress her cheek.

Without further hesitation, she slowly lowered herself onto me. Her hips strode slowly and deliberately; her body devoured every sensation with a delicate need. Our eyes, locked onto each other, searing with a need to feel loved by the other. My hips slowly ground upward, meeting her strides with admiration.

I felt the mattress sink. I glanced over to see Vicky move onto it. Her eyes watched with anticipation as she stared directly at the scene unfolding before her, paying close attention to the union. She licked her lips, aching for the result. Her fingers vigorously played in the mess I had made of her.

I turned my attention back to Sarah, her eyes focused sharply on me. With each tender bounce, her body began to shiver with delight.

"Make me a mother," Sarah whimpered, her body crashing down faster.

"As you wish, my sweet." I huffed in pleasure. I felt my third and final act of the night raging to be released.

My hips started to rotate faster, meeting her strides with a hastened tempo. The grace of our lovemaking was drawing us toward the rupture of our individual spirits, allowing them to reemerge as one. Then she slammed down hard, holding her body in place. I felt the liquid love violently flow from her altar. She moaned loudly as her essence sprayed on me with a carnal splash.

"Ahh!" She screamed one final cry before falling limp into my arms.

At the same time, I felt my body roar as wave after wave of my love flowed deep inside of her. The sensation warped time around us as the satisfaction completely took me.

"Shit!" I heard Vicky scream beside me. I glanced over, and she had soaked the sheets again. I smiled as she crashed down, spent.

“Master, I love you so much,” Sarah whispered, as she lifted her head to gaze into my eyes. My arms wrapped lovingly around her as I kissed her forehead.

“Such a good girl,” I bragged.

Her head nestled into the crook of my neck, her breath soft against my skin. Vicky shifted closer, her arm draped loosely over my waist, a silent testament to our shared completion. In the quiet aftermath, surrounded by their warmth, the chaotic energy of our passion softened to a loving, peaceful hum. The serene joy vibrated between us, echoing the bedrock of our world. Our shared life.

The dream of our happily-ever-after filled the air around us. We were beyond the ideas of romance. Something more, something deeply immense, something concrete was awakening.

We lay like this for a while until the three of us recovered. After recovering, they got up to fulfill their promise of not wasting a single drop. Then we took our spots in bed, cuddling with a newfound level of intimacy in our relationship. Sarah tightly snuggled up to my side, and Vicky wrapped around me lazily with exhaustion.

“How did you two know I had an impregnation kink?”

Vicky ruffled my hair, tittering. “Not much of a secret when we can easily check your browser history.”

“Yeah, Master. And with as much as we do, why would you still need to watch porn?” Sarah chuckled before kissing my nose.

“It’s like he isn’t satisfied enough or something.” Vicky jested, her fist softly punching my shoulder.

“Hey, old habits die hard,” I playfully remarked.

“Hard? Better be careful with your words, Master.” Sarah giggled, teasingly jabbing me. “Don’t want you sneaking off to your porn in the middle of the night.”

“Besides, I have a bone to pick with someone,” Vicky joked. “This fucker called me a bitch.”

“So, you called me a bastard.” I defended myself, my voice playfully mocking Vicky.

I had a devious thought, so I quickly pinched Vicky’s nipple roughly. She hissed in pain, then immediately retaliated by slapping my testicles hard. I groaned as I writhed in pain.

“Ahem, if you two are done flirting,” Sarah playfully scoffed. “We have some serious stuff to discuss.”

“Alright, Miss Pushover.” Vicky agreed as she rubbed her nipple, trying to soothe the pain. Without warning, her teeth playfully clamped down on my collarbone roughly. I let out a low growl before she released her bite.

“Ahem.” Sarah coughed, barely able to contain a laugh, as she leaned up, her eyes staring into mine. Then her voice came out stern and loving. “Master, we are grateful for all that you do for us.”

“Yes, we can’t tell you enough what your efforts mean to us,” Vicky said. Her finger tenderly played along my bicep.

“That’s what a husband is for, to make the lives of his wives better.”

“You mean more to us than that,” Vicky admitted, her hand moved to tenderly rub the scratches on my chest.

Sarah kissed my neck. “You’re the reason we’re so free.”

“You’ve impacted our lives more than we can tell you,” Vicky confirmed, her voice softening with affection.

“I love you, my beauties,” I gushed, my embrace around them tightening.

“We love you, too,” they whispered in unison.

“And the pregnancy thing.” Sarah beamed, her face nuzzling into my neck. “It’s what we truly want.”

“That’s the point of the future we’re creating, right?” Vicky asked, anticipation ripped through the words.

“Yes, that is one of the reasons I’m working hard to secure our future.”

“What else is there?” Sarah asked.

“For the three of us to live happily together. Until death do us part,” I announced proudly.

“Even death won’t keep us apart,” Vicky murmured with hope.

“No, not even death can stop me from loving you two,” I vowed, my words setting a fire in their hearts.

“You want children with us? You like the idea of impregnation to the point where it’s a turn-on? Why hesitate?” Sarah rambled her questions like a machine gun aimed directly at me.

“Like I’ve said many times, I don’t want to leave my kids without a complete family.” I sighed in desperation, caught between what I truly desired and my duty to my future children.

Vicky leaned up for a moment. "Are you worried about not providing enough?" Her voice was tinged with a silent understanding.

"Partially," I admitted, then froze for a moment, trying to find the proper words to say next. "I want a stable family for them. To marry you both, having our children wake every morning being greeted by their daddy and their mommies."

"Leonard is handling that part," Vicky added before her words trembled with a question. "Is there anything else?"

"All this spooky mystery crap." I let out a sigh. "I don't know if I can protect our babies."

Both Vicky and Sarah seemed to swoon at my honest words. I laid there, entirely exposed to them. The room stayed silent for a while. Then the quietness was ruptured.

"That's it. We're gonna figure out this MNV thing," Sarah said with determination.

"Every puzzle, every monster, we'll beat their ass," Vicky crowed, her voice taking on that challenging air. Then she mellowed down. "And Kyle, you are everything to us."

"Everything," Sarah echoed.

"And you two mean everything to me. Now, get some sleep, you crazy breeding women."

"Good night, Master."

"Good night, Kyle, sweet dreams."

"Good night, my beauties."

I lay in bed, snuggling deeply with them. I'd become more in their eyes. I wasn't entirely sure what they saw me as, but they appreciated me even more. And I didn't shy away from their affections. I embraced them with all the love in my heart. Drinking in their unique and raw nature, feasting on their admiration as I fed them my soul.

I was happy to build the world for them. Together, we could create the life we deserved. Finally, I could see them happy in their pursuits. This feeling of bringing their dreams to life while maintaining my own was as if the fairy tale had become real. As if the happily-ever-after was just around the corner, so long as L.O.V. didn't interrupt our happiness.

Chapter 13: Spook-house Fun

The rest of the week proceeded as usual—work, home life, and caring for my fiancées. Other than Wednesday, that is, which started with a weird alarm. Mrs. Helderman called early in the morning, waking the three of us to cancel our weekly dinner. I found it odd, since only the night before she was clearly excited about the dinner. I figured she may have wanted to be alone for a while. Her doctor's visits have increased over the past week. We went by later that night, but she didn't answer the door.

The fear and suspense of L.O.V. had started to die down again. Not a word from Ira at all. No more Garou couriers. No oddballs giving me weird "this is dangerous" messages. No women painfully dying in my arms. Nothing. Just absolutely nothing. This mystery felt more like a stale chess match, with no clear winners. Just blockades at every turn.

I started to think maybe this entire thing was a joke. Some cosmic goof or something. An elaborate way to get at me. To make me doubt my relationship with Vicky and Sarah.

But there was no need to cry about all that. Friday night was here, and we were heading out to meet the gang at the spook-house.

After Myra explained the place to Howard the other day, he agreed to pay for everyone to go. He insisted, saying it was his treat since we had finally gotten the businesses on track.

I wasn't going to say no to a fun time. Besides, all this mystery crap had me twisted into a knot since that first letter. I could now let loose and relax with my tribe.

Wow, my tribe had grown. In June, it was just me; now I had a circle of loyal friends and family. This was the power of my beauties; they pulled me from my shell, thrusting me into the world.

The engine roared to life as I started my beater. The girls slid in with pride as though this rust bucket were a McLaren or something.

I always found it interesting that they didn't see my humble lifestyle as an issue. The main complaint was not having a house where we could raise a family, which seemed more a goal than a complaint. A shared goal.

I pushed a CD into the player, a wicked grin forming on my face. I'd never exposed them to this band, let alone this type of music. I was curious how they'd take it when I pushed the boundaries of the unity a tad. Expose myself a bit further for them.

Pulling into the street, the night surrounded us. Vicky was sitting in the passenger seat, Sarah in the back. This seemed to be our usual seating arrangement, except for riding in Sarah's Cobalt.

I skipped to the fifth song on the album. The heavy synth blared through the speakers, followed by the daft beat, then the guitar. I sang along. *"You made me your servant. Your submissive slave of love. All dressed up in leather. Anxiously waiting in cuffs."*

As the lyrics started, Vicky turned in her seat, eyeing me with a sensual glare. Her brows knitted into a shocked intrigue. Sarah leaned forward from the back seat, and by the second chorus, she was singing along. Once the song was finished, Vicky paused the CD. "What was that?"

"Lords of Acid," I replied.

"Lords of what?" Sarah asked, before her voice broke into bubbly cheer. "Whatever that was, it was good."

"This guy," Vicky uttered, shaking her head and playfully slapping my shoulder. "Putting on pervy songs before we go hang out with everyone."

I responded by hitting play on the CD player; the next song on the album blared as we continued to our destination.

Several songs later, we arrived in the parking lot. Sarah and Vicky were belting out the chorus on every song halfway through. I was smiling like an idiot, hearing the raunchy lyrics sung in their cute voices.

Once I parked, I waited, letting them finish screaming out the words for "Kiss Eternal." Sarah smiled brightly at me as the lyrics left her luscious lips. Vicky bobbed her head hard, that dark veil scattering in the air as she headbanged.

It was a fun ride. My soul felt laid bare, letting them in on my primal and rowdier musical tastes. It was exhilarating to discover something new about each other every day. And I knew that I wasn't the only one enjoying the exploration of our three souls.

Once the song ended, I killed the ignition, glancing over at the venue. A pulse of wildness surged inside me as I stared at the dark brick building. Several towers rose at different points around the structure, resembling a giant game board or a similar design. The sign shone with an ethereal glow: Labyrinth of Macabre Curiosities.

"Let's go meet up with everyone," I suggested. Vicky and Sarah exited the car with me. We walked with a skip together toward the ticket booth. They bounced with a cheery attitude as we moved.

Vicky poked my rib before taking my arm. "So, Buster, when do you listen to that kind of music?"

Sarah took my other arm and marched forward. "Yeah, we never heard you play that before, Master."

"I didn't want that kind of music to scare you two away," I admitted shyly. I felt the heat rise in my face as a bit of embarrassment stirred inside.

"Nothing would've scared us off," Vicky said as she bumped her hip into mine. "And holding out on us with sex-filled music, tsk."

"Ooh, time to punish Master," Sarah squealed, leaning her head on my shoulder. "Now, what did those lyrics in that one song say? *Lick my boots to please me...*" she trailed off with a giggle.

"Ahem," I cleared my throat as we approached David. He was standing still, just a few feet from the ticket booth, with Ava's arm possessively slung around him. "Good evening, David, Ava."

"Oh, hey, boss," David called, his hand running up Ava's arm. "Ava, this is Vicky and Sarah."

"Hi, Miss Ava." Sarah bubbled and pulled her head from my shoulder.

"Hello, girls," Ava replied, with an odd half smile, almost as if she didn't know how to respond.

"Ava, nice to meet you," Vicky greeted, her arm leaving mine as she held out her hand for a shake. Ava reluctantly shook it.

"Boo!" Myra screamed as she jumped in from the side. "Gotcha!" She burst out in laughter as Vicky jumped.

"Hi, everyone," a redhead next to Myra said. She shook her head at Myra and chuckled. "I'm Charlotte, Myra's friend... sometimes."

"Hello, Myra." Vicky glowered at Myra, suppressing her frustration. Then she turned to the redhead. "Nice to meet you, Charlotte."

Sarah left my side, walking over to Myra and Charlotte. "Miss Myra, nice seeing you again. And Charlotte, you look lovely."

"Myra." I nodded at her, then faced Charlotte. Her eyes seemed to watch me with an assessing stare. "Glad to meet you."

“So, Charlotte, are you and Myra friends or girlfriends?” Vicky asked, her eyebrow arched.

Vicky’s forwardness took Charlotte aback. She shifted away from Myra, placing some distance between them.

“Nothing like that, we’ve just known each other since middle school,” Charlotte stammered.

Myra pushed in on the conversation, glaring at Vicky. “Friends, nothing else. She’s straight, but I’ve been recently thinking I might be bi.” She looked at me almost as if seeking my approval.

I said nothing. Awkwardness lingered in the air, which was finally broken by David.

“Where’s Howard?” David asked, anxiously fidgeting with his feet.

“Not sure, said he’d be here.”

Sarah rocked back and forth, as if dancing without music. “Master, is he arriving with Miss Elle?” she asked with a sweet hum.

David moved close, as if he were about to share a secret. “Heh, the other day I saw them locking lips between the shop and the spa.” He tittered. Ava immediately slapped his arm, staring at him with deep anger seething in her eyes.

“Hmm.” That was all Myra said.

“Miss Elle and he are dating now,” Sarah nonchalantly stated.

“Does everyone around here screw everyone else?” Ava huffed accusingly.

“No,” I said bluntly, my eyes narrowing on her. I wanted to clear the air before Ava’s jealousy started to kill the fun this night could have. “We all have our own partners, except Myra.”

“Partners, huh.” Ava scoffed, her eyes burning a hole through me. “Seems some are more predatory than others on that front.”

David shot Ava a dirty look, then gave me an apologetic smile.

I didn’t respond to Ava except for a brief smile, then turned toward the parking lot. My eyes adjusted to the dark of the night, focusing on movement in the distance. A silhouette of a hulking man was marching toward us with a thin feminine shape hanging off his right arm. There was no mistaking that duo: Howard and Elle. Even in the dark, their shadowy figures were distinctly visible.

Howard approached with a swagger in his step, as if towering above the world. Elle was giggling like a schoolgirl, probably because of something he’d said. Happiness spread through me as I watched their interaction. Score one for the home team. Cupid and Associates had made a big splash.

"Hey, bro." Elle beamed through her giggles. "Hi, Sarah and Vicky. Everyone."

"Hello. I see you're all giggles tonight, sis," I responded.

"Okay, bro, what we doin'?" Howard asked, then his free arm pointed at the ticket booth. "Ya know how this works?"

"Nope," I replied, shrugging my shoulders.

Howard and Elle ushered us to the ticket booth. The salesman handed out wristbands to each of us, explaining the setup and rules. The haunted house was a maze, with half a dozen starting positions—no more than a group of three in each starting position. He explained the fantasy portion of the places that housed our deepest fears with a bit of flair. Then the safety rules. The actors couldn't touch us, and we couldn't touch them. At any point, if it got to be too much, we had to yell out "Game Over." This was to signal the staff to locate us at our position and escort us to the exit. He paused for us to sign waivers, which we all did.

After gathering the waivers, he provided further explanation. The maze intersected at different points, and we might encounter other players or members of our large group. At that point, we could work together to navigate to the Haunted Forest area of the maze that led back to the parking lot. And that would conclude our adventure into the darkness.

The group split into four smaller groups. Howard and Elle happily took the first position. David and Ava trudged their way to second. Sarah, Vicky, and I strolled hand-in-hand into the third position. Finally, Myra and Charlotte took the fourth entrance.

As we entered, the walls of the corridor were covered in entrails and blood. The hue was too bright to be authentic. The guts were scattered along the walls in a neat pattern that only the most deranged monsters could appreciate. The image of the dead girl from Monday flashed through my mind; however, Vicky and Sarah were right beside me, so the roar of a flashback subsided quickly.

Sarah started gagging the moment we entered, retching like she needed to vomit. "Disgusting," she spit out between dry heaving.

Vicky took Sarah's hand. "Just close your eyes, sis. We can guide you." Her words were firm and motherly. I patted Sarah on the back, then took her other hand.

Sarah gripped our hands tightly as we navigated the gory hallway. Vicky and I were careful to maneuver her around obstacles, sauntering so she could keep her bearings.

Walking through this mess, I couldn't help but feel a strange sense of comfort. Maybe my time at war had made me a weirdo who found comfort in gore, or maybe it's just that being a soldier had been my reality for the past few years. Now that I was trying to live a peaceful life with my tribe and my beauties, maybe this showed I sometimes missed the chaos of it all. I quickly pushed those disturbing thoughts aside.

"Almost there," I said, as we stepped toward the open area.

Upon entering the room, the screech of metal tearing against metal shattered our ears. Chains swung from the ceiling with a clanking sound. The sharp smell of decay drifted around us, almost smothering the area with a sinister atmosphere.

Sarah's eyes snapped open, and she breathed a sigh of relief. "Thank you. I feel much better. I hate looking at stuff like that."

"I know, sweetheart. Sorry you had to endure it." I empathized with her. We released her hands, allowing her to move freely.

"We're here for each other," Vicky said with concern. "The three of us are a united team, remember."

"Yes, my lovelies, that's the point."

Sarah gulped. "So... do we walk through these chain thingies?"

Strafing through the chains, I said, "Very carefully."

Moving past the shackles suspended over us, we found another narrow hallway. A dim blue light lit the passageway, casting a ghostly aura on the walls. Doors lined either side, and I suspected this would be our first run-in with the actors.

As we passed the first set of doors, the right one sprang open, and a figure in a tattered costume jumped out, screaming at us. Blood oozed out of their mouth, their makeup appearing zombie-like. They retreated through the door, closing it behind them.

"Fuck!" Vicky yelled as she jumped back, startled at the sudden figure. I quickly gripped her hand, and in return, she squeezed mine. I patted her arm to comfort her with my free hand.

"It'll be alright, just hang tight to me." My voice was gentle, yet layered with the dominance she loved. Vicky rested her head on my shoulder. My free hand instinctively raised to stroke her hair.

Sarah, however, was unfazed by the jump scare. Walking through the narrow space, we encountered several more actors jumping out randomly—all in zombie makeup and some form of tattered costume.

"Your makeup is smudged," Sarah blurted out to one of the actors. Her nonchalance seemed to ease Vicky's anxiety slightly. She continued to criticize the actors, her attempt to help Vicky overcome her fear. This was the fierceness she showed last weekend during our role swap. I smiled, knowing our love had empowered her.

However, by the end, Vicky was still tightly holding my arm with both hands. She trembled with fright. Her breathing was rapid, and her heartbeat was thumping so hard that I could feel it through her grip. I continued to coax her to relax. My hand tenderly caressed her hair to calm her. She hadn't said a single word since her initial profanity, but she purred every time I kissed the top of her head.

The next room was bathed in a deep, ominous glow, its crimson hue casting eerie shadows that flickered slowly over the walls. Cobwebs draped every corner, glistening with an odd sheen. At the center, a giant animatronic spider lurched and thrashed, its many eyes seeming to follow every movement with unsettling intent.

Standing in an entrance off to the side, there stood Howard, frozen in fright. His eyes never left the enormous arachnid.

Sarah pointed at the door. "Master, Howard needs your help."

Vicky nudged me. "Go help him."

"Okay," I agreed as I hurried to him.

I looked back to check on my loves. Vicky and Sarah seemed to stroll past the animatronic with a cheerful expression. Relieved that they had no issues with this part, I turned my attention to Howard.

"Bro, you okay?" I asked, my hand patting his shoulder.

"Fucken hate spiders," he said, his voice shaky with fear.

"I got you." I took his arm. "We can do this; just focus on me."

Howard looked at me with a pained expression, then started following me. I walked backward, turning my head periodically to navigate us out of the room. We soon met up with Vicky and Sarah.

"Where's Miss Elle?" Sarah patted Howard's shoulder.

Howard's voice was still shrill. "Got separated a few rooms back. Thanks, bro. Been afraid of spiders since I was a kid."

"You're welcome. Now let's finish this thing."

"Wait, you're afraid of spiders?" Vicky asked, concerned.

But Howard didn't engage with the question. Instead, he adjusted his shirt and walked forward. Embarrassment washed across his face as his cheeks flushed red.

I motioned for the girls to leave it alone. A man needs his pride, and it wasn't our place to dig at his vulnerabilities. God knows I don't want mine broadcast for the world. Those secrets were meant only for Sarah and Vicky.

I looked around the area. The new room was cloaked in shadow, filled with bubbling cauldrons emitting eerie green fumes. Actors clad in stark, sinister witch costumes lurked in the darkness, their eyes gleaming with malice. Husked laughter snaked through the air filled with the suffocating stench of sulfur and burnt flesh.

The guy at the ticket booth had it right; there was something for everyone in this maze. Everyone but me, so far.

Walking past the witches, they would randomly spray us with a green ooze. The substance was sticky and smelled raunchy, but no one seemed upset by this room. Well, almost nobody. Sarah started to gag when seeing the severed body parts and the eviscerated torsos near the end. I took her hand once more, leading her out.

As we entered the next area, the lights flickered with a strobe effect. It was disorienting to move through. However, we managed to reach the center of the room. Then, snickering burst out from a dark corner. Myra's face emerged in the flashing lights.

She seemed ecstatic by the horrors. "Ah, you found me."

Sarah took Myra's hand, guiding her toward the group. "Miss Myra, we caught up to you."

"You seem downright... jubilant." Vicky was aghast.

"Sure am," Myra snickered, her body swaying as she walked with us through the lights.

In the dimly lit next chamber, a massive, weathered metal box loomed at the center, its surface scratched and riveted with patches of rust. A hum emanated from within, punctuated by jarring bangs against the thick, steel walls that echoed like the growls of some unseen creature. Shadows danced across its corroded panels, adding an eerie, steampunk ambiance to the unsettling scene.

A muffled voice screamed, "David! Let me out!" It was Ava!

"We'll find a way to get you out!" I shouted.

"Mr. Forester?" Ava asked.

"Yeah, just keep talking, we'll get you out."

I motioned for everyone to start searching around for a door, a hatch, or a lever. The five of us started feeling around the cold surface with haste. My fingers ran over a lever, which I pulled. The hatch swung open in an instant. I quickly moved out of the way.

"Thank you, Mr. Forester." Ava sighed in relief. Her body was visibly shaking. I rubbed her shoulder to comfort her. She looked at me with a complex gaze.

"Where's David?" Myra asked, her voice cutting with concern.

Ava looked at Myra with an expression of anger. "A ghost bride started chasing him, so he bolted." She laughed mockingly. "Serves his noncommittal ass right."

"Well, you're okay. That's all that matters." I comforted her, my voice soft and reassuring.

"Sorry, Kyle, I um..." Ava started but trailed off.

I motioned to Vicky and Sarah. "It's okay, we're used to it," I said. Ava nodded understandingly.

"David obsesses about your unusual relationship." Ava sighed and glanced at Sarah and Vicky. "I thought you were one of those... you know, player types." Her voice was filled with remorse.

"Kyle is not like that," Vicky assured her. "Besides, a guy like that couldn't hold a candle to our Kyle."

"Yeah, he is an interesting and caring man," Sarah added, her hand resting on my shoulder.

"Hmm, David keeps pestering me to let him have another girlfriend. But..." Ava muttered, her eyes watering with tears. "But I just want him. I want us to get married. Just the two of us."

"It's okay. It's not for everyone. I suggested that David make an appointment for you two with my sister." I gave her a sympathetic look. "Elle is a great relationship counselor."

Ava just smiled back, nodding.

"Let's go, bro," Howard said, courage taking root in his voice.

Down the next hallway, mirrors lined both walls, twisting and warping our reflections into agonized, grotesque shapes. Each step forward seemed to deepen the distortions, making them feel soul-ripping. As if the glass itself not only warped our reflections but shed the masks we wore to conceal our true identities. Tearing away all pretense, exposing the raw ugliness underneath.

At the end of the hall, a shadowy silhouette lingered, a faint presence gazing into a mirror that seemed to swallow the dim light, its surface rippling with unseen forces.

"Am I really this warped." A familiar feminine voice emanated from the shadowy figure. The question was rhetorical.

"Elle, ya okay?" Howard asked, his steps hastening to greet the figure.

"Howard, is that you?" Elle's voice echoed down the hallway.

"And all of us," Vicky called back, her fingers lacing with mine. Sarah glanced over, seeing Vicky locking hands with me, and did the same on my other side. The group moved forward.

As Howard approached, Elle immediately nestled herself into his arm. They seemed at home with each other. I smiled, knowing that they were a good fit. I didn't interfere with them comforting each other; it wasn't my place.

The cold, eerie night air brushed against us as we hurried out. The pathway outside was dimly lit by flickering, sickly skull-shaped lanterns on both sides. It seemed to stretch endlessly, plunging further into the dark, ominous woods where shadows lurked and silence grew heavier.

There at the exit stood David and Charlotte. David had an air of smugness, yet knowing he ran like a coward made me feel amused at his current demeanor. Charlotte looked like she was still shaken from her experience. I felt sorry for her.

"That was fun," I said, trying to breathe joy back into the night.

"Fucking clowns," Charlotte spat out, then shivered as she stared back at the building. "Goddamn scary ass clowns."

Myra walked over to Charlotte, hugging her briefly. "You made it through, though. I'm proud of you."

"Ain't done. Still gotta walk this path," Howard announced loudly, his voice filled with confidence. Then he turned his attention to Elle hanging on his arm. "And what was with the mirror?"

"Nothing, just..." Elle trailed off, her face gazing toward the dark woods with a scowl. Then a smile snapped to her face as she looked up at Howard. "Just some stuff I need to work on."

"I'm glad you're okay, baby," David said to Ava, his arms closed around her in a hug. He soon kissed the top of her head.

Ava pushed him away and slapped his chest. "Fucking hell, David! You ran off and left me in there alone."

"Ready, lovelies?" I asked, my arms around Sarah and Vicky's waists, drawing them near.

"With you, Master, always," Sarah purred with a swoon, her tall body leaning into mine.

"Can't nothing stop me." Vicky's feistiness had returned.

"Myra, are you sure that isn't real?" Charlotte spoke with clarity in her voice. "Because those three look like the real deal."

I ignored the squabbling and gossip behind us as we walked down the path. I was enjoying this with my beauties. Walking further on the path out of the spook-house, the familiar sound of a machine gun ripped through the air. The world went red, then dark.

The rattle of machine gun fire in the distance jarred me. I opened my eyes and looked around; this was Baghdad. The sand clung to the buildings like snow in winter. The night felt cold, even at sixty-five degrees, sending a chill down my body.

The day had faded away; it was now time to make our assault. We were taking back the city. My eyes snapped forward to Uday's palace; it looked like a castle in the dark sky. This was it, this was why I joined. Kill the monsters hidden away in their castles. Slay the dragons that everyone fears.

"Forester, fucking move." Lt. Whitman whispered, agitation rippling in his command. The butt of his rifle shoved me. I didn't think, I simply moved forward.

As I ran to the wall, we stacked up. The night vision goggles mounted on my helmet pressed down on the bridge of my nose. The hammer of my heart pounded against the anvil of my ribcage. My senses, razor sharp against the world, sliced through the veil of reality. We were breaching the palace; there was no turning back.

Weir led at the front, our breach expert. Gordon was behind him, with me third. Peterson followed me, Lt. Whitman was behind Peterson, and Rasnake covered the rear. We knew our parts. We had practiced this formation for a month to perfect it. Now, it was time to perform and demonstrate our capability.

Without any further communication, Weir kicked the side door in, and we advanced into the room. My pulse quickened as we entered. The first room was clear, no one inside. Lt. Whitman signaled for us to continue. I felt my body move without thinking, as if it already knew the rhythm of this place.

My weapon moved forward, pieing the corner. Nothing. I turned back, motioning the assaulting element to advance. Just as they were moving into place, I heard Arabic down the hallway. I quickly motioned my unit to halt.

"Allaenat ealaa al'amrikan! Aqtilwa!" *The lead insurgent screamed. I didn't understand most of it, but I did understand the last word: "kill."*

My finger squeezed the trigger, the round flying from the muzzle of my weapon. I watched the lead royal guard's head snap backward. His body fell with the impact. I started spitting round after round down the hallway.

Lt. Whitman started screaming commands, and I followed every word without hesitation. My body was no longer my own; I was a weapon. Moving in position here and there, shooting everyone who wasn't us.

Somehow, through the chaos, we made it to the main hall. Two large staircases curved around the central area. Perched on the second floor was a machine gun nest.

"Fucken' RPK stairs!" Gordon howled.

However, it was too late; the ratta-tat-tat started to rain down on us. Peterson barely looked at the second floor before his helmet was pierced. Blood splattered on the wall behind him, shredding the flesh off his skull. His face was no longer there as the spray of bullets ripped through his head.

Their weapon turned toward Whitman, and in that moment, I dove, knocking him to the ground. I felt something whiz by my back, grazing my body armor. I assumed it was rounds from the crew-serve above us.

"Damn, fucking close." Whitman's nervous laughter briefly eased the tension. I rolled off him as we crawled to take cover behind a wall.

I desperately scanned the area. "Fuck! Where are our guys?"

I spotted Weir, inching up on the machine gunner. Gordon was laying suppressive fire to distract the guy.

Then we heard it, a metallic clank against the stone floor.

"Grenade!" Rasnake yelled before lunging at the sound, cradling the explosive. His body muffled the boom, giving us a chance to do this. I wasn't going to let his sacrifice go to waste. I raised my weapon and began laying fire.

I felt the hatred boiling over inside me, screaming, "FUCK YOU, MOTHERFUCKAS!!!"

Weir closed in on the nest as his weapon quickly dispatched the shooter. The night wasn't over, but we had made it inside. I moved to check on Rasnake. Turning him over, there was nothing left of his torso; it was as if someone had spooned out his insides.

Then I felt it, like a baseball bat being slammed into my chest. I looked up; another Haji had started shooting at us. I fell back, landing on the cold stone floor. I was winded, but the armor saved me. I lay on the ground as the volume of the world faded out.

I was flat on my back. The cold ground beneath me was like an ice wall against my spine. My head was pillowed on something warm and soft. I felt two hands gently petting my hair, and a third caressing my face with care. I took a deep breath, inhaling all the chilled air into my lungs.

I heard two voices start to speak—a tender, soft voice and a smooth, sexy rasp.

"Game over!" the tender voice yelled desperately into the night.

The rasp echoed with agitation, burning deep. "Fucking game over!"

It was silent again, as if the voices were waiting for something. Then the chatter started back.

"Do you think Master is back?"

"He's quiet, now," the raspy voice said. "So, I don't know, sis."

"Oh, Master, come back quick," the soft voice sobbed.

"Don't worry, he will."

I opened my eyes, looking up to see that a redhead was staring down at me, her emerald eyes tearing up. My head rested neatly in her lap as I was on the ground. A brunette emerged on the side of my face, her sapphires studying me.

Where was I? What happened? The acrid smell of sulfur clung to my clothes, and I could feel a sticky, cool substance on my cheek. Was that the green goo from the witches?

But then, the taste of sand on my tongue lingered with desperation. The machine gun fire, the screams. Rasnake's hollowed out torso... All of it slammed into my core, into my soul like a phantom punch. Was it real? Was this?

The hand of the brunette cupped my cheek, her thumb gently stroking my jawline, pulling me back. Vicky... my fiancée, Vicky.

"Don't nut up on us completely," Vicky whispered, her soft command felt more like begging. "We still need you. Still love you. Our everything."

The redhead's tear-streaked face hovered over me, lovingly watching me. Sarah, yes, Sarah, my other fiancée. I was engaged to two women. These were the women I loved with my entire heart.

"Say something, Master, please," Sarah pleaded, before she leaned down, planting a kiss on my forehead.

The flickering of the skull lanterns shimmered in my face. I wanted to speak, but no words came to the surface; only a ragged gasp escaped my lips. The echoes of gunfire still rattled deep into my being. As my vision sharpened, I saw a figure emerge—a staff member or actor from the spook-house. He approached, his face weary with concern.

"Is he alright?" His voice was a cacophony of concern and guilt.

"Yeah, he's al'ight," Howard said from the side. Although his voice seemed confident, I detected a slight tremble in it.

I lay there recovering, regaining my wits. The nightmare, the memory, had gone as quickly as it came. Leaving only the concerned and worried faces of my beauties and my tribe. My chest was still sore with the lingering phantom pain of the round that struck my vest. But I was here, not there. Yes, here, safe.

"I'm fine," I finally announced, my head still buzzing.

"Let us help you up," Vicky mumbled, getting to her feet. Her hand grasping mine, tugging me upright.

I quickly stood with her help. Sarah followed me up, her hands on my back to stabilize the move. Their care was firm and steady, the way I always needed after an episode like this.

"What the..." David muttered. He stood in shock as his jaw hit the floor. "Is he okay? What was that weird shit he was screaming?"

Sarah eyed him with a dangerous stare, then turned back to me with a bubbly smile. Vicky shook her head at him, wiping tears from my eyes that I hadn't noticed.

Each took an arm, bracing me as I gained my equilibrium. Their touch grounded me, pulling me back from the depths of that memory. They were my salvation, my home. I finally realized this was the entertaining haunted house, not the bleak deserts of war. I didn't need to be a killer here to simply survive. I was a friend, a brother, a leader, a lover. Not a soldier anymore.

"Ya good, bro?" Howard's concerned voice broke through the chilled silence. Then he gave a slight chuckle. "Thought ya might stab a guy or sumten', ya know."

Managing a weak dismissive wave. "Nah, just cut his ear off, then make a necklace out of it." The heaviness around me slowly lifted. I felt Sarah's hand tighten around me. "I'm alright, things just got a little too real for a moment."

Sarah and Vicky supported me with a loving caress. They both gazed into my eyes with a look of worry, as if searching for the man they loved. My image reflected in Sarah's emerald eyes and Vicky's sapphires. Inside, I felt the warmth of their care melting me.

"I'm okay, swear," I said before inhaling a deep breath. The worry on their faces faded.

Vicky stared at me longingly, her fingers tracing my cheek. "I'll make you a special dessert when we get home. One that will make sure you know where home is." She growled with a flood of relief, but a sensual tinge hung to her voice.

"You're safe, Master," Sarah reassured me, her face nuzzling mine. "We're here. All of us are here for you." She pointed toward the small crowd gathered around. Surrounded by the others, a concerned awkwardness lingered in the air.

"They're amazing," Myra whispered to herself. "No wonder he loves them."

I glanced around at the distraught faces of my tribe. Elle watched in silence, her face etched with understanding. Howard seemed confident on the surface, but his eyes were a storm of worry. He soon pulled Elle close, his massive arm enveloping her with care.

David was stunned, his eyes glowing with confusion. Ava had tears falling, and she gave me a brief smile. Those two stood with arms locked around each other.

Charlotte glanced back and forth between me and the staff member, seeming torn and unsure if everything was all right. Myra's eyes darted around Sarah, Vicky, and me, formulating some new understanding.

The staff member gave me a once-over. Once satisfied that I hadn't caused an injury to myself, he asked. "Sir, are you sure that you don't need water? Or to sit for a while?"

Vicky shook her head. "He's good. We got him," she said assertively. "Now, can you lead us to the parking lot?"

For a moment, I could see the enjoyment on her face as she took control of the situation. A light chuckle escaped my lips as the power dynamic shifted in her favor for just a second.

"I'm fine, just ready to go," I muttered, nodding a thanks to the staff member. My arms caressed the women at my sides: my women, my beauties, my wives.

The night air was refreshing and cool against my skin. I drew a breath of it to expel the ghosts of the past from my core.

Following the actor, we walked silently down the path, forming a semi-wedge as the haunted attractions faded. The dark, winding trail through the trees now felt different. The carved skull lanterns flickered with a new glow, no longer monstrous but like guiding lights in the darkness.

I kept my mind on the present. I focused on Sarah's gentle hand, caringly pressing into mine. The way Vicky's fingers curled around my bicep, trying desperately to remind me of my strength. Their perfumes enveloped me in sweetness, extricated me even further. The crunching of leaves under our feet as the nine of us moved along the path filled the air with sound.

Reaching the parking lot, the guide peeled off. His tone with his final statement was one of creepy satisfaction. "We appreciated savoring your souls here at the Labyrinth of Macabre Curiosities. Until we meet again in the warrens of shadows."

As soon as we moved across the parking lot, I felt a hand reach from behind, tugging on my shoulder, halting my movement with Vicky and Sarah.

"What the hell happened?" Ava's voice roared near my ear.

I turned around, facing my tribe. Vicky let my arm slip from her hands as they balled into fists, ready to strike. Sarah just kept her fingers intertwined with mine.

David rudely chimed in. "Yeah, the fuck was that?"

I carefully looked over the tribe, then, with a reluctant sigh, I began to explain. "A flashback, I have PTSD," I admitted with shame. My words hung in the air for a moment as everyone processed what that meant.

"So... so, you're crazy? Like, psycho kill... killer crazy?" Ava stuttered, her eyes widening in shock, hand traveling over her mouth. Her words caused Myra and Charlotte to take a step back from me.

"No," Vicky responded abruptly, her expression now a cool, calm one, as if to discharge the accusation. "It means he has a conscience about what happened over there."

"Master is troubled by the things he did and saw, that's all," Sarah added, her fingers tightening on mine. Then her voice boomed. "If you got a problem with that, we could settle it now." She growled fiercely, seeming ready to fight.

Vicky looked at Sarah with a prideful yet worried gaze. Then she turned her attention back to the crowd. "He's still the same man from ten minutes ago that you all seemed to like," Vicky said, grief slicing through her lips. "The only thing that's changed is you now know about some of his troubles."

"Are the meds working?" Elle asked, her face serious, her voice professional. Sarah seemed at ease as Elle spoke.

"Yes," I replied with a simple answer.

"Then why the freakout up at the haunted house?" Ava asked guardedly. "All that screaming... the weird shit you said."

I didn't answer, I didn't know how. How do I talk about something I don't have a memory of? Tell them that it was alright, while I didn't even know what happened?

"He plays out what happened in his mind," Sarah answered for me, with glacial frustration. "The things he talked about, they happened to him. He relives it, talking through the fog of his mind. That's how we get to know the horrors that he is seeing. Some noise must've triggered him."

Myra, with a look of defeat in her eyes, turned to Charlotte. "I can't compete... they know how to handle him. But I gotta try."

No more questions were asked as everyone was frozen in thought. Then Ava broke the stillness. "You... you better not hurt anyone," Ava stammered, fear still laced in her voice.

"Ya being dramatic," Howard spoke up with a boom, his eyes glaring at Ava. "Just go home, all of ya." He sighed.

"Yeah, Ava, let's go," David coaxed as he tugged Ava's arm. "Kyle wouldn't hurt anyone," he said with sympathy in his voice. "See you Monday, boss."

She stared at me for a moment, then followed David's lead. Her head occasionally turned back to glance at me as they headed toward their car.

“Kyle, I...” Myra trailed off, her eyes drooping before suddenly igniting with an odd kind of resolve. A crooked smile slowly spread across her face. “See you next week,” she purred, then hurried after Charlotte, who was walking away.

“Ya three have a good night.” Howard gave a knowing look in my direction. He seemed to understand the emotions the ostracizing caused me.

“Goodbye, girls. Take care of my brother,” Elle said, her voice carrying a gentleness. “Be good, li’l bro.”

On the ride home, my mind was rippling with thoughts.

That wasn’t just a haunted house attraction; it was a reminder—a statement to me—that the darkness I left behind was only a breath away from this life, this peace. It called to me, trying to pull me back into the abyss. L.O.V. was a tangible manifestation of this endless cycle and the early death it seemed to promise.

I felt a shiver thinking about how they looked at me, my tribe, my people. It felt like that dark sea swallowed my heart. Was I really that frightening? How would it change things if they saw me like that? Seeing the real me, the monster I could become.

I couldn’t let that consume me. Not when I had my fiancées. Not when I was finally starting to build our three-way life the way we wanted. I had to stay strong for them. For our new tribe. Everyone was counting on me. I had to prove I was the man worthy of their trust and understanding.

Besides, I was planning to have children with my fiancées. The marriage was just a stone’s throw away if Leonard could win the court battles. The career dreams of my wives were coming true. I had secured the finances that would help raise our kids. I needed to get back in there and saddle up for the ride because my white picket fence–dream of marrying these two women was just inches away.

Chapter 14: Three-Sided Coin Flip

Saturday morning came fast. Last night, after the spook-house incident, the girls had me wrapped up in their passionate touches and compassionate whispers. Vicky and Sarah made sure that my special dessert left me completely satisfied.

Their soft scents, mixed with the musk of lovemaking, pulled me into what was real: our life together. The three of us indulged in pleasures that the other two could give and freely gave to each other, with enthusiastic, reciprocated affections.

Their soft caresses touched me deeply, igniting the fire in my heart. Our silent confessions of love and unity echoed in the bedroom. No words could express those emotions. Only the tenderness of our affections was able to communicate at that level.

Then we lay in bed, conversing and dreaming about the big house we wanted. The way the light would break into Vicky's art room as she painted happily, her music bouncing off the walls. The garden that Sarah would lounge in, reading her novels under the warm glow of the sun. The dozen or so children the three of us wanted to fill the house with noise and cheer.

And how much love would be shared not only between the three of us, but also with our children. This dream was our shared goal, our happiness. This was who we were—together, loving each other, standing united and strong against the finality of life.

When we finally succumbed to sleep, lovingly embracing each other, the night felt serene. The warmth of their bodies against mine as we drifted off to dreamland soothed the terrors within.

I awoke feeling well-rested, the night lingering on my body and in my soul. However, today would be anything but rest. Breakfast went in a flash as I wolfed down toast and eggs. Sarah and Vicky were surprised by my early and hasty cooking, since we usually slept in on the weekends.

I reminded them that Elle needed me to be her backup for Jenny's visitation exchange. Sarah and Vicky wanted to come, but I didn't know what craziness might ensue, so I advised them to stay home. They were upset but understood.

Elle swung by after breakfast to pick me up. Sarah gently kissed me, while Vicky shooed me out with a playful swat on the butt.

As I got into Elle's SUV, something felt off. Her clothes were slightly sloppy, her hair a disheveled poof on her head. And her eyes burned with... fear? Anxiety? Anger? I couldn't tell, but I figured it was most likely from the episode I'd had the night before. It was highly embarrassing that my tribe found out about my PTSD that way. And I was still nervous to face anyone other than the girls.

As we drove to the meeting place, a park on the other side of town, Elle discussed her excitement about seeing Jenny.

Elle weaved in and out of traffic. "I can't wait to hug her."

"It's been four months. I bet Jenny can't wait to see you and play with you. Do you have any plans?"

"Ice cream first, then McDonald's."

"Ice cream first? Aren't you doing that backward?"

"Nah. Besides, who's the parent here?" Her eyes briefly moved off the road to glance at me. She had a tightness around her mouth I hadn't noticed before.

"Alright, alright. You win, Sis," I stammered in jest. My hand waved in the air. "I know you spoil her rotten. She's your kid."

Elle took a slow, deliberate sip of her green tea, her gaze staring out in the distance for a moment. Then she chuckled to herself before saying. "You know nothing, Jon Snow."

"*Game of Thrones*? Really?" I laughed. It was a stressful day for her. I had to be the supportive brother she needed.

Elle put her bottle back in the console before explaining. "I've been catching up on it."

"It's a good show. I didn't think it was your type of thing."

"Hot guys, sex, and gore." Elle turned the wheel sharply. "Definitely my thing." A flicker, quick as lightning, crossed her eyes, something hard and cold, then it was gone.

"Maybe I should watch it with Sarah and Vicky."

"I think they'd like it," Elle said, glancing at me briefly with a smile not quite reaching her eyes. "They like your sword-and-sorcery pervy ass, anyway."

I thought about our life together. "Yeah, they kinda do." I chuckled.

"Kind of, little brother? Last night, both of those girls looked like they were going to smack Ava into oblivion."

"Maybe," I replied, falling into a sullen mood, remembering that the tribe had seen my breakdown. "What did I do last night?"

"Nothing, really." Elle was dismissive, yet gentle. "You jumped into the ditch, then shouted about Patterson... Peterson, something like that, and a rattlesnake..."

"Peterson and Rasnake, men who died on my first deployment," I corrected. "Along with many others."

"Is the therapy helping?"

"Yes, and so are the meds," I answered in a dull voice, feeling exposed. Then sarcasm rose in my voice. "And yes, before you ask, Sarah and Vicky hound me every day so I don't forget to take them."

"Damn, chill," she said. "It's good that they take care of you."

"Hey, Sis, do you..." I trailed off, trying to find the courage to ask what I needed to. "Do you think that everyone believes I'm Ted Bundy, now?"

"Bro, your brain is fried from war. But that doesn't make you a psycho killer or whatever." Elle sighed, her hand falling to rest on the stick shift. "It just means you have a long road to heal from whatever happened over there."

Heal. Holly used that term a lot. Was I healing? I thought I was. But then last night proved maybe the wounds were still bleeding, that I was still capable of being a killer, a monster. I looked out the window, watching the people we passed. They seemed unaware of what was happening half a world away. The battles that were being waged for them, the sacrifices made for them.

"I'm trying."

"That's all you can do," Elle said, her words filled with sisterly affection. "Just keep doing what you are, things will get better."

Elle turned on the radio. "Now, turn that frown upside down, and sing with me." She smirked with mischief as a Britney Spears song started to play. "Come on, I know you know the words."

Elle started screaming out the lyrics. I smiled, shaking my head. She may be a decent therapist, but her horrible singing voice would make dogs cry. However, I couldn't help but sing along with her, if for nothing else than to drown out the sounds of an animal dying coming from her lips.

"*You drive me crazy. I just can't sleep. I'm so excited, I'm in too deep. Whoa oh oh, crazy, but it feels alright.*"

We continued singing for several more songs, goofing around together after each one ended in our duet car concert. I was sure that our improvised car karaoke was the stuff of nightmares, poor kids we passed having to hear that screeching. However, from time to time, I would notice Elle with a tense grip on the steering wheel, often so tight her knuckles would be whiter than snow before she relaxed them.

Arriving at the park, Elle turned the radio off. Her eyes instantly fell to the playground equipment, scanning for Jenny. She muttered something under her breath, almost inaudible. I could only make out "fucking piece of shit husband" before her voice trailed off into a low hum.

I turned in my seat, my eyes studying her. She seemed worried, her hands visibly trembling. Her eyebrows knitted into an anxious, almost hesitant scowl.

"Hey, you got this." My hand fell on hers. "Besides, I doubt he will try anything with your serial killer brother here." I smiled brightly at her, trying to pull her back to the happy sibling moment we just shared.

Her face relaxed as the corners of her mouth tugged up. "Okay, Ghostface, just don't gut him quite yet."

We exited the SUV, and I gave her a reassuring pat on the back. Then our feet moved in cadence with each other. I walked beside her, like the strong younger brother she needed me to be.

As we walked along the sidewalk, I saw it. Of course, he was already parked there; there was no mistaking that car. With shiny dark paint, it was a very unique vehicle. Like a black rose in the desert, it was the single sight of elegance against a drab city backdrop. The futuristic, sleek appearance contrasted hard against the ruin of a building next to it.

The feeling of hatred poured deep into my heart. My heart was no longer smiling as it had been the night before. Instead, the icy chill of ire had eroded the warmth. The frozen depth of war remained on my shoulders. And Stephen was where that hatchet desired to bury itself, deep into his skull.

Snap back, Sergeant. Relax. You are here to support Elle and ensure that Jenny's exchange goes smoothly.

As we approached, Stephen sat on the bench overlooking the playground, unaware of us. I followed his gaze to Jenny. She ran up the pirate ship with a boy, both pretending to sword fight. This tugged at my heart, softening my tough military exterior, warming the cold inside me, and chipping away at the icy shell on my soul.

The pirate ship was proudly moored right between the swings, the spinning merry-go-round, and the monkey bars, creating a lively hub of adventure. Laughter and the cheerful squeals of children echoed joyfully throughout the park. Along the edges, near the busy sidewalk, parents lounged on benches, smiling and chatting as they watched their little pirates and explorers having the time of their lives. This was a joyful place bursting with energy and happiness. I hoped that nothing bad would interrupt this cheery atmosphere.

I turned back to Stephen, noticing he was in casual attire, which I had never seen him in before. He wore a green baseball cap, a T-shirt, and blue jeans—a stark contrast to his usual business suit.

Elle's hands began to tremble more, her face red with rage. She leered at Stephen, then she stomped up next to him. "Where the fuck is my daughter?" She growled, her voice sharp and angry.

"Elle," Stephen gasped as he jumped in his seat, startled by her harshness. Then he settled back, relaxing on the bench, pointing toward the playground. "Playing."

Elle pointed her finger at Stephen's nose. "You have some nerve making me pick her up here."

This seemed crazy to me. Wasn't it Stephen who was the aggressive, violent one? Why was Elle acting like this?

"It's a public place, dear. We shouldn't fight and make a scene."

Elle, seething with anger and hatred, transformed into a shrew. "Don't fucking start with me! And don't ever call me dear again!" Her voice began attracting attention from the park attendees.

She launched into a tirade of belittling remarks about Stephen, criticizing everything from his sexual performance to his workaholic tendencies. Yet, she never mentioned the abuse she had confided in me about. He didn't speak, but took every cutting word. Was this a calculated move, or had years of this simply worn him down?

I stayed silent, trying to understand this attack on Stephen. He hadn't done anything wrong. What the hell was going on? As this unfolded, all eyes, from the parents to the children, narrowed in on us. I felt embarrassed. Was this the same Elle I was singing with minutes ago?

The unhinged screaming and verbal abuse Elle was slinging felt like an ambush or an IED. The sands of Iraq and the snows of Afghanistan began to touch my soul again. And it wasn't Stephen causing it; it was my own sister.

The spectacle she was creating started to push my nerves to the brink. She was beginning to trigger another flashback. My heart raced like a dragster, my eyes narrowed sharply. Muscles tensed with the hunger for a fight. *Calm, Sergeant. Calm down. Sarah, Vicky, Sarah, Vicky, breathe in, breathe out. Just relax. Sarah, Vicky, they are your home. Be at peace. Just breathe.*

My breathing slowed, my heart rate calmed. My muscles relaxed. I was starting to gain control over myself. I hadn't slipped into another flashback, so maybe I was in the clear.

Then clacking heels marched across the sidewalk. I looked over to see Naomi, her face scrunched in defiance of Elle. Great, what was she doing here? This was going to get even crazier, my sister and my future mother-in-law at each other's throats.

"Shut up," Naomi sharply commanded, her voice low yet hard against the profanities from Elle. Her eyes flicked briefly toward me with a gaze of deep, worried concern. "Just shut up, Elle."

Elle was stunned into silence—as was the park. Not even the sound of children playing was heard.

"Ahem," Stephen cleared his throat, his cheeks burning red with embarrassment. He quickly scanned the crowd, then turned to Elle. "Please have her back by seven tomorrow night. She has school on Monday."

"Oh, just brush it off like always," Elle growled through gritted teeth, her eyes red with anger. "Go hide behind your little skank."

"Skank, huh." Naomi spat, her nostrils flaring. "Want me to show the world who the real skank is?" Her words rippled with accusation and provocation, causing Elle to reel back with worry,

I finally forced my way into this mess. "What's going on, Elle?" My hand tugged on Elle's shoulder.

"This asshole and his slut, that's what's going on."

"Hmm..." Naomi's only word in defense of Elle's accusation. She pulled her phone out, fidgeting with it.

Stephen stood up, his demeanor stronger than it had been a moment ago. "Naomi is here to make sure the visitation exchange goes smoothly."

I was sure that his newfound confidence was from having Naomi as his backup. Vicky's mother carried an air of authority. I was reminded of when she told me love could change the universe, and how powerful that made me feel.

And somehow, I was feeling that again. "Sis, you came out of the gate slandering him." My gaze drifted back to Naomi, who was still scrolling through her phone. Then I turned my focus back to Elle. "Stop acting like this. We're here for Jenny, remember."

Naomi held up her phone so only I could see; a video was playing on the screen. She had muted it, or the lewd acts the couple engaged in would have been heard by every parent and child here.

I leaned into her. "Mom, porn? At the park?" I whispered, trying not to draw the onlookers' attention to the content.

"Son, take a closer look," Naomi implored, her voice somber, her purple eyes holding a difficult regret as she met my gaze. "Does the woman look familiar?"

I took her hand and pulled her phone closer. My gut twisted. It was clearly Elle—the face of my elder sister who had protected me. The one I looked up to, the person I wanted to be like when I was a kid. Now my idol was exposed in a compromising and humiliating way. Disappointment surged through my mind, followed by a cold, unsettling realization that I'd never truly known my sister.

I shoved the phone back at my future mother-in-law. "So? My sister's love life has nothing to do with me."

"Darling, your sister is nothing like you." Naomi sighed, her hand gently touching my arm. Her expression softened with regret at having to show me the video. "She doesn't have your sense of loyalty." Naomi reached her hand out briefly, caressing my cheek with a mother's care. "Your commitment to the love in your life."

Elle exploded. "Loyalty? You want to talk about loyalty?" Her gaze fixed on me as her jaw clenched. "My brother is fucking two women!" Her voice was harsh and accusatory as she moved aggressively at Naomi.

The way she said that last sentence felt like a knife piercing me. Was she really not okay with me being with Sarah and Vicky?

Stephen stepped in between them. His hands pushed their shoulders gently to separate them.

"Naomi, enough!" Stephen growled at her, his voice falling like an employer talking to a subordinate. Then his gaze fell pitifully on Elle, exposing the complex mix of emotions he harbored for her. "Calm down, Elle," he said gently.

"Calm down?" Elle screamed, hatred seething deep in her voice. "When are you going to tell Kyle about your little experiment?"

I glanced at her, confused. Then, I looked back at Stephen. He and Naomi gazed at each other with shock and panic. Elle saw this and decided to land the blow.

"Yeah, that's what I thought!" Elle spat with rage, mocking them with disdain. "Your L.O.V. project or whatever." She had to jab in one last hateful comment before stomping off to the playground.

I stood in a daze. Project L.O.V.... the memo, the dead woman. What did Elle know about the experiment? How was it connected to me? Did Elle realize I could be a clone? Did she know if I was or not? Did she know if I was going to die? If there was a cure? A way to stay in this world with my beauties? Why didn't she tell me?

Naomi cleared her throat, shaking me from my thoughts.

"Mom, tell me about L.O.V."

Naomi looked me over, her eyes soaking in everything. Then she smiled warmly. "Son, your heart is pure and honorable." Her words were motherly, laced with affirmation. She turned toward the playground, toward Elle. "The same can't be said for your sister."

"Mom." I reached out to her shoulder. "Tell me what L.O.V. is."

Naomi's lavender eyes pleaded for me to leave the subject alone. But I couldn't, not when even Elle knew more than I did.

"Please, Mom."

"I'll be at Stephen's house today; he needs my help with something," Naomi said, almost as if it were an invitation. It was apparent she didn't want to talk about it here or now.

"Jenny, dear, time to go," Elle announced loudly. She forcefully took Jenny's hand. My niece complied as Elle began to make a charged, brisk beeline for the SUV.

"Bye, Mom, gotta go." I gently squeezed her shoulder. Just as my hand dropped, she rushed in, hugging me. The motherly embrace caught me off guard, but made me feel her actions today were sincere. I hugged her back.

"I'm sorry, Son. I shouldn't have shown you, but you deserved to know." Naomi's voice was shaky with remorse. "You know in your beautiful heart what's right. Be the good man my daughters chose," she advised, her voice filled with a mother's hope and a hint at the burden she carried, before releasing me. "Take care and be strong."

As I dropped my embrace, my gaze fell on Stephen, his face drawn with a worried look as he watched Elle take Jenny away.

"Stephen." I nodded a farewell, acknowledging the awkwardness of the situation Elle had caused.

"See ya, Kyle." He forced his pout into a remorseful smile.

I quickly trudged to Elle's truck. My head hung low, not wanting to make eye contact with anyone. The embarrassing family dispute that they all witnessed was like a public gutting of everything I stood for. All my values, all my hard work, erased in moments by my sister. My flesh and blood.

I couldn't understand the storm of emotions ripping at my insides. Was it the feeling of embarrassment? Anger? Betrayal?

As I approached, Elle was aggressively struggling to get Jenny buckled into the booster seat. She was muttering harsh things to Jenny about her father, but Jenny ignored it. Without saying a word, I gently moved Elle out of the way, fastening the seatbelt with a smooth ease. Elle stomped to the driver's seat, starting the engine.

"Uncle Kyle, I've missed you so, so much." Jenny's soft voice was a breath of fresh air. She waved her princess doll at me. "So did Princess Lulu."

My genuine joy to see Jenny forced away the previous scene and put a grin on my face. "Me too, Bootyhead. I missed you bunches and bunches. And Princess Lulu, I hope you finally married the prince." My words fell short of the enthusiasm I wanted.

"Are you coming with us? Mama says we're getting ice cream. I want a swirly cone, and Princess Lulu wants a chocolate shake."

"Of course," I replied, rustling her hair. "I'm going with you. Let me jump in up front."

I shut her door and quickly took my place in the passenger seat. Elle peeled out, her anger still boiling. We sat in silence, the engine and Jenny's conversation with her doll were the only sounds in the cab. What could I say? What was there to say? Elle exploding for no reason. Her dismissal of my relationship with Vicky and Sarah as mere sex. She knew it was more than that. And L.O.V....

"Sis." I faced her, my eyes studying her demeanor. Her grip tightened on the steering wheel, bracing for what I would say next. "What do you know about L.O.V.?"

"Nothing, really," she responded, a hint of anger soaked into her words. "Just that you were to be a test subject."

"Nothing else?"

Braking at the stop sign, her gaze pivoted at me. "No, dammit, nothing else." She gritted her teeth, as if I had accused her of lying. "Are you siding with that pathetic couple?"

I shook my head. But not in response to her question.

This wasn't my sister sitting next to me. She wasn't my sister the clinician, the relationship therapist, the believer in love. This was a hateful pod-person; nothing about this stranger resembled the Elle I knew. "I'm not siding with anyone. And I don't think they're a couple." My words were stern with that NCO strictness.

Elle's face snapped back to the road as she punched the gas pedal. "I guess you're the fucking relationship expert now, huh?"

She was harsh, attacking me with undisguised cruelty. I swallowed it, trying to understand her. Understand this hate.

"Speaking about relationships, what was that you said at the park about mine?"

Elle's face littered with worry, as if she were a child caught in a lie. "Don't know what you mean."

She knew damn well what I meant. "You don't approve of my relationship with Sarah and Vicky, do you?"

She gave a fake chuckle. "What kind of question is that?"

"A real one. You seemed hateful in how you dismissed it as just sex"—I lowered my voice so Jenny wouldn't hear—"just fucking."

Elle sighed, her hands loosening on the wheel. "It's not fair, you don't get judged for what you want. But me... I'm judged as a slut when I do the same thing."

"I'm in a loving relationship, and we're judged all the time. But what was implied about you was not the same thing." I was trying to be sympathetic as I came to grips with this new version of my sister. "When was that video taken? After you two split?"

Elle coughed, trying to hide a sob. "No, just days before Jenny and I came to your place to meet Vicky and Sarah." She lowered her head. "The same day Stephen confronted me with that video."

"Cheating is not the same as what I'm doing. I'm in a committed relationship with my fiancées, and we love each other." I asserted, my voice full of disappointment. "We understand each other and support one another. We're building a life together. It's not some sex thing or toying around; it's love. Real love."

Elle chuckled maliciously. "You think that's love? Spending your nights screwing two women?" She paused, her voice starting to crack with hoarseness from all the screaming. "Polygamy, by definition, is toxic, cruel, and perverse to the very idea of love. A boy like you is only concerned about getting laid."

She was pissing me off. I've never wanted to hit a woman, let alone my sister, but she was pushing me to a place where I might. The way she dismissed everything about my relationship, calling it toxic and cruel, hurt. Then, a direct attack against my achievements, experience, and age to invalidate them. Like she was deliberately trying to emasculate me to make herself feel better.

"I'm a man, have been since the day I swore in," I said through gritted teeth, my muscles were beginning to tighten. "And my relationship is far from cruel or toxic."

Elle went quiet. She seemed to realize her "boy" statement invalidated my military service and all I endured. "Kyle, I– I– I didn't mean it like that." Elle stuttered, her voice softened from the bitterness she just spat at me. But I couldn't care less now.

"Let me out," I demanded with cold, sharp determination. My hand hastily unfastened the seatbelt.

"Uncle Kyle, stay. Mommy didn't mean it. You can't walk home. Stay, please," Jenny pleaded, her eyes welling with tears.

I wanted to stay and comfort my niece, but I had to get far away from this stranger wearing my sister's face. Leave before I did or said something I'd regret.

I turned in my seat. "It's okay, Bootyhead, I'm used to walking. We did a lot of it in the Army." As I turned to Elle, my voice rippled with that icy chill again. "Let me out, goddamn it."

"Fine," Elle hissed as she stomped on the brakes, sending us all jerking forward. I braced myself just in time, with my hands slamming against the dashboard. "Fuck you and your whores!" Her last hurtful words rendered my decision to leave absolute.

I opened the door and jumped out of the vehicle. Jenny's sobs followed me out. Before I could completely close the door, Elle sped off, nearly taking my hand with it. I didn't know what to do or how to help my sister and niece. I felt powerless.

As I made my way to the sidewalk, the anger inside started to subside. I stood there for a moment, trying to gather myself, figure out my next move. I hailed a taxi, deciding whether to go home, follow Elle, or... Naomi subtly invited me to Elle's old house.

“Where to, kid?” The driver asked as I slid into the seat, the leather making a creaking noise. I breathed in a breath to calmly give him a destination—the smell of fresh lavender hit my nose.

“2115 Heartwell Avenue,” I said, my mind barely remembering the street address for that house. If I wanted answers about their involvement in L.O.V., about myself, and to find out about MNV, it was the only logical choice.

As the cab pulled out, I felt the sting of my sister’s actions deep inside my heart. And Jenny was caught in this web, which weighed on my heart even more.

I shifted to stare out the window. My mind was a fuzzy haze. I was trying to piece this together. Find answers to the feelings troubling my heart.

How could Elle be this way? What caused all of this? Were the past few months an act? She had not only seemingly accepted my relationship but was friends with my fiancées.

Stephen wasn’t what I thought he was or what Elle had led me to believe. Was my sister manipulating me? Weaponizing me against her husband? I thought about the events a few months ago, how he came to me. I suddenly realized that he hadn’t been trying to taunt me. No, he had been trying to ask for help. How could I have missed that? My rage and hatred for him blinded me, consumed me. When he tried to get close to me, I snapped at him, not giving him a chance to open up truly. And then there was the fact that he defended me, tried to save my job with Mr. McKellen.

As the cab rounded a corner, I thought about the implications of Stephen and my mother-in-law being involved in the conspiracy I had found myself in. The danger L.O.V. posed to my life, my relationship, breached my thoughts like a battering ram.

Could Naomi give me the information I needed? Could Stephen? I had to try. I had to try to find answers. No, I *was* going to find answers. I was determined to solve this so that Vicky, Sarah, and I could live a long, peaceful life together—our happy life, happy marriage.

Chapter 15: Family Revelations

After arriving at Elle's old place, I paid the cabby, giving him a generous tip. He waved me on with a smile, then drove off. The ride over gave me plenty of time to figure out what to say, what to ask.

I turned to the house, where that distinctly shaped futuristic car was parked in the driveway. The outer material catching the sunlight had strange sparkles. Its seamless panels radiated a deep allure, almost inviting a person to touch and discover the way in.

Shifting my attention away from the vehicle, I stood on the sidewalk for a moment, my eyes studying the brown bricks of the two-story home. The rosebushes under the large bay window brought color to the area. The large, dark door once invoked a sense of dread, having to spend any time with that man. Now it seemed more inviting than my own sister. Maybe it had always been?

I watched as the trees rustled in the autumn breeze. Elle once told me that she picked this place, right after Stephen got his promotion, for the way the light flowed into the living room through the trees in the front yard.

I moved forward, my feet not feeling my own. The walkway underneath my boots sounded with each heavy footfall. As I made it to the porch, the large door swung open. My mother-in-law stood tall against the frame, her purple eyes following my movements.

"I knew you couldn't stay away." Her bright smile gleamed as the sunlight washed over her face.

"I'm here for answers."

"Of course you are." She nodded, motioning to invite me in. "He's in the study, don't mind what you're about to see. We were just starting on a project."

I walked into the foyer, my eyes immediately spotting Jenny's backpack. It hung, lonely, on a hook near the door. I smiled for a moment. Then quickly frowned, thinking about what craziness she was enduring from her mother at that moment. And I was the guy who left her to that.

"It's not your fault," Naomi said flatly. I glanced over at her. Her eyes were on the bag like mine were, then she turned to me with a sigh. "Anyway, I've to get back to work."

She opened the door to the study. The room was simple, with a wooden desk near the window overlooking the backyard and a computer on the workstation's smooth surface. The walls were filled with schematics of various devices. Two shelves on the opposite wall held portraits of a happy family: some of Stephen and Elle's wedding, some of Jenny, and some of all three of them. This home office felt personal, like all his work was for them, his family.

Stephen was sitting in a chair in the middle of the room, facing away from the door. His back to me, he seemed so fragile, so small. Not intimidating at all.

"Where did you go, Naomi?" He turned in his seat and his eyes widened when he saw me. "Why is *he* here?"

"Be nice, Mr. Dolion," Naomi replied. "My son is here for answers. I told you he had gumption."

"You think he should be seeing this?"

"Oh, hush, it's not like we're doing anything wrong," Naomi bleated. "You just need a little adjustment. Stop being a crybaby."

She moved to the toolbox in front of Stephen. She leaned forward, taking his left arm to examine it. Her eyes traced along the limb, as if it were some electronic device.

"What's legal going to say if he opens his mouth?"

"Nothing," Naomi released his arm forcefully. "My daughters chose to love him freely, and by extension, I trust him."

"Fine, let him stay." Stephen huffed, his head shaking with disbelief. "But if legal comes down on us, I'm throwing Reginald's favorite under the bus."

"Throw me under the bus, huh. I'll just be transferred back to the Black Forest to dig up new technologies." She gloated, almost as if she wanted to go to this forest place. "I miss my research anyway and grow tired of cleaning up your messes."

Wait, Black Forest? Wasn't that an exclusive exhibit at the gala? Yeah, the one that Ira pulled me from before the girls and I could venture in. I snapped back to the present. Naomi picked up a package, ripping it open, and retrieved a scalpel from the plastic.

"Whoa, what's that for?" I asked, taking lightning steps to her.

She held her free hand up, signaling a halt. "The protoskin can't be repaired without removing it."

Proto what... the hell was she talking about? Before I could ask, she quickly lifted Stephen's arm and made an incision.

"Wait! What are you doing?" I shouted.

She stopped to look at me. "Sweetie, relax. You'll see in a moment what's under the synthetic dermis." Then she went back to slicing Stephen's arm. The scalpel pierced deep into the flesh, yet no blood came. Her casual demeanor was as if she were cutting a piece of meat in the kitchen. Each slash was exact and sawing deeper.

I stood still, trying to trust her, trying to understand. But then there was no understanding. She surgically peeled the flesh off his arm; my breath hitched in my throat. The bone wasn't bone. A sleek, bluish metallic frame lay underneath the flesh. It was a robotic hand, ghoulishly resembling a human skeleton. Shimmering along the cold metallic surface was a bluish tint, reminding me of that scimitar at the museum. I sighed, letting the breath flow, my eyes focusing sharply on the limb.

Stephen's fingers reflexively twitched, a faint, synthesized clicking sound clattered like a tiny machine starting up. Each joint was an advanced, complex motor I'd never seen before. He wasn't just a man in a chair.

A jolt of a memory flashed, a sickening déjà vu feeling. Nothing I'd experienced, but from a movie I'd watched with Vicky and Sarah a few weeks ago. The scene from *Terminator*, the T-800 revealing his endoskeleton. That theatrical horror now felt immediately real. My stomach churned as a chill of unease overcame the warmth in the room. My blood ran cold, with terrifying realization. This was no damn movie. This was real.

Questions swirled in my mind for a moment. Stephen had a robot arm? Was he a robot? No, he was Jenny's father, how could he be? Breaking through my thoughts, I finally spoke with a hoarse voice. "You have a metal arm?"

"Yeah," Stephen replied, annoyed.

"Why?" I asked, my curiosity boiling over. "What happened?"

"A lab accident. He saved many lives that day," Naomi interjected proudly, as she picked up a screwdriver. Then she glared at Stephen with annoyance. "And you, Mr. CEO, hold still. This is tedious enough without you jerking around."

I moved to the other side of the table to face the scene. I looked Stephen in the eyes. "Okay, but how did you get the arm?"

Naomi nodded, as if to say "trust him." His eyes narrowed at her with agitation, then gazed at me with nervousness.

"Right after Jenny was born, a lab caught fire. I saved everyone I could," Stephen started, but then paused for a moment, his mind frozen in the memory. "But the flames neared the plasma canisters, igniting the liquid tritium, causing a chain reaction explosion." Stephen paused again, a tear sliding down his cheek.

Naomi stopped with the screwdriver; her eyes drifted from the arm to me. "Then, ol' Reggie himself sent Dr. Dolion to a medical research facility."

Doctor? Stephen has a PhD? Really? And Reggie? Wasn't that the name Ira recited to himself?

Stephen sniffled, then glared at me. "Yeah, he gave me my arms back. I spent two months in and out of surgery for the implants. Then three months in recovery and rehabilitation."

"Elle never said anything about this," I sighed, my eyes studying the man in front of me. He seemed like a whipped dog, tail between his legs.

Stephen choked back a tear, then explained. "Of course not, she didn't know. ITI informed her I was away on business. A research project that could take months."

"That's crazy," I replied. My mind was in disbelief that corporations could hide a person away for months.

Stephen continued. "After those painful months, I got home. Elle greeted me with a happy smile, or so I thought. Jenny was just under a year old at the time." Stephen paused, his sad eyes fixed on the family portrait before him. "Later, when I went to the bedroom, I found used condoms she had carelessly discarded in the trash."

"Then you started beating her?" My voice was laced with anger.

"No, he ignored it, like an idiot," Naomi interjected, her tone warm yet sharp. "Chalking it up as a marital hiccup."

"I'm not the monster you wished I was," Stephen spoke softly, yet his words were louder than if he screamed. A familiar shame of being a monster rose inside me as he continued. "I stayed silent for a few years, ignoring the 'late nights' she had at the office, the weekend trips she took, and the expenses to high-end restaurants. I figured it was my punishment for working so much, disappearing for nearly half a year. That was until..." He trailed off.

The conversation stalled, heavy with the weight of Stephen's testimony. My mind, reeling from the betrayal he described, flashed to Vicky and Sarah. My beauties. My fiancées. My everything.

The thought of hurting them like that, of carelessly disregarding their trust, was like a bullet to the heart. We laughed, we cried together, we were united. I would never—could never—cheat on them. And I don't believe they would betray our love ever, either. Our union was different from this room, this tortured hollow confession. The love we shared wasn't just a feeling; it was a sanctuary—an unbreakable, eternal promise.

"For Christ's sake," Naomi said. "If you're not going to tell him, I will." She picked up a tool, focusing back on the arm.

"Tell me what?"

Stephen gulped hard. "Until she started leaving Jenny at my parents' house to go on her rendezvous. I could stand the pitiful and disdainful stares in our social circle." He sobbed, his free hand reaching out, pulling a picture from the shelf. His fingers softly caressed the picture frame in front of him. "Even enduring mockery and brazen insults from her lovers was easy. But Jenny... I couldn't stand for her abandoning my daughter."

The information filled me with a newfound repugnance for my sister. My stomach turned and my heart screamed with indignation. "Elle just left her there at your parents?" I huffed in disbelief.

"Yes." When he looked up from the picture, tears had filled his eyes. "One time, when my parents were out of town, she left Jenny alone in a hotel lobby. At least she paid the front desk clerk to watch her." Stephen's pain was immense, intensely pouring from his eyes.

The reckless actions of my sister were a far cry from those of Sarah and Vicky. Their relationship was completely different from ours. We treasured every moment spent together as if they were precious. Our days were filled with uplifting each other; Elle, on the other hand, tore Stephen down into nothing. I started to understand what genuine, healthy love looked like—fierce and protective.

"I received..." Stephen continued, but the tears overwhelmed him. A sprinkle of tears splashed on the picture.

I glanced at the portrait in his hands. Stephen was on the left with his arm lovingly around Elle, who was holding Jenny. I sighed, feeling a strange, futuristic nostalgia to have my own family portrait like that. Then my mind pulled back to the infidelity and irresponsibility of my sister.

"What happened?" I asked, my voice shaking with an emotion I didn't know how to describe.

Naomi's face twisted with revulsion as she chimed in. "Your niece told the front desk she was tired of waiting for her mommy and asked to call her daddy." Naomi paused for a moment, admiring her work on the robotic limb. "Once the clerk learned who Stephen was, they called him directly."

"That's..." I was speechless. Was my sister truly capable of that? The thought tore holes in my stomach and a sickening buzzing whistled in my ear. No. Not Elle. She couldn't be this kind of monster. But then, my mind flashed to her actions today. The cold hard truth of what Stephen was saying started to settle in.

My hands clenched as the soldier in me burst through. The protective instinct to safeguard our future children surged through me. I could see them in my mind: small, perfect, safe in the arms of their mothers, Sarah and Vicky.

Their love for me was already unyielding, their desire for a family, our family, was pure. There was no doubt they'd shower our babies with a kind of love Elle could never comprehend. This thought was a shield I pulled close to defend against the darkness of my sister. A prayer, and vow to the unborn children I longed for.

"That's your sister," Naomi said emotionlessly. She gracefully placed the skin back on the cold, metallic skeleton. As if putting a glove on a child. Then she looked up from the arm to Stephen. "Do you have any protoskin sealer?"

I stood there for a moment, dazed. What would my fiancées make of all this? With as intensely as they feel about children, and their need to bear mine, would they be angered? Would it affect their friendship with my sister? Would they hate her?

Yeah, they'd be pissed. I felt a fleeting need to escape, to feel Vicky and Sarah. To know the world was not as dark and miserable as this. Taste the color they brought to the world around us.

"In the top drawer," he replied, pointing at the desk. She quickly retrieved a tube of flesh-toned substance. The liquid inside the tube perfectly matched Stephen's skin tone. Naomi opened it. She traced the nozzle along the seam of the cut flesh, rendering it gone. Instantly, his arm looked normal again.

"There, like new." She beamed loudly with triumph in her voice, "Now, will you stop whining?"

Stephen nodded as he flexed his hand for a moment. Each finger moved with a smoothness that seemed very human-like.

I needed to stay, to get answers. Secure the life I was building with my fiancées. I took this quiet moment as my chance. "L.O.V., what is it?" I didn't have time to dance around the topic anymore.

Stephen eyed me with a cautious stare, his mouth open to speak, but not a word came out. Naomi, having put the tools away in the box, smiled at me with a warm glow as if she were happy that I cut through the chatter to ask.

"Uh... it's a... prosthesis project... for soldiers." Stephen stammered, his voice hollow and nervous.

"Why did Elle say I was part of the experiment?"

Stephen sighed, his head hung low. "You were a candidate to receive a prosthetic." He explained, hesitantly and unconvincingly. The weight of his words was light, flimsier than a paper plate.

"I have all my limbs, all my organs," I said, my arms outstretched as I spun around slowly. "So why me?"

"Not all prosthetics are physical, Son," Naomi butted in, her smile wide. "Some are made to heal the soul. To touch the heart in ways we can't with modern medicine."

Stephen eyed Naomi with a sharp look. "Touch the heart, huh?"

"Um... okay," I replied, then paused my hand reaching to scratch my head. Heal the soul? What does that mean? I cleared my throat. "Heal the soul? Touch the heart?"

"Yes, replicate life's most precious bonds," Naomi said, eyeing me with a motherly yet mischievous grin. "Son, everyone deserves love and compan—"

"That's enough, Naomi," Stephen growled, his voice burning with frustration as he placed the family picture back on the shelf.

"If you say so, CEO Dolion," Naomi slowly enunciated, annoyed by his interruption.

"Good, at least you remembered I'm your boss while you're at ITI." Stephen huffed, seeming triumphant. "Now be a good little assistant and fetch me some water."

It was apparent there was a power play between these two in the corporate world. I wasn't sure what it was, but the tension in the room was thick like molasses.

Naomi shot him an insincere smile. "Yes, boss," she said with mockery as she started toward the door. "Just remember, boss, those who stand in Love's way will feel her wrath. And she's a bitch with the fury of the universe."

Stephen stood, placing his baseball cap back on his head. "If there is nothing else, Kyle, I have some things to tend to."

It was evident that "show and tell" was over. I would get no more answers from him. Staying and asking for more might cause issues. Besides, I needed to go home. To bathe in the love of my beauties after a day like today.

"Thank you," I said, my voice soft with sympathy. "For sharing that with me."

"Don't thank me. What I shared ruined the image of your sister for you. Ruined the image of the mother to my child." A single tear flowed down his cheek. "I hope you can see yourself out."

I left, feeling a pang of deep regret and pain. This man was honest with me, at least about my sister. Then he gave me that paper-thin prosthetic crap about L.O.V., an annoying blockage.

However, all I wanted at this moment was to feel Vicky's and Sarah's presence. Go home to them, where the world felt real, in our love. A love that was far less complicated, less messy. Just simple. Caring for each other in the way we do.

"Have a great day, Stephen," I said with sincerity. As I entered the hallway, I turned. "And I'll find answers about Project Lineage Oversight Vindication." My voice echoed throughout the house.

I heard Naomi burst into hysterics from the kitchen. "Told you he's smarter than you thought," she yelled back.

I exited the house, feeling that I had learned something that could help with the L.O.V. mystery, though I wasn't exactly sure what. Naomi hinted that the clones served as a form of emotional prosthesis. For some reason, the thought of AI girlfriends flashed in my mind. And what Howard had confided in me about wanting a clone to download his AI girlie in—

No, I need to leave. I needed to consult with my wives about all this. They may have answers. They're brilliant women, so maybe... maybe we can figure this out together.

Circling my mind was the blatant, selfish, and irresponsible person my sister had become. I had to get home and talk to the girls about today. Heal with them, because I knew this would hurt them.

Stepping out, following the sidewalk, I pulled my phone from my pocket. The warm glow reminded me of the warmth I felt in their arms. I sent a text.

[Master] Saturday 11:14
Wanna pick me up???
[Vicky] Saturday 11:17
Where r u?
Isn't Elle bringing u home?
[Sarah] Saturday 11:18
How's Jenny?
[Master] Saturday 11:19
No, at Stephen's house
I'll explain later
[Vicky] Saturday 11:19
Fuck did u kill him
[Master] Saturday 11:19
No, just pick me up
[Sarah] Saturday 11:20
On our way

Stepping into the street, the warm sun gently kissed my skin as I sat on the dusty roadside. My hand reached down, feeling the rough texture beneath my fingertips. The air was thick with the scent of asphalt and blooming roadside flowers. The day was nearing lunchtime, and my stomach grumbled softly, reminding me I hadn't eaten since the early morning hours. The distant hum of cars and the chirping of birds filled the otherwise quiet scene.

The ground beneath me felt different. I wasn't sure how, but my heart felt heavy as I waited for my ride to whisk me away—waiting for my beauties to take me home, rescuing me from this day. Where would I even begin to explain? How would I start?

The world around me felt dark and unwelcoming, contrasting the brightness and warmth I felt with my brides-to-be. A longing to taste their tender kisses lingered on my lips. The feel of their warm arms wrapped securely around me was missing from my soul.

Our loving connection beamed with honest joy amid the chaos of my sister's turbulent life. And L.O.V. still held mysteries, but in their embrace, I found my sanctuary. My home was with them. And home was now the agenda.

Chapter 16: Fain Stalwart

A red glint flashed before me; it was Sarah's car. The Chevy came to a screeching halt in front of Stephen's house. I was surprised how fast they'd made it to me. It usually took thirty minutes to get here from the apartment, but they arrived fifteen minutes after I sent the texts. They must have thought I was in trouble. I was... just not the kind they were worried about.

I didn't hesitate; I quickly opened the door and slid into the back seat. Getting in, both my beauties looked back at me with concern, and in that instant, the chaotic roar of the day fell quiet. Warmth washed over me, cascading my spirit with affection. Even under their worried gazes, I felt at home, the craziness slightly lifting from my soul. With them is where I truly belonged—comforted by the simple hum of their presence.

Sarah pouted, concerned. "What happened, Master?"

"Did you fuck him up?" Vicky chimed in, her voice a strange mix of excitement and worry.

"I didn't fight with Stephen." Their faces brightened a bit.

Vicky scratched her temple. "Did you kill him?"

Sarah elbowed Vicky. "Why would you ask that?"

Vicky rolled her eyes. "Because Kyle can easily take Stephen, duh. As his wives, we need to know if there's a body to help hide."

I couldn't help but chuckle. "No, I didn't kill or fight anyone. When we get home, I'll explain. Just let me stew on it until then."

"We're not going home yet." Sarah beamed with a smile as she turned back around in her seat. Her hands excitedly gripped the steering wheel.

Vicky sighed as she turned back to the front. "Miss Pushover wants to have a picnic."

"Sounds good, I'm hungry."

The streets passed by as Sarah drove on. The ride to the picnic area was mainly silent. Vicky was in the passenger's seat, glaring back at me, every so often, as if I had punched a baby. Sarah focused on the road, humming to herself. And me, well, I just watched out the window, trying to sort out my thoughts.

Revving with a howl, the engine clapped against the blurring streets. My mind wrestled with the jarring insanity of the morning.

Elle was extremely rude and belittling to Stephen, treating him like he was worthless, her face contorted in spite, making her appear monstrous. The cruelties she screamed deformed her entire soul.

Integrity is the key to who I am. My sister's actions are in direct opposition to my values. I growled at the audacity of her disloyal sexual affairs. And the claws of the beast inside tore at its cage, seething with fury to rip her apart for abandoning Jenny. Fucking disgrace. Then Elle's jealousy of *our* relationship stung worse than a bullet wound. I don't know how to hate her, but I want to so badly.

Naomi showed me that video, then regretted it. Her alliance is... a mystery. And L.O.V., a prosthesis of the mind? The absurdity would have been comical if it didn't feel like a direct threat to the precious, fragile love that Sarah, Vicky, and I shared.

As we neared the city's edge, the scenery began to look familiar. I was sure we were heading toward the lake. It was a sacred spot for us, because after taking them there for the first time, we confessed our love to each other. The waterfall was a concealed wonder where our love felt limitless, unchained from the bonds of society.

Sarah slightly turned her head as she started to ask me for guidance. "Is it this right coming up?"

"No, the next one, just over the hill." I leaned forward in my seat, pointing ahead. "You two really want to go to my spot?"

Vicky nodded. "Wouldn't be sitting here with Miss Pushover if I didn't." Her sharp words held more than a hint of happiness.

"Yes, it's a beautiful place, Master." Sarah beamed with her bubbly attitude, her body swaying in her seat. "Besides, being away from the city might do us some good."

The light of our love shone brightly in my heart; they knew exactly what I needed. They anticipated this need, almost as if they predicted how my day would unfold.

"Did you think today would go bad?" A smile tugged at my lips, knowing the solace retreat would infuse peace into our souls.

"Not exactly, but sis wanted to have a picnic ready for dinner," Vicky explained, as she turned in her seat to lovingly glance at me. "She started making the sandwiches after you left. So, when you texted us, we decided to do the picnic now."

"Are you ready to talk, Master?"

I decided to let them in but would wait to shock them until we were safely stopped, after traversing the winding roads to my spot.

"Watch those sharp corners, we can roll into a ditch if you're not careful," I explained before sitting back in my seat. "And we'll talk about it once we get to the waterfall."

As we hit the dirt roads, Sarah expertly navigated the curves with ease. She was a better driver than I was, at least it felt that way. Vicky just stared at me in silence, studying my mood. It seemed she was trying to guess what had happened today.

"Can we turn on the radio?" I asked, trying to distract from the odd, silent atmosphere of the car.

Vicky immediately turned around, her hand twisting the knob on the radio. Soon, the car was filled with Lords of Acid. I chuckled to myself. Maybe... I shouldn't have introduced them to this music, as they seem to be addicted to it. Just maybe.

As the fourth song on the CD started, we reached the overlook.

Beautiful as always. The rocks gently cradled in the soft embrace of the sand. Trees surrounded all sides with bare branches, readying for winter's chill. Leaves soared in the autumn breeze like magical green ships sailing in the air. The grass shimmered with a vibrant, lush green, alive with promise. The sun cast a warm, tender glow across the lake at just the right angle, causing tiny sparkles to dance on the water's surface as if echoing a hidden heartbeat. The sky was a deep, calming blue, dotted with small, drifting clouds that moved slowly, like hopes gently floating by. It felt like the warm environment I needed to escape the day's insanity.

Sarah parked the car on the ridge, and we hustled out. I grabbed the heavy cooler with the food and drinks from the trunk. I started to move around toward the front of the car.

"I got the chips and sweets," Sarah announced with excitement as she grabbed a bag. She started skipping toward Vicky.

Vicky tossed a blanket over her shoulder, then started marching ahead toward the woods. She halted, turning back to me. "This way, right?" she asked, her voice smooth with a subtle hint of affection.

"Yes, just down that path," I responded.

Most of the trees were nearly bare, the leaves having littered the ground from the change of season. Surprisingly, the cycle of life offered a refreshing tenderness. The soft crunch of leaves under our feet as we walk down the path made the space feel more hidden, less crowded than the city, more at peace than my mind and heart.

As we stepped into the clearing, the majestic waterfall roared fiercely, its mighty cry echoing through the forest. Sunlight danced on the rushing rapids, casting an explosion of color that shimmered like a living jewel. Below, the water crashed against smooth rocks, frothing into a luminous, creamy cloud that swirled with a mystic aura. The air was infused with the gentle, calming scent of autumn's tide, wrapping us in an embrace of nature's exquisite beauty. This was the peaceful environment I needed to rest my mind.

Vicky spread out the blanket on the sandy beach overlooking the waterfall. I placed the cooler on the ground just at the edge of the blanket. Sarah sat next to the cooler on the left, with her bag beside it. Vicky sat on the right, her right knee propped up.

I took my place in the middle of the blanket, my eyes drifting between my beauties and the breathtaking scene of nature before us. We moved in sync, like a ballet of understanding for each part we played. Sarah handed out the sandwiches, while Vicky tossed everyone a can of soda. I opened the bag of chips, placing it between my legs for everyone to grab a handful whenever they wanted.

We sat in silence as we ate, our souls drinking in the wonder of the world around us, connecting our silent appreciation to the unspoken words of affection between us.

"So, tell us what happened." Vicky's raspy voice was filled with concern. She perfunctorily took a bite from her sandwich.

"It's... complicated." I tried to think of how to break it all down.

"How so, Master?"

Vicky swallowed her bite. "Yeah, did you slice and dice?"

Sarah shook her head. "Vicky! Let him talk before you go all out in your gore-fest fantasies."

"It started off okay." I popped open the soda and took a sip. "Elle and I were laughing, even singing on the ride over to the park."

Vicky leaned toward me, her sandwich hanging between her fingers. "Then what happened?"

"She started yelling at Stephen, but he hadn't done anything."

"What?" Sarah's brows knitted with confusion. "That doesn't sound like Miss Elle."

Vicky flailed her sandwich around. "Yeah, that douche must have done something."

"Nope. I watched all of it. He barely said anything." I took a bite of the sandwich, chewing fast. "Just sat while she belittled him."

"Belittled him?" Sarah sank her teeth into her sandwich.

"Yeah, she talked about how he couldn't please her in bed, then screamed that he worked all the time. It was wild."

Vicky sipped a soda. "How did you feel seeing her like that?"

"Like I didn't know her. Like she wasn't my sister. But that's just the start."

Sarah stopped midbite. "There's more?"

"Yeah. Naomi—Mom—showed up."

Vicky momentarily choked on her sandwich. "My mom?"

"Yes. She told Elle to shut up, then showed me a video of Elle cheating on Stephen."

"Miss Elle is a cheater?" Sarah was crushed by the revelation. "But... but she is a relationship counselor, a savior of love."

"She cheated, admitted to me in the truck that the video was taken just days before she first met you two."

"That's sick," Vicky said, sorrowful and angry.

I felt the anger boiling over. I was unsure how much more I should tell them about Elle. I didn't want to place a wedge between my fiancées and my sister. But was it me doing it? Or was it her? They need to know, they deserve to know. Vicky said no secrets.

"Gets better, Elle also admitted that not only is she jealous of our relationship, but she doesn't actually approve of it." The hurt and betrayal ripped at my heart. "At one point, she said that our relationship was perverse, toxic, and cruel."

"That can't be," Sarah said. "We're friends. She supports us."

"Fucking bitch, lying to our faces," Vicky spat out. "If I get my hands on that two-faced slut... fucken' bash her skull in."

"Whoa, chill out!" I was angry with my sister, but still...

I put down my sandwich; my anger was overshadowed by my need to take away their pain. My hands reached out, caressing the back of their heads. My fingers lovingly threaded through their locks; each stroke was an unspoken promise—a vow always to be their strength. A tear for their pain threatened to fall, but I choked it back.

I cleared my throat. "On a positive note, we still have each other... So, fuck 'em. Fuck what the world thinks. Remember?"

I wasn't just saying words; it was the unyielding truth of our defiant love. A shield against the world's judgment, one I carried proudly. Their broken spirits, cradled in my loving touch, were the only things that mattered.

"Yeah, fuck her cheating ass and the dick she rode in on." Vicky savagely ripped a bite from the sandwich in her hand.

"Master, does she really not like us being together?"

"She dismissed my loyalty to our relationship, claiming that I'm only... How did she put it?" I tamped down the anger and betrayal. "A boy trying to get laid... or something stupid like that."

"What a spiteful bitch to say something like that to her own brother." Vicky sniffled, burying her face in my shoulder. I reached around her waist, giving her a gentle squeeze to remind her that I was there for her.

"But Master, you... We've done so much."

I pressed a tender kiss on Sarah's crown. "I know. And our love is more real than anything my sister could ever comprehend."

A moment later, I kissed Vicky's head too, a reaffirmation that their hurt was my hurt, that our joy was also always shared.

I relaxed, allowing the warmth of the sun and the gentle October breeze to settle within me as I held them close, calming them with my tenderness against their broken spirits. The golden rays beaming down bathed us in a warming sauna, deepening our connection. The soft roar of the waterfall, the revitalizing embrace of nature seemed to wash away their muffled sobs. Our bond felt even stronger, fortifying the solidarity of our relationship.

After they cried for a moment, they sat upright again. Sarah grabbed a handful of chips, crunching them loudly as she relaxed back. Vicky finished her sandwich, then stared out at the water, her blue eyes sparkling as the light reflected in them. Both of them seemed to be deep in thought. I finished my sandwich, then grabbed a fistful of chips, popping them in my mouth.

"Want to know why I was at Stephen's? And what I found out about L.O.V., today?"

"Um... yes." Vicky eagerly met my gaze.

"Yes, Master. Why did you go to Stephen's house?"

"Elle mentioned that I was in some kind of experiment, naming L.O.V. But that was all she seemed to know," I explained, falling to lie on my back. My hands folded behind my head, pillowing it against the cool blanket surface. "This freaked out Stephen and Mom. Then Mom sort of invited me to Stephen's house."

Vicky followed me to the ground, her face pillowed on my chest. "Mom did what?"

"Why did Mama Naomi ask you to go to Stephen's house?" Sarah crashed down beside me, her face nuzzling into my neck.

"Well... implied. So, after I argued with Elle, I took a cab there." I sighed, remembering the harsh final words my sister spat at me. "Anyway, Stephen has a PhD—and robot arms!"

"Like a fucking Terminator or something?" Vicky asked. "I gotta see this."

The thought of their faces when they saw the part where the T-800 exposed his arm to the Cyberdyne guy flashed in my mind.

"Yeah, like that." My arms moved around them, embracing their bodies tightly. "They mentioned Reginald, or Reggie, whom Ira had mentioned. There must be a connection."

Sarah muttered into my neck. "Reginald Payne, the owner of Sentinel, funds the school grant you found for me."

I gasped. "Of course. That makes so much sense. ITI is a subsidiary of Sentinel."

Vicky nuzzled her cheek into my chest. "Anything else?"

"The Black Forest, Naomi mentioned that at one point."

"Wasn't that an exclusive gala exhibit?" Vicky asked.

"It's a forest in Germany, where a strange phenomenon occurs," Sarah announced as she shifted to get more comfortable. "And yes, there was an exclusive exhibit at the gala that we didn't get to see."

"Phenomenon? What kind of phenomenon?"

"The plants have a mysterious black hue," Sarah said, "No one knows why. Anything that grows there turns a dark metallic color."

Vicky added, "The plants turn black. Now that's fucken weird."

"Why does it do that?"

"Don't know, just does," Sarah said, then kissed my cheek. "But there are some weird online rumors about that place."

"What kind of rumors?" I waited with anticipation.

"Weird things. Bizarre stuff," Sarah mumbled, uncertain of how to explain. "Rumors about technologies like microwaves, rockets, and jets came from what's buried there."

"Bullshit," Vicky said. "That sounds like urban legend crap."

"Don't snap at your sister, she's not your enemy," I softly scolded Vicky. "Besides, legends have some truth to them, since your mother talked about digging up technology from there."

“Sorry, sis,” Vicky apologized. “And I guess, legends can have some truth to them. Did Mom really say that?”

“Yes, she was gloating about going back there when Stephen threatened her position.”

“Makes sense,” Sarah interjected as she placed her hand on Vicky’s cheek, gently caressing her. A silent acceptance of her apology passed between them.

“How so?” Vicky ruminated as she swung an arm over me to caress Sarah’s shoulder.

“During World War Two, the Nazis occupied the area around the Black Forest.” Sarah paused to think for a moment. “There are accounts of them leading archaeological digs until the fall of Hitler.”

“Think Ira will know anything about this?”

“That creepy beatnik?” Vicky huffed. “No telling.”

“Master, we may want to find other sources for this kind of information,” Sarah said. “He hasn’t been completely forthcoming.”

“I agree.” Vicky caressed Sarah. “He’s hiding something.”

“True, he does seem to know more than he is giving us,” I agreed, before kissing both of them on the top of their heads. “But I don’t know anyone else I can trust with something like this.”

“How about your new buddy, Stephen?” Vicky’s words were dripping with sarcasm.

“To be honest, I think he was telling the truth about Elle’s behavior.” I sighed in disappointment. “But the moment I asked about L.O.V., he backpedaled. Even lying to me that it was some kind of prosthetic project.”

“So, do we hate him?” Vicky asked. “Or are we... what?”

“I don’t know how to feel about him, to be honest,” I admitted, my eyes looking off in the distance at the waterfall. “He is somehow behind L.O.V., and your mom knows a helluva lot more, too.”

“Good luck getting anything out of her,” Vicky said.

Sarah playfully hit my shoulder. “Mama Naomi isn’t that bad.”

“I didn’t say she was bad, just that she knows more about this L.O.V. crap than she is letting on.”

Vicky intervened. “Anything on MNV or this serum?”

“Nada.” I shrugged, trying to think back if anything was mentioned. “Just what we already got, that it exists and is somehow connected to L.O.V. and that woman who died in my arms.”

We fell silent again, burdened by the unspoken weight of our mystery. The delightful hum of water kissed the rocks, and the sweet melodies of birds played a tender symphony of intimacy.

The cool breeze from the water whispered softly against our skin, cooling the fires within while the sun's gentle embrace warmed us, wrapping us in a swaddling of comfort and deep connection. Our arms entwined, surrendering our minds to the meditation of our unity and love. Our souls were deeply immersed in the caress of each other and the enchantment of the natural world around us.

Collectively, we couldn't completely piece this puzzle together, but we gained a better understanding of the border as a result. And we finally had validation on some of the key players.

Vicky cleared her throat. "Anyone up for a dip?" She peeled off her shirt to expose her red bra. Sarah started undressing as well.

"What? Are we just going to jump in with our skivvies?"

"Why not?" Sarah asked, excited. Then she blew a raspberry at me. "Is Master afraid a squirrel will see his boxers?" she teased.

"If we get caught, you both get a spanking." I laughed as I tugged my shirt off. I slung it at Sarah, pelting her in the face with it.

"Promises, promises. Maybe threaten us with something we don't like." Vicky waded into the water. The light glistened on her athletic body, her underwear hugging her chiseled frame.

Sarah squatted in the water, splashing me with it. "Yeah, like making us watch the ten hours of *Shogun* again or something." Her pose perfectly accentuated her curves.

I entered the water after disrobing to my boxers. "Oh, yeah. Well, you should know that *Shogun* is a classic in cinema history."

"Classic, ha. Don't make me laugh. More like a bore fest." Vicky smirked as she briskly walked toward the waterfall.

"Boring, huh?" I chuckled as I walked toward them.

Sarah began to rush toward the waterfall as I was hot on their trail. Then she turned around midstride. "And Richard Chamberlain sucks." She snickered, sticking her tongue out at me before turning back around, moving faster toward the waterfall.

As we neared the rock wall, they vanished behind the roaring rapids, their figures shimmering through the cascading water.

When I reached their side, the roar of the waterfall enveloped us, a cleansing symphony. They stood drenched and luminous, the torrent weaving over their stunning bodies like silk. Without a moment's thought, I drew them both into my embrace, my arms circling their waists as if they were extensions of my own soul. My heart pounded, not just with longing and desire, but with a fervent gratitude for the tangible reality of our love. The power of it contrasted with the day's revelations and betrayals.

The waterfall poured down upon us, the fire of our bodies soothingly cooled by the water washing over us. My arms were neatly wrapped around them, touching their cores with my fingertips. I admired how sultry the wetness of the rain made them appear. Their eyes stared at me with a dare twinkling under the surface. I knew what they needed, how to make them feel complete.

I pressed my chest firmly, possessively, against Sarah's, feeling the cooling water sluice between us. Her head leaned down, lips meeting mine in a soft, seeking kiss. Our tongues, so familiar, began their graceful dance; the silent song of devotion echoed the waterfall's roar. The sweet wild taste of her gentleness was a balm to my ruptured spirit, purging the ugliness with a pure, unblemished connection. We soaked in the divine power of our kiss, lost to everything but each other, wrapped in the shimmering armor of the cascading water.

Soon her lips broke from mine, and instantly, a feeling of needing more crept into my heart. At that desperate moment, Sarah's hand gently nudged my face toward Vicky.

My gaze shifted to my vixen, her blue eyes glittering with an undiluted fire and a playful challenge, met mine. She moved to close the distance between us. My tongue, driven by an unrestrained hunger, stroked the line of her cheek, a prelude to the devouring kiss I craved. My mouth descended, tracing the curve of her jaw to her plump, inviting lips. Her tongue met mine instantly, igniting our eternal, ferocious feud for dominance. It was a clash of wills, a primal dance that drew us deeper into each other's souls. Both of us always craved this delicious war, fought not to win, but to play. When we finally broke away, a soft, breathless chuckle escaped her lips. A joyful sound that I felt taking root in my heart.

Under the gentle, cleansing drizzle of the showering waterfall, they turned to each other. A silent understanding passed between them. They met in a kiss that was fierce yet tender, a testament to their own deep, intertwined love. Watching them, a swell of elated emotion bloomed in my chest. It wasn't just *my* connection to each of them; it was their connection to each other. A wholeness that completed *us*. In that moment, surrounded by nature, I truly felt it: three hearts beating as one—a shared breath of life, a soul-deep unity that transcended mere words. This was the true essence of our love, vibrant and unbreakable.

As they tenderly pulled from each other's lips, they turned to me, giggling. I smiled brightly at them, happiness filling me.

The water dripped from our soaked bodies as we walked back to the blanket—the fuel of our hearts filled full in each other's presence. The three of us together were the embodiment of love made flesh. The unspoken whispers of our souls mingled into perfection. They were mine; I was theirs. And they were each other's. A perfect blend. A perfect harmony. A perfect love.

Our love reigned, absolute and unyielding, over the shattered pieces of the day. Brightly standing as the true kingdom of the world. There was nothing that could defeat us, nothing that ever would. We loved each other fiercely and truly. And there was nothing wrong with that, nothing wrong with us. It was the world that was mistaken. People like my sister, blinded by their narrow definition of love, are wrong about everything that matters. Wrong about love. Wrong about *us*.

L.O.V., whatever dark secrets it held, could never—would never—be as powerful as the incandescent bonds we shared. The life we built together and continued to build was stronger. The limitless love we shared, showering all three of us, only amplified our strength, fortifying our resolve.

A little conspiracy? It stood no chance. It couldn't break this.

It couldn't break *us*.

Chapter 17: A Favor Asked

The weekend was a whirlwind, reminding us what we were fighting for, the sacred worth it held. The music beat echoed with pulsating affection within our walls. Our bodies tangled and danced around the apartment in a celebration of contrasting emotions. They exhausted all three albums that I had of Lords of Acid.

The quiet moments eased our souls with soft tenderness. The dreamscape of the future rippled through our conversations. Our upcoming battles against this conspiracy finalized our need for each other.

We lounged on the couch, watching movie after movie. Sarah threw popcorn at me when I turned on a horror film. Vicky booed when Sarah started a romantic comedy for us to watch. And I was simply in heaven, seated between them.

At night, our hearts fell to the pleasures we shared in darkness. Soft moans filled the air with a hydration of the soul, quenching our thirst for each other. The shared releases filled the void in all of us, ensuring our three bodies were forever joined.

Monday morning shone brightly with a renewed lease on life. This new information provided us with a better understanding of the mystery. And a need to find a suitable ally that could help fend off the approaching darkness was evident.

After entering the office, Myra greeted me with a half-smile that was barely there. Her eyes darted to David before settling back on me with cool assessment, which lingered for a second too long, tracing a path starting at my eyes, down to my waist, before snapping back up. Her desk had a stack of applications the size of Mount Everest; it seemed like today was going to be a long day. I walked past on the gray carpet, gently gliding over the surface.

David waved me immediately into my office. He gossiped a bit about how Ava was convinced that I could get him hurt. I found it odd that neither one asked about the ordeal at the haunted house. However, I could sense the weight of it in their interactions. Myra kept a noticeable physical distance from me, but she gave me warm smiles. David had a chill to his words. But I left it alone and didn't address it. I figured they would soon forget about my humiliating PTSD moment and go back to normal. That was the hope, anyway.

I had Myra order three dozen coffees from Hot Joes, the cafe that Howard and I owned. This was to prepare for the interviewees who started showing up almost immediately after eight. I could at least offer them refreshments to begin with.

A girl from the coffee shop delivered them quickly. She glanced at my office and smiled at me. I assumed she knew I owned her store. I walked out and gave her a generous tip. Before I could collect a cup for myself, Myra took one straight to my office. I returned to my desk and thanked her. She lingered for a moment with her hip leaning into the doorway, and gave me a strange smile before returning to her desk.

As the day progressed, David and I conducted a parade of interviews, each seeming promising yet not quite a fit. None of the candidates appeared to fit David's ideal subordinate. After nine applicants came in, I called for a lunch break.

The hum of the fluorescent lights was starting to give me a headache. The overwhelming colognes these applicants smothered themselves in were nauseating.

I walked out of the office; my eyes were strained from reading through the applications and resumes. I turned to the row of men still waiting for an interview.

"If you're here for an interview, we'll pick up after lunch," I announced, then followed up with, "If you want a free lunch, you're welcome to stay in the office. We've ordered pizzas for everyone."

"Hell yeah," David cheered from behind me, as he followed me out of the office.

"Myra, can you please call and check on the delivery?" I asked as I walked toward the door. I needed some fresh air. "Oh, and use the petty cash when he shows up. Thank you."

Myra looked up from her desk. Her gaze met mine, holding a spark of amusement. She leaned forward, resting her elbows on the desk, as if settling into the task. Slowly, she picked up the phone. "Right on it, Kyle," she said, her fingers punching in the number. "Earlier, I also ordered a couple of Mountain Dews for my wonderful boss. Consider it a professional courtesy to keep your energy up." She offered a quick, professional smile before focusing on the receiver.

Stepping outside the office, I felt a brief relief. The scent of the city wafted into my nostrils. The sun shone down, bleaching away the shadows in the parking lot. The slight chill in the breeze felt soothing against my skin. Moving to the side of the building, my eyes snapped to the spa next door. I propped against the wall, admiring from a distance the bustling business Vicky had created.

In just under a week, Vicky had assembled a whole staff and was operating massage booths. She even had a chiropractor on the hook to set up shop in her spa. Last night she announced that she was meeting with an aromatherapy specialist this week. I was amazed at how rapidly she was growing her business. All I needed to do was provide her with a building and give her a gentle nudge. Then boom, she blossomed into an aggressive businesswoman.

My mind wandered to what Sarah was up to at this moment—probably dealing with some inner office conflict or another author complaining about royalty payout issues. Or maybe she was daydreaming about attending college and teaching kids.

They were amazing women, and sometimes I wondered how I got so lucky. I stood there for a while, daydreaming about my beauties until the pizza delivery guy showed up, hauling the feast inside. I quickly followed behind. I needed to eat something before starting the next round of interviews.

As I walked in, Myra had the Mountain Dews on her desk, beads of condensation rolling off them. She handed me a bottle, not saying a word, just giving me a polite smile. I thanked her, then moved to the pizza boxes.

I grabbed a couple of pieces and headed straight to my office to eat alone, pulling my phone out to look at pictures of Vicky and Sarah. David stayed in the lobby, conversing with the applicants. Myra was happily munching on a slice at her desk.

After lunch, the grueling interview process continued. Two more candidates came and went, with David exhibiting apparent signs of disappointment. Finally, things turned around.

In the office doorway stood a tall, energetic man, his dark brown hair short and neat. The polo shirt he wore was professional and tucked into his waistline. His khaki cargo pants were neatly ironed, and his gig line was on point. His boots were clean. And his blue eyes held a vulnerable strength that most men rarely showed. He appeared more squared away than the other applicants.

I stood, offering my hand. He immediately shook it with a strong, firm grip. He did the same with David's extended hand.

"I'm Jonathan Letterman." He had a bright smile.

"I'm Kyle Forester, the owner," I announced, plopping back in my office chair. "And that's David Novak, the service manager."

"Nice to meet you. Now, I know I don't have any HVAC experience, per se, but I've worked in construction for a few years. I am really enthusiastic to learn the mechanical side."

"What did you do in construction?" David asked, his pen already scribbling on his notepad.

"Well, just about everything. Framing, drywall, and some electrical. Sometimes, I helped with the mechanical installations."

I watched his movements; they seemed to be the most honest we had had all day. "So, by help, you mean what?" I quizzed.

"I ran the power lines, built the return base. Even ran the copper, but I didn't braze it."

"You understand what all that means?" David cut in, intrigued.

"Of course, and a bit more. High voltage and low voltage controls, the refrigeration cycle. Things like that."

As we continued with the interview, I couldn't help but feel that Jonathan was focused a lot on me. I couldn't tell if we knew each other or not. I didn't remember meeting him, but for some odd reason, his mannerisms seemed familiar.

Then, while we were discussing wages, the thought hit me. Maybe he was a clone? A product of L.O.V. possibly? I couldn't tell. But when he mentioned working on the construction of the ITI building downtown, his eyes had a brief glint of strangeness to them as if he were hinting at something.

After Jonathan left the office, David turned to me. "That's the guy. That's who I want to hire. He's fucking awesome."

"Okay, it's your call. But let's finish the interviews first. Tell him to hang around for a bit."

"Thanks, boss," David beamed, as he hugged me. I embraced him back. Myra happened to glance toward the office at the right moment, witnessing this exchange. She snickered to herself before pretending to go back to work.

We called in the next interviewee. The final two interviews yielded the same results as this morning.

After finishing the day of interviews, David found Jonathan and took him to Myra. She printed off the paperwork and sent Jonathan to an open table to fill it out. David disappeared into the bay, I assumed to smoke, since he was barely able to take a drag all day.

I stood to stretch. Then, I filed the other applications away in the file cabinet near Myra's desk. I was sure we would grow by the new year and would need more employees. Calling these guys back would be easier than trying to advertise again.

Just as I was walking back to my office, I heard a familiar voice from the door. "Forester, I thought that might be you."

My mouth agape and eyes widened from disbelief. There was no freaking way. Immediately, I did an about-face, instinctively saluting the voice out of habit, which Myra chuckled at. I quickly realized I was at attention and eased back into a normal posture.

"Lieutenant Whitman?" I asked, the shock in my voice rippling through the almost empty office space. "What brings you to Dallas?"

"Not lieutenant. Pinned my railroad tracks after Iraq," Whitman announced, his words seemed faintly guilt ridden. "Got out as a Captain last year. Now I'm an electrical engineer."

"Electrical engineer, sounds fancy for a grunt," I joked; an embarrassing snort came through my laugh.

"Shit, talk about fancy," he exclaimed, his arms waving around the office. "You own a business? Impressive."

Walking closer, I recognized the weariness of war on his face. He seemed to have aged a decade since I last saw him. I hugged him. His arms wrapped around me, both of us knowing that this hug was to reassure us that our actions in combat weren't evil.

"Damn, Kyle, you're all hugs and rainbows today." Myra snickered behind me.

We released our brotherly embrace, aware that we had spectators. I glanced over at Myra, who was typing on her computer. Then, to Jonathan, his pen scribbled fiercely on the paperwork.

"Where does an electrical engineer punch the clock?"

"At the moment, Sentinel, actually, the subsidiary, ITI."

Whitman's words hit me like a physical blow, my mind immediately registering the L.O.V. connection to ITI. Was this the universe's way of screwing with me? A man I trusted with my life walks into my shop and works for the very people I'm trying to dig up secrets on. Undoubtedly, a divine comedy at play.

"Elle's husband, well, ex-husband, is the top guy there," I said, trying to hide the shock of his employer.

“Oh, is it that Stephen cat? Yeah, he’s a real stickler and a pain in my ass. Always questioning everything in the electrical systems I design.” Whitman shook his head. “Elle... who’s that? Your girlie?”

“No, my sister. The one who always sent the entire platoon care packages.”

He snapped his fingers and smiled wide. “Yeah, with the lipstick kisses on the boxes. I remember those.”

“Yep, yep. Speaking of girlies, um... Well, I’m engaged,” I gushed, a fountain of happiness bubbled over.

“No fucken way. Don’t tell me it’s that... what’s-her-face?”

I waved my hand dismissively. “Regina? Hell no. I’d never marry that dependa tramp,” I answered. “This is gonna sound crazy, but I’m engaged to two women. Like, at the same time.”

“Wha-what? Uh, by engaged, you mean rings, wedding dresses, shit like that?” Whitman stammered, stumbling over his words. His eyes were wide, like they were trying to soak up the information.

“Unless you know any other kind of engagement. I don’t, so yeah. Rings, the whole shebang.”

“Well, congratu-fucking-lations, brother. That’s... Wait, are you sure you’re Kyle fucking Forester? The guy who was so hung up on that Regina girl? I mean fuck. Two? Jesus fucking Christ. Does your dick ever get to rest?” Whitman rambled on for a while like this.

I wondered what Vicky and Sarah would make of him. The atmosphere seemed wild by his rant about my relationship, sparking life into the dull office. And I enjoyed the celebration; it reaffirmed my thoughts that this relationship was right.

Myra couldn’t contain her laughter at his rapid-fire remarks. I heard Jonathan burst out with a snicker here and there, his eyes occasionally darting up from his paperwork to watch the animated Whitman. If he really worked for ITI—I had to ask—to cash in on that favor, breaking this happy moment with the direness of L.O.V.

I cleared my throat, interrupting his hilarious tirade. “Hey, about that favor you owe me.”

Instantly, his face fell to a serious look. “Sure, uh... whatever you need, brother,” he said in a soft voice.

“In my office. It’s more complicated than my engagement.”

All eyes were on us as we entered my office. I felt the sharpness of Myra’s judgment on me. I closed the door, then walked behind my desk, sitting in my chair.

"Please sit." I gestured to the chair in front of my desk. "You may need to, with what I've got to show you."

As he sat, I took a copy of the L.O.V. report that Ira gave me and placed it on the desk. I pushed the paper toward him. "Read this, then we'll talk."

He immediately pulled the paper closer, his eyes focusing on the report. As he read, I heard him mumble the words to himself. After he read it over twice, he looked up at me with a confused look.

"Genetically identical... This is about some illegal shit here."

"Yeah, illegal cloning experiments. Your employer is behind it."

"Okay, and how do you fit in this mess?"

"To be honest, I really don't know. I guess I may be one of those... genetically identical things."

"I trained with you, deployed with you," Whitman reminisced, his words felt like he was trying to understand something. "You were clumsy at times, but a good soldier. Maybe a little wild with that group of yours, but a good man."

"Will you help me?"

"That's not even in question. I owe you my life, so of course." Whitman's voice was full of despair. "But I don't believe this clone crap, not about you anyway."

"Here's what I need." I didn't want to ask him to get involved, just like I didn't want my beauties involved, but he was someone I could trust. "Any information on L.O.V., anything on something called MNV, and any mention of a serum, just things like that."

"You just need information?"

I sighed with hesitation. "Yeah, that's all."

"Shit, piece of cake." He chuckled as a smile grew across his face. "I'm in all their systems. Give me until the end of the week, and I'll slap a thick folder on this desk with everything you need."

"Thank you, brother." Relief washed over me. "It means a lot."

We exchanged numbers. Then he gave me a huge smile.

"You gotta let me meet these two women that tied you down. I mean two, you lucky bastard."

"Hopefully soon. They are crazy gorgeous, and so interesting."

"They have to be interesting to want a poly relationship. So do they act like sister-wives?"

I smiled. "Yeah, sorta. They were best friends before we got together. Now we're a unit, moving completely in sync."

"That's good. Invite me over sometime, maybe dinner or something." Whitman stood. "I'll see what I can dig up. In the meantime, keep your head on a swivel, brother."

"You too, Lieu... I mean, Captain." I replied, the NCO tone edged in my voice.

I watched him leave, whistling as he opened the door. The puzzle pieces would be in my hands soon. All I needed was to figure out how everything fit together. Will the picture be a terrifying apocalypse? Or just be a minor setback? Either way, we were officially REDCON-1 on the offensive. No more waiting for answers.

I glanced at the clock, and it was close to sixteen-thirty. Perhaps I should call it a day and send everyone home. Besides, I was missing my loves. I needed to feel their arms around me. Whisper to them how much I loved them, needed them, adored them—cherishing every inch of their wonder with rivers of my affection.

I stood from my desk, walking out to the lobby. David and Jonathan were huddling around Myra's desk. She was inputting the information from his paperwork into the computer.

"Hey, let's call it a day," I announced to the room. "I'll pay everyone for a full day."

"Almost done," Myra replied. "I'll stay and lock up afterward."

David smiled. "Shit, boss, ain't gotta tell me twice." He beamed as he moved away from Myra's desk. He headed toward the bay; I assumed he was going to lock the bay doors.

"You too, Jonathan," I added. "See you at eight."

Jonathan nodded. "Good night, Kyle. See you in the morning."

"Good night."

I left the office and moved through the parking lot straight to my work truck. The sun was closing in on the horizon, and in another hour and a half, it would be setting.

I sat in the truck for a moment. I watched David scurry into the van, pulling out in a rush. Ava had probably already called him. Jonathan drove away in a silver jeep. I glanced back to the shop. Myra was still seated at her desk, fingers flying over the keyboard.

I pulled out of the parking lot. I needed to get home; tell my beauties we had a new ally in our battle against the conspiracy. On the drive home, my mind was filled with excitement that we had another ally against the L.O.V. conspiracy. I had a secondary source of information. Ira couldn't monopolize the flow of information anymore. Crap, I have to meet him in the morning.

The road swiftly took me home where Sarah should already be and Vicky would soon be arriving. We'd have time to spend enjoying the night together. Maybe watch another movie or play a game.

I turned into the apartment complex. The truck slid into its spot with ease. But as soon as I parked, a figure rushed up and ripped open the passenger door, quickly jumping in, then closing the door.

My annoyance level shot through the roof as I looked over to find Elle sitting in my truck. Fuck. I really didn't need this shit.

"Jenny and I had an awkward visit." Her voice was strained.

"Elle, I don't want to see you yet," I replied flatly.

"We need to chat, Bro." She turned to me and reached for my face. But I slapped her hand away, the sharp crack echoing.

I didn't have time for her manipulation. But I also couldn't toss her aside. She was still blood. Even if those things didn't mean a damn thing to her, they still meant everything to me.

"You have five minutes. Then, I'm calling the police to have you hauled off." I pulled my phone out, placing it on the dash. The accusing blue glow filled the cab.

"Kyle, you can't treat your sister like this." Her voice was laced with hurt. I chuckled at the irony.

"You're not my sister," I stated firmly, my words cold and hard, each one a deliberate blow. "I don't know you anymore."

"I am your sister," she insisted, her eyes pleading.

"Are you here to mock my relationship, again?" My voice rose with disdain. "Or gloat about your new sexual conquests?"

"I'm sorry, Kyle." Elle averted her eyes, which were welling with tears. "I never meant to hurt you. I... I don't understand it, and maybe... Maybe I'm jealous." She choked back tears.

"I'm not the one you need to say sorry to," I retorted, my voice filled with icy daggers. My gaze was unwavering. "There's a five-year-old girl who needs to hear it more."

"I know. I'm a shitty mother." Her shoulders slumped. The tears turned her mascara into streams that flowed down her cheeks.

"More than that, you're a shitty person."

"Can we start over?" she pleaded as she reached out to me again. I swatted her away for a second time.

“Start over?” I shook my head, the pain evident in my voice. “I don’t even know who you are. That girl I was raised with, my sister, she doesn’t exist anymore.”

“I know,” she began. “I’ve a lot to work on—”

“I don’t care,” I growled, my words were a low rumble. “Look, who you are doesn’t mean a damn thing. To me, you’re a pathetic scumbag who abandons her child for some cheap sex thrills.” My words were a brutal hammer against her fragile excuses.

“I know... I... Kyle, are you going to tell Howard?” she asked, her voice trembling with fear. She nervously pulled her hand to her chest, as if to guard her heart.

“No. Hell no. I’d never tell him.”

“Good, thank you. He means a lot to me.” She sighed in relief as her hand fell limply from her bosom.

“I don’t care what it means to you. You’re not the reason I’m keeping quiet.”

“Then why?” she asked, her brows furrowed with confusion.

“He’s a good man, with a good heart.” My mind filled with the blight my sister might rip into his life. “It would hurt him to know who you really are. And I’m not going to be the one to hurt him.”

“You’re really not going to tell him?”

“I won’t have to,” I explained, my gaze fixed on her. “Because you’re going to be the one to tell him yourself.”

Her eyes widened in shock, as if I’d plunged a knife into her heart. “Kyle, I...” she sobbed. “I can’t. I won’t. I need him...”

She ranted about all the rationalizations of why she couldn’t tell Howard. My mind faded from her droning words. I had hoped she would agree and we could move past this, but she refused.

Wasn’t it just a few months ago that she was the one who told me to be honest with my girlfriends? Now she refused to explain the truth of her divorce to her new boyfriend—the hypocrisy.

Her integrity, or lack thereof, pushed me to my breaking point. Integrity was more than a word to me. Sure, I screwed up a few months ago, but continually abandoning a child and a marriage for the fleeting whim of passion, that’s a different story. I really didn’t have the patience to hear her empty lies anymore.

“Stop with the excuses!” I roared, interrupting her crocodile tears. “Mom and Dad would be disappointed if they were still alive. Get out of my truck, you’re not welcome near our happy home.”

The truck was filled with sniffles and sobs for a moment. Then she gained her bearings once more. Her body shifted toward the door. Clutching the door handle with a shaky hand, she looked back at me, her eyes not meeting mine.

"Goodbye, brother." She opened the door. Her sobs echoed in the parking lot. I watched with clenched teeth as she trudged toward her vehicle. After she got in and drove off, I sighed in relief.

I sat in the truck for a while, her acrid perfume lingering. The chill of my own disappointment in her iced the air. A frustrated pity for her rose in my chest. The way she played the helpless victim while being a hateful and calculating person gnawed at me. Her sharp manipulations were like claws and fangs, ready to rip anyone to pieces. She took no accountability for anything that went wrong with her relationship. Hell, this charade showed she never took responsibility for herself.

The way she berated me when my beauties called me Master. When I wanted to call the police on Stephen, she stopped me, saying she would go to ja... Fucking idiot, jail, the word is jail. She would go to jail. It's easy to spot now, seeing her as the abuser. I should've seen it with her volatile outbursts.

The stupid mind games she played on Howard, I bet, were her thing. Play little mind games with her affair partners. Even that cynical crap she said about love at Vicky's birthday dinner. And back in July, what did she say about Jenny? She seemed happier without Elle. My sister was just feeling guilty for abandoning her daughter.

God, so disgusting that she was abandoning Jenny, her own daughter, to play hanky-panky with some random stranger. Fucking sick bitch, only a lowlife would do such a thing. Goddammit! How could I be so blind to how selfish and pathetic my sister was? To how damn cruel she could be.

I felt my muscles tighten, my eyes sharpening. Was I getting this worked up? *Calm Sergeant. Stay calm. Just breathe. Sarah, Vicky, Sarah, Vicky, breathe in, breathe out.*

I just hoped Elle wasn't spreading her toxic cruelty to her clients; that would be a travesty. I had to stop worrying about my poisonous sister before I got myself worked up again.

Think about something positive. Kids, yeah. Vicky and Sarah would be lovingly running everywhere, trying to corral our wildlings. The satisfaction of watching the mothers of my babies happily caring for our young.

Perhaps the house would look like a war zone when the kids finished their day. Legos tossed about, dolls on trial for treason, and small cars piled up on the highway to the kitchen. Nerf darts flying across the living room, and me lying on the floor playing dead for the ninety-ninth time in a row. Or the clash of plastic swords swashbuckling between the den and the back patio. With me, in a pirate outfit, charging forward, leading my little buccaneers to the prize that awaited us. I couldn't help but feel happy at my silliness.

I figured most of them would take after me, of course, with my super wit and charming good looks. Or if I was lucky, they'd inherit their beauty and intelligence from their mothers; God knows those women are certainly more intelligent than I am.

I had to stop daydreaming about the future and make it happen. Make sure those two wonderful women felt how much I cherished them. I had to get out of the truck and go home.

I jumped out of the truck and hurried across the parking lot toward my salvation. After entering the building, I bounded up the stairs but stopped when I heard a faint whisper echo down the corridor, causing me to freeze in my tracks.

"I don't care if he's getting close; minimize the injuries to the casualty." If it weren't for the acoustics of the stairwell, I might not have heard the frail voice. "And remember, no collateral damage. We don't need bodies stacking up, drawing attention to this." The familiarity of the voice hit me: Mrs. Helderman.

"Wanda? Is that you?" I called as I started up the stairs again.

"Kyle, my boy, yes." Mrs. Helderman's voice rang loudly down the stairs. "Was talking with a nice young man who may get an apartment on our floor."

I made it to the landing. Standing at parade rest next to Mrs. Helderman was a fit, muscular man. He wore a green T-shirt and green tactical pants. His boots looked government-issued. He seemed ex-military or paramilitary. At least he looked the part. The air around him was permeated with that carbon smell of gunpowder blended with diesel fumes—reminiscent of a battlefield.

For some reason, I wasn't as calm as I typically was in the presence of a fellow servicemember. Instead, I felt something in my gut, like it was saying "beware of this guy."

I extended my hand to him. "I'm Kyle. I live next to Mrs. Helderman," I said, staring into his eyes. The brown hues were cold with the iciness of a killer.

He didn't say a word, nor did he shake my hand. He glared at Mrs. Helderman briefly, then walked past me down the stairs. My eyes followed his every movement until he was out of sight.

Live here... Yeah, here. Maybe I should keep my sidearm in the nightstand again. Just in case I need it to protect Vicky and Sarah. Protect them from a guy like that.

I turned to Mrs. Helderman. "Feeling better?" I asked, gently, trying to hide my distrust of that man.

"Yes. And don't worry. I'll come by for dinner on Wednesday." She replied, a wry smile tugging at her mouth.

"Well, the girls want to try cooking a duck for Wednesday night's meal. Not sure how that will go, but I guess we'll find out." I tittered, trying to smile.

She started walking toward her apartment. "Sounds nice. Tell those lovely girls I look forward to it."

"Good night, Wanda," I added, putting my key in the lock.

"Good night, my boy." She responded, then paused for a moment before entering her dwelling. "Be careful." Her last words were chilling, almost prophetic in delivery.

I stood there for a beat, processing the guy I met on the stairs. He seemed squared away, like special forces or something. If I must fight him, I may not win. But I will make damn sure he remembers the tussle. I just hoped Sarah and Vicky could get away fast enough if it came to that. His demeanor suggested a sharp determination. I would need the forty-five, not the nine, if I wanted to stop him.

And what Mrs. Helderman was saying, "minimal injuries"... What did that mean? What was she really doing with that guy? The old lady had become strange these past few weeks. Like a ghost of the caring elderly lady with an enthusiasm for romance that she once was. I pushed all that out of my mind, opened the door, and headed inside.

Chapter 18: Game Night

Entering our cozy home, a phantom effect surprisingly illuminated the space. Our apartment was now bathed in the glow of black lights. As I closed the door behind me, all the props, both spooky and goofy, took on a ghostly aura. This was a calming and fun sight. It felt like Halloween had come early.

Under this new lighting, I admired the decorations even more. I felt the weariness of today's encounters drift away. This was a tangible expression of our shared joy, a defiance against the outside world—a perfect reprieve from the dangers beyond these walls, a night that was perfectly us.

I figured this might be Sarah's doing. Only she could turn a simple evening into something warm and magical. I inhaled deeply, taking in the new environment and the scent of something delicious.

"Sarah, are you home?" I asked, peering through the eerie glow.

"In the kitchen," she announced with excitement. "I made finger foods for dinner."

I walked to the kitchen, my eyes still adjusting to the effect of the black light. On the counter, there were several trays of different foods: small ham chunks, salami, pepperoni, a plethora of unique cheeses, and crackers lining the outside of two trays. There was even a full veggie-and-fruit tray, complete with the small dill pickles I liked, which had been sliced into bite-sized pieces. Sarah had put a lot of thought into this.

I scooped up two crackers and some meat, quickly making a tiny sandwich. "Why are we having finger foods for dinner?" I asked, then popped the cracker sandwich into my mouth.

"Gaming night, Master, didn't Vicky call you earlier?" Sarah swiftly picked up a tray as she headed for the living room.

"Gaming night?"

"Yeah, we decided to kick your ass in *Halo*," She placed the tray on the coffee table. "I take it she never called you."

I took out my phone and opened my call list. There it was, plain as day. A missed call from noon while I was outside trying to get some fresh air. "She did call, but I missed it. Sorry, sweetie."

"Well, tonight is game time, and Master"—her voice roared with ferocity—" you're on my hit list."

"Am I?" I grabbed a tray and plopped it on the coffee table. "Sounds like a young lady is asking to be spanked fifty times over."

She walked toward me, bumping her hip into mine. "Booties are meant to be spanked, Master." She grabbed another tray. "Ooh-wee! And tonight, yours will be redder than a cherry."

Under the black light, her eyes gleamed with pure mischief. A look I knew meant nothing but trouble—and pure delight.

"Such big threats for someone bound to get stomped."

Sarah walked past me, her shoulder lightly bumping into mine. She turned to me and blew a kiss. "Uh-huh, talk is cheap."

The door sprang open. Vicky walked in, her eyes locking with mine. Then she turned to Sarah, her chin tilting up with arrogance.

"Has he been talking his shit yet?" Vicky smirked as she closed the door. "Saying we're defenseless little girls."

"Uh-huh," Sarah murmured, then her voice boomed with that sexy innocence. "Sis, he's already threatening to stomp us."

"His balls smashed under our heels is the only stomping happening tonight." Vicky laughed maniacally. "Anyone want a drink before we start?"

"Just a Mountain Dew for me, please," I replied, then playfully added, "Hold the ball stomping."

"We'll see," Vicky replied. "Sarah, want anything?"

Sarah bounced for a moment before speaking. "Besides the sweet taste of victory?" She turned to me with an evil grin, then back to Vicky. "Yeah, a Sprite, please, and thank you."

I got the last tray of food, placed it on the coffee table, then sat in the middle of the sofa. Tonight was shaping up to be fun.

But I realized I had so much to tell them. Did I really want to ruin this? The girls seemed so excited, and the fun gaming banter was already picking up. However, the frustration of not being able to place Jonathan's familiarity bore into me. Mixed with the unease of that guy in the hallway set off danger alerts. No, I needed to wait until game night died down. It was time to enjoy the competitiveness of my beauties for a bit before thrusting us all back into darkness.

"Is talk all you two can do, or are we gonna play?"

"This mothahfucka," Vicky playfully barked. "Sis, get the controllers. I'll be right there."

Sarah blew a raspberry at me, then went to gather the three controllers on the entertainment center. She bent over, placing her ample rear in my view. My head tilted in admiration of the lovely sight. She snapped up, her eyes fixed on mine.

"Like what you see?" Sarah asked, her voice soft with a slick sexiness. "Tsk, maybe if you win... but I doubt you can."

My chest tightened with a sweet ache, a mixture of desire and playful joy of being teased by my beauties. So, this was their game... yeah. I playfully clicked my teeth.

"You're just trying to discourage me, but it's not gonna work." My hand reached out to her. "How about handing over the controller, find out about your ifs..."

Sarah tossed a controller in my lap, a wicked grin slowly curling across her face, knowing she'd nailed my jewels. Then she snuggled up on the couch next to me.

Vicky brought the drinks, setting them on the coffee table. She made sure to put mine just out of reach, forcing me to lean forward. "Oops, guess you've got to stretch to get it. Sorry." She plopped down on the other side of the sofa.

Sarah reached across me to hand Vicky a controller. For a moment, they shared a knowing glance. They were plotting. But that didn't matter; they'd soon find out about my skills.

"It's fine," I responded, my fingers already manipulating the controller. "Slayer match, right?"

"Yep, now prepare to die." Sarah giggled.

"Bet your ass," Vicky added.

"What are the stakes?"

"Hmm..." Sarah purred, her index finger playfully tapping her chin. "If you win, we'll give you a special treat."

Vicky purred back. "But if we win, you give us both full-body massages. Feet, too."

"Okay." A slick smile formed on my face. "Seems like a no-lose scenario for me, but... you're on."

Inhaling a large whiff of their intoxicating perfumes mixing around me, I knew what I needed to do. Tonight they were mine.

The match started, and at first, I was on top, but soon the tide changed. Death after death, I was beginning to fall behind. They were ganging up on me, as I expected. However, it wasn't just in-game; they also employed other distraction tactics—more sexy ones.

Vicky would sometimes "accidentally" caress and pinch my thigh, her fingers sending jolting sensations up my leg, right before Sarah killed me. Sarah would lean over, pressing her cleavage against me, the soft weight tempting my resolve, blocking my view, just as Vicky found me. Then they would take turns periodically kissing me, stealing my breath, to distract me from the screen.

But I wasn't going to let their antics avert my attention from the goal. A victory over them in the game ensured I could claim what was mine from those sexy bodies. I had to be a little smarter if I wanted to be the victor.

My character ran to a cave. Hiding deep inside the rocks, I set up an explosive trap at one door and an automatic turret at the other. Just as they thought they had me, boom, double kill.

"Gosh dang it, he set traps?" Sarah bellowed as her character died. "Master thinks he's slick, but my rocket launcher can fix that."

Vicky growled as she spawned back in. "Shit, fucker had a turret at the other door. I'm getting the Needler."

"Oh, thought you two were gonna stomp my balls," I taunted. "Guess that was just shit-talking, huh?"

"Cocky bastard," Vicky smirked as she pulled the controller up, readying for battle. "See how smug you are after this."

"Rockets away!" Sarah yelled, jumping with excitement in her seat as she launched her barrage.

"Say hello to my little friend," I said with my best Scarface impression. Then I wasted both of them again with the chain gun.

"Damn, a fucking chain gun." Vicky squealed. She leaned forward, her eyes on the TV. "Get the tank, Sis, I got a plan."

"Already there," Sarah responded with desperate determination. "But I can't get to him in that cave."

"Don't worry about that, just be ready to blast his dick off."

"Ain't no dicks getting shot off today," I said, my words dancing with mirth. "Especially not mine." I finally caught up to them in terms of kill count, but a coup ensued. Vicky started rapidly killing Sarah to boost her kill count.

"Hey, Sis, stay on target," Sarah bleated, her voice hoarse from all the loud banter.

Vicky glanced over before huffing. "Hey, nothing. He's catching up. I'm just getting ahead."

"Yeah, by sacrificing me," Sarah complained, then she picked up a pillow. Before I knew it, I was smacked in the face with the feathery cushion. "Sorry, Master, that was meant for her."

I placed my controller on the table and turned to Sarah. Then I leaned in, my hands tickling her ribs. She started wiggling and laughing uncontrollably.

My hands tried to get through her defenses to attack with more tickles. "Oh, yeah? I think you were trying to cheat."

"Haha, no, haha. I swear, for her."

Then I was pelted with squishiness again, this time on the back of the head. The pillow rolled down my shoulder and onto the couch next to Sarah. I turned to Vicky. "Oh, you want some too." I reached out, tickling her next.

"Ha... damn it, sis... get him." Vicky huffed in between laughs.

As the words drifted across the sofa, I felt two hands reach up and start attacking me with tickles. This broke my assault on Vicky; she took that as her chance to join the fray and began tickling me too. I was now surrounded and entirely at their mercy, a joyous prison in their arms.

"Okay... Okay... I give... I give."

They halted their attack. We fell back on the couch, bodies tangled, hearts pounding with a shared, exhilarating warmth. Wrapped up together, laughing, it was these times of elation that I felt the pulse of us, the righteous form of our love. We were more than partners; we were an orchestrated symphony of joy and chaos.

These fun moments were like a gateway into our relationship—playfulness that encompassed our profound, deep love. Each smile, each laugh, was a wave of elation soaking through the fabric of reality, making every shared experience feel special. Every touch was a reminder of the unspoken language we secretly shared. Every kiss was that taste of life blossoming in our souls. And every word was a testament to our bond.

"That was super fun!" Sarah screamed with happiness.

Vicky sighed with relief. "Fuck yeah, it was."

I playfully pouted. "No fair, there's two of you."

Sarah patted my shoulder, then gently caressed it. "Don't be embarrassed that you got your ass beat by girls."

Vicky playfully slapped my cheek. "Yeah, don't be a pussy."

A strange feeling washed over me. I glanced at the door, not wanting any unexpected visitors to catch us off guard. I relaxed when I saw it locked. I turned to my loves, rising on the couch.

"Did someone say pussy?" I chuckled, my voice landing with a soft NCO resonance.

"Nope, you lost." Sarah snickered, then patted my crotch. "The deal was you get it tonight if you won, and you didn't."

"Better luck next time, tiger," Vicky teased. "Now get those hands ready to rub us down."

"Ah, you two cheated."

Vicky pointed at me, wagging her finger. "Rules are rules."

"Fine, you win, a massage it is," I grumbled, then my voice rose with confidence. "But I call for a rematch—with higher stakes."

"Higher stakes?" Sarah's brows furrowed.

"You'll see. Next time, that is."

"Well, Mr. Next Time, it's time to clean up your mess." Vicky chastised before pointing toward the coffee table.

I glanced over to see that two of the trays had been knocked off. The remaining food was now scattered across the floor. It must have happened during our tickle fight.

"If I remember right, I wasn't the only one who caused this."

We soon busied ourselves cleaning up the mess and putting everything away. As we did, I started talking to them about my day.

"Got a new apprentice today. His name's Jonathan."

"Ooh, that's awesome." Sarah cheered as she swept the living room floor. "Is he riding in David's van?"

"Yep, but I got this odd feeling about him," I said, the wet rag in my hand vigorously wiping down the table. "Can't place it, but I have this weird feeling I know him or something."

Vicky washed the dishes. "Maybe he has one of those faces."

"Maybe," I answered, shrugging. But I couldn't help feeling something odd lurking under his youthful demeanor. I brushed it from my mind; I had other things to talk about. Then, excitement rang in my voice. "Oh, my Lieutenant from Iraq stopped by today. He is dying to meet you both."

"Ooh, an Army buddy," Sarah bounced with glee, the broom in hand swirled around for a few spins. "What's his name?"

"Charles Whitman. He was a total badass back in the day."

"What does Whitman do for work?" Vicky asked as she glanced at me from the sink.

"Electrical engineer. But get this, he works for ITI."

Vicky placed a dish in the dry rack, then turned around. "Um... so your Army friend is working for the enemy?"

"Yeah, that's why I cashed in the favor he owed me," I said.

Vicky leaned her hip back into the cabinets, her hands planting on the counter behind her. "What did you ask him to do?"

I took a deep breath. "Gather the information we need."

"Master, do you think it's wise to mess with ITI employees?" Sarah asked, halting mid-sweep.

I moved to Sarah to caress her cheek. "You said we needed allies other than Ira; I got us one that we can trust."

"Okay, but... he can get in big trouble, Master," Sarah lamented, her green eyes sparkling with empathy.

"He's a soldier. He knows the risks."

I pulled Sarah in with a quick warm embrace, locking eyes. A silent oath burned in my retinas, ensuring I wouldn't put our allies, or us, in unnecessary danger. She smiled knowingly before gently pulling away to finish sweeping.

"Speaking of risky," Vicky interjected, shaking her head, giving a dismissive click of her teeth. "Did Elle try to talk to you today?" she questioned, propelling herself forward from the counter.

"Yeah, she jumped in my truck when I got home. But I sent her away." I paused. "Wait, how did you know?"

"She was circling our block in her SUV when I pulled in," Vicky explained, her arm wrapping around my waist. "Are you okay?"

"I'm fine. Just wish I knew what to do with her."

"Meanies like her need to be taught a lesson," Sarah said, still filled with hurt. She put the broom up.

"Maybe," I said dully. Then the protectiveness inside me spiked. "Hey, there may be a new guy on our floor. He seems dangerous. I'm gonna put a pistol in the nightstand just in case."

"Dangerous?" Vicky's arms tightened around me. "How so?"

"Don't know. Just got a feeling. Please be careful around him."

"Master, you're so protective." Sarah swooned as she strolled over to me. Her arms wrapped around my neck, embracing me.

I was enveloped in a tender warmth, basking in the power of their love. My arms gently embraced Sarah, her skin soft and silky beneath my touch, a delicate whisper of comfort and desire. This was my home, sandwiched between the affections of my wives. This was where I belonged. We were more than words could explain. The universe revolved around our love; every star twinkling in the sky was a tribute to the eternal happiness in our souls.

Then Vicky released me with a playful chuckle, giving me a gentle pop on the butt, which brought back our unique playfulness to our intimate moment.

"Time to pay up," Vicky commanded. "Now get the lotion, because we need a deep, *long* rub." She let loose a dark chuckling roar; obviously, she was enjoying this power shift.

"Mmm, Master's hands are so relaxing." Sarah released me from the embrace as she walked toward the bedroom.

"Okay, but my hands have a habit of slipping from time to time," I slyly admitted, the defiance creeping into my words.

Vicky grabbed my hand and gently caressed it. Then her blue eyes snapped to mine with a fiery stare. "Do it, and they might get gnawed off." She growled, then chomped her teeth at me.

"Alright, alright. I'll be a good boy," I vowed, but under my breath, my defiant mischief rose. "Maybe."

I walked toward the bathroom to gather the lotion and soft towels. My fingers were ready to feel their tender flesh under them. To hear their soft sighs of relief as I worked the knots from their muscles. I loved them so much, my beauties. To me, this wasn't just a massage; it was a ritual of devotion manifesting the boundless love I had for them in the physical world.

I may have lost in the game, but I had won in life. This was the real prize tonight, seeing them happy. Not some victory in a game, but the chance to shower them with my affection. Soothe away the tension of their day. Connect on a level that words could never do. A link between souls that only the three of us shared.

As I entered the bedroom, Sarah was already lying on her stomach on the bed, her clothes crumpled on the floor next to her. A sigh escaped her lips as I approached. Vicky settled beside her, turning onto her side to watch me, her gaze possessive and pleased. The backlight glow from the living room barely flowed in, casting soft, intimate shadows.

I squirted a generous droplet of lotion onto my palms, warming it between my hands. The fresh scents of lavender and vanilla floated through the air, filling the room with comfort.

The second my fingers met Sarah's skin, a soft gasp quaked from her, followed by a low moan of holy contentment. The tones were an affirmation of her trust in me, which sent a shiver down my own spine. Her tense muscles began to yield beneath my touch, surrendering to the loving caress of my hands. I moved to her shoulders, kneading gently, feeling the tension melt away under my thumbs. Every stroke was quiet cherishment, a promise of devotion, whispered through my fingertips.

Vicky shifted, nudging my arm. "Hey, soldier boy," she pleaded, her eyes staring with admiration deep into mine. "Don't forget me." Her voice was a purr, a raw invitation.

I stared lovingly back at Vicky, "Never," I said softly.

Leaning down, I kissed Sarah's temple, my lips brushing her hair. I reached across, my free hand finding Vicky's, our fingers intertwining. Passing between us was a silent acknowledgement of the three of us. Always connected, always intertwined.

This... Us, that was my reason for existing. These small moments of joy and play between us. This was the reason we had to fight the world. This happiness fueled our need to fight everything. Our united front against society, to let us be in the three-way love we shared. The struggle of piecing together L.O.V. and preventing its possible damage to this serenity. All of it.

The game was over, the world outside waited, its shadows always lurking. But in this room, under these hands, there were only my beauties. Only our love. A powerful, undeniable current, sealing me to this realm, defining me, making every challenge worth facing. And our love... That was the reason for everything.

Chapter 19: Museum Allure

Last night, I had spent two hours working to relax each of my beauties. My hands tenderly massaged the tension from their bodies. For Vicky's hour, she wanted me to focus on her hands and feet. And Sarah's was focused on her lower back and around her butt. I was sure she added the last part to tease me, and probably to gloat about my supposed loss in the game.

After the massages, we lay in bed, cuddling for the rest of the night, watching a movie. This was a fair consolation prize in the wake of my defeat. Losing was still a huge win when I was with them. I made sure to steal a kiss whenever I got the chance. Finally, we drifted off to sleep. But no dream could ever be as sweet as holding them close.

Morning came, and so was the darkness with it. I had to meet with Ira before work, and I hoped he could give me another clue to this puzzle.

As I stepped into my work truck, the lingering aromas of my beauties remained on me. Sarah's summer rain smell and Vicky's jasmine scent followed me out of the apartment. In the confined space of the truck, it was potent and intoxicatingly pleasant.

I looked over the dashboard, seeing that the day was barely breaking. The sun was starting to rise over the city, washing away the peacefulness of the night.

I wondered if Sarah, with her tender romantic tendency, would appreciate the red hues scattering across the sky. Or Vicky, with her more practical nature, would think about how a bright sky would draw in clients for the spa. Each was unique yet completed me. I pulled out, heading toward the ziggurat in the center of town. I needed to get us answers, to ensure our love was protected.

Morning traffic of businesspeople rushing to work made me think about how busy life was lately: Vicky's spa, Sarah's schooling, and the HVAC business. Those were all good, positive things.

The L.O.V. mystery, though, had the power to unravel our lives, destroy our peace. Even Elle's disgusting ways and the craziness of society affected us. Yet, even though there was still some negativity, it was somehow positive because it brought us closer together. It strengthened our bond and made our love even more potent.

The large building came into focus on the road ahead. I felt fear when I first saw it; now I know it's a lifeline—another person who, I believe, is genuinely happy to see my relationship grow.

Pulling into a parking spot near the museum, I shut off the truck. I hurried past the knights in the fountain; swords locked in that eternal battle. The sun danced across the marble surface of their armor, shimmering with the boldness of courage. Then I passed beyond the dragons standing guard. Their open maws still spilling secrets into the rivers beneath that flowed to the fountain. In the day, this place felt more majestic than ominous.

The need to bring Sarah and Vicky here during the day to witness this sight seemed a necessity. It was enchanting.

I sighed, stepping in front of the large glass doors. With a quick tug on the handle, it opened. Surprisingly, the door was not locked. I figured it was too early for the museum to open. The vast space was still an awe-inspiring sight. The dinosaur skeletons near the entrance still tugged at the child inside me, beckoning me to explore this place. To drink in its wonders.

For a moment, I was stunned at the door, thinking back to the night we were here. Vicky's childhood desire to be a mob boss, and Sarah, a princess in love with a prince. And my childhood dreams of being a pirate, blending the roguishness of Vicky's wild side and the enchantment of Sarah's romanticism. It was warming to know that we fit perfectly together in unity.

As I walked in, a voice bounced across the marble floors. "Mr. Forester?" A redhead behind the circle counter called out to me. The shock rang clearly in her voice.

"Yes, ma'am."

"Wow, you're early." She said, walking from behind the counter. "Mr. Kuolem wasn't expecting you until around lunch."

"I'm not intruding, am I? I mean, is the museum open?"

"We're always open, in a way," she muttered before her voice sprang up. "Um, Mr. Kuolem is in the archive vaults below. You're more than welcome to wait for him, if you wish."

"It's okay, I can come back."

"No, don't leave, it's not necessary," she said, looking back at the elevator. She turned to me. "Mr. Kuolem instructed us to send you straight to him whenever you arrived."

"Okay, so how do I get to the vaults?"

"He's in sub-level three, so press 'B' for ten seconds, then immediately hit '3'; that should take you to him," she instructed.

I walked across the marble floor, my steps echoing loudly in the empty museum. A quietness from the city bustle settled around me as I realized I was the only patron. The eerie silence felt like the museum was holding its breath, waiting for people to arrive so that it could return to life. This was a different feeling than when I was here with Vicky and Sarah during the gala.

As I approached the elevator, I heard the counter lady. "Yes, sir. He's on his way." I glanced behind me, the redhead was on the phone, I assumed to Ira. She gave me a lazy wave.

I entered the lift and pressed the buttons as she instructed. The elevator descended into the deeper, more hidden parts of this place. Parts that few ever saw. Halting on the sub-level, the doors opened with an ease that felt jarring. The scent of something ancient wafted in. A light electrical hum buzzed through the air like a bee.

I stepped out and was immediately greeted with rows of artifacts wrapped in plastic. Briskly moving forward, I couldn't help but admire the vast collection that was stored.

Armor from the Roman Legion. Entire Chariots made of gold. Statues lined up in perfect formation, as if readying for an inspection. This was the treasure that he kept hidden, truly a wonder to boast about. And I was only on one of the sub-levels.

I moved forward, every new treasure that I passed was like a gaze into another time, another place. If Sarah were here, I doubt she could keep her hands off the ancient artifacts. She would be like a child strolling through the toy aisle, grabbing everything in sight.

Vicky would be more subtle and refined, yet the allure of temptation would be too much to deny. She might run a hand over an item here and there, barely leaving her essence on the relics. But enough for the world to know that she had been there.

Then a funny thought popped into my head: Mob Boss Vicky running around in a stolen Roman helmet, chasing Sarah, the coy mischievous princess, through the halls. Meanwhile I, the dashing Pirate King, plotting the course to our new adventure, plunder all that we can along the way. I chuckled to myself, thinking about how our childhoods would have been if we had been together back then.

Maybe I could've taken them to prom, the three of us dominating the dance floor. Their prom dresses flowing on either side of me. I would've been twirling each one around with dazzling grace as we spun through the crowd. Our love would have shone through the high school gym. That would've been a much better night than sitting in the corner drinking punch alone. Or the secret notes in class that would pass between the three of us, plotting our next teenage tryst.

I moved beyond the relics, coming back to the present. Then I heard that distinct voice coming from a room ahead.

"Great work on the Xu Fu mummy." Ira's voice echoed down the corridor to me. "And the restoration on the immortality vials."

"The team is to thank for the restoration, sir." A sophisticated female voice responded.

As I got closer and leaned in the doorway, I saw Ira standing over a mummy; he still had that air of creepiness around him, yet for some reason, I didn't feel like he was harmful. A blonde with her hair in a ponytail and a lab coat stood beside him.

"Ira, I'm here," I announced, walking into the room.

He turned to me with a gentle wave of his hand. "Kyle, just a moment," he said, then pivoted to the woman. In a split second, he turned back with an apologetic smile. "Is it okay if I call you Kyle?"

"Yeah, it's cool."

His gaze drifted once more to the blonde. "Alexandria, your craftsmanship is commendable. Come the new year, your efforts will be honored as the museum's new exhibition." His tone was polished, with an underlying ripple of enigma. "Proceed with Temüjin's sarcophagus. It will dominate the upcoming display."

"Right away, sir," the blonde said, then walked to the back of the room.

Ira walked to me, his steps soft but quick. "Kyle, walk with me."

"Sure." I followed, my feet in step with his. "What's a Temüjin?"

"Temüjin is the birth name of Genghis Khan," Ira revealed, his voice tinged with a scholarly resonance. "He was not particularly bright, especially as he neared the end."

As we continued to walk to the elevator, my thoughts swirled. A dumb Genghis Khan? Didn't the man almost take over the world at one point? A feat like that requires a lot of brains to pull off.

"Ahem, why do you say he was not smart?"

"His sarcophagus was crafted from pure silver. Silver is a metal commonly used for vanquishing evil." Ira began, his voice tinged with intrigue. "Inscribed across the surface was an incantation—a resurrection spell, so he believed. Yet, what the alchemist concealed within was a sealing spell, a safeguard rather than a revival."

"Okay, so what does that mean?"

"It signifies, my friend, that his soul remains forever ensnared within the sarcophagus." An enigmatic smile curled at the corners of his lips. Then he waved me into the elevator. "He shall never awaken anew, nor shall his spirit ascend to the beyond."

"Oh," I replied as I stepped inside the lift. My mind raced back to the gala, remembering the scimitar with symbols carved on it. "Strange inscriptions seem to be a theme around here."

Ira followed me in, then hit the button for the tenth floor.

"Very good." He beamed. "You're quite clever."

"So, are we going to talk about L.O.V.?" I asked, shifting my weight to my right leg.

He glanced at me, his eyes holding an emotion that I didn't quite understand. "When we get to my office," he said softly.

The elevator ride was quiet and seemed eternal as my anxiety rose. I needed answers, which I wanted now, not later. I needed to find a way to protect my beauties, to protect our life together.

The elevator dinged on the tenth floor. Ira waved me out, and we both exited the lift. We briskly moved through the hallway toward that engraved door. A sense of relief started to tear away at the anxiety, knowing that behind it was another piece of this puzzle.

Upon entering, Ira immediately plopped into his office chair, heavy as a stone in water. His eyes narrowed at me, gesturing to the chair in front of his desk.

"Please, have a seat." His invitation was a strange mix of energy and dullness. "Oh, your shirt is on the coat rack by the door."

I glanced at where he motioned, my shirt hung on the rack. It was surprisingly clean, with no trace of blood, as if it were brand new. Pulling my shirt off the wooden phallus, I leisurely slung it over my shoulder. Then I walked hesitantly forward, still intimidated by the prominent angel and devil statues on either side of his desk. I eased into the chair, awaiting his explanation and a clue, if he had one.

"So, who was that girl that died in my arms?"

"Subject Four. The poor soul was never bestowed a name." Ira's voice carried a weight of sorrow. "She'd been lingering near the museum for weeks. I gather she was drawn to you after the gala."

The fact that those bastards who made her never even gave her a name pissed me off to no end. She was human, even if she was manufactured and not naturally born. She deserved every ounce of respect that we afford every living creature.

"Subject Four?" I asked, my eyes narrowing on his face. "Was she a clone like me?"

He regarded me with a measured gaze before speaking in a subdued, cryptic way. "She was a clone, like several others."

"The gala was on a Friday, but she came to me the next Monday," I explained, the pain of her death stirring in my words. "Why did she wait so long to reach out to me?"

Ira shifted slightly in his chair, a quiet sigh escaping him. "Her time was brief, though I doubt she ever imagined otherwise." His voice was tinged with muted sympathy. "The telomeres had long since become irreparable; her body was succumbing to its decay. I assume she knew her time was close."

The weight of her death came back to me in the haunting image of her disfigured face. Those lifeless eyes staring into my soul. The sores that were bursting with green pus. My heart tightened, knowing that I failed to save her.

"Is that what killed her?"

"Put simply, yes," Ira answered, his gaze dropping to his desk, a subtle shadow flickering across his face—an unspoken burden.

"How does it start? The breakdown of telomeres, I mean."

With his head bowed somberly, he softly remarked, "Initial indicators may manifest as the gradual cessation of limb functionality, reminiscent of arthritic decline."

An odd pain spread in my heart as I thought about Vicky's hand issue. I wasn't sure why, but I felt something was missing. Maybe it was them, and that's why I had come alone to speak with Ira again.

"Is that all that happens?"

"No. The respiratory system will exhibit early distress signals, accompanied by cardiovascular irregularities." He sighed with a pained groan. "The spectrum of symptoms is extensive, yet each serves as a subtle warning."

"Fuck, everything just spirals out of control... and then death!"

“Yes.” He raised his eyes, a wry smile sat on his face, poorly masking the depths of his sorrow. “But perhaps it need not be the ultimate fate for others.”

He reached into the top drawer of his desk and retrieved a manila folder. With a loud slap, it landed on the desk.

“Subject Four requested your aid to save the others.” His voice was fragile yet imbued with hope. “This is how you can.”

I opened the folder in front of me, and the immediate MNV stuck out to me. I pulled it close and read over the document.

Project: Lineage Oversight Vindication (L.O.V.)
March 10, 2012

Chief Executive Officer Payne has mandated the utilization of MNV 3.7, designated as the "Red Dragon Project" serum. MNV 3.7, variant 4, referred to as “Elixir,” has been acquired under the supervision of Sentinel. The preceding test subject for variant 4, Master Sergeant Gregory Michaels, exhibited no observable signs of aging. The telomere replication observed with the Red Dragon subject was nearly flawless in each cellular cycle.

Administering the MNV 3.7 variant 4 to all five subjects presents a significant potential to mitigate age-related deterioration, with the possibility of restoring optimal telomere replication. At this stage, it is essential to recognize that variables are unpredictable; the subjects exhibit substantial augmentation and do not fully conform to human biological parameters.

Genetic augmentation of physiological attributes has been implemented across all living subjects to establish distinct body types for individual specimens. Additional enhancements have been instituted to facilitate situational variations in performance. The subsequent augmentations are detailed below.

Subject 01 underwent genetic augmentations involving LRP5, APOE, and ACTN3. Subject 02 experienced genetic modifications to MSTN, ACTN3, and DEC2. Subject 03 was subjected to genetic augmentations targeting MSTN, SCN9A, and APOE. Subject 04 received genetic alterations in

OPN1MW, DEC2, and SCN9A. Lastly, Subject 05's genetic profile includes augmentations to MSTN, LRP5, and ACTN3.

The modifications, as mentioned above, render the side effects of MNV 3.7 indeterminate. This serum was initially formulated for administration in naturally conceived and non-augmented human subjects. Should the treatment fail, there is a potential risk of mortality among all five subjects. Proceeding with caution is advised.

Dr. Lilianna Ambrosio

I glanced up from the document. Ira was no longer in his chair. He'd moved to the window, his back to me. His gaze seemed fixed on the city below, as if in deep contemplation.

Closing the folder slowly, I cleared my throat. "So, MNV is the serum she was talking about?"

Without turning around, he spoke, a hint of sympathy in his voice. "Yes, MNV, or what was once called the Midnight Virus, is indeed the serum she desperately sought you to find." His words lingered, echoing softly against the glass before him, carrying a quiet understanding and concern.

"So, this serum can actually save the lives of us clones?"

He sighed briefly before speaking, his voice measured yet tinged with a subtle compassion. "In essence, yes. It possesses the potential to save the lives of the remaining clones."

"And how do I find this MNV serum?" A desperate question barreled through my lips.

"Dr. Ambrosio vanished days after that report was drafted. I have been unable to locate her," Ira murmured, carefully guarded.

"So, all the clones are screwed?"

"No." He turned away from the window, arms crossed, lips pursed as if contemplating something unresolved. "On the day Subject Four died, I received information that Dr. Ambrosio was attempting to sell the serum to foreign governments currently on the brink of war with the US; Iran is one known buyer."

I was stunned based on my research on her. She was passionate about cloning, even advocating for its legalization. So why did she go rogue if she believed in the concept so passionately? Why sell the MNV serum to our enemies? There was something I was missing.

"Why would she do that?"

"Greed, fear, and a host of other motives—it's impossible to pinpoint her exact reasoning," Ira grumbled. "All I can confirm is that her son has just beaten a rare form of terminal cancer. That's all I know, and frankly, her motives are of no concern."

"Okay."

"MNV was designed to enhance human capabilities," Ira explained, his arms uncrossing, a hint of anger flickering in his voice. "Or in layman's terms, manufacture super soldiers."

My mind flashed with the fables of the Red Dragons while I was in the Army. I thought it was just bedtime stories for Drill Sergeants to tell young Privates, but it seemed that my thoughts about legends holding some truth rang true. This memo proved their existence.

"Okay, exactly how does it do that?"

"While not an expert in molecular biology, my understanding hints that it operates as an mRNA-based agent," he said with a composed yet tense demeanor.

"Meaning?"

"It is the reprogramming of an individual's inherent physical and cognitive faculties to approach the apex of human potential," he explained with an expression of exasperation. "Fundamentally, it employs a genetic modulator that refines specific phenotypic traits. Or, as I previously mentioned, manufactures super soldiers."

My mind buzzed as I tried to understand. Then that online rumor about the Black Forest came crashing into my mind like a 747. "Is this connected to the Black Forest?"

Ira regarded me with a proud smile. He returned to his seat. "What do you know of the Black Forest?" he inquired, his eyes shimmering with admiration as a veiled smile played on his lips.

"Not much, just that it is said ancient technologies are dug up from there. Then they get passed off as modern inventions."

He clapped enthusiastically. "Excellent job!" His demeanor shifted to one of lively excitement that I hadn't heard from him before. "It is also rumored to be a mystic place, a site of immense power beyond human understanding."

"Is the advanced tech coming from there magical?"

"Magic and science don't necessarily orbit in two different directions." His voice was layered with a cryptic excitement. "What was once considered magic has now been revealed as science."

"So, magic is science?"

He leaned forward in his chair, a serious expression illuminating his face. "Not entirely," he declared, his sentiment scholarly yet charged with energy. "There are mysteries beyond our grasp—magic. How do we interpret that magic? Through science."

He waited to see if I were going to disregard his statement.

"Makes sense."

He gave a wry smile. "We utilize this new knowledge of the magic to advance our technologies."

My mind fell into a rhythm with his; what he was saying made sense. At least in a weird and twisted way, things started to click. The conversation I had with Howard about his AI girlfriend came to mind—his desire to bring her to life with ITI's project.

"ITI had a cloned organ project," I said, my voice flat.

He exhaled. "An elaborate facade concealing the true objective: to project an unblemished image to bureaucratic overseers."

Then I remembered Reginald Payne, Sentinel, and ITI were all connected to this "magic" he spoke of. "What part do Reginald Payne and Sentinel have in all this? Besides ITI being a subsidiary."

"Reggie... hmm," Ira grumbled, his voice seeming to fall into one of deep regret. "He was an archaeologist who worked on the Black Forest dig site. In the Eighties, he emerged as the founder of the world's leading technology conglomerate."

I could guess that those rumors Sarah mentioned were true. Where would an archaeologist get the technical skills to not only invent an array of technology but also become the world leader in innovation? He stole it from the ancient ruins. He had to have.

"Okay, so how do I save myself and the others?"

He offered an enigmatic smirk before folding his hands on his desk. "You're on the path," he said, his voice tinged with triumph. "Your Captain friend is making strides—whether he realizes it or not—toward tracking Dr. Ambrosio and the MNV serum."

"How... how do you know about Whitman?"

He observed me with a look of disappointment in his eyes. "I possess extensive knowledge, but please exercise caution; our adversaries are formidable."

"Is there anything else I should know?"

He stood from his chair once more, pivoting back to his window. "Do you love them?" he asked, his words a confused mix of longing and excitement.

"Sarah and Vicky?" For a long moment, neither of us spoke. My mind drifted to the night before, lying in their arms—a warmth spread through me. The way Sarah laughed at the movie we were watching filled me with joy. How Vicky's fingers had laced into mine was like a silent promise in the dark, it felt so loving. I smiled to myself. "Yes, with every ounce of my being."

"Good. Remember what the Jerry told you, that all living beings require love." His words were upbeat yet cryptic. "Without it, all things will die. Subject Four was unloved. Her death is a reminder of that fact."

My mouth fell agape. How did he know what a homeless person told me? I barely remembered that guy, yet Ira seemed to know the entire incident and possibly know this Jerry intimately. I wanted to speak but couldn't. Ira turned briefly and gave me a friendly wave goodbye, then turned back to the window.

I knew I would get no more answers from him. He'd given me quite a lot today. And I doubted that he was willing to share more. I stood from the chair, picking up the folder. Walking to the door, I couldn't help but feel something was off. Then it hit me. He once was in love. I turned on my heel, then halted.

"What was her name? The woman you loved?"

He let out a deep sigh. His head turned, but he didn't quite face me. "Arella," he whispered longingly.

"Tell me about her. Is that why you're helping me?"

He turned around, exposing a single tear running down his cheek. "She was a researcher in Israel. We fell in love, and for a time, it was beautiful. I wrote poetry for her every day."

His scholarly attitude seemed to fade, replaced by a human quality, as if the façade of the all-knowing curator was now that of a hopeless romantic.

"What happened?"

"Many years ago, we disagreed. She fled, taking my passion for poetry with her." Ira softly lamented, then he slowly turned back to the window. "To answer your question, seeing you with Sarah and Vicky, watching how much love the three of you share, it resurrected that piece of me."

Silence spread across the room for a moment. I felt the power of the love he had for this woman and the hollow ache of its pain in his office—a life of quiet loneliness, a fate that I once shared with him. I glanced around, and the room felt warmer for some reason, as if the soul of it was beginning to mend. I stared at the rows of books lining the shelves. This was a tomb; hidden inside was the broken, dead heart of a man, Ira. However, it now appeared to have a faint pulse. I smiled.

"Maybe Genghis Khan isn't lost forever," I said, my voice carrying that NCO resonance. I turned toward the door, my mind fixed on the love I shared with my beauties. Happy that it could inspire another to renew their view on what it means to love.

"Goodbye, friend," I said as I opened the door.

I heard his faint whisper. "Bye for now, my friend."

I walked to the elevator feeling a sense of relief that this mystery was starting to come into focus. As the doors of the lift opened, I stepped in. My hand immediately moved to press the ground floor. The doors closed, and the elevator shook for an instant as it descended. Surrounded by the glass enclosure, the air felt thick with relief. I inhaled a deep breath, clearing my lungs. The soft elevator music seemed alive with hope.

My mind was trying to wrap itself around the morning's revelations. Reginald was behind L.O.V. with his Black Forest technology. Dr. Ambrosio fled with the lifesaving serum. And Ira confirmed that Whitman was on the right trail to save my life and obtain the MNV serum.

A happy ending was possible, my happily-ever-after with Sarah and Vicky. That big house, filled with laughter and joy. The dozen or so children who would all call me Daddy. The beautiful, heart-melting smiles that would constantly be pinned on my loving wives. I clutched the file in my hand as all of that started to seem closer.

I arrived back at work, which seemed dull after I met with Ira. David, with his perpetual five o'clock shadow and years of HVAC wisdom, and I spent most of the day getting Jonathan up to speed. Jonathan showed an eagerness that was youthful but determined. We showed him different temperature-pressure charts, explaining how the ambient temperature outside can change the pressures.

David tried to explain how refrigerant is metered. However, his lesson was a confusing mess due to the use of technical jargon. So, I stepped in to simplify the subject, breaking it down into practical steps. Jonathan's brow smoothed, and a look of understanding finally crossed his face as I spoke.

Then they got a "no heat" call, Jonathan's first repair call. This left me alone in the office with Myra. She seemed to warm up to me after the office was emptied. She brought a Mountain Dew to my office. We chatted for a bit, her cold blue eyes never leaving me.

Her obsession with my military career was apparent, as almost every question she asked was related to it. A familiar tightness began to coil in my gut, the ghosts of the battlefield whisking through my mind. I felt as though she was reaching for the causes of my PTSD, but I made sure to keep the answers lighthearted. A practiced smile was plastered on my face to keep things polite.

I threw in a firefight here and there, a generic burst of adrenaline, but none of the ones that still haunt me. None that carried the screams waking me from my sleep on those bad nights. Those painful memories weren't meant for her. The only ones who got to see my pain, the only ones worthy of seeing inside my soul, were Vicky and Sarah.

Then she started to probe into my relationship. I explained some things about the dynamic, about how we live. But nothing too personal, nothing that could be used against us. Then her questions did get personal.

"Do Sarah and Vicky ever get jealous of each other?" she asked.

"Um, no. They've been like sisters long before I met them. They don't get jealous of each other."

"But, I mean, do they get jealous of each other when it comes to you? Surely the little green monster must rear its ugly head when one realizes you've"—she raised her eyebrows—"'paid more attention' to the other."

I reeled back from that. I almost didn't answer it, but I felt like I needed to protect my fiancées. "I pay equal amounts of attention to both of them."

"Come on, Kyle, you must play favorites sometimes."

My patience was wearing thin. "No, Myra, I don't."

Finally, she asked a more direct question about sex.

"How is your... um... bedroom life with *them*?" Her eyes darted to the desk right where my crotch would be, then back at me. Not only was this question unprofessional, but it felt like a violation of the trust Vicky and Sarah had in me. I felt very uncomfortable.

"Did you just ask about my sex life?"

"Come on, Kyle. A threesome is so unusual," Myra purred, her voice a low invitation. The seductive look she gave me was as if she were offering me a forbidden treat.

"The relationship feels natural for *us*." I hoped that would put an end to that uncomfortable line of questioning. But it didn't

Her gaze sharply lingered on me, assessing my reactions. "How *do* you manage two beautiful, *sexy* women? It must take everything you have to keep them happy." Her face beamed with a crooked smile. "It must get so exhausting, you *poor* thing."

"Myra, I'm not going to discuss my sex life."

She leaned closer, her eyes staring intensely into mine. "Secrets, huh?" she whispered in a conspiratorial tone, leaning over my desk. Her voice then boomed with a forced, cheerful explosion. "You must have some method of keeping those fires burning. Most men can barely keep one woman satisfied, but here you are with two." Her eyebrows arched up.

With all her movement, the smell of her perfume wafted over to me. I recoiled back in my chair, gaining distance from her advances.

"We need to put an end to this conversation." She had crossed a line, and it caught me off guard. How was I supposed to handle this?

"You must feel very..." she trailed off. "Unique. Like a hidden island. With all the focus on *them*, how does all that... *love* make *you* feel, deep down?" Her elbows propped on my desk, her face fell neatly into her palms. "Do you ever get to be the one... *taken* care of? *Your* needs met?"

"Myra, enough. We have a healthy, loving relationship. And let's leave it at that." I cleared my throat. "Now, weren't you working on an account to invoice?"

My redirection appeared to hit a nerve. Her mouth pursed, her eyes studied me, like she was attempting to reassess my resolve. Abruptly, I felt warmth on my knuckles as she placed her soft hand on mine. A sudden, cold weight fell upon me, making the atmosphere feel even more claustrophobic, suffocating. I couldn't react; I didn't know how to. I didn't want to cause a scene, but the unease she caused made me wince. My face turned away from her.

I prepared myself for the confrontation to explain that she needed to leave my office. However, luckily, the guys returned at that moment before I had to get nasty.

Myra quickly pulled her hand away, her face flushing with realization as though she had been in a trance. "Sorry, boss. I, uh..." She stood up and hurried back to her desk, glancing over her shoulder with a worried look. "Please don't hold this against me."

I let out a breath I hadn't realized I was holding. A wave of relief quickly replaced the lingering unease. My mind immediately drifted to Sarah's warm embrace and Vicky's knowing glances, a safe harbor against the whirlpool of this office chaos.

I watched her retreat to her desk, a knot in my stomach loosening. All I wanted was to be at home with my beauties, cuddled on the couch in their warm, comforting embrace. Where life made sense, where love was abundant.

Myra's actions caused conflict within me. At first, I considered firing her, but that might be too hasty a decision. A messy termination like that could lead to rumors or unfounded accusations. I'm a man and her boss. Everyone wants the villain in that type of situation to be a powerful man preying on the weak, innocent woman. The drama practically writes itself.

I could add cameras to the office to protect myself and my relationship. I'll call about that after the business account gets flowing. I also thought of not staying in the office alone. Regardless, it was clear I needed a second person in the office. Myra was great at the job, and I didn't want to lose her. I needed to hire someone else to prevent being left alone with her.

I didn't want a chance for anything to be said about infidelity. I didn't want to explain something like that to my beauties. Just the thought of seeing the lights dim in Vicky's understanding sapphires or the heartbreaking tremor that would cross Sarah's lips if they even thought I cheated would crush my heart completely. I had already vowed to myself never to betray their trust, never to betray the love we'd built.

I didn't want a false accusation to damage our beautiful life together. I told Myra that afternoon to put up an ad for a duct fabricator or metal worker. That way, I could keep another person in the office and avoid any suspension. Avoid hurting my beauties.

When I got home, the simple sight of Vicky's favorite throw draped over the sofa and the scent of Sarah's lavender candle burning grounded me to what I was fighting for. It was more than an apartment; it was our home, our sanctuary—the one we built on shared laughter and quiet understanding. I immediately explained to Vicky and Sarah everything that Ira and I had talked about.

Showing them the report on MNV, they instantly concluded that we needed to get the serum. Their voices were filled with an urgency that I had never heard from them.

Sarah explained the enhancements part of the report. The clones each received different combinations of enhanced strength, speed, agility, alertness, and intelligence. She speculated that each clone receiving only three of the five enhancements might be a precautionary measure against the aging process.

Vicky, for some reason, kept looking at her hands; her fingers softly tracing invisible lines on her palms. I figured they were bothering her again; I needed to convince her mule-headed ass to see a doctor.

I was about to explain that Whitman was on it when I received a call from him. He said that he had good news and wanted to meet me for lunch the next day.

After hanging up, I continued to explain, telling them that Whitman had good news. Their voices had an urgency I'd never heard from them. They pleaded for me to meet with Whitman.

This wasn't just about my life; it was about the future... our future. And the future of the "others," if I knew who they were, I would surely ask for their help.

The rest of the night, we sank comfortably into the sofa, cuddling together, watching a movie. Vicky curled around my bicep, and Sarah laid her head in my lap. Sarah would snort from time to time as she laughed. Vicky cackled so loudly at one part that I thought all the glass in the apartment was going to explode from her booming ruckus. The exhaustion of the day hit all three of us, so we went to bed, wrapping ourselves in each other, crashing hard.

Chapter 20: On the Trail

We woke up late, so I was buzzing through the apartment trying to get out the door. Then I made my way to the office in a flash.

Today, I accompanied David and Jonathan to perform a tune-up on six rooftop units. I worked on four of the units by myself, while David taught Jonathan on the other two. David stood over Jonathan, directing him on what needed to be done while chain-smoking. Jonathan seemed to grasp the information, his hands easily navigating the machines.

By lunch, we were all ready for a break. David just finished his thousandth cigarette, flicking it off the roof. Jonathan was packing up their tools, then slung his tool bag over his shoulder. David picked up his and let it ride at his hip. They soon approached me.

"Hey, boss, can we head out for lunch?" David asked, his breath smelling of cigarette smoke.

"Sure," I replied, then took my wallet out. "Here, take the company card, get something for both of you."

"Thanks, boss." David accepted, the smile on his face curled slightly as he placed a cigarette onto his lips.

Jonathan's eager student face fell, giving me a look of sadness. "You're not coming, Kyle?"

"No, I have a business lunch with a client," I explained.

A quick comforting thought of the coffee-laced kiss I shared with Vicky this morning and the way Sarah kissed my cheek before I rushed out the door flashed through my mind. A quiet touch of the happiness we shared before I dealt with the craziness of today.

"But next time, I'll save you from another Ava story."

"Ah, boss, I don't always talk about her," David whined, then lit his cigarette.

"Sure, you don't," I joked, my sarcasm drizzled into my words. "See you guys back at the office, unless we get a call."

"Bye, boss."

"Be safe, Kyle."

I jumped into my work truck, backed out, and left the commercial building. The road was surprisingly not that busy at noon. The drive was smooth, with no traffic to get caught in.

My foot on the pedal fell a little heavy, causing me to speed across the highway. This was probably due to my anxiousness to get the information Whitman might have. Not just about his safety, but for the peaceful, loving future I envisioned with Vicky and Sarah. Every mile closer to answers felt like a mile closer to our shared dream. Closer to the life we were building.

My hands flexed, then tightened on the steering wheel with determination. The low hum of the engine was a dissatisfying drone compared to Sarah's breathing beside me at night or Vicky's raspy laughter. I missed them already, a familiar ache tearing at me, reminding me that they were the reason for this fight.

I caught a glimpse of my ring finger as I looked at the dashboard. The thought of marrying them, wearing my wedding band openly, was a tangible reminder that they were my entire world. The reasons for everything I do. The reasons for my every breath.

When I arrived at the restaurant, I noticed that it was swamped. This was most likely Whitman's way of being clandestine. The noisy public area could conceal our conversation. And the bustling place to prevent someone from seeing the exchange of data. A brilliant play. His tactical mind was still intact.

I walked into the place. Simple cardboard Halloween decorations were strung around the host booth.

Before I could say a word, the host motioned me to follow him. The aroma of steak and burgers surrounded me as I followed behind him. He must have been informed ahead of time, because he rushed me straight to the table where Charles was seated.

Whitman looked up from the menu. "Forester, how are you?"

"Good," I said, sitting in the opposite chair. "How's it going?"

"Interestingly," he began, but was interrupted by the waitress.

"Afternoon, gentlemen. What are you boys drinking?" The waitress asked, her caramel skin shimmering in the fluorescence of the restaurant.

Whitman smiled at the waitress. "A beer for me, thank you."

"Mountain Dew no ice, please, ma'am."

"Alright, I'll get those out," she replied, her finger pointing toward the menu. "You boys might want to try the steak; it's terrific." Then she walked to the back.

He leaned forward low as his eyes looked directly into mine. For a second, the noise of the restaurant faded. The crisp picture of Sarah's worried frown and Vicky's determined gaze as I read out loud the MNV report flashed in my mind. That was my motivation: to see them smile. To remove those worried looks.

"So, I downloaded the data you needed," he said in a low voice.

"That's awesome, where is it?"

He shook his head. "Not awesome."

My eyes widened. Crap, did he get caught? "What's that mean?"

A slanted smile crossed his face. "It means ITI takes data security seriously."

"Okay, so... what happened?"

He leaned back in his seat. "I plugged the flash drive into my laptop, then ka-boom, a fried computer. And to top it off, the flash drive literally caught fire." Then he went quiet, his body stiffening as he looked over.

"Here you boys go." The waitress interjected, placing our drinks in front of us. "You ready to order? Or do you need more time?"

"No, I think we're ready," Whitman said before taking a sip of his beer. "Steak well done, and can I get a baked potato instead of mashed potatoes?"

"Yes. And do you need steak sauce, hun?"

"A1, please," he replied, handing her his menu.

"And for you?"

I handed her my menu as well. "Steak, rare, and let me get a side of mac & cheese, please."

"Okay, I'll put that right in." She beamed, giving a brief victory smile. Then she turned on her heel and headed toward the back.

I watched the waitress walk away. There seemed to be a brief pause in the conversation, allowing my thoughts to drift again.

I wondered what they were doing at that moment. Sarah was probably reading a romance novel at her desk, making her sigh in contentment. And Vicky was likely immersing herself in reviewing the spa's financial figures, trying to secure the chiropractor as a permanent fixture. I smiled faintly, a warmth spreading through me before I focused on Whitman.

I turned to him. "On the phone, you said you had good news."

"So I talked to a CIA buddy of mine," he boasted. "You know that weird guy who was taking our POWs after we bagged them."

“Yeah, if I remember right, he was a little scary,” I reminisced, my hand wrapped around my glass, my thumb rubbing on the cold surface. The screams of the insurgents he interrogated still haunted my dreams sometimes.

“Well, he found information on a scientist trying to sell high-end designer weapons to our enemies,” Whitman said, his gestures becoming even more animated. “Then he talked about the possible place MNV was being stored; apparently, MNV and the serum are the same thing.”

“Cool. Is this going anywhere?”

He gave me a serious look. “Welp, about two dozen agents descended on that place armed to the teeth.” He paused for dramatic effect.

“You gotta stop dragging out your stories. Just tell me.”

He smirked, his head playfully shaking. “Ha, but it makes this fun. I feel like a real spy.” Then his face got serious, and his tone reflected the expression. “Do you miss it?”

Do I miss it? Was he talking about the war? A phantom ache surged through the old wounds on my body. Sometimes, I guess I did. Things somehow made more sense over there. At least there was a clear bad guy, and we knew what was at stake. Civilian life was a messy labyrinth, with no clear distinction between good and evil. It was simply a matter of deciding and hoping for the best. There was no order, no discipline, and camaraderie was scarce.

“You mean war?” I asked. “Some days.” The admission felt like a betrayal of the life I was building with Vicky and Sarah.

“Me too. I think men like us are built to fight. Destined for it.” He picked up his glass and took a sip.

His words hit me hard. But then I thought about the life I was building with Sarah and Vicky. The joyful hum Sarah had when she cooked. The way Vicky would lovingly stroke my hair late at night when she thought I was asleep. The easy laughter that filled our daily life as we bantered. The passionate nights I never wanted to leave. The house we dreamed about—the kids we wanted to have.

All of that poured into my soul, reminding me that I was more than a soldier. I was a loving husband, a friend, a leader, and a business owner. And maybe one day a father.

“Maybe, but I’m trying to live peacefully.”

"Peaceful? Really?" He placed his glass back on the table. "Because this doesn't seem peaceful. Maybe the fight follows us."

Maybe the fight had followed me, something I carried back from the edge of the world. I was lost in my thoughts for a moment, thinking that perhaps that world of secrets and killing was never going to fade from my life.

Then Charles broke me out of my thoughts. "Anyway, the warehouse was empty; their raid found nothing."

I threw my hands up in defeat. "None of this is good news. Do you have anything at all?" I was getting discouraged. I needed my home to be a safe place. I needed to keep my wives safe, the two incredible women who were my entire world. I needed to protect our love. Being with them was a blessing that I never thought I was worthy of having. Yet they were there; this was more than a mere mission for me. This was my life. I was starting to feel like it was a mistake to involve Whitman.

"Impatient, are we?" He chuckled, then took a sip of his drink.

"Well, yeah. This is life-or-death stuff, bro. No offense, I'm starting to feel really let down."

Whitman caught something out of the corner of his eye and went completely silent. The waitress placed my plate down, then his. Finally, she pulled a bottle of A1 from her apron.

"Can I get you boys anything else?"

"No, ma'am, I think we're fine," I answered.

"Alright, you boys enjoy."

I smiled at her. "Thank you."

She walked away, then Charles started the conversation again.

"Hmm, well, this should change your mind." He cut into his steak, then stuffed the piece in his mouth. "I contacted a private military contractor, a guy I deployed with to Afghanistan. Turns out he already has a client paying him to track one Dr. Lillianna Ambrosio, the rogue scientist that the CIA raided the safehouse of."

"A merc is tracking this scientist... and how does that help us?"

He waved his fork at me. "You know, you're not the only one who has favors to cash in." His eyes sparkled with enjoyment.

"Just get to the point." I bleated, pulling a scoop of mac n' cheese into my mouth.

"He's close to nabbing her. When he does, I'm his first call."

I swallowed my bite. "So, what's our plan after he calls you?"

"How's your waterboarding skills? Just kidding, maybe." Whitman chuckled, then the chill hit his tone as his command voice came through. "But seriously, we conduct an interrogation and find you those MNV vials."

"Sounds squared away. Any risks involved?" I asked, my mind immediately picturing the big house, the children, the life I was building with my beauties. I couldn't risk that.

He looked up from his plate, brows furrowing with concern. "We're literally kidnapping a mad scientist who has connections to some very bad hombres."

"Fair enough,"

Loading butter onto his baked potato, he sighed. "That's not including using *creative* methods to extract information. So, it's safe to say the risk assessment is high."

I nodded, the weight of his words settling deep in my gut. High risk means high stakes for the future. For Sarah's future as a teacher and Vicky's future as a businesswoman. For the peace we needed. And for the loving life we deserve.

"I see your point," I said, looking over, seeing an elderly man watching us. So, I decided to switch to a different topic. "Oh, on a brighter note, Sarah and Vicky are excited to meet you."

"Really?" His voice was filled with surprise. "That was fast." He stuffed a forkful of baked potato into his mouth.

"Dude, we don't have secrets in our relationship."

He put his fork down, then leaned forward. "Wait, do they know what I'm doing for you?"

"Uh, yeah. Why? Is it a problem?"

"No, just weird," he said, relaxing back.

"How so?"

He shook his head; his eyes filled with a complex emotion that I couldn't understand. "Wife number one never could keep her mouth shut with Op-Sec. So, I never told her shit. Then wife number two said I never shared enough. Even though I shared more with her than I did with number one." He sighed. Then his voice rose a bit. "It's weird how you guys are so open and honest."

"Isn't that how marriage is supposed to work?" I asked, tilting my head slightly. "Complete honesty and openness?"

"That's not been my experience." He sighed, then took a bite of steak. "Women are never satisfied with the information you share."

"Can you elaborate?"

He looked at me for a long while, a storm of emotions spinning in his eyes. Then he sighed. "My first wife wanted me to be so stoic that I couldn't even cry in front of her." He was breathing heavy as if he'd run a mile. "It freaked her out if I showed any emotions at all. After I had a big PTSD breakdown, she left me, saying I wasn't man enough for her anymore."

"That's fucked up. What about wife number two?"

He shook his head, looking down at his plate. He ate two more bites before he looked up at me. "Wifey two, yeah. She allowed me to open up, sure. But later, when we argued, she weaponized my emotions against me," he said, his eyes stinging with tears. "Then she filed for divorce and ran off with our son's teacher."

"I'm so sorry, bro," I said.

He shook his head, then feigned rubbing his nose to covertly wipe away his tears. "Hey, don't go all sappy on me. I'm fine."

"Are you sure?"

"Yeah. Besides, seeing the look on your face when you talk about your girls..." He trailed off, then a genuine smile spread across his gloomy face. "It helps to see real love reflected in someone's eyes, glowing around them like a supernatural aura or something. Gives me hope that I can still find mine."

"Wanna hear something funny?" I asked, finishing my steak.

"Sure." Whitman's fork hovered over his baked potato.

"The other night, I was playing *Halo* with them, and damn did they cheat."

"Why would they cheat?"

"Well, we had a bet of sorts. Long story short, I lost and spent two hours giving them massages."

"What... No, you don't do that to me," he pleaded, biting the meat on his fork. "You've got to explain this whole story to me."

"We were on the couch; they were shit-talking the whole time."

He finished his plate, then took a sip of his drink. "Shit-talking ain't cheating. Spill it, Forester." His brow arched with intrigue.

"I'm telling you, they're vicious. I was dying left and right."

A smile broke across his face as he side-eyed me. "You were always great at *Halo*. In the barracks, you kicked everyone's ass."

I huffed, then breathed in a deep breath. I already opened this can of worms. Might as well tell him.

“Well, they kept rubbing all over me, trying to distract me from the game. Like hands-on-my-thighs, tits-in-my-face kind of way.”

He started to cackle. “You got your ass handed to you in the game and on the couch.” He shook his head, then laughed louder. “And I can guess the bet: sex for you and massages for them.”

“Yeah, that was the bet.” I chuckled, finishing my plate.

“That’s funny,” he said, starting to come down from his hysterics. “Yeah, I need to meet the two women who can kick your dick in the dirt on *Halo*.”

“Hey, whose side are you on?”

He smiled, averting his eyes, as if trying to hide from shame. “The winning one, of course.” He took out his wallet, tossing a few bills on the table. “Well, I gotta go, bro, take care. I’ll call you when we get the package.”

“Roger, just be safe, Captain.”

I paid half of the bill and left as well. Walking back to the truck, I felt somehow everything was going to be alright. Even if I had to get my hands dirty, I could still live a good life with Vicky and Sarah. The sun was glowing with hope and a subtle hint of dread.

Once inside the truck, my phone rang. I pulled my phone from my pocket and answered it.

“Kyle?” The Boston accent mixed with a southern twang bellowed through the phone. It was Leonard, Howard’s father.

“Yeah, what’s up, Leo?”

“Can ya swing by my office sometime today? I got a few things for ya to sign that need to be turned in ’fore your court date.”

“Sure, I’ll be by in a few.”

“Good, see ya soon,” Leonard said. The rustling of papers could be heard on the receiver.

“See you in a bit.”

I raced to his office. Even though L.O.V. and Dr. Ambrosio were lingering overhead with the possibility that I might need to become a soldier once more, today had a silver lining. Leonard was moving forward with legal actions, progressing my case to sue the state. Maybe I could marry both my fiancées. At least the hope was there.

Making it to his office was easy, as he was only about ten blocks from the diner that Whitman had picked. I spent about an hour at Leonard’s office. We went over the paperwork in extreme detail; he didn't miss a thing. Before I left, he asked me one more time if this was the path I wanted to take.

I turned around, my thoughts flashing to Vicky and Sarah. The way their spirits joined so perfectly with mine. The loving life we could live together in our blissful joy. Crafting a new form of romance, unconventional but healthy and full of happiness. And the beauty of the children we could have. I smiled as I told him with unequivocal certainty that I did want to take part in this legal battle.

Our love was worth it. Worth risking my reputation. Worth risking my business. Worth falling back into the darkness. Worth risking my life for. Our love was worth everything.

After exiting Leonard's office, I walked to the truck and turned on the ignition. I sat for a moment, processing everything, before sending my fiancées a text.

[Master] Wednesday 14:12
Got lots of good news :D
[Sarah] Wednesday 14:14
Awesome
[Vicky] Wednesday 14:16
Good, busy right now
Tell us when we get home
[Master] Wednesday 14:18
Okay will do
Gotta go back to work anyway
[Vicky] Wednesday 14:18
Me too, see you soldier boy :P
[Sarah] Wednesday 14:18
Be waiting, may give you a snack 😉

I chuckled, thinking about what mischief Sarah was planning. And that playful "soldier boy" from Vicky alluded to a similar attitude. I needed to be careful because they might be plotting something crazy. But for now, I had to get back to the office. I put the truck in drive and off I went.

On the way to the office, I couldn't help but fantasize about the wedding. Of course, I still had to win the case, but I was confident we could win. At least I hoped.

Once at the office, Myra was filing her nails at the front desk as I walked in. Her eyes followed me with a strange glare, which I ignored. I greeted her with a polite nod and smile, then trekked on. I heard David's voice coming from the bay, so I decided to eavesdrop for a moment.

David was in the bay, a cigarette in his mouth, with Jonathan, reviewing various electrical issues they might encounter during the upcoming winter season. I watched from the doorway, amazed at how well David explained the system failures and the methods for correcting them. After listening for a while, I decided David was doing a great job, so I took my leave, heading to my office.

The rest of the workday was dull; we didn't have a single call. I spent hours searching the web for information about arms deals, but I came up empty—there was nothing about Dr. Ambrosio or MNV. Maybe I wasn't digging in the right spots. Or perhaps the sale was hidden in the dark web? I had no clue how to access any of that.

I shoved the keyboard on my desk, frustrated by the fruitless search. I leaned back in my office chair and took a deep breath. Then I decided to pull out my phone and scroll through the pictures.

I found a selfie with the three of us in the shot. In the photo, I was in the middle with a big, cheesy smile—the kind that says "I am happy to be their man" sort of cheesy grin. Vicky was on my right, her tongue out licking my cheek, Sarah on my left kissing my other cheek. We were definitely a weird throuple... At least we had fun being weird together. We now had to fight in the courts for our right to marry. But it would be worth it in the end.

I sat for a while staring at the pictures on my phone. Seventeen hundred came quickly, and so did the end of the day. All my employees left in a rush today, most likely due to the dull afternoon. After locking up, I headed home.

On the drive back to the apartment, I passed by many houses with jack-o'-lanterns on the porch. Halloween was a week away. I was excited to share the experience with Vicky and Sarah. And I was dying to see them in their costumes. The spooky vampire and the lively elf.

Chapter 21: Halloween Triune

Opening the door, the place felt strangely empty. Mrs. Helderman wasn't here, nor were my fiancées. Instinctively, my alertness sprang to life as my muscles tightened for a fight. I felt a weird knot in my stomach as the vigil of being a soldier filled me. My heart began to pump rapidly, and my blood felt like liquid iron coursing through my veins. Considering the darker things I might be required to do to save our bliss, I couldn't help but think that there were invisible traps. The potential loss of my loves began to weigh on my mind, causing concern about what could happen.

Then the scent of pumpkin spice wafted over to me, lingering in the air with an autumnal, sensual feel. The room flickered with candlelight, casting a dim, primal dance on the walls. My eyes scanned the apartment, falling on a piece of paper taped to the bedroom door. I walked in, closing and locking the apartment entrance behind me. Moving to the bedroom, a sensation of anticipation began to replace the dread. The parchment was a letter.

> *Master, Miss Wanda canceled on us again. So, we planned something different. Take a shower first thing. Scrub every inch, you dirty boy. Clothes are in the bathroom already. No peeking. And don't try to come into the bedroom, we locked it—you naughty-naughty man. Anyways, once you're done, we'll be waiting.*
>
> *Sarah & Vicky*

Feelings of awe and wonder about what they had planned soothed my mind. My muscles relaxed as my heart slowed to a steady rhythm. Since Sarah's text hinted at a "snack," I figured they might have something up their sleeves.

I could hear heavy breathing and soft moans from the bedroom. It sounded like they were busy enjoying the pleasures of each other. I shook my head; they were already engaged in a sweet moment. At least the love was being spread around in our relationship.

Trying the doorknob, I found it was locked as the letter had promised. Too bad I couldn't watch. I wanted to break down the door, take from them what I knew was mine. But I felt that maybe I shouldn't disturb their time together. Let them enjoy each other without me.

I resigned myself to following the instructions in the letter and trudged to the bathroom, frustration etched into my face. *No. Don't pout, Sergeant. You have a mission. Clean up for this new plan.*

As the door closed, my clothes peeled off with haste, then were tossed in the hamper. Noticing a hanger on the door with an outfit I didn't recognize, I eyed it with curiosity. But I quickly turned my focus to getting clean, turning the shower water to warm.

The water splashed against the gray tiles as I stepped in. I dangled my head under the spray, feeling the soothing cascade of water wash over me. Palming the soap into a lather, I scrubbed every crevice. Washing away, at least for the time being, the dirtiness of what I might have to do to save this relationship. Once I ensured that my body was clean, I turned off the shower. Drying off quickly, I stepped out of the tub and moved to the door, inspecting the clothes they had laid out for me.

A white ruffled shirt, the kind that you would see an aristocrat from the 1700s wear, and black faux leather pants. No underwear, their usual insistence. No socks, no boots. So, this outfit was purely meant for their entertainment. Spraying myself with their favorite cologne, I smiled. The shirt slid on with ease, but I struggled to wiggle into the tight pants.

My eyes glanced into the mirror, and I admired how I looked in this outfit. It was different, but romantic—sensual, even. I looked like a buff male model on the cover of a spicy romance novel. I wondered if this was how they saw me. Romantic and strong?

I took one last glance in the mirror, admiring the style of the clothes they had chosen. Turning to the door, I opened it, and my beautiful brides-to-be immediately greeted me. The sight of them caught me off guard for a moment, forcing my heart rate to speed up to a lightning pace. All the blood in my body instantly rushed below my waistline. Jaw falling to the floor in amazement.

Vicky was seated on a chair at the dining table. Her confidence radiated in a tight black dress with a high, spiky collar, reminiscent of a vampire temptress. The fabric contoured that chiseled body, making her seem more alluring. The dark brunette veil concealed half her face, but those blue eyes stared at me with the hunger that stirred within her. She gave me a quick, seductive smile, exposing that she was wearing her vampire fangs. This sent a sensual shiver through my manhood, my throat begging to be bitten.

Sarah kneeled on the floor, her emeralds shimmering with an unspoken longing that needed my attention. Her face was a beatific smile, dizzying in its brightness, and her hair was pulled behind pointy elf ears. She wore a small black French maid outfit, complete with a small white apron. The costume clung to her curves with a delicate grip, accentuating her features with sharp dedication. The fire burned higher within my soul. I craved to touch her.

As I neared them, the intoxicating aromas of their perfumes mixed with the musk of sex filled my nostrils. Inhaling deeply, I was hit by a combination of Sarah's summer rain and Vicky's jasmine scents. The faint aroma of their wetness wafted alongside the tenderness of perfume. Smirking knowingly, my arm reached back to close the door behind me, just as I was enjoying the heavy arousal their smells invoked.

"Good evening, my lovelies," I croaked, my voice cracking. I cleared my throat, trying to regain my composure.

"Good evening, Master." Sarah purred, her eyes locking with mine. "Tonight, we have something special for you."

Vicky inched forward on the chair, her legs spreading, inviting my gaze to her exposed flower. "Special, yes, Sire. Very special."

"Hmm... interesting," I said in a smooth, dominant tone, running my hand through Sarah's red hair. "So, what brought this *special* to us?"

Vicky ran her hand down her neck, then slowly down the V of her cleavage. "We know Halloween is a week away, but..."

Sarah nuzzled my hand as I stroked her hair. "Tonight is a special Halloween just for you, Master," she said with sexy innocence.

I stared seductively at Vicky. "So how does this go?"

"Simple, I'm your sexy vampire sired by you. But..." Vicky uttered with a smooth rasp dripping with sensuality. She stood from the chair. Her hips swayed as she slowly walked toward me. "You have to earn my servitude." She playfully chastised me as her hand stroked my cheek. Then she gave me a soft slap, her eyes ripping at me with a silent dare.

"And you?" I asked, looking down at my fiery redhead.

“I’m your devoted elven maid,” Sarah whispered, her hand reaching up to caress mine. “I’m at your command. Your desires, your will, unlock my salvation.”

I had so much to tell them, so much to discuss. I wanted to explain everything about what Whitman found on the MNV serum. I needed to inform them about our court case moving forward so that we could proceed with our wedding. That our three-way marriage was starting to look like a reality, that the life we were building together was finally within reach.

Vicky noticed my awkward silence. Aggressively, she moved her hand down my body before gripping the crotch of my leather pants. Unzipping my fly, she eyed me with a predatory stare. Her fingers reached in. The heat of her digits grazed my masculine prowess. With a forceful jerk, she freed my manhood from the tight pants. Grasping it in her hand firmly, the pressure made my passion rise.

At that moment, the outside world was rendered into oblivion. I was lost to myself, knowing only them. Knowing only that we belonged together, belonged to each other. Our love, our passion for one another, poured over me like a spiritual vehemence—my desire to be with them, to feel whole with them, consumed my mind.

Vicky stroked me for a moment, then released me. Gazing down, her eyes pierced into Sarah’s. “Drink from your Master, elf slut.” The words felt like needles of challenge pricking deep into Sarah’s lust.

“His pleasure is my delight.” Sarah acknowledged the command as her face moved close, nuzzling her cheek along my shaft. “Master, may I taste you?”

I peered down at her; those large doe eyes sparkled with an endearing gaze, fueling my need for them. “Yes, my sweet,” I growled with dominance. “Taste me.”

Without hesitation, she took me completely into her warm mouth. The soft heat pulled at me, as the moistness ripped through my being. Sarah grappled the back of my thighs, her lips sliding to the base of my member.

Vicky instinctively laced her fingers in Sarah’s hair, pushing her head faster and harder. She looked at me with a twinkling passion reflected in her blue gems. Without warning, her lips crashed into mine with a sensual fire. I was automatically locked in combat with Vicky’s mouth as Sarah worked my scepter with fervent enthusiasm.

With a warrior's savagery, Vicky's tongue fought me. The fray of our eternal struggle waged on until my kingship took dominion. After I claimed my victory over Vicky, she pulled away from our kiss, squatting next to Sarah.

"Good little elf slut," Vicky teased as she softly stroked Sarah's hair. With a hard yank, she pulled the red mane. "Your Master tastes good, doesn't he?" she asked, her words felt sexually accusatory, laced with a playful jealousy.

Sarah answered with an incomprehensible murmur as she continued to work me in her mouth. Her cheeks closed in around my shaft tighter. I felt loved and admired, knowing that both regarded me with such passion and need. The playful jealousy hinted at Vicky's admiration. The solid approval from Sarah further strengthened my affection for them.

Vicky flung Sarah's hair free as she stood. Soon, her sexy vampiric body walked toward the kitchen counter, retrieving a riding crop. She turned around, her grip on the black leather tightening slowly. A loud smack rang out as she hit the riding crop in her palm. A wicked smile tugged on her beautiful face as she marched back to us.

"Now, now... little elf sluts can't go without punishment," she boasted in a sexy voice, softer than usual. She ran the crop along Sarah's face, tracing her cheekbone. "Can they?"

Sarah replied by shaking her head as she continued to work my shaft. The walls of her throat moved, sending a powerful sensation along my length. Then she lifted on her knees, exposing her rear to the air. A loud pop echoed through the room as Vicky landed the crop on the soft flesh of Sarah's bottom. Jolting forward with force onto me, Sarah took me deeper with a muffled moan vibrating along my member. This pulled me closer to the edge.

"That's enough, elf. We don't want Sire to be too tired, do we? Vicky said, then sat back down in the chair. "Now"—she spread her legs wide, exposing herself—"come pleasure me."

Sarah pulled away from my organ, drool sloshing onto the floor. I quickly felt neglected, my manhood left without attention. But I soon found joy as she slowly crawled toward Vicky. With her rear high in the air, I could see the roundness, the perfection under that short skirt. Admiring her pink, glistening wetness, my feet moved on their own, following close behind. I found joy at the sight of

Sarah's head sliding between Vicky's legs, her tongue whipping along the folds.

Walking over to Vicky, her eyes snapped to mine. She leaned her face down, on level with my rod. Then the crop made a cracking sound as Vicky gave Sarah another swat. I rubbed my neglected manhood along her vampiric lips. A plea rippled in my eyes, my desperation on full display for her. A fanged smile grew across her face as she cracked Sarah with another strike.

She looked down at Sarah, admiring the attention she was receiving. Then her eyes found mine as she looked up at me. A feigned innocence played in those sapphires. "Sire, do you need my attention too?"

I didn't say a word in response; instead, my tip pressed to her lips. She accepted my silent reply by opening her mouth wide to encompass my girth. Wrapping my hands around her head, the digits laced into her dark veil. I bucked my hips into her face, forcing her to take the entire length. A noisy gagging sound wailed from her while the cracking of the crop sounded once more.

This wasn't a raw desire binding us to the acts; it ran far deeper. A merging of three souls filling the void inside each other. A love piercing through reality with the most primal of human instincts. Vicky's blue pools stared at me as she worked my shaft, showing a powerful connection between our power dynamic. Sarah's soft moans onto Vicky filled the air with an unspoken trust. Together, we were one entity, one being.

Vicky pulled my length from her lips, a bead of saliva trailing out. She moaned loudly as Sarah's tongue worked her body into a frenzy. With each lap of the tongue, her thighs tightened around the crimson wonder between them. I stepped back, stroking as I watched the spectacle of the first orgasm from this special moment.

"Fucking elf... make... me... cahh.." Vicky screamed between breaths, her body trembling with delight. "Cum... cum... I'm..." An eruption of Vicky's fluids flooded Sarah's face. The warm liquid drenched Sarah as she happily lapped up every drop. Vicky collapsed on the chair, her body going limp for a moment.

After Sarah finished cleaning the mess, she lay down on her back, propping herself on her elbows. Her shy face peered pitifully at Vicky. "Madam vampire, this maid is in need." Her voice held a sexy plea.

Vicky turned to me; her eyes filled with a forceful desire for my permission. “Mmm, what do you think, Sire?” she asked, her words dripping with sensuality.

“I think our maid has earned a treat.” The dominance rolled smoothly from my lips. “But make sure my pretty little vampire is on all fours,” I commanded, my finger tenderly running along her cheek, “for me to use.”

“Yes, Sire,” Vicky agreed. She soon hastily acquiesced, sliding from the chair, crawling toward our elf maid.

Sarah’s feet planted on the floor, arching her knees up as Vicky entered her space. Without preamble, Vicky’s tongue began to viciously attack Sarah’s wetness, forcing her to moan in pleasure.

“Ah... Madam vampire... Right there... ah...” Sarah huffed as her hands wrapped around Vicky’s head, pulling her closer.

Watching Vicky’s ample rear sway in the air seemed like an invitation. I moved into place, kneeling behind her. My member rubbed along her soaked entrance, as her left hand shot back, pulling her cheeks open to accommodate me.

Rushing deep inside, I filled her with every inch of manhood. The heat of her walls was moist with the saturation of her previous climax. My vampiric bride squealed onto Sarah’s warmth as I started my rough treatment of her body. A cacophony of moans spilled from her lips, reverberating onto Sarah. Her muffled cries of ecstasy sent a shiver throughout Sarah’s body.

Ravaging her with every inch, my pace hastened to the tune of her pleasurable sobs. Quakes of passion fluttered between our three bodies, as we lost ourselves in the pleasures of our trinity. This was more than sex; it was a physical reaction to how deeply profound our love ran through our flesh—a cherishment of the unique desires we held for our unity.

Gripping her thighs tightly, my hips roared toward her love cove with fierce aggression. My vampire would feel the wrath of her Sire, as my raging desire burrowed deeper into her wild womb. With every thrust, she jolted forward onto our maid, forcing the pleasure to be shared equally.

Sarah’s long, silky legs twirled as they wrapped around Vicky’s head. Her dark veil was now smoothly rooted between the soft, milky thighs of her beloved maid.

Then a whimper of surrender bellowed from Sarah. "Ooh... fuck... I'm... cahh.... cumming!" she squealed as her body tensed, trembling as the sensations bombarded her. The explosion of her love spewed onto Vicky, covering her in the heavenly essence.

Vicky's face lifted from Sarah as she began to pant. Her chin dripped with the warm drink of our lover.

"Sire... fuck me... fuck me harder!" she panted, her breathing shallow as her body rapidly flew into the next orgasm. Her head turned back, eyes flicking to me with desperation. "Fucking show your dirty vampire... show me what my body is for!"

"Yes, my blood sucking vixen," I howled, the pounding of my stem raged rougher and faster. I was determined to get both of us to release.

Sarah watched us with anticipation as Vicky's body became animated. She bucked back onto me with a furious need. A sprinkle of her juices began to drizzle onto me.

"Aah!" Vicky barked with a heated rasp. "I submit, Sire!" she yelled as the power of her body rippled, submerging me in her vampiric amrita. Feeling the affection coursing, a final deep thrust landed before my potent bolts shot deep inside her.

I pulled away, my pelvis soaked with the immortal fluids of my yielded vampire temptress. Slumping back, I watched Vicky clean Sarah with the tenderness that our maid deserved. I enjoyed the loving exhibition before me, the power of love on full display.

After Vicky had cleaned Sarah, she turned to me. "Thank you, Sire," she whispered, her eyes filled with deep admiration.

"You were wonderful, my love, my sexy vampire."

Vicky sat up, hovering over Sarah, sitting her freshly seeded womb down to be cleaned. Her face turned to me. "May I?" she asked apprehensively. Her tongue flicked over her left fang, signaling her desire. I knew what she wanted: to fulfill her vampire fetish. To bite me.

"Yes, my lovely," I agreed, walking over, kneeling beside her. My head tilted, offering her my throat.

With slight hesitation, she leaned forward, her teeth clamping down onto my collarbone. A painful pleasure surged through me, feeling the fangs piercing my flesh. She suckled on the spot for a moment, drinking in my essence before releasing me.

Virile power tore through me as her vampiric desire concluded. Stirring back to life, my manhood grew strong once more. I had given her something no other ever had: the freedom to express her secret kink. Burning higher, the furnace of my joyful agony was teetering on the final act.

The resurrection of my desire was now fostering a hardened compass arrow toward my elf. I gently nudged Vicky to move, a reminder that there was one last ride on this special night. She complied with my unspoken command without complaint; a satisfied smile was deeply rooted in her face. Pulling away, a drop of blood trickled from the corner of her lips.

Moving into place between Sarah's legs, my member tenderly descended into the depths of my elven bride. Slowly sinking deeper, prayers of love filled me. I felt the soft silk of her moist cave envelop me with a tranquil embrace. The sensation was an empyrean of warmth.

The milky skin of her breasts was exposed as her hand pulled them through the top of her maid's dress. Rosy-flushed nipples stood erect in the middle of her dark, pulsing areolas. The titillating nature of her arousal tore into my sight, rendering her yearning a silent plea. Her vivid eyes scanned the room to find Vicky; her gaze reflected with spiritual longing.

"Madam, this elven servant wishes to feel the sting of your love as Master softly takes me with his affections." Sarah whimpered as her forearm cradled her breasts. Her soft pleading eyes fell back to me. "Master, I want to feel your gentle lovemaking inside me while her harsh crop punishes my bosom."

I leaned down, my lips claiming hers with warmth. Her tongue lashed out, meeting mine with the wings of angelic revelry. Remnants of Vicky's essence lingered on Sarah as I tasted her kiss. The passion of gratitude exchanged between our mouths, indulging the intimacy of our union. Her hands roamed over my back, caressing me with the wanton pining of both innocence and furious exploration.

I leaned up, breaking from her lips, focusing solely on her pleasure. "As you wish, my sweet," I whispered with an affectionate dominance.

The steady sympathetic rhythm of my hips slowly gyrated into her. Cracking through the air, the first of Vicky's strikes landed right on Sarah's erect nipple. The unique sensations enhanced her feminine power, catering to her individual need to feel my gentle love with Vicky's harsh admiration. An erotic weeping bellowed from her lips into the room, stirring the united feeling of how we completed each other.

Each deliberate sting of the crop on Sarah forced a howl to slip from her. Pestling deep within her, the loving motions drew us both closer to a final escape. She was ascending higher to her prominent place as the heart of our trio. The restraints of her often youthful, naïve spirit had been unlocked; she was innocent and wild.

Then, with a loud yelp of ecstasy, she burst her frustrations onto me in a flood of duality.

"Ah... I love... I love you both..." Sarah screamed as her body convulsed with the cascades of pleasure.

The warmth of her release pushed me to my final edge as I thrust deep inside her. Blessing her with my theurgic hot love, my sacrament flowed with divine fury, filling her altar. I groaned in pleasure, completely sealing the form of our celestial merging.

Vicky leaned down, planting a tender kiss on Sarah's forehead. "I love you both, too," she replied, as she pulled back.

"You two mean the world to me, my home," I explained, rolling from Sarah. "I love you both more than I know how to say."

Vicky soon took her place between Sarah's thighs, cleansing the mess I had made of her.

It wasn't just the physical warmth of their bodies that grounded me, but the sense of belonging. With them, the claws of the beast inside me stopped ripping to the surface. The vigilance and ire of the soldier were soothed into a tranquil calm.

They saw past all my flaws to the beating heart under my exterior, down to my soul, where I longed to be accepted, to be loved. I may not know how to say it to them, but I knew they felt it.

Once Vicky was sure that every drop was received, she retrieved her throw blanket, which was hanging from the back of the couch, and tossed it over us. She cuddled onto my left side as Sarah nestled into my right. We lay in silent revelry of our special night for a while. The unspoken connection of our souls breathed into our lungs as we enjoyed the presence of being together.

I lay there thinking about why this was so precious, something that I needed to protect at all costs. They were everything to me: my home, my future, and my life. There was nothing that could stop me from marrying these two wonderful women. Nothing at all.

Waves of emotions washed over us—our mutual comfort. Knowing we can truly be ourselves in this love. No judgments, no crazy toxicity. Just shared admiration. We could all feel cherished and vulnerable, each of us strengthening the other two.

They were the treasures I sought my entire life, more valuable than anything. We weren't just lovers; we were architects of a beautiful life. We were adventurers seeking our truth in a world of lies. Living in blissful harmony, our bountiful and fulfilling love.

I broke the silence with my curiosity. "What made you two think of this?"

Vicky rubbed my collarbone where she bit me. "Well, when Mrs. H canceled on us, sis decided we should play dress-up," she explained before gently kissing the bite mark. "And play out the kinks we wanted to try."

"So, these were the kinks you two mentioned when we bought Halloween stuff?"

"Yep," Vicky answered, then her tongue lapped at the blood on my minor puncture wounds. "It's more than a kinky thrill," she rasped, her eyes serious as they met mine. "It's... symbolic. Feeling your blood, your life mixing with mine, it makes me feel utterly, irrevocably linked to you. In ways that transcend physical touch, like our souls are truly merging."

Sarah nuzzled into me. "And I craved to be spanked like the elf maid in my book. Feeling gentle love and barbaric passion at the same time. It sounds strange, I know," she admitted, her voice soft with a hint of shyness. "But feeling your steady, loving presence, Master, while Vicky's firm hand reminded me of her strength... it... it makes me feel completely seen. Like all parts of me, the tender and the savage, are not just accepted but cherished by you two. It's a kind of surrender that feels incredibly safe and loving."

I smiled, knowing that their desires were satisfied and that we could come together to create a loving environment for each other. This was the entire point of our love, though I couldn't help but feel left out earlier.

"What were you two doing in the locked bedroom?" I inquired. The perverted affections of my question had piqued my interest in exploring how their dynamic functions when I'm not around.

Vicky softly smacked my chest. "Girl stuff." She gave a quick evasive response. Sarah simply giggled like a naughty schoolgirl caught red-handed.

"Girl stuff, hmmm..." I teased, my voice a playful murmur.

Vicky pinched my nipple with a flirtatious twist through the ruffled shirt. "Hey, Buster, you're not the only one who gets to take advantage of having two sexual partners."

Sarah lovingly purred in my ear. "Yeah," then she burst with a giggle again for a moment. "Jealous?"

"No," I firmly stated, my arms wrapping around them tightly. "Why would I be? We're a throuple." I tightened my cuddle to make sure they felt my warm, loving embrace. "That means that the three of us deserve to love the other two equally."

"A mature way to look at it, Master." Sarah sighed in a swoon.

Vicky licked my wounds once more. "Mature and sexy."

"I've been called sexy but never mature," I smirked, planting a kiss on the top of their heads.

"But it's more than equal, Master," Sarah purred, tracing circles on my chest. "It's the way we make each of us feel uniquely cherished, even as we share in our three-way relationship." She paused, sighing. "Like we bring out different beautiful parts of each other. It's a love that expands, not divides."

"And it's knowing that even when we are apart, there's this link holding us together, an unbreakable bond between us," Vicky added, her voice dropping to a low, husky whisper. "The feeling that there is always a home to come back to, a place where we're truly understood and protected no matter what."

Sarah playfully slapped my chest. "That's why we chose you. The way we understand love together is beautiful," she said.

"You texted saying there was good news." Vicky acknowledged, her thumb rubbed along the puncture wounds.

"I finalized some paperwork with Leonard today," I explained, then paused for dramatic effect. "We're proceeding with the lawsuit. Hopefully, we win and can be a married throuple by next year."

"So awesome." Sarah beamed. "Married to the two loves of my life. I can't wait."

Vicky smiled; she was more restrained, but I could see in her eyes that the joy was bouncing just as much as Sarah's. "Cool, I'm excited to see how it goes." Her voice choked on a sob of happiness.

"Our beautiful future together is getting closer." My excitement couldn't be contained.

Sarah licked my ear, then charmingly bit it gently. "Don't forget, Master, you owe us children."

"Mm-hmm," Vicky hummed before rasping. "Yeah, you gotta knock up your wives like a productive husband."

"Alright, alright." I surrendered to their demands. "But kids come after we buy a house. This apartment is already at capacity."

Vicky reached her arm across me to caress Sarah's face. "Sis, I think he's trying to gyp us out of our beautiful babies."

"Uh-huh, sounds like an excuse to me, too," Sarah responded.

"Hey, that's not fair." I protested, then sighed loudly.

"What?" Vicky smirked. She pulled her arm back from Sarah, then started to caress my collarbone again. "Can't handle your wives teaming up on you?"

"Get used to it," Sarah mocked, then she blew a raspberry at me. "Women's liberation. We can unite against you."

"Oh, yeah," I replied, my hands sliding down to tickle their ribs.

"Haha, sis, get him!" Vicky yelled. I was bombarded with tickles from all sides.

"Ah, okay. I... I give."

"Good." Sarah stuck her tongue out. "We can keep our power."

"Girl power," Vicky mocked, playfully jabbing her finger at me.

We settled back down in our embrace, the warmth of the cuddle soothing our minds. I kissed their cheeks as they cradled into me.

Sarah hummed as if remembering something. "How did your meeting with Whitman go?"

"He is close to finding the MNV serum but..." I trailed off. I didn't know how to tell them about the dangers of what I might have to do. The coldness that could consume me. It was more than the soldier rising from the grave I put him in; it was a protective fear. "It means," I said, my voice heavy with the weight of it all, "I might have to revisit my former self. And I'm afraid it could jeopardize this... us." I gestured to our entwined bodies.

"You might have to act on your soldier skills," Vicky said, her voice strained. "That's why we're here. Kyle. We've told you before, you don't have to carry this alone. Whatever battle lies ahead, we face it together. We shield each other, or as you say, be each other's sword and shield. Fuck the world, it's us versus them. Remember?"

A warm feeling washed over my heart as I felt entwined in our protective union. But I still had a leery feeling that the soldier in me might harm them if I fully opened his cage.

"Let us be your peace, Master," Sarah said. She reached across my heart, patting my chest. "You won't lose us. This... us... our home is with each other. No darkness can shade the light of our love. No monster can take the feeling of home we found with each other. Not even the monster you think that you are."

"Yeah," Vicky jumped in with a smile. "Ain't nothing getting a chance to wreck our home. We'll kick whatever ass we need to long before it's an issue." She agreed, as her fist softly crashed onto me.

"You felt this way before. Remember when we first met your sister?" Sarah soothingly asked. "You felt bad about how things went. But we saw you as a good man then, and even more so now."

"Yes, a good man," Vicky bragged, a motherly warmth spread across the air. "Remember, being formidable is not the same as being a monster."

Sarah kissed my cheek. "And we protect each other, that's what makes us stronger," she whispered, the heat of her breath a calming caress on my skin.

"That's right, we protect each other," I added. The soft NCO resonated in my words.

My stomach growled, interrupting the moment. I felt the pang of hunger. I was starved, and I was sure they were too.

"Hey, what's for dinner?"

"Crap!" Sarah yelled as she jumped up from our cuddling. "My duck!" She ran toward the oven. Vicky started to laugh hysterically.

"Damn," I said, sliding up on my elbows. "The duck has been in the oven this entire time?"

"Haha, yeah," Vicky laughed as she popped her fingers. After the popping, she let out a low, painful hiss.

"Hands still bothering you?"

"It's getting worse," Vicky lamented as she stared at her hands. Looking up, she gave a brief smile. "But nothing I can't deal with."

"Master, she really needs to see a doctor," Sarah interjected as she started carving the bird.

"I know," I replied, feeling guilty. "But she won't listen to a damn thing."

"Maybe *she* needs the crop next, Master," Sarah responded with a bubbly innocence, winking at me. Sliding a piece of duck into her mouth, she moaned with delight. "Mm-mm, the duck turned out perfectly." She announced.

"Thought you might burn the damn bird, Miss Pushover," Vicky quipped as she started to get up. She made her way to the kitchen and ripped a chunk from the duck. "Took you forever to cream those panties in the bedroom."

"At least wait for me to set the table." Sarah slapped Vicky's hand away from the duck. "And maybe Master has a better tongue, Bratty-pants." She stuck her tongue out at Vicky.

"Uh-huh," Vicky replied.

I shook my head. "Why am I lying by myself on this cold floor?"

"That's what you get," Vicky mocked, her sharp wit jabbing at me. "Doctors, what a joke."

"Well, dinner is ready," Sarah announced, moving the duck to the dining table. "That means you, too, Master. Chop, chop."

"Okay, I'm coming," I said, getting to my feet. Folding the throw blanket neatly, I draped it on the back of the couch.

"Cumming huh?" Vicky placed the silverware on the table.

"Want to test me for another round, missy?" My voice was smooth in that NCO fire. I placed three plates on the table.

"Ahem, flirting happens between the hours of..." Sarah giggled, shaking her head. "Just eat."

After cleaning up, I helped them out of their costumes. Sarah's elf ears initially gave us an issue; we had to use a lot of alcohol to loosen the cosmetic glue. But once the glue dissolved, they came right off. Vicky had to drink several cups of hot coffee to get the denture paste on her fangs to soften. And my pants... Each of them grabbed a leg and pulled it for several minutes before they budged.

Then there was the issue of bandaging Vicky's vampire marks on my collar. Even using multiple band-aids, any movement would pull them off. This was a continued joke throughout the night.

The rest of the night was filled with warm cuddles and stolen kisses. We watched a movie on the couch. Sarah laid her head in my lap, my fingers combing through her crimson locks. Vicky curled around my bicep, snuggling with warmth onto me. I intermittently kissed the top of her head as the movie picked up.

This is what I need to protect and why I wanted the MNV serum from Dr. Ambrosio—the reason I needed to live. Our moments, big or small, felt like heaven, and marrying both was more than an honor; it was like ruling our universe. I had to find a home for our life to grow, a place for our children to thrive. My purpose was to live happily with my two wives and our children—our family.

Around ten, we all felt tired and crashed into bed. In each other's arms, we felt the warmth of our love. I knew what I had to do. What was needed of me was dirty. But for them, I would fight dirty.

Chapter 22: Confidentially Unassuming Day

Thursday was dull at work; we didn't have any service calls. David stayed in the bay. I brought Jonathan into my office to watch some online training videos. Myra didn't say a word to me, but her eyes kept fixating on my office with odd gazes.

Later that evening, the apartment was filled with incense and aromatherapy gadgets that Vicky had brought home. Her idea was to test the products on us before offering them in her shop. Sarah wasn't too happy being overwhelmed by the many different scents at once, but she endured it. It got so thick and overpowering that we had to open the windows to air out the apartment, allowing the therapy fumes to escape.

To kill time, we decided to go out for dinner at Red Lobster. Afterward, we swung by Ground Zero, the gaming shop I liked. Both Vicky and Sarah insisted, seeming curious about what the place was like. Once there, Sarah mingled with the guys at the gaming tables. Vicky stayed next to me, curious about what trinkets the shop had.

Sarah happily talked with the patrons, trying to find a group I could join for a *D&D* session. She was loud and lively, almost intimidatingly so. But one guy chatted with her for a while and invited the three of us to join a session sometime. When his girlfriend arrived, Sarah instantly shifted her attention to her. They talked about romance novels nonstop, annoying the other patrons.

Vicky and I looked through the *40K* section. Her eyes shone with a dark intensity that reflected the twisted figures. She quickly bought a starter pack of Chaos Marines and a paint set for herself, saying it was a way to improve her artistic skills. But I could tell she mainly liked how the miniatures looked, monstrous and brooding.

We left the gaming store and made a final stop at the gelato café. We ordered different treats and found a booth to enjoy them. We laughed, taking turns scooping bites from each other's cups. When arguing over whose turn it was to take a scoop from mine, Sarah playfully smeared a spoonful onto Vicky's face—prompting Vicky to pinch Sarah's thigh in retaliation. They shared a gelato-filled kiss to make up. It was fun watching them play and flirt. I wasn't left out either; both shared similar ice cream kisses with me.

Once home, the overwhelming aromatherapy scents had faded. We snuggled into bed, singing random songs before falling asleep.

Well, I howled the lyrics with my terrible singing voice. Luckily, no L.O.V. craziness interrupted our time.

Friday morning broke in quickly. Vicky was already gone by the time Sarah and I woke. She wanted to set up the aromatherapy and incense displays before she opened the shop.

Once at the office, I was greeted with a seductive glance from Myra, which I immediately ignored. David and Jonathan were in the bay for most of the morning, until we received a repair call that Myra immediately dispatched to them.

Feeling that something might go wrong, since I hadn't found a fabricator to remain in the office yet, I decided to do a complimentary autumn preventative maintenance on the spa. I picked up my phone and sent a text.

[Master] Friday 10:02
Does the spa want free autumn maintenance
[Vicky] Friday 10:04
Sure
[Sarah] Friday 10:04
No fair ☹
I need maintenance too
[Master] Friday 10:05
Be there in a minute
Later I'll give you both a tune-up 😉
[Vicky] Friday 10:05
Naughty boy :D
[Sarah] Friday 10:06
ATM a foot rub would do ☹

I stuffed my phone into my pocket and walked to the entrance. I was determined to maintain my home life, protect it at all costs. I felt a sting of worry that Whitman hadn't contacted me about his contractor buddy tracking down Dr. Ambrosio or the MNV serum. But I pushed that from my mind.

"Going to do an autumn maintenance on the spa," I told Myra as I walked past her. Her eyes dimmed as she watched me leave.

"Okay," she answered, then her voice rose a pitch higher. "Want me to make an invoice?"

"Nah, I own the building. I don't see the point in charging myself for servicing my own units."

She nodded in agreement. Her face, filled with dejection, looked back at the monitor. I exited the office, went to my truck, and grabbed my tools.

When I arrived at the spa, the place was teeming with activity. Clients piled into the shop one after the other. Mostly middle-aged women, all of whom seemed content with how the staff treated them. Her business was more alive than mine. I smiled to myself, proud that my fiancée was able to blossom like this. However, the large number of people pulled at my senses and made me leery.

Quickly, I made my way to the back to avoid the crowd. I opened the inside unit and began working on it first. The roar of the people on the other side of the wall made me nervous, but I pushed through. Everything with the unit appeared in nominal condition.

I bumped through the crowd, heading outside to inspect the outdoor unit. The calm, open breeze contrasted with the densely packed feeling inside of the spa. I felt more at ease away from the ocean of bodies encapsulated inside the walls.

I was halfway through the maintenance when a shadow cast down upon me. I glanced up, spotting Vicky watching me. She was standing with her hips cocked to the side. The sunlight danced in those blue eyes, exposing a playfulness. And that chiseled face was aglow with a sense of pride.

"Miss Schein, what can I do for you?" My professionalism was laced with a sensual dominance. "More to the point, to you."

Vicky crossed her arms as she studied me for a moment, feigning a pout. "What would your fiancée say about this flirty behavior of yours?" she softly asked in that dark rasp.

She obviously wanted to role-play, or at least flirt a bit. I turned from the condensing unit, feigning ignorance. "Which one?"

A wicked smile grew across her face. "The redhead."

I averted my eyes for a moment, then stared directly into hers. "Probably tell me that I deserve a taste of what's between those muscled thighs of yours." The NCO dominance soaked through my words.

"Yeah, what about the brunette?"

I smiled a foolish grin. This was fun. I wanted to see how riled up I could get her before she lost her professional composure. With a coltish shrug, I stared deeper into her eyes. “Eh, she’s a pushover.”

Vicky grabbed my ear and tugged it with enough force to make it clear she was semi-serious. “How about now?” she asked, her rasp sounding a little annoyed but still playful.

“Okay, okay,” I conceded; the discomfort from her tugging my ear served as a reminder that she could be rough. “Not a pushover.”

She tugged a little harder. “And?” Her one-word question was a sexual challenge I was eager to meet.

I was enjoying this lively exchange. A defiant response wormed through me. “A strong, badass *bitch.*” It dripped with sarcasm.

She tugged even harder. “Bitch, huh?” Her voice was a medley of playful spite.

“Woman,” I corrected. “A strong, badass woman.”

She released my ear and patted the top of my head. “Good boy.” She walked off with a victory strut. Her hips swayed, deliberately seductive, a show of her sexual prowess. At the corner of the building, she turned around. “And by the way, Mr. Forester, my name’s soon to be Mrs. Forester.” She spat with triumph.

I shook my head, my mind narrowing in on payback. You may have won this round, but tonight... ooh, tonight you’ll feel my wrath deep inside you. Weeping with pure ecstasy as I punish that hard body of yours. Tonight, my lovely, tonight. *Get back to work, you horny oversexed bastard.*

I turned my focus back to the unit. It didn’t take long before I finished with the maintenance. There was nothing wrong with the spa’s heating system. Everything checked out fine. However, Vicky’s employees didn’t like that I sweat them out by running the heating for thirty minutes. A minor complaint that I was sure she was more than capable of handling.

As I gathered my tools, David’s van returned. Walking back to the shop slowly, I cooled the fire my dark vixen had ignited. On the surface, anyway. But my heart, my soul, was burning with desire.

The rest of the day went back to a slow, grinding halt. David came into my office, praising Jonathan for figuring out the issue with the unit. However, he said that Jonathan seemed depressed, so I pulled him into my office to speak with him.

“David said you did excellent on that service call.”

His face was filled with a weary look, his eyes drooped as if he were grieving. But beneath the sadness, there was a strange, watchful intensity in his gaze, like he was deciding what to say.

"Yeah, maybe. I just did what you guys showed me," he replied with a sullen tone, his gaze averting to the door.

"Hey, is everything alright?" I asked. Echoing off the walls, my concern reverberated in the room.

"Yeah... I mean... well... in a way, a life is on the line, I guess," he stammered, his eyes not meeting mine. "But..." he trailed off.

I leaned forward in my chair. "If you don't feel comfortable talking to me, I understand." Then I had an idea. "Why don't you take the rest of the day off? I'll pay you for the full day."

"Are you sure?" he asked, finally making eye contact with me.

"Go home and take care of yourself," I motioned to the door. "If you need more time off, we can discuss it tomorrow."

"Thank you," he said before leaving my office.

No sooner had Jonathan left than David immediately burst into the room with a look of confusion. "Boss," he said, closing the door behind him. "What's up with that guy?"

"Don't know, but I gave him the day off."

"On the drive back from the job, his girl called him," he said, glancing at the door, then back to me. "Think it's a lovers' spat?"

"Don't worry about it. He'll tell us if he wants us to know."

"Okay, boss," David replied, then he pepped up. "Good news. Ava and I have our first couples' session with Elle next week."

The sheer mention of my sister's name made my skin crawl. However, I forced a smile. "That's good, I hope the therapy works."

"Me too," David sighed, then he patted his pocket, the one he kept his cigarettes in. I knew that meant that he needed nicotine.

"Get you a smoke," I said. "We can talk more in a bit."

David left my office and headed to the bay. I turned to my computer and scrolled through the internet. I tried looking up information on the Red Dragon unit; maybe something about L.O.V. or MNV would be found there. But I got nothing.

I spun in my chair for a minute, then pulled out my phone. I scrolled through photos of my beauties and wondered what they'd look like in wedding dresses. Sarah would likely wear cowboy boots. Vicky, defiant, would put on a spiked collar to contrast the white dress she wore. Yeah, that would be them.

David eventually came back to my office to gossip about his relationship. An explosion of color burst in the room as his face lit up.

"I decided to get Ava a ring." He pulled out a small box and opened it, exposing a stunning diamond ring. "Whatta you think, boss?" Seemed he and Ava were getting along better already.

A smile tugged at my lips. I was genuinely happy for him. I was speechless for a moment, then the words came. "It's... awesome."

"You think so?" He stared at it. "I know it's not fancy but..."

"But you love her. That's all that matters."

A voice boomed from the office door. "Aww, you got her a ring," Myra cooed, her hand traveling to cover her mouth.

"Yep," David cleared his throat before announcing, "Gonna propose next week."

I stared at Myra for a moment, and with a flash, I looked at David. "Congratulations." I shook his hand. "I can't wait to be at the wedding."

"Thanks, boss." He choked up. He stared to the floor before looking back up. "I'm nervous she might turn me down."

"You can't fear rejection with something like love. Go for it," Myra said. She never took her eyes off me. An odd, knowing smile flashed across her lips.

"I'm sure she'll say yes," I added. "Nothing to worry about."

Myra gave me a wink. Then she turned to David with a beaming smile. "Some people just know when they've found the right person." She swooned, her words seemingly directed at me. "Willing to endure any pain just to hold them."

"Exactly," I righteously answered Myra's pointed words. "When you find them, you just know, and nothing can take that from you."

At that moment, I felt completely secure in my relationship with Sarah and Vicky. Myra saw the happiness on my face and gave me a venomous glare for a moment, then walked away. Sitting at her desk, she watched me with an intense gaze.

David stayed for a while longer, asking me various questions about the proposal. How to dress, what to say, when to kneel, everything he could think of. I answered them all with sincerity, giving him hope about his future with Ava.

After a while, David moseyed back to the bay, hiding there for the rest of the day. I left him alone, letting him soak in the reality that he was about to be an engaged man.

Myra walked toward my office many times but was reluctant to enter. She would retreat to her desk, only to try again a few minutes later. I wasn't sure what she wanted, but I left it alone. I didn't want to engage in anything that could be misconstrued.

Hours passed and the workday finally came to an end. David rushed out in a flash, racing home to be with Ava. Charlotte picked up Myra, and the two of them lingered in the parking lot for a while. As I was about to leave the desk, I received a phone call.

Answering it, I was immediately greeted with a familiar loud boom. "Hey, bro." Howard's voice came through the receiver.

"What's up, bro?" I asked, sitting back down.

"Something big just came up for sale. I thought ya might wanna check it out."

Intrigue settled over me. "What is it?"

"That house across from mine is up for sale."

I thought back, remembering the white stone house trimmed with black onyx. It was gorgeous, with a tower on either side. A long driveway led to a detached garage. I knew it had a huge backyard, but I wasn't sure how big it was.

My interest was piqued. "No way. How much?"

"One point five."

I sat stunned for a moment. "Thousand or million?"

He laughed. "Million, dude. One point five million."

No way I could buy that. A million and a half... Nah. That was way outside my budget. "Bro, I don't have that kinda cash."

"Ya don't need it." He huffed with exasperation. "With the HVAC business, the coffee shops, and that investment portfolio I helped ya build, ya can leverage it to get a loan."

Is it possible? He must be pulling my leg. "I can do that?"

"Yeah, I'll show ya, it's easy."

I needed to see the inside first. Make sure this was the right fit for us. "Okay, but can I do a walk-through first?"

"Sure, when ya wanna do it?"

I thought about Vicky and Sarah, mostly Sarah, since she worked a regular nine-to-five. The weekend would be best if I wanted to take both of them to see it. "Can your real estate guy set it up for Saturday?"

"No problem, just bring the girls. They might want to see it."

Then the thought entered my mind. Play this off as if Howard were buying the house. That way, if we liked it and I could afford to purchase it, I could surprise them. "Hey, can you be there too?"

"Um..." He hesitated for a moment. "Yeah, I guess. Why ya need me there?"

"Can you pretend to be the one buying it?"

The phone went silent for a second, as if he were in deep thought. "Oh, I see. Ya planning sumten'?"

"Sorta," I admitted. "If I buy it, I want to surprise the girls when I hand them the keys to our new home."

"Ya always romantic, bro. 'Em girls are spoiled." He chuckled before his pride entered his voice. "Sure, I got ya."

"I try."

"Hey, ya know what's wrong with Elle?"

My mind scurried about for a moment. I wanted to be honest and tell him everything that Elle had done. Who she truly was beneath her mask. Damn it. Play it cool for now. Feign ignorance.

"Why?"

"She's been different since the visit with Jenny."

A flash of how happy he was with her ran through my mind. The bright smile that never faded from his face when he was in her presence. I couldn't be the one to take that from him. Not when he'd just found a way to be sociable, and a person to love.

But he had to know, right? It wasn't fair to him to keep that a secret. The conflict of the matter twisted my guts into knots. I felt like I might throw up. Should I tell him or not?

No. Not yet. I had to give Elle a chance to redeem herself. Maybe she'd have the integrity to be honest with him. Have faith.

"You'll have to talk to her about it," I answered in a dull voice.

The line went quiet again. Then his voice boomed once more. "Thanks, bro. See ya on Saturday."

"Be safe, bro. And if you can't be safe—"

"Then be deadly," Howard finished saying before hanging up.

After hanging up, I left the office, ensuring it was locked and secure, finally ending up in the truck. Seconds before I started the ignition, my phone buzzed again. Without looking at the caller ID, I answered it, assuming it was Howard calling me back.

"Damn, bro, I haven't even made it out of the parking lot."

"Kyle Forester," a strange robotic voice came through the receiver. It sounded like someone using a voice changer. I glanced around the area to see if someone was watching me, but saw no one.

"Yeah. Who's this?" I shifted in my seat, feeling uneasy.

"Ambrosio and the serum are close," the voice explained. I felt a chill rip down my spine. Dr. Ambrosio and that fucking serum. How did this pipsqueak know about that?

"Don't know what you're talking about."

"If you want to live a long, peaceful life with your fiancées, you will listen," the synthesized voice coldly stated.

Was that a threat? I wasn't sure if this was a threat; it didn't feel like one. Even through the odd electronic disguise, I could hear a pang of sympathy in the voice.

"You know a lot about me, but I don't know you."

"Who I am doesn't matter; lives hang in the balance."

For a fleeting moment, I felt a weird Déjà vu, then it passed. Growing annoyed with the games, I sighed. However, that last part was genuine. Subject Four gave her life to find me, asking me to get this serum for the clones, for myself. To save *us* all.

"Okay, so now what, Mr. Nobody?" I spat with more aggression than I had intended. I detested these damn spy types. Why can't we just run into battle, shooting each other? Quicker, less messy.

"Go to 1411 Irving Boulevard," the voice articulated, "Play the hero, save them all," the voice mocked. A hard click sounded.

I sat there for a moment, my mind a swirl of thoughts. Should I go? Is this a trap? Who the fuck was that? The beeping of the line pulled me back to my senses. Turning my phone off, I reached under my seat and retrieved my 9mm. Good thing I had my concealed carry license. It might come in handy.

Stowing the sidearm into the back of my pants, I started the ignition. This was it. Do this, Sergeant Forester, save your family. Put this mystery, this nightmare, to rest.

Chapter 23: Clarity Within Grasp

Driving to 1411 Irving Boulevard, the address I received in that mysterious phone call, my mind drifted back to this morning. The sweet taste of Sarah still lingered on my lips. And a fleeting smile curled on my face as I remembered the playful exchange with Vicky at the spa. Focusing back on the mission, I ripped myself out of the warmth of those memories.

Glancing around, I was on the outskirts of town. The strangeness of isolation gouged at my senses. This area looked almost abandoned, with old, worn-down factories and warehouses that had paint peeling from their surfaces—a reminder of the golden era this district once experienced, but now long dead and buried. Passing these distraught buildings was like walking through a graveyard at night. I pulled into a structure with the tarnished number "1411" bolted into the awning.

The red brick was cracked and brittle, shadows crawling across its surface. Moss usurped the wall, as if nature itself despised this place. The windows' shattered glass lay scattered, remnants of what once was, as if time had eroded memories away. No soul had cared for this forsaken structure for years; it stood abandoned, shadows whispering of secrets best left concealed, and hope long extinguished.

The sky held a red-orange glow, signaling that it would soon be dark. With the approaching night would come a huge issue... or it would make for a tactical advantage against whatever lay ahead.

I killed the truck engine, contemplating my next move in the setting sun. Should I call the police? Yeah, bright idea, genius. Tell them what? A robot told me to come to this place in search of the "super" soldier serum. To save what? A bunch of clones that I don't know? Ridiculous. They wouldn't just laugh at me; I'd be thrown in the loony bin. No, I couldn't involve the police, not yet anyway.

But I could call Whitman. We're both soldiers, brothers from the same unit, baptized in blood, hardened by the fires of war. Yeah, he would be the perfect backup right now. I pulled my phone up and dialed his number. But disappointment washed over me when it went straight to voicemail. FUCK! I sent him a text message giving a brief explanation with the address.

Flipping through my phone's photo gallery, I thought about my beauties to bolster the courage to do this. The brightness of my redhead and the sultriness of my brunette filled me with happiness. For a moment, my mind lingered on alerting my fiancées, but I quickly dismissed the idea.

They would probably worry and try to talk me out of this. But it had to be done. Or worse, they would insist on coming, placing them in whatever danger lies ahead. I was a soldier, trained in combat. They were civilians. I knew we swore to protect each other, but I couldn't risk putting them in real danger.

My mind wandered to Subject Four, her lifeless body tearing itself apart. She deserved a name, a life. She deserved better—more than what she was given.

If her fate were to be my end, I would've been okay with that a few months ago. But now... Now, I must live. Live to see Vicky paint a dazzling masterpiece, to feel Sarah's warm embrace again. Live for the life we're building. Buy them that beautiful house. Have children with them. Grow old with them. Die as an elderly, happy man in their arms. I was going to save myself, save my relationship, and save the other clones.

Looking toward the sky, I sought a final word from the heavens. I prayed, not to a god but to the spirit of the wronged.

"I accept your dying request, Subject Four. I'll fight for you, for all of *us*. Please forgive me for taking so long."

Opening the door with a purpose, I walked toward the building. The smell of burned rubber and oil filled the air. My hand grabbed the pistol from my waistline as I rushed forward, stacking, alone, on the brick structure. Rubbing my bare ring finger, my thumb reminded me once more of why I needed to do this—my plan to marry them both.

Preparing to breach, I pulled the weapon in close to my chest as the close-quarters training kicked in. My heart beat a hole in my chest, and the blood in my veins boiled with absolute clarity. My mind, sharp and focused, was ready.

I tried the door, which was unlocked. I pulled it open, conducted a quick scan, and retreated behind the outside wall. It was clear, so I went in.

The interior reeked of mold and sewer fumes; the air was alive with darkness that made my skin crawl. A maze of obsolete electronics and ominously tangled cords snaked through the vast, foreboding space. Mountains of tube-type TVs, VCRs, and old computers towered about ten feet high, creating a tactical maze.

I paused, listening intently for any signs of movement or voices—nothing. Steeling myself, I resumed my sweep, prepared for whatever might hide in the shadows. Ready to fight for my love.

As I came to a clearing in the clutter, I saw a makeshift table. The glow of a laptop radiating from the surface drew my attention. I scanned the area to ensure it was clear. Once I was convinced it was safe, I approached the device. A copper scent wafted up from the plywood. I glanced around, finding a pool of blood spreading near the glowing screen. This was fresh; it hadn't had time to congeal.

The computer was pulled up to some form of a biochemistry diagram. I had no idea what the hell I was looking at. But I assumed it had to do with the L.O.V. or MNV. Shifting my weapon to my offhand, I started to scroll through the document. Sarah's smarts could probably translate this crap for me.

Abruptly, the aromas of gunpowder and diesel suddenly filled the air, forcing their way into my nostrils. Then two loud bangs sounded from behind me, and the screen went dark.

Instinctively, my weapon shifted back to my dominant hand as I turned around. My eyes were still adjusting to the sudden darkness, but I saw movement. Firing two shots in the general direction of the movement, I heard a painful feminine hiss. The voice sounded vaguely familiar, but I couldn't place it.

My eyes narrowed as they finally adapted to the dark room again. "I know you're there," I said, pulling my weapon up to get a bead on any targets. "Might as well show yourself."

"Someone wants you alive," A husky man's voice echoed in the space. I couldn't pinpoint the location. "It's best if we don't meet, for your sake."

Shit, were there two of them? A guy and a chick? *You're outgunned, Sergeant.* Fuck it, there was no turning back now.

"Good, I don't want to kill either," I grumbled, my head on a swivel, scanning the area. "Let me have the MNV serum, and we both can go home."

"Vicky and Sarah do make a good home," the man mocked, his voice still seeming everywhere. "I hear they have a wild side too."

Damn it, this fucker knew about my brides. Who the fuck was this snarky bastard? *Where the fuck is he? That's it, Sergeant, keep him talking, making him give away his position. Then go all Audie Murphy on the fucker.*

"Yeah," I murmured, my blood burning with the anticipation of a fight. "What would you know about that?"

No response came. I circled the area, trying to find a decent vantage point, seeing only piles of electronic trash.

Then the husky male voice boomed from the entrance. "Good night, Sergeant."

I turned just in time to see two silhouettes backlit by the streetlights outside: a tall, manly figure and a hunched-over shadow disappearing into the darkness; they were gone.

Running toward the door, my left hand swiped the laptop as my right hand punched my weapon forward. By the time I got outside, they were gone. Fuck!

Under the streetlamps, I could see that the laptop was toast. Two perfectly placed bullet holes hollowed the machine. One round penetrated the center of the screen, and the second obliterated the hard drive. It was useless now. I threw the thing to the ground. Whoever they were, they were well trained. That was for sure.

I walked cautiously across the street to my truck. As I got to the middle of the asphalt, I heard a loud boom from behind me. The rippling force threw me to the ground beside the vehicle.

Goddammit. Picking up my gun, I stood, my ears ringing from the explosion. Turning back, I saw the building was ablaze. Luckily, I was far enough away not to be harmed by the blast.

Wait... Far enough away... His mission wasn't to kill me... So, what was it? A warning? A message? Get to Dr. Ambrosio and the serum before I do? Destroy the evidence? The explosion. He waited for me to get clear of the building before detonating it. That bastard was still close. The game was ongoing.

My vigilance automatically kicked in, and I looked around. He could be in any one of these dilapidated places, watching. The thought sent an icy, piercing chill down my spine. Probably with a weapon pointed straight at me, a bead on my head.

There was no way I could effectively cover that much ground by myself. Leaving would be a smart move, Sergeant. But the soldier in me, the part that wanted to put a bullet in his skull, was screaming to stay. To fight, to kill. No, Forester, go home. Leave. Now.

Since his mission was not to kill me, I should've been safe enough to leave. I hastily got into the truck. My hand fumbled in my pocket before finally retrieving the keys. The engine roared to life—a welcome sound that did nothing to calm the adrenaline coursing through me.

I peeled out, my eyes darting around. Happy, you rat bastard? I'm leaving. Glancing through the rearview mirror, the street was hauntingly empty, except for the burning husk of a warehouse. A surge of fleeting minor relief washed over me.

Turning onto the main road, heading back to town, back to my home, my loves. The accelerator was flat to the floor as the weight of the events rested heavily on my foot. The truck was coming up to speed, creating distance between me and that desolate place.

My vigilance, a byproduct of years in the service, kept me checking the mirrors for any sign of pursuit. But there was nothing, just the distant glow of taillights far ahead, and an empty, dark road behind me. Maybe my instincts were wrong; perhaps I was safe.

My heart was still racing. Thoughts ran rampant in my mind. The fight was still fresh in my soul. I needed to calm down.

Come on, Sergeant, calm yourself. Sarah, Vicky, Sarah, Vicky, breathe in, breathe out. Just thinking about my brides soothed me. I was starting not to need the mantra, but it had become a welcome habit now. My mind drifted to the wedding, wondering how they would style their hair. The flowers... *Roses? Jasmines? Carnations? Maybe a mix? And the house, yes, the house, buy that for them, see their faces glow. Deep breath in, then release.*

A low, soft laugh escaped me, a final levity to quell the excitement, and I found myself smiling. Vicky, knowing her darker, dangerous attitude, would have gotten hot and bothered by that experience. Not now, Sergeant, think.

Ira, the man with answers, I had to contact him. Tell him the stakes had grown; there were more players in the game. Then see what he could dig up later, use his network or whatever to search those places.

My eyes flicked to the rearview mirror once more to ensure that I wasn't being followed. Blindingly, two monstrous headlights beamed straight into my eyes. I turned my head to get a better look.

A strange-shaped vehicle with its snarling grill was barreling toward me. The damned thing was reminiscent of an MRAP, but with the futuristic sleekness of Stephen's fancy sci-fi car. Sentinel... the fuckers. Probably one of the toys they designed for military use.

I turned back around, my eyes darting to the speedometer. Shit, I was doing one-oh-five. If a normal driver drove that sci-fi monster, there'd be no way they'd catch up to me. But as I looked in the mirror, he was closing fast. It was no longer a matter of speed; this wasn't a chase. This was a hunt.

A sudden, deafening horn blasted through the night air behind me. The sound wasn't a polite greeting, nor was it a warning. This was another taunt—a declaration of war between two combatants.

In a fraction of a second, my mind went back to the warehouse, back to that mocking voice. "Someone wants you alive." Yeah, that's what that scary fuck said. He wasn't lying. Killing me wasn't his mission. It was to stop me, prevent me from getting closer to the truth. Incapacitate me. Knock me out of this cloak-and-dagger game. Or at the very least scare me away. Well fuck you, buddy.

I turned the wheel sharply and veered off onto a side road. Let's play, motherfucker. If you want me, come get me. The truck tilted on two wheels, almost rolling, but I caught the apex of the road in time. Speeding down the stretch, I glanced back.

Goddammit, that armored beast made the turn with accurate ease. How the hell could it handle so well? What the hell was that thing made of?

I tried to find something to give me an edge. I spotted a small alleyway ahead. It could rip off my side mirrors, but I needed to escape.

As the turn came, I yanked the wheel to the left fast, pulling the nose of the truck into the narrow runway. The metallic scraping sound screeched, echoing in the closed-in area. As expected, my mirrors would need to be replaced, a problem for a different time.

Darting to the rearview mirror, I spotted that the tank-like toy had stopped at the mouth of the alley. Eat shit, kid.

Eyes locking forward, a wave of satisfaction and relief bore into me. But my heart was still thumping with the rhythm of combat.

You had your fun, soldier, now come down from this high. Calm down. Breathe. Now, get your ass home safely to your fiancées.

As I made it to the end of the alley, the hood of my truck barely emerged before I saw glaring lights on my right. I turned my head, only to see that the futuristic vehicle was at full ramming speed.

The adrenaline burned through every fiber of my body. My hands gripped the stirring wheel tightly, trying to maneuver this rig. But it was too late, I had no time to react.

Slamming into the passenger's side with great force, the beastly vehicle ripped into the side of my truck. Crumpling the sheet metal like paper, a sound that rattled my bones with terror.

Jerking forward, my face crashed into the deploying airbags. Then my head tossed to the side, slamming against the side window, which instantly disintegrated. Intense pain wracked me as a pulse of horror rippled in my mind.

An eruption of sound boomed through the cab as it began to flip and spin. Glass shattering in a crackle, the raw metallic sound of the pavement biting every part, and the dinging of the safety alerts tore through the night.

I felt weightless, floating in the cab, banging around like a rag doll. My world was now a kaleidoscope, twirling with lights flashing into the broken windshield. Then it stopped.

I was barely conscious, noticing that I was inverted. A warm liquid ran over my face. My vision was blurry, scarcely able to see lights in the darkness. Weakly, I pushed onto the dashboard, trying to get out, but it was no use; I was pinned by something.

Feeling woozy, I resigned my struggle, as Lady Death seemed to be closing in. I didn't want her seduction, her cold touch. I wanted, needed, to feel the warmth of my beauties, my brides-to-be. I started to fade into the darkness.

A bellow of noise came through, a singular line back to this world from the nothingness.

"Check his pulse," a vaguely familiar female voice demanded. "That car stunt could've killed him."

I tried to open my eyes, but couldn't. The feeling of two icy fingers touched my throat, sending a repulsive shiver through me. I tried to protest, to speak, but was rendered silent by my state. I could only listen to their exchange.

"Your precious dove is still alive," the husky man's voice echoed, then frustration burrowed in his tone. "Satisfied?"

"Good, because Reginald promised Kyle's survival. If Kyle died, I would have had no problem terminating you."

My survival? Why? My head pounded, my muscles swelled with pain. The fading sense that I was leaving this reality lingered. I struggled to stay conscious enough to hear the reasoning.

"Yeah, okay." A manly growl pierced the darkness. "Besides, I know my mission: spook. Throw the kid off the trail. This accomplished that, didn't it?"

"You almost killed him. And explain the scientist?"

A dark, menacing chuckle erupted for a moment. "She wasn't part of your pathetic pity," he mocked.

"What does that mean?"

"It means your boss, Reginald, wanted her dead," he explained, almost remorseful. His voice rose with agitation. "And don't give me that look. You can't shame me for putting a bullet in that traitor."

Were they talking about Dr. Ambrosio? The feeling of sleep was trying to take over, a drooping sensation. *Fuck, stay alert, Sergeant. Come on, just... stay alive. Hold on, stay here, in this world. Stay with your fiancées.*

"Ambulance should be here any second," the female voice said.

"How do you know?"

"I alerted them at the warehouse, then called them again to give the location. Time to go."

"Goddamn spies always playing both sides," he grumbled. I felt the turf of my hair being yanked. "You know, this caged birdie is tougher than he looks; he might be a problem later." I felt another cold hand wrap around my throat, applying slight pressure. "What if I finished the job?"

"I said withdraw, soldier," she commanded the man with a hateful sharpness. The metallic sound of a weapon being cocked echoed in the darkness.

My head was shoved back as the hand retreated from my neck, and the fingers released my scalp. I heard rustling and the sound of heavy steps fading into the night. But the woman's presence was still warm next to me.

"You're safe, now, little dove," she whispered with a motherly sweetness. "Fly back home to your loves." I felt the warm pressure of a gentle kiss land on my forehead. Her steps followed behind the man.

Finally, I was alone. The sirens sounded in the distance as I fell deeper into the darkness. I'm sorry, Vicky, Sarah. I wasn't strong enough, skilled enough to live for you. I love you, know that. I love you two more than I can ever put into words.

Fading away, the noise was eventually gone. I was gone. Drifting away from the world, pulled closer into the dark abyss, yet my heart fought, clinging to Vicky's strength and Sarah's warmth.

Chapter 24: Souls Unite

Waking from a distant dream, the rotor blades kicked up the sand beneath us as my litter was hoisted into the Blackhawk. Weir, Donovan, Gordon... Where were they? Were they still in the HUMVEE? Damn it! I knew they were dead, the IED had murdered them, but... They deserved to be home, laid to rest with honors. Their families needed to mourn their loss. The flags, folded neatly, should be given to their loved ones as a symbol of their sacrifice—an offering in remembrance of brave men. I struggled through the pain of sitting up. To find my men, my brothers.

"Hold him down!" the medic screamed over the rotor.

Instantly, I felt the hard shove back down. The cold surface of the litter sent a shiver along my entire body.

"Let me up!" I screamed, my arms flailed. "My brothers... let me see my brothers!"

"Specialist, they're dead!" the soldier above me yelled, his hand holding a needle. "Now, settle the fuck down!" His final words before I felt the prick pierce through my arm.

"The fuck was that?"

"Morphine!" he said as the helicopter ascended. "Trust me, Specialist, you're gonna need it when the adrenaline wears off."

"Why?"

"You're not fucking Superman," he yelled, yet his voice held a strange form of sympathy. "Bullets don't bounce off your ass."

I went silent; the weight of his words filled me. The adrenaline had pushed me to fight harder, eliminating the bastards that slaughtered my brothers. In that moment, in the firefight, I felt powerful. But as the pain settled in, so did the realization of my mortality. You're not indestructible. You're a man, flesh and blood.

Looking down, I saw that my vest was gone. Blood soaked through what was left of my uniform. It had been cut into pieces, bandages wrapped here and there. Fuck. I lay back listening to the hum of the helo. The wind whipping through the open doors felt soothing against the pain in my body. But the pain in my broken heart, nothing was working to calm that.

I failed. Failed my men, my... As I was in mid-thought, a flash of two warm smiles seared into my mind. Another failure, yet I couldn't understand how or who...

The pain in my body started to fade, but my soul was without salvation. Throbbing, piercing sensations from a life not yet realized crawled up. A love somehow destined, fated to me, yet out of reach, was filling the void inside.

After a while, everything became fuzzy as I drifted into another world. No longer in Iraq, I was floating somewhere else. Somewhere calmer, softer, filled with vulnerabilities and care. Reborn as something different, bathed in affection.

The force pulled me toward a large house, as if a magnet was ripping me closer. Children were running about, playing, laughing. Joy was spilling over in the chalice of life; all I needed was to drink in its flavor. Savoring all that sweetness with admiration was the simple price for such an ambrosia.

The closer I got, the more the static cleared. Emerging like Valkyries, like angels, the faces of two women came into focus with crystal clarity. They filled my vision like a fever dream. A joyful redhead and a sultry brunette. Both exuded everything I cherished.

They spread their arms, embracing me with warmth. The loving aromas of summer rain and jasmine filled my senses. I was uncontrollably drawn to these two women. Kisses landed like arrows hitting a mark. The first one was tranquil, born from something almost heavenly. The second one was fiery, writhed with an all-consuming passion. The saccharine taste of strawberry wine from their lips lingered in my heart.

I couldn't tell what was going on. But for some reason, this felt more real than the war, as if I were in a memory. No, not a memory. A different state of being. A warmer place. A safer place. With love showering me, enveloping me. Consuming me whole. Their love... Who were they?

For some reason, the names Vicky and Sarah crossed my mind. Then a tidal wave of memories flooded in. They were my loves, my fiancées. I was more than a soldier to them. I was more than anything; their eyes saw the true man I was. And they... they meant everything to me.

My life was theirs; every ounce of my soul belonged to them. And they belonged entirely to me as well. Mingling, merging, we became one. One soul, one entity. An indistinguishable trio, a trinity of divinity bursting like a nova through the heavens.

As we drifted closer to the house, exhaustion tugged at my eyelids. Darkness crept in. Then, without warning, I was out.

Opening my eyes, the brightness was a searing sight. The steady rhythm of a pulsing beep softly droned around me. The pungent smell of disinfectants filled the air. *Where am I?*

Before I could investigate, a light snoring rumbled from my side. Glancing over, I was greeted by a red tuft of hair, immediately knowing it was Sarah. She was sleeping, slumped over the bedside.

Scanning the area, I found myself in a white room with monitors displaying information about me. My arm was tethered to an I.V., slowly dripping fluids. Following the walls, my eyes continued to search. Finally, I found Vicky, standing at the window, peering out at the city with an uncomfortable stance.

"What... uh... what happened?" I asked, sitting up in bed. The slight movement felt heavy on my chest as a dull ache rippled through my ribs.

Vicky instantly turned around, face already streaming with rivers of tears, a smile growing on her weary face. The red patch next to me began to move groggily.

"Master," Sarah started, but her voice choked with emotion for a moment. "You were in an accident." Her hand reached out to caress mine. Her muscles seemed tense, twisted with anxiety. "When they called, we didn't know if you were..." She choked with a sob before slightly regaining herself. "If you were alive."

"We thought we'd lost you. For a moment, the world... our world disappeared," Vicky admitted hoarsely, her body calm again. "You got a concussion, three cracked ribs, and some scrapes," she calmly said, but the worry in her eyes fell upon me. Walking toward the foot of the bed, she assessed me. "How do you feel?"

"Never better." My voice stirred with the soldier's stoicism and my affection for them. "Now that I'm back with you two."

"Don't fucking do that. Don't play this off with that macho man crap." Vicky scolded me with harsh motherly worry. "Does it hurt?"

"I'm... sorry. I didn't mean to worry you, either of you," I lamented, the sting of their hurt fell on my heart. "A slight dull pain in my chest and stinging in different areas," I answered thoughtfully. "But I'm okay, for the most part. I'm with you two, that's all that matters."

The pain in Vicky's blue pools was fading, replaced by a hopeful sparkle. Sarah's tense posture relaxed, her body visibly softening.

Vicky leaned forward, her eyes slowly looking me up and down, as if seeing me for the first time in forever. "Luckily, someone called an ambulance quickly after the hit and run."

My mind faded back to the moments before things went dark. That man, that woman. Who were they?

"Not luck," I whispered, the faint memory of my assailant's conversation coming into focus. "Someone planned this."

"Who?" Sarah sobbed, gently caressing my cheek with her soft hand.

"No idea, but it's related to L.O.V."

"How the hell is your accident related to L.O.V.?" Vicky asked, her eyebrows furrowed.

"I got an anonymous call, some weirdo with a voice changer." I sighed, the silliness of my actions now plain to see. "They told me to go to a warehouse; the MNV serum was supposed to be there."

"Master, you... you should've called us," Sarah stammered, her voice filled with hesitation.

"What were you doing going at this alone?" Vicky asked accusingly, hurt ripping through her facade.

"I didn't want you two to get hurt," I lamented, my voice cracking as I fought back tears. "I made the right call, obviously," I said, motioning to myself lying in the hospital bed.

Vicky rolled her eyes, before her face softened. Sarah just stared at me with a pitiful glare.

"Did you find anything, Master?" Sarah tenderly asked.

"A laptop with some chemistry stuff, but it was destroyed. They shot the damn thing as I was looking at it." I paused for a moment, my mouth feeling dry, smacking my lips to hydrate my tongue. "They blew up the building. I left; they chased me in some weird... MRAP. Then... well, this."

Sarah gasped in surprise; Vicky took a deep breath and sighed heavily. The room went silent as the information settled in.

"Fucken bastards," Vicky mumbled angrily. "How dare they do this to our man!"

Sarah kissed my cheek. "Master, you have to tell the police."

I thought for a moment about her proposition. But what could the police do? ITI and Sentinel were both large companies with substantial financial resources. Even Ira, as scary as he is, didn't dare make a direct play against them.

"We can't." Vicky moved to the other side of the bed. "For all we know, they own the police. Billion-dollar company, remember?"

"But… but they hurt Master." Sarah glanced at Vicky, desperate.

"Vicky's right, Sarah." I could see the pain ripping through her eyes. A stream of tears flowed down her cheek. "They're too powerful for simple solutions."

"Did you get a good look at them?" Vicky asked, hardened with righteous indignation, yet the undercurrent of vulnerability and concern rippled like quakes in a pond.

"I never saw their faces," I said, my mind racing to remember any detail. "But it was a man and a woman, that much I know."

"Guy and girl, huh?" Vicky snarled, her jaw clenched tight. "You take the fucker; we got the whore."

A laughed, though it was painful. Still, it was much needed. Vicky stared at me; her soul filled with a fierce fight. As my laughter settled, I felt a thirst.

"Water, please," I begged. Vicky brought the cup from my bedside to my lips. "Thank you, my lovely. But settle down. No Ellen Ripley crap today, we can't just thrash everyone we see."

Slamming the cup on the table, Vicky sternly eyed me. But her hardened facade was cracking as tears started to roll again. "Why the hell not? They did this to you. If they fuck with one of us, they fuck with all three of us."

Sarah, feeling the unity Vicky was inspiring, became animated. She punched her hand, then her face wrinkled with a wickedness I'd never seen in her before. "Yeah, we protect each other."

"Yes, we do," I cheered, the elation of having my beauties near washed over me. "But the accident wasn't a direct kill shot. They wanted to scare me. This was a warning."

"A warning? This?" Sarah indicated the hospital room.

"Fuckers don't want Kyle to figure out L.O.V.," Vicky concluded, her head shaking with agitation. "Fuck 'em."

"They're also highly trained, way better than me. They have some serious hardware. The vehicle that rammed my truck was some kind of advanced military tech."

"But if we can't get the police involved and we can't fight them… What do we do?" Sarah asked, her voice low and hoarse.

“Simple,” I replied in that NCO tone, my eyes darting between both of theirs. “We pretend it didn’t happen, go back to normal.”

“The fuck? Do nothing?” Vicky exclaimed, her voice rising with annoyance. “Sit back and let these assholes get away with this.”

“Not exactly.” My hand gently touched hers. Instantly, her face softened; her eyes stared soulfully at me. “We let them think they’ve won, for now. But we make more intelligent moves in the future.”

“Like chess, Master.” Sarah filled with brightness as if she had an epiphany. A hint of her bubbly side showed as she bounced in place. “Plan a safer, more informed and calculated approach.”

“Exactly.”

“I don’t like sitting around doing nothing,” Vicky muttered, her hand caressing my arm.

“We won’t be,” I said, a smile tugging at the corners of my lips. “We’ll be building our future, together, the three of us. They can never take our love from us.”

The room instantly radiated with warmth, and their weary faces both broke out in smiles. Leaning over the hospital bed on opposite sides, their arms squeezed gently around me into a hug. The sweet aromas of summer rain and jasmine wafted around me. Taking a deep inhale, I was instantly intoxicated with affection. And the heat of their bodies was a comfort that I desperately needed. They were so close to me that I could feel their hearts beating.

But this wasn’t just a hug. Sarah’s touch was a tender promise, a soft warmth that melted away the ice in my veins. Vicky’s embrace was a fierce shield, her strong muscled arms a testament to her unwavering loyalty. In that moment, the sterile air of the hospital faded. I wasn’t an injured man in a bed; I was a man cherished, a man loved, a man whose soul was being mended. Stitch by stitch, the twin forces of their affection sewed my heart back together. As their bodies enveloped me, I didn’t just feel them physically; I felt their souls intertwining with mine.

The crash, the mystery, and the threats faded like a dull noise. The only thing that mattered was this moment, this embrace. I needed to live, not for some mission, but for the future we pledged. The promise of living together in our love. Happily, together in our marital bliss.

“I love you, Master.” Sarah sobbed.

I looked up, my vision still a bit blurry, and saw her tear-streaked face. But the tears weren't painful any longer; they were filled with happiness. I reached up and gently brushed a tear from her milky cheek. The warmth of her skin contrasted with the sterile air of the hospital.

"Always, Kyle, I will always love you," Vicky softly said. I glanced down; her eyes filled with tears, but that vigorous rasp didn't falter. She poured her fierce love into the room, mixing with the tenderness of Sarah. I was caught in between, glowing with a light that connected the three hearts.

"I love you both. Now and always," I declared as my arms embraced them with a tight wrap of my love. Passionately, the desire to taste their kisses took root in my heart.

I leaned up to Sarah, and her face met mine. Our lips met in a moment of pure, gentle reunion. Her kiss was like a soulful melody, a whisper of affectionate warmth. She was my heart, and at that moment, I felt it beating strongly again.

When I turned to Vicky, her eyes blazed with fierce possessive love. Her mouth claimed mine without a word, a kiss of roaring flames that demanded a response. It wasn't gentle; it was a battle for dominion, a clash of tongues that spoke of a burning, untamable admiration. She was my spirit; the kiss reignited the fight inside us.

Breaking away, I smiled at how strong our unity was. Every day with them was a constant, never-ending deep affection. Falling harder and further each day in love.

A silent appreciation of each other filled the air. The room was aglow with the affection of our life, forcing all shadows to recede. A beacon of harmony hummed, passing between the three of us.

Then Vicky leaned up, playfully punching my chest. "Next time, if you go off all lone wolf, I'll beat your ass." A slight chuckle escaped through her sternness. Then her voice deepened in that dark rasp. "We're a pack, get used to it."

"Yeah, Master, we're in this together." Sarah high-fived Vicky.

"Damn, I'm all injured and messed up, lying in the hospital, yet somehow my fiancées are still teaming up against me."

"Wives," Sarah corrected. "You're our husband, even without the wedding. So, please, Master, don't scare us like that again."

Vicky walked to Sarah, her arm wrapping lovingly around her. "Dearest husband, you upset our wife," Vicky lightly scolded.

“*Our* wife?” I smirked; the feeling that the relationship was growing filled my soul with even more joy.

“We’re not just marrying you,” Sarah announced, looking into Vicky’s eyes, a deep, loving gaze lingered in both their faces.

An unspoken emotion filled the space between them as their lips met. They shared a brief, loving kiss that seemed more a gesture of relief than one of passion. Pulling from each other’s lips, both gave each other a mischievous, knowing smile. The sight of our three-way love expanding swelled my heart.

“We’re marrying each other, too,” they said in unison, their voices beaming with happiness. “And yes, we’re both mad at you, right now.”

Seeing them united like that was refreshing. Fun even. I smiled with a goofy grin. “Okay,” I said, trying to play off the elation bursting inside. Then a funny thought came to me. “But dinner better be ready when I get home.”

“The nerve of our husband,” Vicky scoffed playfully, shaking her head. “Thinks he can go slay dragons all by himself. Then expects us to slave away all day in the kitchen. Hmm...”

“Mm-hmm. When he gets better, let’s teach him a lesson,” Sarah said.

Vicky’s sensual gaze snapped to me, her head tilting slightly. “I think the crop will do nicely to mark his cute ass.” She rasped, her tone that of a dark vixen. “What do you think, sis?”

“Hey now, poor pitiful, injured husband over here.” I pouted, feigning a hurt expression.

“Ooh, yeah. Pretty red marks on that cute butt.” Sarah smirked, her smile a mix of warmth and playfulness. “Sis, didn’t he promise us beautiful babies?”

“That’s right, dear husband,” Vicky mocked, her finger wagging at me. “You still haven’t put a bun in our ovens, yet. Tsk-tsk.”

I shook my head. Even in this situation, they remained as cute and playful as ever.

A knock came at the door, and a middle-aged doctor entered holding a chart. His face held a hopeful but exhausted look. He seemed tired, as if he’d been here all day.

“Mr. Forester, you’re awake,” he said, shifting between my fiancées, then back to me. Stepping close, he began to examine me. Checking the monitors and my bandages.

After looking me over, he said, “Your injuries aren’t severe, but we’ll hold you overnight for observation. If all is well in the morning, we’ll discharge you.”

“Thank you, Doctor.”

“And which one of you is Mrs. Forester?” he asked with a smile.

“We both are,” they said in unison. Their unified declaration made the blood in my veins burn with the fires of love. Both... They were both my wife and each other’s wives as well.

The doctor’s brows instantly furrowed with confusion. He seemed momentarily unsure of how to proceed. Gaining his composure, he continued. “Well, okay,” he said, then cleared his throat. “Whoever’s going to look after him will need to know a few things. I’ll swing by in the morning before his discharge to explain.”

Vicky and Sarah both nodded, acknowledging his words.

He exited the room, and seconds later, it exploded once more with banter. We talked into the night. Vicky explained some of her spa ideas for expanding services to clients. Sarah had finally gotten her class itinerary for the spring semester. Both were animated and passionate about their chosen career paths. I was amazed and impressed by them. They were gems so rare and precious. They mentioned the dream house during the conversation, which sparked my memory.

“I really need somewhere to do larger paintings,” Vicky lamented, as she sat on the chair by the window.

Sarah, seated in the chair beside my bed, blew a kiss across the room to her. “We’ll have it sometime, sis. Besides, I still dream of my garden to read in.”

“Hey, reminds me,” I interrupted, taking a sip of the water. “If we get out of here in time, Howard asked me if we’d do a house walk-through tomorrow.”

“Why?” Vicky asked, lounging back on the chair.

Damn, what do I say? Uh. I didn’t want to tell them it was actually me who was thinking about buying it.

“He wants our opinion on the house across the street from his,” I answered, my voice hollow, barely hiding my true intent.

“Howard wants our opinion on a house?” Vicky asked, her eyes strained, as if not convinced.

“Ooh, that pretty one with the white bricks?” Sarah bounced, asking with elation. “I’ve been dying to see the inside.”

"Yeah, that one."

"*He* wants us to see it..." Vicky murmured, then that dark vixen came through, dripping with sexiness. "Or *you* want us to see it?"

Crap! I was caught. But maybe I could recover.

"Just... let's do the walk-through, please. For Howard."

"Yay! I'm going to see that pretty house." Sarah bubbled with joy, bouncing in her chair.

Vicky didn't respond; she simply eyed me with suspicion. Her knowing gaze seemed to guess my true intent, that the house was meant for them. I sighed to myself, thinking how hard it will be to surprise her in the future.

Later, when the laughter and talk died out, the room was still. The city lights outside the hospital window seemed to blink with a sinister brilliance. I lay deep in thought on the hospital bed.

I looked at Sarah, hunched over the bed, sleeping peacefully beside me. I watched her soft, angelic face in her sleep with a deep emotion of admiration. Her gentle kindness was a balm to my soul, a silent, vulnerable strength that held us together.

Then my gaze shifted to Vicky, who was curled up in the chair by the window, a silent guardian. She was fiercely protective, even in her sleep. A warrior in her own right. Her fiery spirit ignited my own, a passionate force that made us all feel alive.

They weren't just two women; they were two halves of my heart. One, the peaceful calm; the other, the righteous storm. Together, we were that feeling of home in each other. The thought of losing this love, this life, was a pain greater than any battlefield. It was a wound to my soul. The immortal essence of our love was worth fighting for.

All the gifts that we bestow upon each other are our rewards and privileges for devotion. Our love is only for the three of us, ever expanding and equally shared. We were evolving into something more than I thought was possible. They weren't just mine, they were each other's. And I was theirs completely, irrevocably.

Our love was powerful and unapologetic, a beacon shining brightly in the darkness—a shield against all the world.

The taste of Sarah's gentleness, the passion of Vicky's fire, and my guiding hand grounded us. It was our fortress, our home. Living for each other, protecting each other. We're not just fiancés; we were everything to each other.

The deepest essence of my beauties holds the loam-kissed sweetness of all our battles won. Their eyes, sparkling gems reflecting triumph, speak of victories yet to unfold. Kissed by their lips, I tasted the quiet peace where our foes would lie in timeless repose.

Soon, this daunting mystery shall be resigned to its final resting place on the earth. Then we may joyously wed, a union of three weary travelers. For we, a loving, united throuple, sail the cosmic currents of revelation. Infinitely, our bond transcends all divinity. No force can still the unquenchable thirst that binds us, three souls eternally entwined, destined for each other's embrace.

Bound in flesh, each touch becomes a sacred cartography of the union where our love endlessly flows, and pleasure knows no bounds. Melded in mind, our collective thoughts forge an alchemical life, sculpting the very fabric of our shared reality.

Three hearts chained together, silently thrumming the melody where power, both primal and tender, blooms like a rose in the dawning new age of love. United in soul, forever sealed to one another, not by ancient deities but by a shared, unyielding flame—our union showers the universe in an endless, radiant cascade of joy. We are the architects of a reality far grander than any singular being, having truly stepped into the boundless fields of what it means to be more.

The future of our love was more than a desire. It became our drive to fend off the world. To solve the mystery that lingered between us. The answers to this puzzle would soon be in our grasp.

We make it our quest to always protect and cherish each other as the shimmering lights in life. I vow never to betray their trust. I pledge my honor to my beauties. For what we have is beyond love; it is the bliss where three souls unite.

This encounter was a warning to us. A reminder of how fragile things could be, that our home was not yet truly safe. Tonight, an unspoken oath was passed between us; no monster, no matter how powerful, would break this. Nothing could, that was the mission from here on out.

Our journey through life together was just beginning. These shadowy figures tried to extinguish our light. Little did they know their actions had forged a new weapon, unyielding unity. Three hearts beating as one, three souls in sync, ready for war.

Made in the USA
Coppell, TX
08 March 2026

73441481R00174